FICTION RESERVE.

23. JAN. 1987

-7. MAR. 1988

21. MAR. 1989

SBS. 4/90

D1491985

AUTHOR	CLASS
PETERLEY D	F

TITLE	No
Peterley Harvest	18514531

Lancashire County Council

This book should be returned on or before the latest date shown above to the library from which it was borrowed.
**LIBRARY HEADQUARTERS
143, CORPORATION ST. PRESTON PR1 2TB**

a30118 026806574b

PETERLEY HARVEST

Peterley Harvest

The private diary of
DAVID PETERLEY

Preface by
Michael Holroyd

Secker & Warburg
LONDON
In association with the
Arts Council of Great Britain

First published in England 1960 by
Hutchinson & Co. (Publishers) Ltd.

This edition published 1985 by
Martin Secker & Warburg Limited
54 Poland Street, London W1V 3DF
in association with the Arts Council of Great Britain

British Library Cataloguing in Publication Data
Peterley, David
Peterley harvest : the private diary of
David Peterley.
I. Title
823'.914[F]   PR6066.E73/

ISBN 0-436-36715-7

© Richard Pennington 1960
Preface copyright © Michael Holroyd 1985

LAST COPY
18514531

02680657

Printed in Great Britain by
Redwood Burn Ltd, Trowbridge, Wiltshire

SL	SL-P ...
SA	SO ......
SBS 4/90	
SB 4.85.	SP ......
SK 11/86	SY ......

Preface

Peterley Harvest was first published on 24 October 1960. The book had a curious history and, shortly before publication, stories began to appear in the press declaring it to be an elaborate hoax.

The jacket of the book contained the information that David Peterley was the only son of an old Quaker family that had 'lived in the Chilterns and been neighbours of Milton and the Penns'. He had left College in 1924 at the age of twenty-two and, despite 'having been trained to no trade or profession', gone to work in a solicitor's office. To escape the tedium of this work, and as an alternative to marriage with a woman of his father's choice, he set out to see the world and, after staying some four years in Australia, returned to England in 1930.

From 1926 to 1939, when he went back to Australia, Peterley kept an extensive diary, re-writing the personal passages so as to produce a 'more or less continuous autobiographical narrative' which, we are told, the editor Richard Pennington further abbreviated for publication. The first four years of this diary are dissolved into Mr Pennington's Introduction, and *Peterley Harvest* 'the private diary of David Peterley now for the first time printed' opened in June 1930 as David Peterley disembarked at Liverpool.

This framing of the book provoked much bewilderment. Readers were not told whether or when David Peterley had died or how his papers came to reach McGill University in Canada. They were told that since 1946 Richard Pennington had been head librarian at McGill University. But by including an anonymous drawing in profile of David Peterley as frontispiece, and a photograph of Mr Pennington on the inside flap of the jacket, the publishers were giving away too many clues. The drawing showed the young man whom Mr Pennington describes in his Introduction as having the 'slight irregularity of face that women find handsome, especially when matched with blond hair and blue eyes'. The photograph of Mr Pennington revealed a dark-bearded, middle-aged man who was described as having been at different times a publisher, sailor, printer, university lecturer and frequent speaker on Canadian radio and television. Yet were these not likenesses, light and dark, of the same man? If so, it would give point to such jokes as the Peterleys having been near neighbours to the Penns (which when added to Milton almost gives you Pennington), and the remark made by a friend to Peterley while on a visit to Prague 'that it was a pity my name was David, and that if it had been Richard I could have become the second Richard of Prague'.

Confirmation of this single identity appeared to have been provided by the copyright line which simply read: © Richard Pennington. It seems unthinkable that a sometime publisher and printer would have allowed such a line to appear had he wished to float a forgery—he would have used the more discrete tactics of *Madame Solario* or *Letters of an Indian Judge to an English Gentlewoman*. *Peterley Harvest* is not in fact a forgery but one of those 'fakes' that present autobiographical material with the foreshortening and ambiguity of an imaginative work —what Wordsworth meant by the phrase 'to throw over incidents and situations from common life a certain colouring of imagination, whereby ordinary things should be presented to the mind in an unusual aspect'.

The unusual aspect of *Peterley Harvest* gave its first reviewers an appalling headache. They did not know what to make of it 'unless, of course,' hazarded the *Sunday Times* literary editor, 'the diary is really the work of Richard Pennington'. Even then, how was one to evaluate such a strange enterprise? Some papers gave it cautious notices ('has atmosphere' noted *The Guardian*) or retaliated with venom: 'The harvest of David Peterley was sour grapes' commented *The Times*. Others left it alone. It is easy to feel sympathy for those literary editors who at short notice found themselves in this predicament, but their fears of becoming the dupes of a sinister literary plot now seem exaggerated. Philip Toynbee, for example, who declared that he had never really been taken in for a minute, his scepticism having been awakened early on by the frontispiece (you can't get much earlier in a book than its frontispiece) obviously *had* been taken in and felt let down. 'While I could still believe that it was dealing, through however many curtains of romantic gauze, with a real life and a real person,' he wrote in *The Observer*, '. . . I wanted very much indeed to know who he was. But as soon as I had concluded that he was nobody at all I found *Peterley Harvest* a serious strain on my patience. Did the author foresee such a reaction? . . . how could he imagine that the hoax would work? How could he dare to introduce his figment to men and women of authenticated flesh and blood?'

Toynbee was particularly sensitive to the danger of literary victimization, having been much mocked in the late 1950s for the generous welcome he gave to Colin Wilson's *The Outsider*. Determined not to be taken in again, he was aggressively on guard against some of his own best instincts. There was, too, a genuine problem of category. Was *Peterley Harvest* a novel autobiography or an autobiographical novel? And does it matter whether the book is a memoir or fiction or an ingenious amalgam of the two?

Short of the *Hitler Diaries*, this question has seemed to matter less in the last twenty-five years partly because there has been considerably more cross-fertilization between fiction and non-fiction. This process has enriched our recent fiction, most remarkably perhaps the novels of Peter Ackroyd, Beryl Bainbridge, Julian Barnes, D. M. Thomas and Thomas Keneally whose *Schindler's Ark* was marketed in America (under a slightly different title) as non-fiction and in Britain as a novel. Writers of light fiction, too, have added to the enrichment of their work by introducing people from history to fictional characters from the books of other novelists—a notable example being the co-operative sleuthing of Sherlock Holmes and Sigmund Freud in Nicholas Meyer's adventure *The Seven Per Cent Solution*.

Many American and British novelists, from Truman Capote to Piers Paul Read, have taken on the non-fiction thriller. But the benefits of fictional devices to serious non-fiction, from the days of André Maurois's romanticized version of Shelley to Norman Mailer's pastiche of Marilyn Monroe, have seemed more dubious. With *Peterley Harvest* there was an additional problem because unlike recent fictional diaries such as *Nazi Lady. The Diaries of Elisabeth von Stahlenberg 1933–1948*, or fictional autobiographies such as Robert Graves's *I, Claudius*, or *Danny Hill. Memoirs of a Prominent Gentleman* (edited by Francis King) and Margaret Forster's 'edition' of Thackeray's *Memoirs of a Victorian Gentleman*, the book mingled well-respected literary figures still alive in Britain with private characters who, if not invented, were surely concealed like the author himself under pseudonyms. *Peterley Harvest* therefore seemed suspended between the fictional diary that has a well-established place in English literature and such fraudulent productions as *The Whispering Gallery*, those anonymous 'Leaves from a Diplomat's Diary' whose author had been prosecuted in the late 1920s on a charge of attempting to obtain money under false pretences. The author of that hoax, reputed to be Lord Birkenhead, turned out to be an actor named Hesketh Pearson. In a subsequent book of breezy reflections on the craft of biography called *Ventilations*, Pearson gave examples of how the non-fiction writer may use his fancy to improve on fact—a perversion of Wordsworth's prescription, which Pearson renounced for solid Johnsonian principles of biography once he became a professional biographer himself in the 1930s.

It seems to have been Mr Pennington's aim to shake these Johnsonian conventions, which had become somewhat fossilized by the twentieth century, and use more ambiguous combinations of methods to achieve his particular artistic ends. He writes in his Foreword that the justification of *Peterley Harvest* is to be found 'in the revelation of the inner life of fugitive images in the mind and fitful impulses of the heart, that inner life which with most of us goes unrecorded and which it is the aim of the official biography to conceal'. This is very similar to Virginia Woolf's view of traditional life-writing which she parodied in her fantasy-biography *Orlando*: 'Directly we glance at eyes and forehead, we have to admit a thousand disagreeables which it is the aim of every good biographer to ignore ... all these sights and the garden sounds too, the hammer beating and the wood chopping, began that riot and confusion of the passions and emotions which every good biographer detests.'

There had been a number of experiments in the late 1920s and early 1930s— among them Harold Nicolson's delightful vignettes *Some People*, Lytton Strachey's psychological melodrama *Elizabeth and Essex* and A. J. A. Symons's detective mystery *The Quest for Corvo*—all designed to find more imaginative and adventurous ways of writing non-fiction. What these authors were trying to do was to release biography from the mechanical processes of the card-index, the confinement of chronology, the heavy impedimenta of reference notes and bibliographies as well as from all the pompous paraphernalia of nineteenth-century Lives and Letters that had made the getting of information their chief priority and locked up biography in the reference library. *Peterley Harvest* does not even have an index. We are told that it is 'strangely one-sided,' that 'all the memorable things are omitted' and that 'as a record of living it is absurdly false'. 'I do not believe that the choice of entries for a journal is made *à votre insu* by your subconscious,' writes the author, 'and therefore is a true revelation.' But this declaration cunningly prompts a reaction that the diary nevertheless is a fantastical revelation, since the entry goes on to describe all those convivialities that it states go unrecorded. Of course, the biographer must respect facts, and these may be independently authenticated; the novelist seeks a truth that may be verified by his own vision and the imprint that the novel comes to make on the minds of readers. By finding legitimate ways of managing the facts and incidents of life with the imaginative techniques of novel-writing, Harold Nicolson, Lytton Strachey and A. J. A. Symons had wanted to put biography back on the English literature shelf. *Peterley Harvest* is another attempt to combine the advantages of both worlds by attaching the substance of biography to the freedom of fiction.

A number of the facts may be checked. It is a fact, as Peterley writes, that in 1937 Graham Greene was chosen to edit an English imitation of the *New Yorker* called

Night and Day, and it is a percipient comment, in view of the coming success of *Horizon* and the brief existence of *Night and Day*, that Cyril Connolly's talent might have better fitted him to be its editor. The bibliographical information concerning the British poet Robert Nichols' career is factual; the biographical asides surrounding that drunken social outcast, the Australian poet Christopher Brennan (whom J. C. Squire believed to be an invention of David Peterley's, and who is now recognized as Australia's first poet of international significance) may be checked against a long manuscript in the Mitchell Library at Sydney—by Richard Pennington. Gwen Ffrangcon-Davies did take the part of Etain in Rutland Boughton's opera *The Immortal Hour* in 1922 with Peter Shelving's designs; and since she also acted in a play called *Spring Tide* which opened at the Duchess Theatre on 15 July 1936, we may safely bet that this play was, as Peterley reveals, co-authored by J. B. Priestley under the pseudonym Peter Goldsmith. Richard Pennington's slip here, by failing as editor to move Peterley's diary from June to July is almost an invitation to the critic to misunderstand his methods. For in terms of such events we are reading an accurate account, including some unorthodox items that find no place in official biographies and academic bibliographies. It follows that Peterley's record of the Czechoslovakian crisis in the late 1930s is historically true, and Harold Nicolson's attitude, though more sympathetically presented in his diaries, not unfairly shown. But there is no mention of Peterley or Pennington in Nicolson's diaries or in James Lees-Milne's two-volume biography of Nicolson.

There is no mention of them, or of this book, anywhere. They do not appear in the biography of Arthur Machen by Aidan Reynolds and William Charlton, though *Peterley Harvest* has some vivid pages on Machen. From this biography, published three years after *Peterley Harvest*, the facts of Peterley's narrative may be verified. There was, for example, a dinner held in his honour at the National Liberal Club on 29 October 1937. Pennington can introduce Peterley to it because Pennington was actually Gladstone Librarian at the National Liberal Club. He gives a fuller description of the event than the biography which contains nothing so wonderfully evocative as 'the night of Machen's punch'.

The most arresting picture of a writer in *Peterley Harvest* is that of A. E. Housman delivering his Leslie Stephen Lecture, *The Name and Nature of Poetry*. Every fact that Pennington uses, from the date and the time to the presence of Quiller-Couch and Will Spens, the Vice-Chancellor, may once more be checked from works subsequently published such as *The Letters of A. E. Housman* (1971) and Richard Perceval Graves's excellent biography *A. E. Housman* (1979). *Peterley*

Harvest has been overlooked by Mr Graves (who uses the evidence of commentators such as Frank Harris): but who can doubt that the non-existent Peterley was among the audience at the Senate House that May afternoon in 1933, and that we are reading an exact, first-hand account from this invisible man?

'Housman rose, placed a brown-covered small octavo pamphlet (of paged proofs?) upon the reading desk and immediately began to read. He spoke slowly, with precision, in a pleasant, even, low, but clear and well-modulated voice, not raising his eyes, and frequently twitching the pamphlet up to the top of the desk, and holding it there with one hand. Even at the witty points he did not look up or change his tone, but kept the outward severity of face and the evenness of voice. Only twice or thrice did his voice falter or change: when he read the stanza "Take, oh take those lips away" and Blake's verse about the lost traveller's dream under the hill, and once when he recalled the time long past when he had composed the last poem of the *Shropshire Lad*: then he was checked for a moment, and brushed his eye with his hand. And there was a solemnity at the end when he bid adieu to literary criticism—and to the world—with the words "Farewell for ever".

Housman is of middle height, spare of figure, with severe, sharp-cut, well-complexioned face, with thin white hair and white Edwardian moustache and dark black eyebrows. In profile the head is remarkably elongated at the back. He wore a very dark-grey suit, with stiff upstanding collar folded right round the throat, and long stiff cuffs. He spoke for seventy minutes, and the applause at the end was fervent and enthusiastically prolonged, and repeated after the formal thanks of the Vice-Chancellor; and throughout the whole reading there had not been the least stir in the audience, so intent was it upon each word, so conscious of the importance of the occasion, so enthralled by this marvellous discourse. I am immeasurably the more content with life after having heard and seen Housman, and am certain that there can be no comparable experience possible now. I am sure that this greatest of living Englishmen will be great even among the dead.'

Housman is especially a poet for the young and it is appropriate that he should appeal so deeply to the Peterley who doubts at the end of this journal whether he has grown more mature. 'One develops a worldly wisdom for the struggle for existence; but this is cunning rather than maturity,' he writes. '. . . I am in danger of staying too long in the aesthetic stage, where one should not linger too much.'

Housman, no less than the Welsh wizard Arthur Machen with his magical brews, was a splendid solitary figure from the past who had become stranded in the twentieth century, as Peterley feels himself to be, and was consoled in his isolation with the timeless sounds and sweet airs of our literature. He valued poetry as Peterley values the music that fills so much of this journal: by its non-intellectual power to 'transfuse emotion', as Housman expressed it, bristling the skin, shivering the spine, constricting the throat, watering the eyes: and by its power to summon up 'something older than the present organization of his [man's] nature, like the patches of fen which still linger here and there in the drained lands of Cambridgeshire . . .'

Peterley too feels the need of something older than twentieth-century organization, something represented by the eighteenth-century house which carries the same name as himself and which, he writes, 'I cannot help thinking nobler because less commercial, and because rooted in the soil'. With Peterley himself we reach another layer of this book, which cannot be authenticated against records but must be measured by its imprint on our minds and emotions. What Richard Pennington attempted to do was to create an Englishman of the Imperial decadence, a contemplative aesthete, incapable of action, who self-consciously reflects the mood of an inglorious period of English history. 'Peterley [the house] seems now to be merely the symbol of an England that is lost for ever,' Mr Pennington makes David Peterley write before casting off for Australia early in 1939. 'The *entre-deux-guerres* is joining the Edwardian age and the nineteenth century as history. There does not seem to be any present, apart from this waiting for the first shots of the second war. Time and a future may still exist abroad; but here there is only suspension of time and movement, a mere waiting. I shall go abroad.'

To establish David Peterley as a figure pinned to this transitory period of decline, and mirroring it through his idle and unpurposed life, Richard Pennington makes him come and go from the other side of the world, and assigns him to that class with most 'downward mobility', the upper class. But this invention of a historical character is superseded by something more personal, a Yeatsian image or mask of the anti-self. 'We are made up of all the things wished for as well as all the things achieved,' he writes. One may imagine the people whom Mr Pennington saw while employed as librarian at the National Liberal Club: and imagine how in his mind's eye he followed them from the club into the country and a different world—a world he comes decorously to inhabit as David Peterley and which, being longed for passionately, becomes not something merely outside himself, but a part of his being. 'Do you know, I had the feeling at Peterley of being in another century', one of the visitors to this make-believe house remarks.

It is a romantic past, like an extended evening, gentle and melancholic, that Mr Pennington conjures up around his *alter ego*. In David Peterley he gives us, not someone simply caught between two wars, but a character adrift between two centuries. Peterley feels that 'the eighteenth century was right in its horror of mountains, as in most things. Civilization is connected with the river valleys.' He loves the dead ceremonies of the Church that, having had all meaning rubbed away by the twentieth century, 'have gained instead a pacifying perfection like that of Byzantine frescoes or Raphael paintings, that soothe but not inebriate.' He wants transportation to be 'slowed down rather than speeded up,' suspecting that there may be an inverse relationship between speed and the cultivation of the mind. With his own cultivated mind and from his privileged (if reduced) situation, he understands the word 'uneconomic' to mean something that, while not making money, is capable of fulfilling our human needs: 'My advice would be: If it's uneconomic, let's do it. Most things that have given most satisfaction to human beings have been uneconomic—cathedrals and gardens, plays and paintings.' Peterley's interests lie in the rural society built upon an agricultural economy. 'The life of the village and of the small country town I know and love, and think the only life worth living,' he writes: 'the life of the industrialized world is a blank.'

David Peterley's romantic preoccupation with the past pulls against his romantic attraction to Polly, a middle-class musician living in London and belonging very much to the twentieth century—'the only woman for whom I have any passionate feeling'. It is, as he admits, 'the attraction of the unknown', and it makes him come alive in the present. But: 'marriage would be unthinkable: one does not go to Sydenham for wives.' At the beginning of the narrative he has married Jane, a lady better suited to the style of the house than the personality of David Peterley himself. But after this empty and passionless union is ended, it seems as if he will repeat the error by sacrificing Polly to his obsession with the past and marry another well-cast mistress of the house. The emotional suspense is tightened by Peterley's exquisite hesitations. 'I viewed this theoretical future all the way back to London,' he writes at one moment in the event-plot, 'and found the pros and cons so nicely equal that the scales refused to kick the beam and solve my hesitations.' As the story develops, Peterley shows himself to be a connoisseur of indecision, procrastination, and all the sensations of vicarious experience. 'Life is cruder and simpler than you imagine,' Polly rebukes him. But it is not simple for Peterley, a creature of the imagination, who hovers agonizingly between his hopes for the future and regrets for the past, knowing life to be the risk of choosing, 'and having that choice we are the slaves of the anxiety it occasions'.

Eventually he is impelled into action by Hitler who both opposes order deriving from the eighteenth century and threatens existence in the twentieth century. The Nazi element in the diaries is introduced early through Peterley's 'Cousin Richard'. David Peterley is not taken in. 'I bought a paper and read of a blood-bath of more than oriental amplitude that the National Socialists have been enjoying,' he writes in the summer of 1934. 'There seems to be less of the Puritan Ironsides about this new party than Cousin Richard would have us believe.' Cousin Richard, 'who's always as full of the hot gospel from Munich as of Niersteiner,' asks Peterley whether he would like to receive an invitation to a Party Rally at Nuremberg, but 'I felt bound to refuse this so flattering offer, and rejoined Polly in the street below . . .'

Until the later years of the decade it is the pleasures of private life that absorb Peterley. 'We lingered amicably my charming companion and myself in the deserted lounge behind the closed shutters,' he writes during a visit to France in 1934; 'and if Hitler had at that moment been reported crossing the Rhine I doubt if I should have been disturbed.' But the shutters must eventually open. The journal skilfully plots the change of emphasis from private into semi-public life. There is a horribly convincing account of the effect of Hitler's speech-making on a Viennese audience in the autumn of 1938. 'I knew that voice. I had heard it before in days when it held an appeal and had a fascination. Its power was still there to charm men's ears, and I had to admit that I was listening to one of the greatest orators of the world . . . the venom in the mind of the orator spilled over into his voice and my companions of the Viennese café were in a murderous heat. The spells of the enchanter were still terrible, and these fat lazy pub-crawlers had turned into man-haters, with their blood pounding in their arteries, their eyes strained and bloodshot, and their sagging muscles tightening under the stimulation of the chemical secretion of their glands.' This must have something of the effect produced on 'Cousin Richard'. But the Munich Crisis opens his eyes: he is disenchanted with his Führer—and Cousin Richard joins David Peterley, the two in one, in forming a political group for the defence of Czechoslovakia.

The politics of *Peterley Harvest* offer an unfashionable counterpoint to *The Orators* or *Down and Out in Paris and London*. 'The young Auden, the young Orwell, longing for signs of change, angry and impatient at the persistence of in-grained forms of social injustice or inequality of wealth, speak of the same world as Peterley's but seen from the opposite angle,' John Wain has written. 'There is no evidence that Peterley worries about social injustice, or thinks about it at all, for that matter.' With whatever undertow of self-disapproval, Richard Pennington rises from an inferior social position through the phantom figure of David Peterley. His Peterley wants reaction rather than reform, 'and books on economics and sociology therefore have no meaning for me,' he writes, 'and the plays of Mr Galsworthy bore me, and I cannot share the conscious worries of Fabian reformers.' He sees himself as an individualist and spectator of the current scene, though he belongs very much to that age of Proust and Dunne's *Experiment with Time* as he calculates the effect on his emotions of the present drifting into the past, and tries 'not to think of the future'.

Much that is severely hostile to this position and critical of Pennington's 'frozen caricature of yourself' comes through the letters of Peterley's friend Alice Peers or 'A.M.P.', who blames him for his empty egocentricity and terror of commitment. Peterley's political views are expressed with deliberate arrogance. 'I am sitting in cafés and enjoying the life of the senses and the mind,' he writes as late as June 1938. 'But, after all, that is exactly what all politics are: only the administrative machinery for making possible. The only justification for Mr Chamberlain, Herr Hitler, and M. Beneš is that they enable me to sit under the castle of the Winter Queen on a summer night drinking wine, and wasting time, and enjoying that strange game of arranging words so as to form an image for the listeners to guess the meaning of, and feeling that emotion of contentment and quiet desire that comes from watching handsome women.' This view of politics would sound more sympathetic if it insisted on everyone's right and opportunity to sit in cafés, for it is not so far from Dr Johnson's

> How small of all that human hearts endure
> That part which laws or kings can cause or cure.

Like Johnson, Peterley has inherited a vile melancholy—'that very paralysis of will which prevents your voluntary escape from it'. As the record of these years grows darker, so Peterley's accidie intensifies and his speculations on the elusive nature of happiness become more rarefied. Walking through London in the spring of 1938, with the sense of being on the snow-line of a new ice age, depression overwhelms him like a black wave. 'Whitehall is a gloomy street,' he writes, '. . . and at night dead as the Acropolis; and my own past and the past of history came up like a darker cloud in the dark night, and I seemed to be walking in the ruins of a buried civilization.' Whitehall was Mr Pennington's place of work at the National Liberal Club—the club where the mysterious Peterley sometimes drops in to brood or entertain his guests. The formality of belonging to this disappearing world oppresses him, but 'when it passed away I am not sure,' he writes in the autumn of 1938; 'nor whether it was merely my world that has vanished, or the world of all the people around me. I suspect the latter; and that it was almost certainly the Führer who uttered the spell that dissolved the baseless fabric.'

It is a tribute to the strength and sensitivity of Richard Pennington's writing that Peterley's journey through the 1930s does not irritate or depress. The structure of the book is many-layered. It includes an anonymous diary within the diary, letters from known and unknown people, a ghost story by 'Cousin Richard', a short story and a few poems by David Peterley, more than one love affair, some travellers' tales and an intermittent narrative of historical events. These layers of fantasy and actuality give the work a complex satisfying texture, and reinforce the central theme at private and public levels. Listening to the King's abdication speech on 12 December 1936, Peterley records: 'I shall long remember the shudder that ran through the celebrities . . . when the phrase "the woman I love" came so awkwardly out of the mechanical box. I felt it too.' He feels and will remember it because the King's moral dilemma has been a magnified version of Peterley's own risk of choosing.

To solve all the riddles of *Peterley Harvest* would need a Preface by Mr Richard Pennington himself: and perhaps, after all, that would only add to them. Shortly after the book's first publication, and greatly to the publisher's dismay, Mr Pennington had it withdrawn and destroyed. Such an act recalls Arthur Machen's words to Peterley: ' "The job of the literary man—at least I've found it so—is inexpressibly painful, nervous, laborious, with more of disappointment and despair than happiness. Only your belief in the value of the written word supports you; and it needs all your strength of will to cling to that belief in this country." He showed me a book of newspaper cuttings: "These are the unfriendly reviews." It was quite a large book.' It may be that adverse criticism had some effect, but there are likely to have been other reasons for its withdrawal, some of which (in the spirit of Peterley) were vicarious and some regretted. In any event, a few copies had been bought and others sold abroad before the edition was suppressed, and these so appealed to the common reader that rare copies were soon fetching greatly inflated prices. In 1963, Mr Pennington issued a small new edition in Canada without the frontispiece and with the title page slightly amended. Until now, there has been no other printing.

John Wain has likened Peterley to Boswell—'not the Boswell who hero-worshipped Johnson but the Boswell who filled volume after volume with the fascinated shredding-out of his own moods and emotions, who once noted 'I should live no more than I can record', as if the only value of experience were to provide pabulum for this delighted connoisseurship of the vintages of his private cellar. Of such grapes is the Peterley Harvest composed.' What the brew lacks in Boswellian robustness it makes up for with its ingenious sensibility, its urbanity and gamesmanship. It may also be seen as one of those rare hybrid works, blending realism with romanticism, the serious and the tongue-in-cheek, of which the fore-runner was George Borrow's *Lavengro*—a book that also had in its beginning few appreciative critics and some vituperative ones.

Whatever its forebears, *Peterley Harvest* fits perfectly into the Arts Council Reprint Library. This already includes fiction and non-fiction books by Norman Douglas, Wyndham Lewis, William Gerhardie, L. H. Myers and J. B. Yeats, and is designed to rescue maverick work such as this remarkable exercise in ventriloquism for the general reader and give critics a better opportunity for assessment, of which this Preface is only the beginning.

Michael Holroyd

Foreword

Among the Peterley family papers now in the McGill University Library
The Journal of David Peterley covers the years of his life in Australia,
in England, and in Prague, the years from 1926 to 1939. The full journal
is more an archival collection than a diary, since almost nothing was
excluded from its pages, and the description of an evening with a poet or
a mistress may be followed by a tradesman's bill (unreceipted), or the
plan of a yacht he built for the Bulli sands, or a newspaper cutting of a
suicide. So that by 1939, when the journal ends, it had grown to six
bound volumes, seventeen folders, and a bundle of Czech documents.
ments which fill the red box now in the manuscript collection at
McGill.

But in 1939, on his last voyage, he selected the passages dealing with
his private life and wrote them out again so as to produce a more or less
continuous autobiographical narrative. He expanded some brief entries,
compressed others, and prudently changed the names of some of the
personages, since all of them were living people and some of them still
are. There was only one important change of text: the scenes at home in
England were transferred in the rewritten version from the actual family
home to the old one in Buckinghamshire, which in fact had long ago
been pulled down, and which he seems to have taken pleasure in
rebuilding in the journal.

Even this greatly shortened version I found much too long for publication, and as editor I have shortened it still more by replacing the narratives
of weeks and sometimes months by a précis of my own. And I have
omitted the whole of the long Australian volume and replaced it by my
brief recapitulation 'Botany Bay', the defects of which should therefore
not be attributed to Peterley. I have avoided as much as possible other
editorial interferences, such as the explanatory footnote, since after all
it is not the factual biographical story that justifies the printing of an

intimate journal. That justification is to be found, if at all, in the revelation of the inner life of fugitive images in the mind and fitful impulses of the heart, that inner life which with most of us goes unrecorded and which it is the aim of the official biography to conceal.

Richard Pennington

McGill University

Botany Bay

ON APRIL THE THIRD 1926 David Peterley sailed for New South Wales, an action he seems to have regarded as hazardous and praiseworthy, although in fact he stepped out of a car at Tilbury Docks and into a comfortable, and first-class, cabin of the P. & O. *Chitral*, from which he emerged six weeks later in Sydney to begin that unsteady course of sentimental vagabondage that so careful an analyst of the human heart should have known would end in disaster.

The voyage to Botany Bay was in former days an alternative to capital punishment; but for Peterley it is the alternative to marriage. He recognizes, the first adventurous impulse over, that he has left England to escape the tedium of a solicitor's office and marriage with the woman of his father's choice. And it is not long before life as a lawyer in London, with a young society woman as a wife, does not seem so contemptible when compared with all that New South Wales can offer. He experiences a nostalgia and an ennui which not all the sunlight and surfing can overcome.

The photographs show him as tall, and with that strength and slight irregularity of face that women find handsome, especially when matched with blond hair and blue eyes. And if he fills his journal with a melancholy indifference to the pleasures of life, he takes no great care to avoid them. There are as many social evenings as solitary ones; and until the relationship with Mrs. Innes Kay he leads the life of any young man whom mothers with daughters think worth encouraging, and who do not know that this is precisely the situation from which he fled in flying from England, and who are not aware that he is living with Mrs. Crosslé during Dr. Crosslé's absence in London. Nearly the whole of this first volume of the diary is devoted to his life with Betty Crosslé, an effortless adultery that even her husband's return does not interrupt. For Crosslé proved to be a man of literary tastes, a musician, and a diarist. Peterley finds him sympathetic; and, having shared a wife, they go so far as to exchange diaries. They spend the week-ends discussing Beethoven; and

9

it is probable that to these musical interludes by the sea Peterley owed that preoccupation with music that played a dominant part in his life.

But even a well-conducted *ménage à trois* has its strains and stresses; and in April 1927 Betty Crosslé returns to Ireland for good, and Peterley goes no more to Bulli. His life is now much emptier, until Dr. Rundle, who had been a complaisant chaperon at Bulli in Crosslé's absence, introduces him to Annabelle Innes Kay, the young wife of a socially prominent solicitor. This intellectual beauty is little to his taste at first. He is alarmed to find so much physical charm allied to a 'chastity of mind to which one is nowadays not accustomed', and he dismisses her as a 'Récamier on a Sydney sofa' and 'a princess of a Chinese opera', which may be an unkind reference to *Turandot*. He lets the impression that she had been so careful to make fade from his mind. And this he can afford to do, since he has made the acquaintance of John Gunn on the morning ferry that takes them both across the harbour to the city from Cremorne. Gunn is a senior member of an accountancy firm, and a book-collector; and his wife, as Peterley soon discovers, 'is the most sprightly, pert, pleasure-loving, party-haunting young matron ever mated with a banker, and with mischievous eyes, the richest of chestnut curls, and the neatest of figures. I would keep her in a bank vault if I were a banker.'

Between Mrs. Gunn and himself there develops what was probably an amused flirtation on her part, but on his a feeling that threatens at any moment to become more serious. The Gunns live on Cremorne Point, just across from his own apartment, and in time they offer him a part of their house. He accepts, and moves in his books and hangs his pictures.

The letters from his father, that are dutifully pasted in the diary, keep him acquainted with affairs at home—harvesting and the changes to the grounds, including the restoration of the stone summer house into a bookroom for Rose, the gardener's daughter. She has left her boarding school because of poor health; and to Peterley's astonishment his father talks of sending her to Switzerland or Egypt. With news of Rose are mingled references to the Miss Leigh from whom he seems to have run away, in exiling himself to New South Wales, and there are hints that an Australian marriage would not give much pleasure at Peterley:

'As you know, we have ploughed and harvested here for eight generations, and I should be sorry to think that we are not to continue. Your grandfather was at one moment tempted to remove to North America when a Miss Raines, an actress whom he had failed to convert from musical comedy to agriculture, ran off to Scotland with a young guardsman she preferred. Commonsense and the charms of Miss Fairfax prevailed, and our continuity was preserved. Whether this of itself is something estimable I am not ready to argue, but am content to accept as an article of faith. I hope we have not been spared the Yankees only to fall among kangaroos.'

Sometimes in a letter a family closet is opened and the customary skeleton is to be glimpsed; as when his father describes the visit he has just paid to Bordeaux for the wedding of Great-uncle Matthew's natural daughter. And on one occasion there arrives a six-page letter, duly pasted in the diary, that could have been labelled 'A Father's Advice to a Son on settling in a distant Colony'.

'My dear David,
        The last words and testament I suspect to be a literary device; although in the days when, unhastened by surgery, one died slowly and could find one's family close at hand, it may have been possible; but death today comes commensurate with the speed at which we live, and families are scattered to the four corners of an empire, so that I thought it more sensible to give you my opinions now when you have time and may have the wish to consider them, rather than later or too late. You may, of course, come to conclusions quite different, but quite workable as far as you are concerned.
        As the first of a man's relationships is to the State, I commend to your respect whatever form of government you live under. The attainment of order and stability is such an achievement among human beings, and these qualities so precious, that nothing should be done to destroy them, and if men were wise, they would be willing to sacrifice much, including some of their freedom, for them. No revolution produces the State it dreamed of, because its dream was part of the old order of things; and a new order comes into being with the successful revolution, in which that dream is no longer valid. Nor have I ever been convinced that revolutionaries were actuated by love of their fellow-men: it is contempt and hatred that shine in their eyes. Their belief that they must drag up the lowly and poor to another level is proof they despise them, instead of viewing them with respect and pity as does the wiser and more benevolent Church.
        As you should support the State (and I do not regard a Monarchy as necessarily opposed to the common will), so you should not

weaken the authority of a Church. The temptation to do so is very strong in one's younger and irresponsible days; and it is because one confuses the institution with religion. The latter is wild, solitary, and dangerous; and these qualities belong naturally to the desert, and there the uncompromisingly religious man will find himself, with anchorites and atheists and mystics, and also with all the dangers of the desert: the unearthly vision, the distorted echo, the voice of the tempter, and madness. It is not wise to despise a Church for having ordered this wild emotion and linked it to morality. To enact the cosmological drama on the stage of a chancel and imprison the godhead in a chalice is surely a piece of life raised to the highest aesthetic level, and worthy of your admiration: much play-acting you applaud is far less effective, and I suspect less beneficent. Nor I, nor you, will solve the problem of good and evil; unless perhaps we are unconsciously solving it each time we walk down the avenue to the church that I and my no less perplexed ancestors have maintained.

As for your conduct in the world, you will find that for most men the world is really the world of their profession; but you should try to be one of those that can move in other spheres than their professional one, and can mix at ease with the broader minds who from time to time escape into the freer society of the educated men of all kinds, the world of the London club and the London dining-room. For this you must be able to talk entertainingly, be attentive to women, and undertake your share of hospitality. If you choose the right people, your time and money will not be wasted; but I do not mean by "right" those whose prominence is merely social and not intellectual as well.

In your dealings with your fellow-men, it is wise to remember that they, too, will have their private dreams and unconfessed ideals, but that they are engaged in the struggle to maintain their standard of life and their personal dignity, and to protect the household gods. If you attack any of these, you must expect to encounter all the malevolence of which our human nature is capable; but if you are careful to respect these very natural self-interests, I think you will be continually surprised at the normal kindliness and even altruism of human beings.

I imagine that it is unfashionable now for parents to address their sons on the subject of women, except by means of the smoking-room story; but, as this is an English convention, I shall ignore it. If you are well read in Classics and French literature—for our own will not help you much here—you will know almost all that can be known about women, and it will be of little use to you.

Your encounters with women, if you are wise in your choice, are likely to be the most pleasant episodes of your life, if you conduct them properly; and otherwise, the most unpleasant. It is necessary to remember that if women surrender—and they do, of course, much more readily and oftener than our conventions admit—it is because they look in return for kindness and sympathy and solicitude, which are for them as imperious a need as sexual satisfaction is for us. They ask for nothing else; and if you cannot make this return, you should not continue the liaison.

You need not assume that a physical intimacy necessarily entails marriage, and it is prudent to be cautious of any woman who refuses to admit the separateness of these two things, unless it is the woman you intend to marry. Living with women cannot usually be postponed until marriage is convenient, and it is advisable to give some thought to the choice of a mistress. I am of the opinion that the most satis-factory way is to select from the wives of your older acquaintances, or at any rate from the young wives of older husbands. These are often neglected by busy or indifferent men and are eager for a companion-ship which is as much intellectual as physical. They will have an experience and an ardour from which you will benefit, and they are usually wise enough not to risk the loss of their position by demanding that you abduct them from their homes. But to avoid any danger of this, you should take care not to undermine their respect for their husband.

I am assuming you would no more dream of having recourse to whores any more than you would hire for an evening party a dress suit that has covered the private parts of any tradesman or commercial traveller.

I have gone to great length to say what I suppose could have better been said in the simpler phrase: fear God, honour the King, and be chivalrous to women. With all our political science and our sociology, we have not really progressed beyond this, nor do I believe we ever can.'

Peterley is greatly impressed, but by its style; and shows no sign of letting its precepts influence his conduct. He comments: 'The old man must certainly have found it hard to unpack his heart of all these words, and I should love to know where he got the fine phrases about the liturgical drama. I'd also like to know the early sowings that have produced this late crop of wisdom.'

Sailing remains his chief pleasure and interest; but when he is not sailing, or conversing on sofas with young married women, or filling his diary with metaphysical speculations and literary criticism, he has two other diversions to occupy his leisure: the search for Christopher Brennan, the lost Australian poet, and the founding of a repertory theatre in Sydney. He eventually succeeds in both. 'I found Australia's finest poet in Australia's worst slum,' he records; and he rescues the drink-sodden remains of what had once been the country's foremost scholar and writer from the back bedroom of a dingy rooming house in Woolloomooloo. He brings together a small committee of lawyers, doctors, and university men to create a Brennan fund to provide food, clothes, and shelter for the destitute poet. And to help the rehabilitation he introduces him to the houses of his friends, who listen enraptured to Brennan's conversation that carries them far from the Australian shores to Athens or Alexandria or Provence on a spring morning, or down the byways of the eighteenth century. They listen and forget the pathetic spectacle of the fallen scholar with a second-hand morning coat buttoned too tightly across his huge chest and across the dicky that conceals the absence of a shirt. Peterley takes him to the Innes Kays at Point Piper, and brings him to the Gunns at Cremorne; and both these literary ladies are enchanted by the poet he has rescued from the docks. For Peterley's first impression of Mrs. Innes Kay has changed, and he is spending more and more time with the woman he had dismissed as a '*précieuse* out of time and place'. The choice of sofas is in fact becoming more difficult, whether on the north shore with Mrs. Gunn or on the south with Mrs. Innes Kay. Brennan had not suffered from this divided mind. He had fallen, as he thought, in love with Dorothy Gunn; and one day he presents himself at her door with a bunch of faded flowers, a shaven face, and unlaced boots; and very ungratefully tries to win her favour by exaggerating Peterley's entanglement with the Calypso of Point Piper.

As a result of this indelicate intrusion Peterley has to retire from the domesticity of the Gunn home and take shelter on the other side of the harbour in a small public house where the only other permanent lodger is Radcliffe Brown the anthropologist. Whether from solitude or propinquity (for he is close to Point Piper) his friendship with Mrs. Innes Kay develops into a passion, the less restrained because hopeless, that shadows the rest of his two years in New South Wales. The diary is little more than a monologue on his love for a woman who can resist every temptation except that of being rapturously adored. He adopts all the usual and useless remedies: travels in the Victorian highlands; goes sailing alone; wanders solitarily up-country; and finally comes back uncured and asks her to divorce, and offers her marriage. She refuses. For nearly six months there is no entry at all in the diary. When it begins again it shows that he has resumed a normal life in Sydney. He appears with Annabelle in public; and spends all his free evenings at her house; but there is henceforward no mention of the unwelcome passion of the year before.

The letters from home at this time are often filled with news of Rose; and he expresses (in his diary) his irritation that his father spends so much time and money on the gardener's daughter. She had been staying in Switzerland in the hope of a recovery of health; and there had made the acquaintance of a young Italian from Milan. They had eloped together and had married at Rome; and Peterley has some grim satisfaction in observing how this setting up the gardener's daughter in a state of life to which she had not been born had proved too much for her. But she had probably realized she had not long to live; for before Peterley leaves Australia he received the news of her death in Rome.

He finds some solace at this time in his work for the establishment of the Turret Repertory Theatre at Sydney; and from being interested in founding a theatre, he grows interested in the acting, and then in the actresses, and in one actress in particular whose dramatic ability he considers far above the average. He surprises himself by proposing to Miss Stella Peters one evening as he is driving her home after a successful first night. But the decisiveness of such an act appals him in his more thoughtful moments, and it is only after a wrestling with the angel of his conscience in the Botanic Gardens that he decides it is his duty to carry the engagement through. He tries to secure support for this courageous determination from Annabelle during the evenings he spends at her home, but not with much success; and evening by evening his resolution weakens and drains slowly away, until the moment comes when with an effort of will he announces to Stella that the engagement is broken, and to Annabelle that he has booked a passage back to England. He spends his last, his only, night with Annabelle—decorously talking in her room that looked out to the Pacific that in twelve hours will be separating them forever; and their long dialogue, with its stretches of silence, ends as the first pallid light of morning defines the groups of trees on the lawn. He takes his leave, and walks down the familiar hill to Double Bay for the last time; and at midday boards the *Makura* for San Francisco on his way back home.

Peterley

1930

June

LIVERPOOL greets the traveller not imperially, not grandly, nor even picturesquely, but meanly, dirtily, dully like all English ports. This is England, busily making bicycles, cotton shirts, machinery, and sanitary porcelain, and too busy to care about any other life than that. The harbours of England—shade of Turner!—are now oily estuaries flushing the sooty walls of warehouses. This imperial and royal island meets the sea without a single noble gesture of monument or esplanade or piazza, with nothing to symbolize the audacity of seafaring, the secular adventure of foreign trade, the solace of landfall. Slums sprawl obscenely on the slopes of what were wooded hills; tenement and factory jostle where the city should be. There is no city; only a maze of ignoble brick and narrow streets that peter out in alleys and dwindle to rows of shabby shops.

If this is the heart of the Empire, it is an empire that cannot last for long, for there is nothing here that is durable. Where are the opera houses a German princeling could build; the paintings an Italian city could produce; the music a Transylvanian peasant can play? Are there statues in their gardens and fountains in their towns? Are their colonies more beautiful for their coming, or only more profitable? Will their operations on the Manchester Stock Exchange save them in the day of reckoning? Is this slum of a city worthy of the human mind?

Scott's imitation Gothic cathedral is no answer: it smells of the electric light of the industrious apprentice; and size has taken the significance out of the design, as a river in flood loses all the beauty of a river. I sleep in a Gothic and grimy hotel; breakfast on bad coffee ministered by a slatternly maid; and catch a train that drags me through débris-littered fields and by the unwiped backsides of factories southward towards a Peterley that does at least represent a life I cannot help thinking nobler because less commercial, and because rooted in the soil.

I had forgotten that my annunciatory letter from Vancouver would not have travelled faster than I, and I could not understand the air of desolation over Peterley when I arrived. The house was closed; there was no one at Gurney's cottage; no one in the garden. In the servants' wing a young girl whom I did not know was sitting reading before the cold kitchen stove. She was so surprised to see anyone that she forgot to be frightened. I introduced myself, but all she said was, 'I'm Mary.' She did not know where the Old Man was, except that he had left four days ago, with Gurney driving. Everyone was on holiday except herself and the young man who helped the gardener, and Boughton who was in charge. I asked if she could manage to look after me, and went through into the house. It was airless and chilly and there were dust-sheets in the two drawing-rooms. I did not venture to use the study, and took temporary possession of the Card Room, and stowed all my luggage there. Father returned on Monday evening. He said he was fortunate to be delivered undamaged, for Gurney in turning into the drive had seen the lighted windows of the Card Room and, knowing the house to be empty, had nearly lost control of the car in his terror. I should not have suspected the old gardener of believing that story about the haunted Card Room. Father showed no surprise at my return, as I expected he would not. There was a rather dry conversation in the study afterwards, although he did go down for a bottle—a Fendant, I noticed. He said he'd taken to drinking it with a late dinner or a light supper. Matthew had carried on at Peterley a habit he had picked up in Valais or Vaud. 'There they drink it with a *fondue*, a hot dish of melted cheese and kirsch which I suppose is digestible after a day's skiing. A light amusing wine, scarcely petillant. Goes well with cheese. Not drunk at all on this side.' He filled up the gaps of silence by random observations and seemed unwilling to mention my four years' absence, perhaps to avoid the embarrassment of asking the wrong questions. He did bring himself, however, to inquire if I'd liked the country. I replied truthfully, no; that the curves of the land were rarely pleasing and that the eucalyptus was the ungainliest of trees, especially when it had been ring-barked and had lost all its foliage and had died to a dead white trunk. 'I can understand. You come to like the slopes you've been accustomed to. I could never admire the steepness of the Swiss valleys. I think the eighteenth century was right in its horror of mountains, as in most things. Civilization is connected with the river valleys.'

He asked what I would like to do, to which I had no answer, except that I had thought of his suggestion of going in with Harris and Harris, and was willing without being enthusiastic. 'Enthusiasm would be a bit out of place among solicitors,' he admitted, and went on to say: 'I should warn you that Peterley isn't as profitable as it used to be. I'm no farmer and perhaps Maynard has had things his own way too long for me to try and change them. I think there's enough for an economical life in London, but it wouldn't quite be enough for a married man. Let me know if you'd like me to speak to Harris.'

And that was all the serious discussion we had. That strong impassive face, as though chiselled in stone with all the surfaces left flat and unrounded, in fact, hated to face the realities and crudities of life with an equal brutality, and preferred any cost that could shield the sensitive mind behind the blue eyes from the suffering such contact with reality would cause. Rather than ask a tenant to do something he legally should do, he would pay himself to have it done; he would keep on a wastefully inefficient labourer rather than dismiss him, or even rudely try to reform him. It was as though he had spent all his life and fortune in painting the rocks of a coast a rosy tint which each light storm washed away.

The study was unchanged; the chairs were still heaped with books that hid the embroidered seats; the desk still preserved its inch-layer of papers. But the large board on the wall had changed its maps and when I got up to look at them I found the French general-staff maps for the Belfort region. 'Still interested in the 1870 campaign, I see.' 'Wrong. Too obvious. You're not likely to guess, although you did it in the Fourth Form. Don't you remember the most critical moment in Caesar's career or hadn't the master an eye for strategy?' He seemed much more interested in this than in my return, as he showed me the meaning of the little flags that stretched from Châlons-sur-Saône to Neuchâtel: 'This was a moment when Caesar was out-manœuvred, out-numbered, and out-marched. He was here'—and he pointed to a place near Langres—'and the Gauls were calling up armies all over the country to crush him once and for all before he could get back to his base in Provence. He had a Gaulish army to the west; there was one to the south concentrating round Autun. He could have retreated east, but that would have taken him into Germany, ever farther from his base. There was only one line of escape open to him—the single pass across the Jura mountains that led down to the Genevan lake; and from there he could take the valley of the Rhône to Lyon. To entrust his army to the steep, narrow, pine-covered defiles of the Jura where they could be surprised and picked off by the enemy was a serious risk to take. But Caesar must have risked it; and he was in fact caught by the Gaulish cavalry, who overtook his rearguard at a place called Alesia. Now the professional historians insist this was in Alsace, which is nonsense. I've been over the Jura with Armand-Périer who is Député for the Doubs, and we are agreed that Caesar was trapped at Alaise near Besançon, right on the gap at Pontarlier that leads to the pass at Vallorbe which brings you down to Lausanne and the Genevan lake. Caesar got away; but it was one of the most dangerous moments of his life.'

We finished the bottle, and separated for the night. The Old Man had spent twice as much time discussing Julius Caesar as in speaking of Australia or the future, and that, too, was the Peterley I had always known. I went up to my room, and from the stairs could hear Father pottering about the study, where he would read for another hour yet, and Boughton asking if there was anything more for tonight, and going round closing up. The pattern of life was establishing itself. The room was just as I had left it four years before: the simple bed, the huge armoire from St. Claude, the writing table and the rush-seated chairs, and Uncle Matthew's Arabian saddle-covers on the floor. I looked out through the window-panes upon the unaltered garden below and the same stars above:

> Vaghe stelle dell'Orsa, io non credea
> Tornare ancor per uso a contemplarvi
> Sul paterno giardino scintillanti,
> E ragionar con voi dalle finestre
> Di questo albergo ove abitai fanciullo . . .*

It is still with a shock of pleasure that I gaze each early morning at the neat landscape, the trim grass, the plum tree nailed to the sheltering wall, the flower borders, and the wood beyond, and enjoy the round shoulders of these beeches and oaks after the angularities of the eucalyptus. This is indeed the England, small, quiet, beautifully assured, that I longed for under the endless blue sky on the limitless plains of the underworld, and I feel contented as I have not felt for years.

I came down the stairs, by the wooden portrait of the 'first George' on the half-landing, through the white hall with its old rugs and time-blackened furniture, into the morning-room where the bowls of flowers

* 'Stars of the Bear, I never thought to behold you again shining down on my father's garden or that I should converse with you once more from these windows from which my boyhood gazed. . . .' Leopardi, *Le Ricordanze*.

22

used to be arranged by my mother and where flowers, with their too-happy associations, are no longer allowed. The chintz of chair and curtain I could swear was the same, and was almost surprised to find that the *Country Life* on the table bore this year's date. Beyond, the small square library of the eighteenth-century house, which a Victorian Peterley had turned into a spare sitting-room for his large family, still retained the nineteenth-century furniture. I walked through and looked out on to the south garden down the avenue of mown turf between apple trees to the paved clearing where the statue should be. How many years was it since this room had known the noise and depredation of children? Great-uncle Matthew's dereliction of duty had left it unpeopled, and if it depended upon me—as it did, as it did—to make good the lack, I began to wonder if it might not just as well become a library again. Perhaps in two or three days' time I could go to London and, without a show of undue haste, see Jane, who by now must have been informed of my return.

'Sydney,
Saturday 17th May

David,
          Since the boat sailed on Thursday I have not dared to face the realization that you are really gone, and I still feel numb as one half awake after an anaesthetic, very quiet and a little dazed, and knowing that pain will inevitably come with full consciousness.

How could I have let you go? How could you go? But the questions are absurd. I made no attempt to keep you; and you could not have been persuaded. I knew all along that this separation would come, and I shall not, like Sister Alcoforado,* give way to expostulations and laments, however moving, in whatever eloquence of prose. Yet like her I do not know how I am to endure all—ah, it is that "all" that hurts—all the future days and nights without you. I am still not in a mood to write: the image of the *Makura* getting smaller in the distance on its way to sea is still in my mind, blurred with my tears like those early films with cinematographic rain. It is a glorious morning and I am writing on my balcony. I wander listlessly round the house instead of reading. I look out from here across Watson's Bay and South Head and wonder where in all that waste of water the

---

* Marianna Alcoforado, the author of the *Letters of a Portuguese Nun*, was, with Mademoiselle Aïssé, one of the two women writers for whom Peterley had a very great admiration.

Makura is now, and whether the gradual process of separation has begun yet for you. I will give you half-way to Frisco, and myself two years. But in spite of my foreknowledge I am on the brink of confessing how much I am still impassioned; how much I have always been, from the very beginning, more than I could ever confess. Now I am paying for my silence.

Annabelle'

I read this in the orchard on a perfect summer morning under the carolling of English birds and it reads like a fragment of Australian literature and as remote from me. The skies are changed. . . . But from this manuscript I can re-create some of the emotion of those days (and yet not so distant) as I might feel for a heroine of Richardson. There was nothing else to do; she was the most virtuous of women since she was probably more moved to surrender than I was to press the attack, and yet she refrained. I am with Milton in not admiring the fugitive and cloistered virtue; and Arnold could not accuse us of not being deeply moved or not deeply feeling. She will finger that lapis-lazuli in her country fields and think of nights at Romano's; and the green jade on a shrunken finger will, like an Arabian charm, summon up visions of nights of oriental luxury—at any rate it will seem like that at a distance of twenty years.

Coming in from a ride over to Hampden I see the envelope with an Australian stamp on the hall table, and wonder if it is wise to listen to this voice from the past and from another world. It is written only five days since I left Sydney; it mentions my radiogram from Wellington—did I send one?—which had moved her to an impassioned outpouring of regrets, for all the things she had not said or done, for all the tenderness she had refused—she surrenders on paper with a warmth which mocks me when I remember the princess of China posed on the sofa in her stiff brocades, holding out a negligent hand to be kissed and turning afternoon tea into a scene from a novel she had not yet written. I was then all fire and adoration before this stylized figure which has now become a woman in love with a character who has vanished from the literary scene.

'I am not brave at all when I think of all the days, the weeks, the months and years ahead with your love only a memory on which my dying heart must unnaturally nourish itself. I am lonely beyond the power of words to tell, and it is only the perfection of these memories that will help me live. It is late in the day and winter outside, and the mind is dull and the body aching and tired; and this is not a proper letter; and in any case it is useless as communication. You would have to be here; but if you were, I dare not think what I would do. It is pitiful that life is so often the denial of itself. It is dark, the only light my little lamp over my writing table; and you will read this in sunlight and the air. I think I am writing from the underworld. Goodnight, goodnight.'

I fold the letter up, and walk in the garden; and an emotion that is blended with the melancholy of early evening floods me and I almost falter in my steps.

The next communication from the underworld is Brennan's. He gives me full powers with regard to all his published verse, to select, edit, expound, criticize, 'as all rights belong to the author alone, the mere publisher having no rights at all', he not very correctly adds. He sends a long disquisition on poetic metre to elucidate 'not my metrical innovations because there aren't any, only developments', and he lays it down that 'stress is not accent. The two must coincide in the majority of cases or there is no verse; but stress is primary.' But he goes on to a metrical analysis of some lines of Milton and I find myself disagreeing. In the absence of a record of Milton's voice speaking the first dozen lines, all discussion of the metres of *Paradise Lost* is a waste of time.

September

Second

The date on the next letter is the 12th of July, and my letter from Vancouver has just reached Sydney, and Annabelle is overjoyed. She writes on her verandah and watches the yachts coming from Rushcutters Bay to the Heads and expects to see *Seabird* sail by,

'and I imagine you on board and that I shall see you in the evening when you return very brown and even more impetuous to tell me of the day and how glad you are to rejoin me at the end of it. But your odyssey speaks of Tahiti and California and I know you will not be rushing up these stairs tonight. But I enjoyed your voyaging since you say how much you wish I had been with you.'

Time is working its beneficent cure, since she goes on to talk of her books and of new dresses, a close-fitting sleeveless bodice with a full pleated skirt reaching to the ankle, and a short plain coat with frilled collar. I am promised a photograph.

I waited for Jane to descend the stairs of the Club where she was living, a white sepulchre of virginity in this cemetery of South Kensington where life was so genteel it scarcely seemed to exist at all. Appearance only: choleric Anglo-Indians, I was sure, brow-beat their little women in back bedrooms; divorcees during drinking bouts slept with good-looking chauffeurs in mews; and ladies in reduced circumstances conducted a dignified withdrawal before Economic Necessity through all the advertisement columns of the daily newspapers. If every room in South Kensington could be instantaneously photographed say at eleven o'clock one evening I wonder by how much the human misery would outweigh the amount of happiness? All this covering plaster frightens me: I suspect unstaunchable wounds beneath. Which was not the right mood in which to receive Jane who came down the stairs very slowly, conscious that this was a critical moment. She need have had no fear: she still was as handsome as her portrait, with that regularity of feature the Englishwoman so often has but with the elegance of figure that she so often hasn't. I said something about my impatience to see her again and asked where she would like to have dinner, adding that I didn't mind where, so long as there was no music. 'Well, that means Soho'; and we went to the *Escargot bienvenu*. Afterwards it occurred to me that music was probably the very thing a young woman would prefer. She seemed very happy; talked a great deal of Peterley and parties and hunting and was polite enough to ply me with questions about Australia. She seems maturer, but still looks on life with that continuous optimism which has always irritated me a little. I left her at her club, said I would ring during the week or arrange a party at Peterley, and walked back across the Park to my hotel trying to find an answer to the question whether I intended to marry Jane or not. I could see no argument against it, and much in favour: she has all the physical graces and the social ones as well; and if she likes the hunting crowd overmuch, that is something I can overlook.

Three months in England, and I am spending more and more time in London with Jane. Our evenings grow later; the dinners in Soho have turned into suppers at the Criterion or the Berkeley; and in midnight taxis it is almost as obligatory as it is usual to kiss. The strictness of her club has become annoying, and there were occasions when, had it not been Miss Leigh, I would have suggested an hotel.

On Thursday she asked if I would like a week-end at Elizabeth's cottage on the Dorset coast, where I could do some sailing with Martin, the sculptor she has married. We went down on Friday in a hired car and Martin and I spent a long Saturday sailing in the Channel. On the Sunday he and Elizabeth went out for a tea-party, leaving the house to Jane and myself. I wonder now if it was by design or not; for, from sitting talking on the sofa in this brief security, we fell to some familiarities and came somewhat closer to facing the problem of our physical relationship which has been troubling me, and perhaps Jane, since my return.

Afterwards, as I was rearranging my tie in the glass over the fireplace and gazing without any emotion at the face mirrored there, I felt that there could not remain much doubt about the solution of our problem and I remarked to Jane that I thought we had perhaps better get married. 'I quite agree,' was all she said.

Martin and I tried a little night fishing, but without success. When we were well out from the coast I was perturbed to discover that he had built the ketch himself with the aid of the village carpenter. A silent drive back to London very early on Monday morning, neither of us making any reference to Sunday's intimate discussion. I am still hesitant at heart and reluctant to make any definite commitment, but fully aware that Jane takes it for granted that we are unofficially engaged.

Here at Peterley I am beginning to feel the physical absence of my undeclared fiancée, and the growing desire dictates letters more passionate than any I have ever written to her before. Katherine is back in England, in Derbyshire, and I ought to visit her, and now no longer have the courage. Had we met first . . . but I cannot see her as mistress of

Peterley, only as a mistress in St. John's Wood, and that will never content her. I could wish unwritten all those fervent letters from Australia, but in the shock of learning of my marriage she is certain to burn them.

October

Seventh

Went in today to see Squire at the *London Mercury* office for an opinion on my Brennan article. He was in a jovial mood, pulled out my chrome-yellow tie and said he wished he had the courage to wear something like that. He found the article with the help of a typist and an assistant editor, and slapped it on the table and said: 'This stuff is good; but you can't fool an old hand like me. I've been in the game too long.' I couldn't understand; and he still thought I was bluffing. 'It's good; but you've made two slips. Look at these lines beginning with lower-case at this date—1895 of all years—and in Australia of all places. You can't get away with that.'

'And what was the other mistake?'

'Oh, the Mallarmé. His influence is obvious; and at that date it's impossible.'

I realized that he really thought Brennan was a figment of my imagination, and it took some time to persuade him that I wasn't pulling his leg. Unfortunately, I still do not possess the rare Brennan volume; and the B.M. does not have it either. It certainly looked suspicious. He said he'd keep the MS. and think it over: 'I doubt if the public here has any interest in this colonial writing. But this fellow, I admit, is different.'

Sixteenth

Squire writes:

'Brennan seems to have been a pioneer of the non-capital-letter-beginning line. Shift his dates on, and you will make him more convincing. Also give him parentage, education, etc. Also some verse of a robuster kind to square with his Johnsonian aspect. Your handwriting is exquisite.'

He refuses to believe in Brennan. Unfortunately I cannot get a copy of the poems. They must be the scarcest item in Australian bibliography.

December

The end of our honeymoon at Peterley. I woke up early this morning and looked out on a cold bedewed world outside. Jane sleeps soundly till eight-thirty always. A charming bride, if with the immaturity or un-sophistication of the English girl in matters of the bedroom. But amusing, even-tempered, industrious. I realize now why (at least I think this must be the reason) she had suggested a private, almost a secret, wedding, with no family forewarned; for when Harris, who has taken over the family affairs, now that the senior partner is ga-ga with age, came down today with Raybold, Jane's solicitor, to discuss the question of a settlement, I discovered that Jane owned more of Peterley than I did. Father's, or Maynard's, negligence had been paid for by mortgages which on every occasion Raybold had taken up; and Harris explained that Timothy had in writing instructed his solicitors to prevent the alienation of Peterley from the family, or if necessary acquire it and add it to Misham. Jane, who must surely have known this, had most conscientiously kept it from me, to ensure at least that I should not marry her for mercenary reasons. She had even sacrificed a proper wedding which would have meant a preliminary financial settlement that would have revealed my financial dependence. However, the mortgages are all cancelled; Jane restores Peterley to me; and all is as old Timothy planned. Harris will remove Maynard, and Knight who farmed for Timothy will manage the two estates. We shall have just enough when my father's income is deducted to run a small house economically in London, and I shall be spared a very junior partnership in law; but there won't be enough for that little flat in Weymouth Street I had described so lovingly and with so little result to Katherine.

I am beginning to tire of this inactive life and to wonder if leaving Australia were wise. Now in its turn Sydney becomes the scene of the Golden Age; and its turbulent pleasures, its crises, the heart-heavy climbs to Point Piper and the tired returnings to Double Bay; the brief ecstasies with Stella; above all, the harbour sunlight and the full sails of *Seabird*; even the old passion at Bulli—how long ago it seems I saw the flame trees at Coalcliff and watched the Pacific break on the rocks at Austinmer —all these gather the rosy light to them and become the lovely past.

To the meet yesterday, Boxing Day, at Chipping Campden, since Jane had written that she thought she would go over and would like me to join her. I came back to London alone, driving through a cold, clear, whitish winter evening; and, undecided whether to make for Peterley or for the empty house at Brook Green, I took the Wycombe road and so came to the turning to Chesham Bois. And suddenly the thought of finding Moira here made me forget my indecision and I turned down the dark lane and searched for the house at the corner among the beech trees where I had last seen her more than four years ago. The family were too polite to show their surprise at this late call, and Moira too surprised to be merely polite as I had feared she might be after the news of my marriage. She was as frank, as unaffected, as responsive as ever; and when she said she was glad Jane and I had married, I believed her. She still has that lovely face that is always radiant with her faith and her idealism, which in her alone of all people I have known do not seem ridiculous. She is all kindness and sincerity and the noblest thoughts; and I should have loved her for these qualities instead of feeling they came between us. She has been studying with Plunkett-Green and thinks of concert performances, 'because one can do so much good to people by singing'. She sang for me some of the Dowland songs which I find rather precious; but I was so content to sit and listen to her just as four years ago that I did not object. 'We must all meet,' she said at parting. 'You must bring Jane next time: we are great friends.'

I have decided to keep this house in Brook Green. Its seclusion, its quiet air, its trees and grass captivate me: a Victorian backwater. A few doors away Seymour Haden lived and etched: may still do. Opposite is the old house of the Queensberry family of ancient infamy, its grounds still unravished by the speculative builder. There is even a public house, Saloon to one side of the door, Public Bar to the other, which serves roast and two vegs. with the midday beer. We bring odd pieces of furniture from Peterley; and the old furniture of Uncle Matthew that I had offered for Katherine's virtue, and hoped might grace our extra-marital flat in Marylebone, now serves for my study. In idleness Jane grows domesticated, and I grow bored, and spend my time in the book-shops, and apply for a Reading Room ticket at the British Museum.

1931

January

Twenty-third

Squire writes that he has decided against the Brennan article, although he can't quite make up his mind about him: 'Perhaps your quotations don't bring him out enough. Try us with something else later on.'

Jane is still the most agreeable, most loving, and lovely of wives; yet it is strange how little difference even marriage makes to the solitude of the soul. One uses phrases, as amusing as one can make them; but one does not really ever say anything of oneself. Or do some people? I begin to think the life of the village shopkeeper in the Midi would be all I could desire. Why is our here-and-now so hard to bear?

May

Twenty-sixth

In Crockett's last letter from Sydney are cuttings from the local papers: 'Society Girl Vanishes. Left Her Home Secretly. Family's Shock. Miss Stella Peters, well-known society girl, left Sydney secretly yesterday afternoon by the steamer *Commissaire Ramel* bound for Europe. Until they received a radio message from the ship at five o'clock that she was well and happy, Miss Peters' family were entirely ignorant of her intentions to leave home. . . .'

I remember Stella's love of newspaper publicity. I remember how easily she could evade her parents. I think I may have given her the

31

impulse to move farther afield; but in any case she had too much sprightliness of mind for Australia, and I'm glad she has escaped.

Twenty-eighth

To Chesham Bois where Moira sang 'Pretty Polly Oliver' and some
Manx and Irish folksongs, but did not know 'Should he upbraid' when
I requested it. Driving back to London I reflected on the attraction
exercised by a woman singing; and how, with a singer, the sexual appeal
is much greater than with an actress. I suspect this to be historically true;
and have always found it true for myself. I still remember with a quite
sharp emotion how I listened to Gwen Ffrangcon-Davies as Etain on the
first night of *The Immortal Hour*. It was such a warm night as this when I
drove back in turbulence of mind and inattention to the road, back from
the Birmingham theatre through the sleeping villages of Warwickshire
and Oxford, and along lonely roads to Peterley, although I saw only the
figure of the singer standing in Paul Shelving's dim green lighting
which seemed to mix with Boughton's music into a flickering brilliance
like an aurora borealis.

June

Second

We met for tea in Kensington Gardens, and I gave her 'Should he upbraid'. It was one of those afternoons of dusty sunlight and warm, still
air; the noise of distant traffic like the hum of insects, and the flow
of life seeming fixed in a perpetual afternoon—the Palace without
its Princess, the parked perambulators, nurses statuesque on benches,
children bent over toy boats on the pond, and old men asleep in the sun;
and at the fringe of the tea garden a young man who leans towards
his companion, who is hatless, with light waves of hair, and whose eyes,
a little troubled, are gazing into the distance, and on whose smooth forehead is the slightest of frowns over the possible meaning of his words.
I look at Moira and am sure she rejects (although she has already enter-
tained it) the suspicion that I might be making love to her. She has rejected the idea as unjust to me, and out of loyalty to Jane. She is the most
innocent of women and the purest of natures; and I adore her and am
tempted to disturb that serenity of mind. And what gives me an ironic

pleasure to think of is that, if once her heart were touched, she would help me willingly to that destructive end.

She brings her gaze back from the distance, looks frankly into my eyes, and changes the subject.

[He begins to complain that he is idling his time away, and although he is helping Gordon Home with his work on the Roman roads, and is busy with the Corpus Inscriptionum Latinorum, the self-accusation is true. He does little but spend his days with Moira, who does little except try to persuade him to do something else, but, as he adds, 'would be unhappy if I did'.

He has established a home with Jane in Hammersmith; but, naturally perhaps, it is not the domestic evenings in Brook Green that the diary records but the hours passed with Moira in Burdon Grove. True, it is music that serves as the excuse to bring them together; and, with his encouragement, she has taken up her singing in earnest; and she is still received in Brook Green. But his embarrassment when sometimes he comes home to find the two women taking tea together reveals that his feelings are more personal and less musical than he imagines.

There is at this time a move to bring out into the open the old, hushed-up scandal of Miss Douglas-Pennant's dismissal from command of the women's auxiliary forces during the 1914-18 war, and Home takes a hand in the organizing, and Peterley with him.]

Twenty-third

Busy with the Douglas-Pennant case. Home lays much of the blame upon one of the P.M.'s secretaries, since Macdonald confessed himself seriously misinformed when Home called on him the other morning. Miss D-P. herself came in to talk over the preparations for the public meeting. She gave me the impression of a woman of a strong, sincere, and inflexible character, who should have been the wife of one of Plutarch's heroes. Lord Danesfort has exhibited the excessive caution of the aged Polonius and will probably do nothing. Hailsham, now that he is leader of the Upper House, will, likewise, not venture his renown in what is merely a question of justice. *The Times* says nothing, nor will not, on account of Lady Astor's friendship with Lady Rhondda. Two newspapers have misstated the day of the meeting, which was correctly and carefully supplied to them. I am beginning to think the press has too much freedom; has abused it, and should be muzzled.

P.H.—C

Twenty-fourth

A pleasant day in Home's study rearranging his books. Miss D-P. called and chatted for a long while. Clever, suave, with a precise orderly mind; and exhilarating to talk with.

The public meeting at the Central Hall, Westminster, for Miss Dreyfus-Pennant was a great success, at least as far as the attendance went. But there had been hints of 'revelations', and many must have come for the juice rather than the justice—the nonconforming puritans especially, who are still mourning Mr. Stead. Williams at last publicly revealed the accusations of lesbianism that had secretly been brought against Miss Pennant. A sudden stir in the hall. Everyone gazed round trying to identify the distinguished and peculiar sinner. The best speech was by W. J. Brown, a Labour M.P., who moved the resolution that the Prime Minister should take immediate action to probe the dismissal of Miss D-P. It is, of course, hopeless from the start. Comrade MacDonald will not do anything to impair his popularity with the hated upper classes, not honest son of the labouring poor, J. Ramsay, he won't. He dare not tackle Lord Weir, who, I understand, has a promise from Government that the question of her dismissal shall never be raised. And in any case Government can't be expected publicly to chastise itself for using one of its political weapons—the whispering campaign. It used it against Casement when it began to lose the courage to hang him, as it had every right to do. It spread the rumour of his homosexuality. It has used it again against Miss Pennant.

July

Eighth

To Moira's for supper, who finds it exciting to be at last independent and alone and in Chelsea, which she believes to be the wildly Bohemian purlieus of the capital. Her innocent heart beats faster at the mention of the actor of small occasional parts in the basement, at the thought of the public house at the corner where reputedly John Ireland downed his pints, and of the studio vaguely to the west where Gaudier-Brzeska worked. I stayed talking till one, and left after the lightest, the almost imperceptible suggestion of tenderness; she not quite concealing a faint reluctance to be left to face the rest of the night alone.

She has none of the superficial charms or prettiness of face that catch the momentary eye on the street, except the slim, the trim figure, and that she covers disdainfully with loose sweaters and drab skirts; but I am not yet so close that I can insist on the light and low-necked blouse belted lightly at that slenderest of waists, and the full pleated skirt that will, when she walks, describe in the air those invisible curves that belong to the highest geometry. She leaves uncurbed the thick light-coloured waves of hair, and her face too often has that serious contentment of the nun, and always the open frankness of the young girl who looks into your eyes with no other meaning than what her words have just expressed. Except when, at some too patent avowal from me, she looks whole volumes of Canon Law. It is when she sings, or is playing, or talking of music, that this grave face has the lovely joy of Italian angels. She is in love with goodness and simplicity. Her room has a Carthusian severity, with piano for prie-dieu, and two wooden Windsor chairs, and her shelves of music; and in the bedroom is nothing but a dove-grey coverlet over her divan and an unpainted chest of drawers and dressing table. I once jokingly offered her an old crucifix for the wall, and she replied that if I gave her one she would certainly hang it, but that in that case she would never let me enter the room. 'While, as it is . . . ?' She came over and ran her fingers through my hair: 'As it is, I'm sure you will never ask me anything that we should both of us regret.'

In Moira's sitting-room, stretched out along the floor, we had a long tea together which talk and the simple pleasure of being with one another prolonged into a Bohemian supper of cold meat and cheese and buns and innumerable cups of coffee. We were talking of Mozart and at one moment Moira got up to play the piano part of a movement of a concerto: 'David, you have no idea how beautiful this slow movement is: you have to hear the strings and woodwind coming in. It's not a pianist's concerto. We must try to hear it. I'm so contented playing to you, although I know we ought not to be together so much.' I replied that the fact that we could spend so much time together harmlessly was surely excuse enough, but she disagreed:

'We are hiding and hoping no one will find us.'

'You mean we ought to have the courage to run away together?'

'You always use the wrong word. It isn't courage.'

I remember also we talked about the daily life being unsatisfying unless time past were continually recalled; and that time remembered ran back to fetch the age of gold—the age of gold that is the racial equivalence of the individual's longing for his lost childhood; and that the most evocative of all the arts was music; and that perhaps human life, that in the living seems so formless and so insolubly tragic, becomes resolved by music into a semblance of unity and meaning.

(Yet now, as I write the next day, I doubt it. Lorenzo meditates on his tomb with no hint of any solution to his perplexity, while beneath him the Night is impenetrable to reason and recusant to hope.* The greatest work is inexplicable. Agamemnon dies, and Cordelia; and even the Beethoven Mass does not close in peace and understanding. There is no permanent happy ending.)

Moira merely answered that I had things the wrong way round: that living comes first and music after, and that if the former is not right, the latter cannot cure the original error. She argued, too, that what appeared the philosophic synthesis occurs only in the flash of intuition or the second of ecstasy, and its very evanescence is a denial that the solution is permanently valid.

August

'David, I am out of money and cannot come with you to *King John*; for I will not have you pay for me. Come instead and have coffee with me, and I will sing to you, and I will play that movement of the Hammerklavier that you find so heavenly and I find so sad. Come between 8 and 8.30 and ring the side bell. Please don't stay late, my dear, for both our sakes.'

'David, my dear, you should not of course have the feelings for me you have; but I cannot be too insensible in return; and I am grateful

* The reference is clearly to the Medici tombs at Florence; but Peterley has forgotten that Night is beneath Giuliano not Lorenzo. Ed.

to you for taking so lovingly the little that I can give. I am sending you this copy of *Songs of the gardens* and I have underlined the date so that you will remember this happy evening and why I gave it to you.

Your Moira'

I cherish these notes which are the very condensations of the airy charm, the almost innocent happiness, of the young woman who is the virgin of the mediaeval tapestry, the lady of the unicorn, the maid that is makeles. But I sometimes wonder is she deceiving herself.

Home told me, at lunch, how he had hired a boat and gone down to London Bridge and inspected all the pillars in order to verify a popular belief that the name 'Trafalgar Bridge' was carved on one of the piers. He found nothing of the sort.

A copy of Flecker for Moira and armfuls of flowers. She is leaving soon, she swears, for Scotland; and I should be in anguish if I believed it. I try to persuade her to abandon the intention. She was almost in tears, and confessed she would only go to cure our growing affection. She has a strange theory that she is destined to cure me of my too fleshly love, by showing me how a woman can be purely passionate: 'You've never known anything but sensual love, and that is why you find marriage disappointing. But I can be in love with you without being unfaithful to Jane, and then you'll realize that marriage isn't merely a question of physical fidelity or infidelity.' I objected that she would suffer just as much as I from the imperfection of such a liaison. 'Of course I should; and that would be part of the experience and good for both of us.' She sang some Elizabethan songs; and we kiss tenderly at parting, and it seems as voluptuous as more fervent embraces, and I wonder if Moira is not more deeply involved, unconsciously, than she knows.

Jane still at Peterley, saying she finds life in London dull without dogs and horses; and once in a moment of exasperation I retorted that I found it equally dull with her friends, who are all estimable people, all honourable, all, but concerned so much and seriously with such trivialities as parties, dances, horse-racing, motor-racing, and flying as to bore me. They drive fifty miles to a country club only to sit down to the wrong kinds of alcohol, to an undistinguished dinner, and to worthless chatter. In Australia I used to long for the intellectual life in England; returned, I wonder where it is to be found. I spend more and more time with Billam, play-writing, or with Finley who is back from Sydney and busy with stage designing; and Jane shakes her head over my Bohemian cobbers.

October

Third, Saturday

A long argument with Moira all this evening, at times bitter; she accusing me of making love to her only because I think it fashionable to be dissolute and unfaithful. She says she will give me her friendship, on condition that I must maintain mine for her when she marries. I think she may be trying to argue herself into the possibility of marrying that school-master who is so pathetically and persistently in love with her, and sends her bunches of wild flowers which she takes care to put in the vase I gave her. If she marries him, it will be because he is poor and undistinguished and unsuccessful; because he is so nobly idealistic; because he needs look-ing after. In fact, for all the wrong reasons. When I mentioned divorce, Moira replied that if I left Jane for her she would refuse to marry me, and added that in fact Jane was fairly content with our liaison, because she could count on Moira's co-operation. 'We like each other more than you as a man can understand.' I was sceptical, and she retorted that I had my ideas of women from fiction; and when I left she added, 'Goodnight, my dear; and be very kind to Jane when you get home.' I walked all the way back, by way of Redcliffe Gardens and along Warwick Road—shades of the Fanes!—and by Olympia, smoking furiously and furiously thinking, but to no comfortable result.

November

'David, darling, it isn't any good. I cannot play this deceiving game any longer. It seemed delightfully carefree at first; but you must have guessed I love you very much, and so you must see that I can't continue being friends with you both. Do not try to persuade me. I shall devote myself to music, and that will help; and you should find something of great use to do, as you could. Please do not ring me up; but I'll be in if you call on your way home tomorrow—to say good-bye to me.

Moira'

It didn't, of course, turn out to be goodbye.

Moira talks of flying to Scotland, again, and I have to muster the most sophistical arguments to turn her from the idea.

'David,

I have thought of all you have said and I begin to feel that you are right, and that it would not be sensible to cast away such a precious gift as our love. I was troubled because I thought I was hurting Jane deceitfully; but I know now that I need not do that; that it would not be noble to go away, but only be making the worst of a difficult situation. It will be hard, darling, to keep a proper balance. We must be strong and help each other, and not meet so often, which is not really necessary. Come here tomorrow instead of at Mervyn's; come as early as you can after three o'clock. I've found two lovely songs in the book you gave me which I will sing to you. We will just be happy and not mention our troubles. Come looking young and happy as you did on Tuesday; it makes me so joyful to see you like that.

Your Moira'

December

Fifteenth

A strange and far too serious note from Moira today. She tells me she can never be disloyal to Jane, but swears she will continue to give me all the love she can, but that it will be difficult:

'If I suffer too much I shall go away; but I will not go until I have to. David, I will with God's help stay with you and keep you with me in his shadow; and if I do not have the strength to resist your pleadings and my own longing, I must go, and we must suffer in separation, and that in time will solve everything.'

We agree not to meet for two weeks. But I am worried, as I always am when Moira invokes the Deity: it means she is about to do something particularly wilful.

1932

January

Third

Moira has gone. I came to Town today when our agreed and lenten period of abstinence from felicity was over. I rang the bell at No. 18 and it was Mrs. Downes who opened the door and said, 'Will you come inside?' 'But Moira?' Instead of replying, she asked me into her sitting-room and bade me be seated. 'Moira left a letter for you; but you know why she's gone?' I replied that I had been afraid this might happen. 'She told me of course all about it.' I waited for the censure which was sure to come; but it was not of the moral kind I'd expected. 'You two should have got married: it was the one thing she wanted. Was it really as impossible as she thought?' And I had to admit that it probably was. The good woman sighed as though the loss were hers, and we sat there futilely, neither knowing what else to say. I asked her what Moira had said on leaving. 'I didn't see her go. She stayed in her room all that evening playing, and she must have left early in the morning. I went up at nine and she was gone,' and after another silence added, 'I hope you'll marry her if you can.' 'If I could, I wouldn't hesitate a moment. It may be possible still.' 'Well, I'm sure I don't want to interfere with your private life, but I hope it will be—her mother's going to fetch the grand piano,' she added incongruously. I took her letter and went; and sadly, slowly, walked along those roads that had once been the stage scenery of our romantic comedy and now, like scenery in daylight, were drab, dusty, and cynical parodies of their midnight selves.

We lead a quiet, rather melancholy life here at Peterley. Jane rides a little, and calls on the neighbourhood. I read, walk solitarily, and avoid the locals. We dine together, but drift away separately, Father to his campaigns in his study, Jane to her sitting-room upstairs, and I usually up to Uncle Matthew's garret of curiosities. Knowles sometimes comes up to the house for chess; and sometimes we drive into Aylesbury for a bad film.

Talking to Gurney yesterday about the grounds and asking about the Tempietta which I notice is still kept in perfect order. 'Your father's orders. He likes to sit there in the sun in summer.' I remarked that it must have wasted quite a lot of money, all the changes in the grounds. The old gardener straightened himself, looked at me and said: 'He didn't regard it as wasted. He regarded it as a duty. I thought it was a bit extravagant at first; but I dare say he was right.'

'At least it helped to make Rose happy for a little while.'

'Aye,' said Gurney, 'generous to a fault your father, Sir, generous to a fault.' And he turned back to the study of his *Chimonanthus fragrans*.

I walked down to the end of the avenue and looked along the narrow clearing through the wood to the little domed building at the end, white against the black trees, and shuttered, like a family mausoleum. Inside, it is as she left it four years ago, the miniature library still on the white shelves, her pen-and-ink stand on the writing table, the empty chair, and the unlit tiled stove.

February

Not two pages in my journal since Moira went to Scotland, so listless was
I. I wrote, sent her my *Granite Sonnets,* and received in reply her descriptive letters which breathed an innocent contentment with life and
Highland scenes and simple happenings. She studies her singing; sings at
local concerts; reads the books I send her, even the ferociously sophisticated ones, with a just appraisal and with equanimity; chides me for my
choice as though to a naughty boy; tells me simply that she still cares for
me very much; sends her love to Jane; and refuses to say when she will
be back. I am heart and soul in love with her, and yet her influence is
so strong I do not have the least desire to break up my marriage, knowing
how much that would hurt her.

> Art thou gone so far,
> Beyond the poplar-tops, beyond the sunset-bar,
> Beyond the purple cloud that swells on high
> In the tender fields of sky . . . ?

The words are not mine this time, but all the longing is.

> O come thou again.
> Be heard in the voice that across the river comes
> From the distant wood . . .

Each week when in Town I go to Charlotte Street where Norman
keeps a bookshop that would be credible only in fiction: a shop complete
with dust, sagging shelves, a broken chair, windows with cobwebs in
every pane through which not even the grey light of Soho comes, and
heaps of books over all the floors, in which like an archaeologist in kitchen
middens you rake for discoveries, and, at Norman's, find them. Working
downwards through a pile of sermons and eighteenth-century philosophy
today, I came upon a black notebook and looked inside and found it
to be a manuscript diary. I bought it and read it with fascination, coming
back in the train to Missenden. I had gone to hear Greg lecture at University College on his principles of bibliographical criticism, and wondered
a little that he thought them so novel as to need such elaboration. Esdaile
was there in a faintly purple waistcoat which I wished I had the courage
to wear.

Sixth

Walked over to Hampden today in a bitter wind, thinking of this
anonymous diary-keeper whose story has so much impressed me and
made me reflect that I, who had always thought of leaving something
well written as the fruit of a contemplative life, have done nothing
except contemplate myself and with decreasing admiration as time passes.
Yet the diary is not a literary work. It is a commonplace enough romance,
such as I suppose is normal in a large city, of the young—what can he
be: apprentice solicitor, young man-in-the-City, or even university
lecturer?—who falls in love with the shop-girl, the Elizabeth Siddal,
whose pose of elegance and sophistication hides all too successfully the
simple shop-girl's heart beneath. She is all the women in all the novels he has
read; she is all the poetry she has never heard of; and when she leaves the
opulence of Oxford Street she goes back to her bed-sitting-room near Euston
Station, from which she longs to escape and to which he hurries each evening that he is free as though to paradise. She finds herself cast for a rôle she
can scarcely support. She often forgets her lines and dissolves into tears.

They take tea in the little Bloomsbury tea-shops with the red-and-
white-check tablecloths and the middle-aged ladies who bring you
buttered scones with the melancholy of women whom a cruel Fate has
driven to this menial service. They watch the sunsets from the seats in
public parks. They part at bus-stops, and meet in Tube stations. They
hold hands in suburban cinemas. And sometimes, after a dinner in a
students' restaurant, they return to her room and talk about their love:
I imagine it is he who talks about his; and time flows away in words and
towards that conventional moment when the spectre of landladies drives
young men away, and he pleads to hold her in his arms, and they lie down
on that waiting bed, and he forgets time and she forgets her assumption
of ladyship, and surrenders. They make love. For him it is annihilation,
extasis, exolution, transformation, the kiss of the spouse, gustation of
God, and ingression into the divine shadow; he has already had a handsome anticipation of heaven. But for her the glory of the world is surely
over, and the earth in ashes. The enchanter's palace of words has tumbled
down. 'She buries her face in her hands, in the pillow, and is crying,
though soundlessly.' He caresses her hair as tenderly as he can and asks
her gently why she cries, and keeps repeating, 'I'm sorry, darling,' but
with no visible effect on her. So he gets up, and thinks he will let her give
full vent to her feelings—are they of love or grief, he wonders? He covers
her with her dressing gown, and sits beside her 'with no consciousness
of guilt myself'.

43

The days that follow are emotionally subdued. They part at an early hour. They go to the British Museum. The diary speaks of his lectures, airs his views about aesthetics (which cause him a great deal of mind-searching), and mentions, with disapproval, the political situation. They attend the symphony concert at the Queen's Hall; they go to the Mansard Gallery for the exhibition of the London Group, and one wonders what mental disturbances aesthetics caused in her. They may not have been too painful, for on a foggy Sunday they walk from Parliament Square to the Tate Gallery—and one remembers Moore's phrase about Old Masters and young mistresses—and that evening they spend together again in her room, and make love. This time there are no tears.

As I read that, I felt, for a moment only, that it was more tragic than the quiet sobbings such a short time before. I am already half jealous on her behalf, and feel infinitely sorry for her. I've read the whole diary, and now that I can see her against that future, I'm like the spectator in the cinema who longs to shout his warning to the heroine, 'Think what will happen in the tenth reel!' But to hell with it, as the Americans say; why should I grow sentimental over this silly young woman? It had to happen; she is so obviously foredoomed by character to be seduced in a bed-sitting-room near the Euston Road. She is fortunate in having a decent fellow as the scoundrel: there's no doubt he's absurdly infatuated.

All the same, she is a pathetic figure, this slender girl with the pretty face, who buttons up her long gloves as she hurries from the shop to meet her distinguished young gentleman at Tottenham Court Road Underground where he is waiting with a copy of Mr. de la Mare as a present for her. I wonder what the poor girl did with it: it isn't something you can display with pride to your friends at the shop, such as a brooch or ear-rings which very faintly foreshadow—one hopes—the eventual engagement ring. Of which there is no mention.

There seem to have been several romantic evenings during this winter in Bloomsbury, and they produce some mighty fine writing in the diary, but also some stirrings of conscience in Doris, for there is a note for Saturday the 18th: 'Long talk on the bed with D. about the nature of love. Tried to explain to her how the physical element is not degrading if kept in subordination to the spiritual side of life.'

On the following Monday he picks up at Foyle's Bookshop a significant title: *Moral values and the idea of God*, but also Donne's Poems. He is maintaining nicely the spiritual and physical balance, but I feel it is a precarious equilibrium. There are touches here and there among the comments on art and philosophy which suggest she is perhaps as much in

44

love as he. He has a slight cold, and she cancels the cinema and insists he go to bed. She comes and serves him hot milk and gingerbread. One evening she devotes to mending the holes in his pockets. The cold turns to 'flu, and she spends her evenings sitting by his bed knitting. Once she leaves rather late, at 11.30, and meets the inhabitants of the upper flat on the stairs, and that worries him a little.

At the end of the year the liaison becomes a little more respectable: he takes her to visit his parents in the country; and after a family dinner the young couple, left to themselves in the drawing-room, look at photographs. The family album, I imagine, showing him at the age of four bent over a sand-castle on the beach, at eleven standing and awkwardly gripping the handlebars of the new bicycle, at Cousin Carola's birthday party—'I was terribly smitten with her at that time'—and at thirteen looking doubly foolish what with his new long trousers and the embarrassment of having Cousin Carola hanging on his arm.

She seems contented with the official recognition which this visit implies. She must also have been a little carried away; for some weeks later back in London he is anxiously consulting the calendar; but the alarm is unfounded.

The diary, and life for the writer, suddenly become more exciting, for he receives an invitation from an uncle and aunt to join them in Bavaria. I wish he had some regard for chronology at other times than those occasions when he fears for his companion's health; but he merely records: 'Wed. Spent last night packing. Called at the German Passport Office and waited one and a half hours.' At the last moment, when they are having dinner at Fleming's, his resolution fails him and he decides to put the journey off for one day and spend tomorrow with Doris. They go to Kensington Gardens and sit on the slope overlooking the lake till nine o'clock. 'A fine sunny day. Memo, to read *The Promenade Ticket* and *Twelve years in a monastery*.' The question of what books to take occupies a page of the diary: 'The choice of books for my travels had given me some trouble, as I resolved that I could not carry more than three; but I felt perfectly satisfied in the end when I had decided to take Plato's *Republic*, the *Inferno*, and *Don Quixote*. I wanted also to take Rhoades' translation of Virgil but could not lay hands on a copy.' I can afford to smile, because I know that he never looked at any of them.

He leaves, but sadly, the next day. Doris comes with him in the taxi to Victoria, and when he kissed her her face was so cold he received a shock. They have the saddest, the tenderest of partings, and she lets him cut off a lock of her hair which he places in an envelope. He leans out of the window as the train moves out and sees her on the platform smiling and waving her gloves until the train takes the curve and she is out of sight. By the afternoon he is watching the flat fields and poplars of Belgium flash by the carriage windows, and he is already beginning to be, although he does not know it yet, someone other than that young man who sadly kissed the cold and apprehensive girl in the London taxi that same—but can it possibly have been that same?—morning.

He is enraptured by the Continent, by the clean trains, the comfortable seats, the politeness of the people. The young woman in the bookstall at Brussels is so friendly and offers so charmingly to stick the stamps on the postcards he has bought that he lingers just too long, and recovers from the enchantment to find his train has left. He sends off a telegram to the frontier station, Herbestal, and follows by another train. The exchange is fantastic: the fare to Munich is four shillings English. He, too, like all travellers, is awed by the Piranesi-like immensity and blackness of the Cologne station at night, in whose cavernous gloom unseen wagons snort and clank. And, like all travellers, he falls in love with Bavaria and thinks Munich the loveliest city in the world: 'The first thing that struck me was the remarkable beauty of the Bavarian people, especially the children, and the delightful picturesqueness of their national dress. Moreover, they all seemed so kind and natural and simple, that I did not feel as if I were in a strange land. I could not for a long time cease from watching the people in their quaint and lovely costumes, and the golden children, so healthy looking and with such regular Greek features. In my mind I contrasted this healthy gay bright throng, so full of colour and beauty, with the sight that would greet one on emerging say from King's Cross or Victoria—the sullen black-coated business men hurrying intently as if it were a matter of life and death, the gangs of crafty-looking loafers, women whose faces are thin, pale and worn, and whose dress is shabby beyond words, children looking half-starved and wretched; the dingy smoky buildings, the close reeking atmosphere thick with petrol fumes and dust, the screeching advertisements on every hand, the vulgar and degraded taste of everything. Then I turned to the brightness of the Munich streets, to the light unpretentious useful buildings, the cleanness everywhere, the blue sky and the sunlight. I felt I had been transported magically to another world.'

It is amusing to watch this Englishman discovering by the comparative method the cancer in the Empire's heart.

He takes the 5.20 express to Garmisch; is astonished at the Würmsee, amazed by the Staffelsee, and is ecstatic by the time they reach the pass into Garmisch and see the Alpspitze. At the hotel his aunt awaits him 'and behind her I saw a tall slender girl whose face interested me extremely, it had such a deep sorrowful look' and he does not recognize the Katie of the old photograph of his birthday party. She is eighteen and passing through what he calls an abnormal psychic state, which is to say that she prefers to walk by herself twenty yards ahead of the family party, finds grown-ups' conversation dull, has a small appetite, and confronted by a fine view sits and gazes at it without talking. Sister Caroline is normal; that is to say she appeals physically to him immediately and he finds in her a young woman who is not only physically desirable but intellectually his equal—one suspects a little more than equal—and he is soon noticing whether she says 'Goodnight' or 'Goodnight, Denis'. For two of these summer months he takes the Bavarian cure, tramping the pine woods, climbing up the mountains, and bathing in the lakes. He talks with Stephens about music, books, communism and D. H. Lawrence (on whom he is writing a book), and sits between Katie and Caroline drinking wine at the Marktplatz Café. The string orchestra plays Wotan's *Farewell*, and there follows the inevitable discussion about Wagner. 'Caroline,' he notes, 'was wearing a very pretty frock of a small check pattern in salmon colour and white, with short sleeves and round-cut neck. Her sunburnt arms are as beautiful as anything I have ever seen.' From Wagner they move to psychoanalysis. They dance. They go home in the rain. He gets up the next morning with a feeling of the inexhaustible grandeur of the intellectual life.

The days pass happily enough in what he calls 'the companionship of charming healthy girls'. It rains of course; and Katie insists on walking bareheaded in the rain, which annoys her mother, probably to her daughter's satisfaction. He accidentally brushes Caroline's arm with his cigar while they watch a dance and is filled with admiration that she does not cry out; and walks home that evening 'thinking about Caroline', and admits to his diary that his thoughts at present are very complex. 'With the constant stream of strange and vivid impressions, the thought of my Doris has always been mingled. Now the thought of Caroline occupies me more than anything else—except, of course, Doris; and the dwelling upon these two personalities, each so attractive in its own way, and the contrasting of them, produces in my mind a very intense, almost ecstatic state of feeling, whose beauty is increased by its complexity.' Captain MacHeath expressed it more concisely.

He goes to see the Badersee, a tiny lake that so captivated the imagination of mad Ludwig he threw the statue of a mermaid in it, and it glimmers there to this day through the clear water, making the traveller wish other monarchs had shared some of that royal hyperaesthesia. The water there is iridescent, with hues of shifting green and pink; and its temperature, they say, never varies; and in the middle is a miniature island, and all round are the woods whose trees are mirrored in the still surface of the lake.

The Passion play at Oberammergau bores him, especially the Prologue, an old man with a white beard and a long sceptre, who declaims at regular intervals; and he sensibly prefers the stormclouds over the Riessersee, that roll away and reveal the newly fallen snow on the summits behind. He is not as critical of the Alte Pinakothek in Munich as he should have been, that overpowering jumble of skied pictures, that riot of Rubens, but it reminds him that he ought to send a postcard to Doris.

He returns to Garmisch and the company of his two cousins, and each night as he walks home to his hotel he realizes more clearly that he loves Caroline very dearly, and he approaches with despair the day when she is to go back to England. She goes, and he haunts the scenes that are associated with her. The long evenings are tedious. He reads Baudouin's *Suggestion and auto-suggestion*, but finds more consolation in Galsworthy's *The Patrician*. Eventually he calls up enough courage to write her a letter: the diary contains the early attempts; it gets finished just before he too must leave for England. But I doubt if it had the effect he hoped. It is too psychological and his divided mind loses itself in parentheses and subclauses. He posts it in Munich, and starts back to England, a changed man who knows that an unchanged Doris will be meeting him on the platform at Victoria. It is there the diary ends.

Ninth
There is a full-rigged model ship for sale in South Kensington, and I go to Gloucester Road to see it; but £300, though a not unreasonable amount for one of such condition and of about 1790 (they claim 1750), is beyond me at present. I walked moodily across the Park and along Oxford Street to Gower Street, the wind bitterly cold and driving a thin rain in my face, and I think of Moira in worse weather than this in the north, who writes tenderly and yet refuses to return. Whether she is waiting for some decisive step from me I do not know; and I could find out only by taking it. I am certain that if I wrote that Jane and I were separating, she would come south post-haste.

.   .   .   .   .

Walking towards the British Museum, I saw on a street corner the name Great Titchfield Street. So this was where the Doris of the discovered journal worked, might still be working. From curiosity, I turned up to the left to see the actual shop. It was commonplace and dull, and seemed quite a different place from the shop in the journal; just as, I thought, if I went in and asked for Doris, and a young woman came forward, I should object: 'But you are not the Doris of the manuscript.' And I should be right; for the one I knew was the adored young woman of the diarist, who had become transfigured by the written word, and enriched by the writer's passion that had been like a filter on a camera lens, but one that puts more colour into the picture instead of filtering it out.

A letter from Dorothea Gunn full of hopes of a return to England for a holiday.

March

First

When I came into the drawing-room at Peterley yesterday before lunch, Jane was reading a letter, and looked up to say that she had heard from Moira. I said 'Oh' with careful absence of inflection; and with an equal casualness Jane added, 'It's all about her wedding.' I stopped still. I could find nothing to say, and steadied myself against a chair as against a shock that had abruptly ended my present calm of life. I remember staring into the tall mirror opposite and seeing my white rigid face as the face of a stranger. I continued to stare stupidly, while a sense of defeat and misery seemed to mount like a tide of blood to the heart.

Jane had meant, I think, to make some play with the letter, and was still sitting by the fireplace reading it; but the silence in the room and my immobility made her look up. This was intended to be the moment of her triumph; but she saw my face and read there in an instant not only my defeat but her own. She knew then for the first time how serious had been my love for Moira, and guessed that the woman lost would be a greater barrier between us than the woman loved. She must intuitively have realized this, for she stood up, put the letter on the table, and without another word went out of the room.

I picked the letter up and folded it, and did not read it. I still have not done so, and probably never shall. Nor did I see Jane again that day, for I left the house and walked purposelessly over the ridge of the Chilterns and down through Princes Risborough where the Oxford plain begins; and when a pub in Haddenham opened I went in and sat there with an untouched glass of beer in front of me, tired from the walk, numb with the news, and empty of everything except the bitter knowledge that all was lost, and lost by my inactivity. It is not Fate we rail against, but our own weakness of will. Had I acted . . . But those acts we conceive in the mind and never carry out are, I am sure, unconsciously rejected because they do not belong to us. We dream of them instead, and say, 'Ah, that is what I should have done.' But the fact that we didn't do it is proof that it was not in keeping with our real character; it belonged only to the 'I' of the life of the imagination. Had I acted, Moira would have responded; but she would have been responding to someone else, someone she thought I was. I remained my real self, and, after writing one literary letter, I sat down and wrote another one, instead of knocking on the door at No. 18 and announcing that my marriage was ended and that I'd come to ask her to join me for life. And now, as a result of my doing nothing of the kind, there are three unhappy persons instead of two happy ones. I had to ring Griffiths and ask him to send Gurney with the car to pick me up. When I came home Jane had left for Town, and has remained there while I walk these woods and try to harden my heart.

April

Eighteenth

Back in Town after sailing with S. along the melancholy Essex coast. The weather chilly and damp; and returning to Maldon, late on Monday, we ran on to a mudbank on the ebb and had to wade ashore and leave the deck-hand to bring her back on the next tide. I find waiting for me a letter from Sydney hinting at a visit by Dorothea sooner than I had dared hope; and I wonder what may happen if the Australian past in the person of Landell's wife returns like the long-lost uncle from the gold diggings in the melodrama.

June

The most satisfying moments are still those, though rarer now, when one rests in contemplation of a scene that is charged with the emotion of time passing—time that inspires our deepest feelings, deep as those fears of not being, of leaving the hospitable world 'and sunlight and the air', of losing precisely that emotion of impermanence. We fear to pass away: we live by this very sensation of passing time.

I sat in Hall listening to the chatter of undergraduates, and felt the joy—which at the time I never felt—of being myself in college. The talk seemed foolish to me now; the recollection of time past wholly pleasing. Times of indifference, of actual discomfort even, become thus radiantly transformed in remembrance.

We have not learned this from Proust: he expressed the generation's feeling. Are we in this late hour of civilization particularly sensitive to time, that our philosopher is Bergson, our novelist Proust, our historian Spengler: is it perhaps a malady—but how delightful a one—of a culture's decline? Time's warning shadow on our path; or a happy gift to ease and drug the sense of doom? I stand under the columns and look across the court, and tarry before returning to that outer world where time is concealed by clocks and sirens and time-tables, dulling the delicate sense. But shall I equally well remember these days of London; the trees of Brook Green watched in moods of depression from my sitting-room; and Holst passing quickly by with his leather satchel on his way to the girls' school, where he occasionally taught; the little restaurants of illicit suppers; and Jane Brown's snack-bar at South Kensington Station, where on high stools we ate our sandwich lunch together; and the house in Chelsea next door to John Ireland where I climbed the stairs with such trepidation for fear of waking the Wades, and where we hushed our voices and handled so carefully the coffee-cups because of the spinster above. Shall I one day go back and gaze along the unromantic vista of Warwick Road and recollect in tranquillity the emotions that filled my heart so fully and with such a living spring of happiness that, now that they have all drained away, I am like the stony creek of the Australian countryside in drought? I think that time will never come.

November

Twelfth

A listless year of which every day has been clouded over by regret for the loss of Moira, who is the only woman I have ever deeply loved, unless it is the losing her that makes me think so, and whose life like mine has flowed into the wrong channel through my inaction. I have remained with Jane without being able to make her happy. She has been marvellously sympathetic; stays much at Peterley riding, gardening, and fostering the village institute; and leaves me to my melancholy in London where I have found some spiritual healing in the monastic quiet of the B.M. and the Victoria and Albert, and in the less monastic company of Cousin R., who is at the university and whose public passions, for the moment, are palaeography, and long garrulous dinners in Soho with Cousin Henry and Sally Satchwell. He took me to a meeting of the 'Colophon', a small private club that dines together and discusses bibliography. He read a paper on the necessity for academic regimentation in England, pointing out that all academic research should be registered in advance at his academy, whose permission should first be obtained for the subjects of theses; that all scholastic publications should conform to a few formats fixed by the academy, and to certain fixed practices for references, footnotes, abbreviations. He startled the audience somewhat by a hope that the dangerous and wasteful liberalism that has sapped the vigour of our political institutions should give place in the world of learning also to a rule of order and an imposed discipline. Esdaile, amused, while half sympathetic, replied very wittily with a plea for the Humanistic freedom of the individual, even though the present academic system was haphazard and uneconomic. 'I love that word "uneconomic". It usually means something capable of fulfilling all our human needs but not making money. My advice would be: If it's uneconomic, let's do it. Most things that have given most satisfaction to human beings have been uneconomic —cathedrals and gardens, plays and paintings. My readers under the dome could give a very poor account of themselves, if called before your academy; but how happy they are in their useless studies!' We also discussed the errors of architects in designing libraries, and the new Cambridge one furnished us with all too many illustrations.

There is news from Dorothea who is already five days this side of Sydney and thirty-seven the other side of Southampton. 'Fair ship that from th' Australian shore . . .' Strange how memorable that poem is—a quality that must come from the strength and depth of the emotions it expresses. And, since Arthur Henry Hallam is the theme, it must be that Tennyson's feelings for him were more than normally strong. So that when Arthur Henry's father publicly disapproved of Shakespeare's sonnets as the poetic tribute to an unnatural love, he may have had another poet in mind.

December

Another melancholy festival at Peterley. Father broods upon the dwindling and dispersed family, and must be aware that Jane and I are not inseparable. And I cannot help remembering the last Christmas here, when I was waiting with a happy expectancy for the meeting with Moira which never came.

We tramp the wet beech avenues together, and go over to Hampden for dinner, and organize a gross eating ceremony for the servants and their village friends; but we are all three quietly unhappy. Jane will probably go to the D.s in Yorkshire for the New Year; but I doubt if I can stand old Sir Matthew's ferocious addiction to religion and hunting. He insists upon attendance at morning prayers in the drawing-room; he is quite likely to quote me the passage in the marriage service concerning the begetting of children; and he is all for smiting the fox hip and thigh as though chasing papists, infidels, and members of the Labour Party over the frontiers of the county. I think I shall join Cousin Judy who is in London alone, Mark being still in China.

1933

February

Eleventh

Spending much of my time with Judy, who has given me the stimulus needed to shake off some of my lethargy, and who is aware of the unsatisfactory impasse our marriage seems to have reached. She lies on the sofa smoking her small cigars, which to my uneasiness she insists on smoking also on buses and in theatre foyers, and tells me that, if only we had had furious quarrels, or thrown a few wedding presents, or left each other vowing never to return, we might have developed a personal life together of some human warmth and some possibility of passion. 'You've been too goddamned polite and nice to each other. Jane ought to have torn your hair out, or locked you out when you came back at one o'clock from your Irish whore.'

I said, 'Sh! she wasn't.'

'Of course I know she wasn't; but all the same she did keep you out of your proper bed and probably out of hers too, which was mean, night after night.'

We go together to all the plays, and at her table I meet the queerest assortment of people, mostly of the Bohemian or the socialist fringe, and some, I suspect, of the sexual one.

May

Seventh

Heard Rimsky-Korsakov's *Snow Maiden* at Sadler's Wells yesterday. I am transported: this is the loveliest opera in the world, which this Empire should have on its permanent repertory at its National Opera House, if it had one.

Alone and infinitely melancholic, and longing for young and feminine company. It is a year and a half since Moira went. It may be the music. It may be that I am older but not wiser. It may be no more than the late stirrings of spring.

Ninth

Caught the 11.50 to Cambridge, and found the city quietly at lunch, and lovely to see again. All the trees a fresh spring green after rain. The raindrops shook down from the limes as I walked from the station, the puddles reflecting a blue sky and the buildings standing out in clear contours in the washed air. Lunched at a cafe opposite King's where a plump woman was eating buns and waiting for the bus, and complaining to the waitress about her parents-in-law. She was a short, fat, vulgar wife of Bath: 'Never have a moment that I can call my own what with them spying and asking questions.' She took a huge bite of bun, which did nothing to check the flow of reminiscence: 'If you go out by yourself they think there's a man at the bottom of it.' The waitress leaning against the counter was all sympathy and nodded with understanding. 'Sometimes they're not so far out,' she added with relish and with bun. 'We're only flesh and blood after all.' I pretended to be reading, as these confessions flowed unprudishly on.

Housman's lecture was not until five o'clock, and I filled the time by browsing on David's stall and at Bowes and Bowes, and buying a Lenci porcelain statue at Faringdon's which I asked them to send to Jane. When I returned at 3.30 to the Senate House there was already a small group waiting outside the doors, which vexed me: I had determined to be first there and nearest to the great man. Some dons had a password that opened the panelled doors and let them in. They opened for us at 4.00, and within a few minutes the whole House was filled, and at the end of an hour dons were having to perch on window-sills and stand at the back and sides. Quiller-Couch found bare lodgment on a bench-end. Exactly at five Housman came in from the Caius side and passed across to the waiting-room, whence a moment later Spens of Corpus Christi, the Vice-Chancellor, led him out and introduced him, saying how great an honour it was for Cambridge that Professor Housman had found it possible to consent to give the Leslie Stephen lecture. Spens is a tall round-faced man with a cheery countenance in which a large flabby mouth seems to have no fixed location but wanders at will below his nose.

Housman rose, placed a brown-covered small octavo pamphlet (of paged proofs?) upon the reading desk and immediately began to read. He spoke slowly, with precision, in a pleasant, even, low, but clear and well-modulated voice, not raising his eyes, and frequently twitching the pamphlet up to the top of the desk, and holding it there with one hand. Even at the witty points he did not look up or change his tone, but kept the outward severity of face and the evenness of voice. Only twice or thrice did his voice falter or change: when he read the stanza 'Take, oh take those lips away' and Blake's verse about the lost traveller's dream under the hill, and once when he recalled the time long past when he had composed the last poem of the *Shropshire Lad*: then he was checked for a moment, and brushed his eye with his hand. And there was a solemnity at the end when he bid adieu to literary criticism—and to the world—with the words 'Farewell for ever'.

Housman is of middle height, spare of figure, with severe, sharp-cut, well-complexioned face, with thin white hair and white Edwardian moustache and dark black eyebrows. In profile the head is remarkably elongated at the back. He wore a very dark-grey suit, with stiff upstanding collar folded right round the throat, and long stiff cuffs. He spoke for seventy minutes, and the applause at the end was fervent and enthusiastically prolonged, and repeated after the formal thanks of the Vice-Chancellor; and throughout the whole reading there had not been the least stir in the audience, so intent was it upon each word, so conscious of the importance of this occasion, so enthralled by this marvellous discourse. I am immeasurably the more content with life after having heard and seen Housman, and am certain that there can be no comparable experience possible now. I am sure that this greatest of living Englishman will be great even among the dead.

June

Third
Days of airlessness and unusual heat and unclouded sunshine, and a strangely clear atmospheric definition. I have been alone at Hammersmith expecting Dorothy, but she has been kept in Lincolnshire. My seventeenth-century studies weary me; I am tired of checking in the P.R.O., and yawning over these badly printed and cropped octavos in the B.M. I walked through Kew Gardens, and was not healed. London repels me when I think of the great slopes of the Risoux and the Bois d'Amont by the Swiss border, and the streets of Morat, and the fountains of Munich, and the view from the *Karlovy most* at Prague. I would like to feel free of matrimony. I would like to be out of England and in love with a young girl.

August

Eventually, I left England and fled to—the Isle of Wight. I live at the little hotel at Yarmouth, and walk in the splendid sun of this prodigal and riotous summer, and bathe and sail in the Solent, and sit on the crest of the windy downs above Farringford, and at evening watch the dusk darken over the still floodwater in the harbour and then go in to read Boswell in the corner of the bow-window that overlooks the village square. But all the time I have longed for the company of Dorothea; until one morning, when at last the rain came up the Channel and sleeted the Solent in grey veils, I caught the ferry on an impulse and came up to Hampton Court where for a week now I have been her guest. We spend all day together. We breakfast, since the weather is so warm, in the garden under the huge mulberry tree which is so old it leans on poles, like an old man tottering on sticks, and drops its purple fruit, fat and swollen like the faces of drunkards, upon the grass. This is the tree that Garrick brought back as a cutting from the mulberry in Shakespeare's garden at New Place when he attended the first Stratford Festival in 1769.

We have a gossiping woman from the village, Mrs. Roddick, as house-keeper, who has grown suddenly more industrious, attentive, and garrulous than ever now that—bless her human heart—she is convinced we are living in sin, and that the bad novels she has spelled through by her kitchen fire are being verified before her sentimental eyes. We do not have the courage to tell her the truth; and we continue to let her give hostages to morality in the fruit tarts she makes specially for us.

Through the hot days the cool Thames flows past the lawn and under the shadowing trees down to the warm brick walls and towers of Hampton Court. We punt on the river, or we lie reading on the lawn when the river nymphs are too numerous and their friends the loitering heirs of City directors have not yet departed. In the evenings the long twilight softens all outlines; the boats glide by, paddled by unseen shapes; the river is a sheet of dull silver with a vein of gold when the harvest moon is reflected. And, when the shapes of the familiar world are blurred, we go in, and from the open casements see the phlox white in the dusk and the stars brightening over the chestnut trees.

After dinner each evening Mrs. Roddick washes up, and then comes with some trivial excuse into the drawing-room and lingers gossiping, as though loath to leave this comfortable house of sin. She smiles approbation on us, and is the veriest pander in all Hampton. I said yesterday to Dorothea that she had all the right conventional ideas, and that it was we who were unreasonably perverse; but all she answered was that my timing was out. 'There nearly was a moment in Sydney; but everything went wrong—or everything stayed right. Sometimes I am almost sorry.'

The dinner at Brook Green with Jane was as polite and formal as I had expected. Jane was surprised to find her guest so obviously not an Australian, but couldn't quite manage to avoid a slight condescension as of an Englishwoman to a colonial visitor. All the same she behaved extremely graciously to someone whom, I am sure, she did not believe to be innocent in her relations with me. She asked Dorothea if she was being taken to Peterley, and, when Dorothea replied that she hoped that Jane would be able to show her round, replied that unfortunately she would be at Ashby, which was a plain hint to me that she refused to act as cicerone to my lady acquaintances. I had to drive Dorothea back to Hampton, and at the door Jane said she supposed I'd be home late.

'Not very; but I think we'll drive by way of Egham.'

'Oh, yes, a much more romantic route,' and to Dorothea she firmly said: 'Goodbye. I'm sure you've enjoyed your stay in England.'

'It's always pleasant to see one's native land from time to time,' replied Dorothea.

I took the long way round because it gave me time for a long conversation, which began by my asking her what she thought of Jane.

'But she's charming; and she's really very kind hearted, although she obviously didn't regard me merely as your friend. Why is it you don't get on well together?'

I replied bitterly that God only knew: 'Perhaps because we're married.'

'Yes; that's probably the right answer. Do you know, the little doctor warned me that if I ever made the mistake of leaving Peter with the idea of marrying you, it would be fatal: you would be cured of your infatuation overnight.'

'Overnight isn't perhaps the right word.'

'No; the nights would be successful; it would be the days that would be difficult, perhaps; I wonder.'

I looked round at her amusing little face with the curls blown back by the wind as we drove towards Chertsey, and felt so happy and so much at peace in her company that I began to wonder too; and wondered how many marriages were truly successful in preserving an emotional relationship in an ever-continuing freshness, or if this was something that in most cases had to be sought outside.

'But, David, I really think you should come to a decision; you can't carry on much longer this ridiculous ménage. It would be kinder to Jane to make a clean break.'

'Agreed. I should have made it for Moira; and now it's too late. The incentive is no longer there.'

'You'll have to make one.'

We came back from Chertsey, and at Halliford stopped to look at the river, it was so fine a night. I couldn't guess what thoughts were in that charming head of curls as Dorothea stood hatless and with coat open gazing at the Thames; but I began to feel an emptiness of the heart that was partly nostalgia for the old days together in Sydney and partly longing for a woman who was not any longer for my possessing. It was at this moment under the dark elms in England that I felt it was indeed a waste of life that we had not, then, accepted the possibility of a happiness that, however transient, would at least have been strong and real and full of life and warmly human, and that was now only a Virgilian ghost haunting a riverside and longing to cross back to the sunlight. I was tempted to turn and take her in my arms, and instead I said, 'Do you know it was here that Edith Nicholls drowned herself?'

After a moment Dorothea said slowly: 'David, what made you think of that? Who was she?'

'She must have been beautiful; she was certainly a very brilliant woman.'

'Did you know her?'

'She drowned herself seventy years ago.'

'Why?'

'Her marriage had been a failure. She tried, I think, to find some reason for living, outside it; and that failed too.'

'If she was so clever, why did she make such bad choices?'

'You couldn't accuse her of that. Her husband was Meredith.'

'The novelist?'

'Yes; the creator of brilliant women. There must have been too much intellect in that marriage: their tenderness probably cut itself on their wits. She was Thomas Love Peacock's daughter. To have inherited his brains and then to find that as a woman you were a failure compared with women whom intellectually you despised—that must have been too humiliating. And you can imagine the sting in Meredith's remarks whenever they got on each other's nerves. She walked one night into the Thames just about here.'

'But why did you think of that just at a moment when——'

'When I should have been thinking of something quite different?'

I did not say that the spectre of our lost happiness in the past had suddenly become the ghost of Mrs. Meredith rising from the cold water, a chilling presence that stayed with us along the dark road to Hampton. I even began to think that perhaps it had kept Meredith company for many years; that to exorcize the revenant and assuage his conscience he had tried again and again to re-create this lovely and brilliant woman in heroine after heroine and give a literary resurrection to the dead wife. Was it Edith Nicholls who rose from the Thames and lived through all the novels?

We were silent until the cottage was reached and we stood under the porch, and Dorothea said that this was almost our last meeting as she would be going back to Lincolnshire for the fortnight before she sailed, and added that these days together had been the happiest of her life. I reminded her that there was still Peterley to be seen before she left. She looked up at me and replied that it would be amusing to see what it would have been like. I drove back in a mood of depression to Brook Green and to Jane and to an existence that never seemed to coincide at any point with my real desires.

Dorothea pleased Peterley as much as it enchanted her. I drove her down yesterday, and she was in raptures at the sight of the long, low house with its tall, white windows set in that mottled stone. From the far side of the lawn, in front, it does look settled and comfortable: the lichened roof has sagged into repose like a dog before the fire; and cornice and parapet have worn by age to the richness of a line in mezzotint; and the classical pilasters at the corners have weathered to the flatness of stage scenery. It is always a surprise to push the heavy door and find beyond it the space and coolness of the hall, the pattern of the marble floor, and the curving staircase giving it an illusion of airiness and distance. Father was most amiable, and made his little speech of welcome about his gratitude to someone whose kindness to his son 'when in nearly foreign parts', etc., etc. Probably his shock at seeing someone so young was so quickly overlaid by the pleasure of looking at a pretty woman that he wasn't aware of it. He called Grace and asked her to take Mrs. Gunn to her room:

'I have arranged for Grace to be in the room opposite, so that you won't feel too lonely in this empty house.'

'I'm sure there's nothing in this lovely house to alarm anyone.'

Father laughed and said there was always the Card Room, and added that tea would be ready in half an hour. Dorothea went up and we were left standing in the hall.

'Very attractive.'

I admitted it.

'Younger than I'd imagined.'

I replied that I thought she might be about thirty-five, adding an extra three years to reassure the Old Man.

'She's English, of course'—as though that made it more respectable.

'Ah, yes, I thought she didn't look Australian.' He went towards the kitchen 'to see about tea', which was something I don't remember his ever doing before: he was obviously going to ask Cook to set out something special, and I was amused at the impression Dorothea had made.

After tea he insisted on showing her round the house himself, and they were gone an hour.

In spite of Jane's absence, Father arranged a 'local' dinner with the neighbours from Hampden, Knowles the Rector and his Italian wife, and Commander and Mrs. Longford, and a Mrs. Roxburgh Smith, who seems to have money and seems to be too often at Peterley. The Hapsburgian formality of these occasions, which wearies me, obviously delighted our 'visitor from the Antipodes', as Knowles insisted on calling her, who was radiant in a black-and-silver dress which artfully set off shoulders which the Commander visibly appreciated.

There was a good Beaujolais which I had forgotten we still had, and the conversation afterwards was not too dull. Dorothea gave some reminiscences of Canberra and of Griffin, its peculiar planner, who curved everything to such an extent that the city seems to have no solid structure but to lie on the ground like a piece of invertebrate sea-blubber. I was doubtful of her accuracy when she described the different quarters of the city which correspond to different salary-groups, the district stretching from Acacia Grove to Juniper Avenue being for the £350 to £399 group, Kookaburra Crescent to Dingo Drive being for the over £400s, while the Civil Service Grade D at £500 and up begins at Platypus Parade, and so on. If this is really intended, it will be the *locus classicus* of the Bureaucratic Mind at work.

Everyone sat till half past eleven, which is late for us; and Dorothea was left with three invitations, none of which she would have time to accept. She wished me goodnight and added:

'David, darling, it was a perfect evening. I love Peterley; I could live here forever.'

And I was tempted to reply that that was exactly what she would now be doing if . . . but which 'if' was it? If we had been more courageous, or more passionate, or more unscrupulous, or . . . These 'ifs' are too melancholy; and I merely replied that she had looked lovely, that I had been happy to see her shine at Peterley, and that it was the kind of evening that it was a pity to part after. At which she went up the stairs but turned at the curve and blew me down a kiss.

The summer is being gloriously prolonged, and we had a late breakfast this morning on the terrace in the sun, the very picture of a settled family discussing how to spend the day most pleasantly. Father pressed Dorothea to stay for the week, and suggested a dinner and a theatre in Town, which ordinarily nothing will persuade him to do.

We walked round the gardens afterwards, Dorothea and I. The size of the barn and the dovecot amazed her, and I explained they were relics of the abbey farm which must once have occupied the site and of which these are the only survivals, apart from the servants' wing which is older than the house itself. We went up to see Rose's little apartment, but it affected us both sadly, the tenantless sitting-room with its chintzes, its little bookcase, and framed prints on the walls—an Albert Moore, a Burne-Jones, a Campbell-Taylor—which proclaimed the poor girl's adolescent taste. At sight of the Temple and its contents, Dorothea protested that the Old Man was being too morbid with his cult of the gardener's daughter. 'If,' she added, 'that's what she really was. It's only because you've given him nothing to drag him away from his study and his military maps. He'd much rather be playing with his grandchild in the garden.'

'Yes; but with the egoism of the old he wanted it on his own terms.'

To which Dorothea retorted with a little too much warmth, 'Well, my God, it's not as terribly difficult or unpleasant as all that to get your wife with child,' which I thought was putting it rather offensively, and we walked on past the stone base without a statue down to the brook without speaking.

When we had asked Dorothea what most she would like to do, she had replied 'visit Lichfield', since her husband's addiction to Boswell's *Life of Johnson* had made this town a necessary place of pilgrimage. So I arranged to drive her down.

Lichfield bears revisiting; it is small, unspoilt, unpretentious—all that a town should be, and that few towns now are. The Johnson statue is grotesque; but that of Boswell is the most humorous effigy in England, pert, self-assured, childishly vain, and ridiculously failing to be impressive: exactly Boswell. The birthplace astonishes by the smallness of the eighteenth-century rooms and the darkness of these old houses, and one wonders what the cost of candles must have been through the long winters. But how beautiful is this miniature cathedral in its little close which is the perfection of all that England has ever managed to achieve in its public arts—a quiet, comfortable, contented serenity. A kind-hearted complacent Ecclesia Anglicana sits here on the ruins of the Middle Ages, still somnolent from the long repose of the eighteenth century, unwakened by Wesley, undistracted by the looms of the Industrial Revolution, undisturbed by Newman, and perhaps unaware of later troublers of the social conscience. These Georgian façades carry restraint to the point of complete silence; and even the classical magnificence of the Bishop's Palace only manages to say, 'His Grace is not at home.'

We went in to Vespers and listened to the clear voices of the choir-boys in the cathedral. The same old octogenarian shuffled decrepitly to the lectern and, like a white-winged turkey, spluttered and gobbled his unintelligible way through the flowery meadows of Jacobean English. The canons stared vacantly at the vaulted roof; the choir-boys nudged each other under their surplices, and whispered profanities, and exhibited surreptitious objects under their psalters. Incredible deities were invoked in fantastic supplications; the biological verities were triumphantly denied, and the cosmic speculations of a primitive tribe proclaimed the accepted faith of an Empire and the only hope of spiritual salvation. And when the three superannuated Bachelors of Divinity, the linen-draper's assistant, the water-rate collector, the retired sanitary engineer, and the novitiates from the seminary had asserted their eternity of duration, their incorruptibility, and their own redemption, they briefly cursed all who differed from themselves and departed to tea and muffins in their respective parlours. And yet, what a lovely ceremony! Its theology one can ignore—for who feels like saving souls at tea-time?—in contemplation of a traditional rite performed with well-bred ease, where music and voices seem to spring up from the columns and mould in air these visible trefoils, spandrils, and pendants in vault and clerestory. We have no national theatre, no imperial opera: we can at least preserve the Church of England.

Dorothea is gone. Gurney drove her back to Lincolnshire this morning, showing not nearly as much repugnance as usual to a long drive in one of these infernal machines. For a quarter of an hour before, we went for a last walk through the garden, but saying little. There was one moment when she was confessing how much she had loved Peterley when she added: 'And to think, David, that if I hadn't been happily married we might—we might—have been living together here. And I think it would have been a success, in all ways.'

I said nothing.

'You believe that, too, don't you, David?'

'Yes, I'm sure it would.' But I wasn't sure at all. It was the last thing I would ever be; even with Dorothea, who surely had everything to ensure sureness; just as Jane had, although with just a spice of feminine— what was the elusive quality: devilishness, contrariety, wickedness, *méchanceté*?—added. I still wasn't sure. The only certainty would be the long and unassuageable regret for a Dorothea whom it was probable I should never see again.

It was brilliant summer, hot, cloudless, a little dusty, bees only breaking the stillness as we parted at the gates and she got into the car which was taking her the first lap of a journey that would end in a climb up the dusty road of Cremorne Point under a hot, cloudless Australian sky. I am writing in my room and the sun is everywhere outside, and melancholy on such a day seems even less bearable when not echoed by the surroundings. This is an end of a period and of a state of mind or heart; and it will be the beginning of something I have no forevision of. I think I will close this journal, and live pragmatically.

September

This, of all years, has been the most marvellous for sunshine. Summer still stays; the air is mild, the sun warm and a pale gold. Vistas in the evening are vaporous, retreating into a romantic haze. I stay at Peterley and sit in the garden reading day after day while Gurney, who is feeling his age, superintends the education of a young gardener. All that is lacking is music, and, from time to time, I go up to Town for this. Sally sometimes plays for me; but what Peterley needs is a Kappelmeister.

October

At Chappell's today I was amused by a friendly altercation between the assistant and a charming young woman who maintained that the score offered her was not the correct edition. I didn't follow the dispute closely, because it became technical, but I could not help looking closely at the girl who was standing by her opinion so stubbornly, since she had a remarkable face, very black hair, dark eyes, a white skin, and a beautifully clear, strong profile. When she had gone, no sale accomplished, I asked the shopman who she was who seemed so sure of her musical knowledge. 'Oh, that's Polly Morel,' as though I would know; and when he saw I didn't, added: 'A pianist. Plays for the B.B.C.'

Providence has perhaps intervened to solve my musical problem. One needs music constantly; and Beethoven is a very necessary strengthening and comfort. At the B.M. today I am enchanted by Dr. Dee's handwriting. It is time there were a revival of good writing again.

I don't know what judgment to pass upon the past month, although I know what the judgment of others would be; and I think it would be wrong. My only conviction is that my actions could not have been different, and that to regret what has happened is an unallowable mental exercise. What happens has the sufficient validity of existence, and an act is, ultimately, as unsubject to judgment as a planet.

Jane returned from Yorkshire early in October and we passed two weeks of uneasy peace together, until I went to Town to begin work again on my seventeenth-century studies which I am in hopes Blackwell will print. I assumed Jane would stay at Peterley until the winter season was well begun; but she came up suddenly late one night, and in the morning, when I was sitting at breakfast reading *The Times*, sat down opposite and asked forthright whether this ridiculous life was to continue indefinitely. It isn't a good time for discussing such matters, and I was a little surprised, and didn't know what to say. She got up and stood by the fireplace and said that she wanted to know if we were to live together again.

'And you know very well what I mean by that, and that a woman needs that kind of normal life as much as a man. Our conduct at present is stupid because we haven't come to terms about it, and we are going on as though nothing is the matter. It's true we seem to have changed in our feelings—or rather you apparently have. Let us accept that; but can't we also accept a more normal life together?'

I remember feeling at that moment an overwhelming sorrow for her, who had to plead so openly, and surely against all her inclination, for what after all were her rights; but in that moment of that rush of sympathy I still realized, as I stared at the printed columns of *The Times*, that any weakness or compromise now would be fatal for us both. I stood up and walked to the window and then back into the room and shook my head.

'No. That would be no help for either of us. The fault's mine, and I'll go.'

For once, for the only time, she was on the point of anger, but even at this moment controlled it and said nothing. I finished my dressing; came back to find her still leaning against the mantelpiece, too sick at heart to cry. I said 'Goodbye', to which she made no reply; and I went out across the Green, and in that abrupt break of routine could not remember whether I took the Underground or the bus, and realized that, in fact, I did not know where I was going.

I went to Judy and got her out of bed, it being only nine-thirty and about an hour before her usual time of rising. She threw me the paper and told me to wait until she had made up; and came back in fifteen minutes looking as fresh as only society women who have been dancing or playing until the early morning seem able to look, with the help, it is true, of a resplendent dressing gown, a frilly kerchief, and a silk scarf wound round the head. She arranged herself on the sofa and said:

'So it's happened at last.'

'Why; has Jane rung you?'

'No; but when you wake me up at this hour, it can only be for one thing. I think it's going to be very hard on her.'

'I agree; but what else was there to do?'

'Well, only one thing; but I imagine you refused?'

66

'Yes.'

'If you couldn't, you couldn't; though God knows your wife's a damnably attractive woman. You'd be surprised if I told you the men who thought so. What do you want me to do?'

'Nothing. I thought I ought to tell you, first. I don't think there's anything that can be done.'

Installed in this dull street behind Gloucester Road Station, which calls itself 'Bina Gardens' because of the square of sooty grass belonging communally to the tall brick houses. No one ever makes use of it, but it offers a patch of dirty soil through which push dispirited lilacs and bilious laurels all green and mottled yellow. Judy had mentioned that one or two respectable ladies in reduced circumstances had this address; and I find that you can take a single room with use of bath, or a self-contained floor. At the moment I have a large front bed-sitting-room, drably furnished. In what was once a large cupboard, behind a chintz curtain, is an electric heater for making tea and coffee. We are like mice nesting in the monumental remains of the Victorian age.

Judy, acting as my representative now that diplomatic relations, like the other ones, have been severed, has arranged for my books from Brook Green to be sent, and the old armchair, the 'wing' one that belonged to Uncle Matthew. Nearly every day I read in the B.M.; dine usually at the Club; and at eleven return to South Kensington, which reminds me of a French cemetery, but one where each daylight *revenant* locks himself into his little mausoleum for the night until he emerges to haunt the day again. In this present depression of mind I have retired to this dry scholastic acre in the fenland of my misery, closing all doors behind me as though to keep the life-giving waters from draining away on the ebb. It is flat desolation under low clouds that bring no rain, the reeds unmoving in the stagnant ditches, and no one passing. I have shut myself up with fugitive royalists hiding in cellars in Gunpowder Lane from the eye of the ailing Protector, and bent all my thoughts to the textual elucidation of Bold and Cleveland. Of an evening, I return to one of my favourites that may not be one of the great books of the world, to *Dichtung und Wahrheit* whose placid narrative, as Goethe in his almost divine egotism lingers tediously over each detail of childhood and adolescence, marvellously contents the mind.

·　　　　·　　　　·　　　　·　　　　·

Heard the fourth symphony of Brahms, and remembered hearing it with Moira, who at the end of the slow movement had turned to me and said, 'There, David, that is what I mean when I say I want my life to be like music.'

Asked H. at the B.B.C. to find Miss Morel's address; and, when I had it, I went the other evening to South London to regions unvisited and unimagined before, and by tortuous and deserted roads, reading the names by gas-lamps, came to the street and found it sloping to still gloomier depths down to what seemed a railway cutting. Returning, I found myself opposite the Crystal Palace which looked gigantic in the darkness: the first of modern buildings, for this is functional architecture at its extremest, being nothing but a greenhouse multiplied by four, with some pagodas from the Brighton Pavilion added, but later, I suppose. When this monster sprawled in Hyde Park before its removal, rib by rib, scale by scale, to Sydenham, these two water-towers were surely not there. Back by bus through the cinematographic murk that is South London. I had no idea it was so large, so lifeless.

I had written to Miss Morel asking if she would be interested in giving a few private recitals. She had replied politely, briefly, favourably, and I suggested a meeting at Buzzard's. She was without hat or gloves, and her thick black hair was let cluster unrestrained round her head, which again impressed me by its strong modelling, by the fineness of the features—the straight nose, the dark expressive eyes, the full lips, all in a marvellously clear white skin; the whole face certainly not English.

I explained the rendezvous was chosen because I had a fondness for their toasted tea-cakes, and she replied that it made no difference to her, since she cared little for tea, or indeed for any meal: 'I should regard it as a waste of time to give very much thought to food'; and she remained throughout very business-like, questioning me, when not yet half-way through my tea, about my musical scheme. But by this time I had become content to sit and talk and watch this mobile face responding alertly to the conversation. When I admitted that these recitals were for me only, she looked up sharply; but I added that she could choose the place, and of course could set the fee. 'It would depend on what I had to play.' I jotted down on a scrap of paper some of my suggestions: the Adagio of Op. 106 and the Arietta of Op. 111, the Sonata in A flat Op. 110, and *Les Adieux*; the Goyescas, some De Falla and Turina, and as much of Debussy as she pleased. She looked at the list and said that several of them were extremely difficult and would need a great deal of practice. 'If you insist on these, I should have to ask two guineas for the hour.'

I think she was hazarding a rate she knew to be excessive and I began to suspect she needed the money very seriously, to undertake so curious an engagement. Her dress, which would be her best, was obviously bought ready-made from a shop in that brick desert of South London. The memory of that dark slope to the railway tunnel impelled me to say foolishly: 'That is too moderate. Say three guineas if you prefer guineas.' And carried suddenly out of her reserve, she smiled and said, 'It sounds more professional.' She looked at my list again this time with only one objection: 'The Beethoven C minor sonata I don't think I can manage; not for some time. I'd have to practise it.'

We took to the cakes, or rather I did, and felt that the ice was broken, although I still considered that the temperature remained low. After a silence she asked, 'Why do you like Beethoven so much?'

'If I were truthful I should have to say it is because he is comforting and soothing.'

'And you don't find the texture of the writing too often coarse and unpleasant?'

'Sometimes; but it's the non-musical qualities that interest me, the philosophical implications.'

'And those tedious variations?'

'You mean the Arietta? They really seem to have a meaning for me.'

She looked at me and lightly laughed, but said no more. She was not going to jeopardize by argument at this time those weekly guineas; but she clearly thought my ideas were ridiculous. I was sorry I could find no excuse to lengthen the interview; and she agreed to meet me in the Brompton Road studio in a fortnight.

At Peterley this week-end, and looking through the books in the attic I found two charming phrases in Wootton's *Parallel between the late Duke of Buckingham and the late Earl of Essex*: 'the inward furniture of his mind' and 'the Armada which did prove but a Morris dance upon our waves'. Such phrases come up like wild flowers in the meadows of seventeenth-century prose. In a bundle marked in Matthew's hand *Misc. MSS.* were some oddments collected squirrel-like. One sheet in a seventeenth-century hand was headed simply *From the Fairfax papers* and contained a stanza which had appealed to the writer in this time of civil war:

> Much better tis in Liberty to dye
> and freedome purchase though with loss of bloude
> then still to live in shame and slavery:
> A noble death should never be with stoode.

Someone, probably Roger when he was laying out the gardens *circa* 1750, had collected works on gardening, and they are still here. One of them is J. W.'s *Systema horti-cultura* of 1683 which has on page 53 a most amusing engraving of the latest improvement in the formal garden, something no gentleman's garden should be without. It is 'a statue of a woman that on the turning of a private cock shall cast water out of her nipples into the spectator's face'. A pity Peterley is without one.

Nothing was said about my private affairs all through this week-end, but after supper on Sunday, as there was no company and I was leaving for Town shortly, Father remarked that he understood Jane and I had decided upon separate establishments. I replied that for the moment we had.

'Once that step is taken, it is permanent. But if you have taken it, I imagine you had no alternative. A pity: there will be legal complications, and we shall have to undo a lot of what we settled in 1931.'

'We have more or less tacitly agreed to leave things as they are.'

'But that can't continue indefinitely. Harris will want it all in black and white.' After some few puffs of his cigar he added, 'The 1931 settlement was extremely advantageous to Peterley.' And that was all he ventured in commentary.

He hated discussing anything that involved a person's emotions; to such a degree that I think he considered even an aesthetic judgment to be an indecent performance. The emotional life was the affair of the individual, and intervention by another would almost certainly be ruinous, because one cannot deflect the personal life without deforming it. He had little faith in the efficacy of environment in influencing the hereditary growth: it could change the personality to some small extent, but what you had as a result was not the improved original but something different; the hereditary potentialities had not been fully realized: there had been a qualitative loss. Instead of x squared, you had x plus y. I imagine this was his theory, unexpressed certainly, perhaps not even formulated mentally to himself. I suspected his strong feeling against an Australian marriage for me; but he had never given anything but the most polite of hints that there were nubile women to be found in England. What worried me as I drove back to Town was that the system did not seem to be successful as far as I was concerned; but at least there had been no unpleasant scenes, and he would never accuse me of hazarding the family estates, and I would never retaliate by saying I had married Jane to please him, which, after all, would not be true.

November

The first of my private recitals took place yesterday, and it was all I had hoped. I listened to what I wanted to hear, and was delighted with Miss Morel's playing, which is exceptionally good. She played the sonatas of Field with just the right delicacy, and, although she had confessed the *Hammerklavier* gave her no pleasure, she gave a lovely performance of it. I had hoped she would come to dinner with me afterwards, but she refused. I handed her a cheque and some suggestions for another recital. 'I hope you've not been disappointed?' I said I was more than satisfied and was willing to continue the arrangement indefinitely; but she doubted she would be free next year. We are to meet next week.

When Miss Morel arrived for this second recital yesterday, I was amused to notice that she had already invested her new earnings in a down payment on a black coat and skirt and a white silk blouse. They gave her an elegant and Gallic outline; and with her dark, vivacious face made her look like an importation from across the Channel. She was punctual again; we entered the studio; she sat down straightway without wasting a minute of the hour and began to play. I had asked for my favourite Haydn sonata, the Beethoven Sonata in E minor, and the rest was for her to choose. She played some Chopin, and some light pieces by Fibich called I think *Stimmungen*. Debussy was played with a delicacy and such perfection of touch that I remarked on it and she replied shortly, 'Oh, the only modern composer for the pianist.'

'I suppose I ought to like him more.'

'Oh, no; you've got Beethoven,' and she gathered her music together, swivelled round on the stool, smiled at me and stood up, ready to go.

I asked if I could give her a lift anywhere and she said she preferred walking; and I went as far as Knightsbridge with her, heartily wishing I could prolong the company of this young woman whose life, with its addiction to music and its austerity, was so different from mine as to have all the attraction of the unknown. But I realized that another invitation to dinner would be refused. From the amusement in her eyes, when we said goodbye at the corner, it was clear she had divined my thoughts; and, deprived of the satisfaction of saying 'No' to an invitation, was enjoying that other satisfaction of showing me my intentions were patent.

In a peace of mind I had not known for two years, I walked across the Park and along the Mall to the Club and ordered a light dinner and a bottle of Niersteiner. The long dining-room, its windows curtained against the wintry Thames, had the calm of a cathedral. In white surplice and high white biretta, the officiating dignitary presided behind the snow-white altar heaped with unburnt offerings for us communicants in both kinds. With hushed pace the lay brothers passed to and fro, and inclined themselves reverently before the Cold Collation.

I dined slowly, and thought of music and Miss Morel, and of Alsatian vineyards, and of our own white wine of Arbois, and of the terrace of the Hotel Arbez at La Cure where we used to sit and sip our wine and watch the warm light lift off the pines of Prémanon as the sun went down behind the old fort. I thought of Miss Morel and of the homely string quartet that met at Dr. Cottet's at St. Claude, and scraped away the winter evenings that were so much longer there than elsewhere, in this town buried deep in the defile of the Jura. In summer we would go to the square and join the statue of Voltaire in watching the citizens play at bowls; until, tired of this, we descended the track that skirted the old fortifications and led back to the old town and the abbey and the high bridge over the Bienne. From the bridge we gazed a hundred feet below to the waters of the river that turned the machinery of the manufacturers of pipes in days before it turned turbines that turned, etc. In St. Claude the sun always set early in the afternoon behind these hills that went up so steeply to a height of three thousand feet on all sides of the town; but in summer a mild light lay in the valley for long after, and the darkness filled up gradually like water rising in a reservoir, the river being the first to vanish in the twilight; and it was then we would go in. But in winter darkness came early, and with it the cold white mists; and after supper we had to sit and content ourselves with books or with pencil and paper in the dining-room while the amateur quartet in the salon produced a kind of music that had no meaning at all for us boys. Once or twice we managed to slip down to the courtyard and pass the concierge unobserved and range through the long narrow street, looking in at the taverns where the citizens at their customary tables sipped and talked for hours in an over-heated atmosphere.

If I went back now, would that little town seem as romantic as then; that river chasm as stupendous; and the train, that with a caterpillar motion descended the tortuous valley, did it really go on over the hills into Italy, as I imagined from seeing on the carriages the name 'Bellegarde' which I assumed must be an Italian place? But one should never go back; the streets are meaner, the hills smaller, and the ducal palace of Great-grand-father is found to be only a desirable detached residence in a select suburb, surrounded by a lawn, some oleanders, and tall iron railings like cavalry lances.

I was still wandering in the streets of St. Claude when one of the officiants approached and in low voice so as not to disturb this gastro-nomic Mass apologized for the telephone call that was awaiting me in the hall outside. It was an irate Judy asking why I had not turned up for dinner. I was still bemused, and foolishly said, 'It was the music.'

'What music?'

'The music in the Brompton Road.'

'David, are you sober and sane?' which recalled me to the reality of Thursday and the realization that this was the day I was to dine with her and discuss the legal problems of the separation.

I travelled in swift rushes and maddening halts in a taxi across to Notting Hill, trying to make up my mind whether to confess I had already dined or pretend I had been detained on business: but then she knew I had no business and I had no appetite. It would be safer to tell the truth.

Judy was still unappeased: 'What was this fairy tale about the Brompton Road?'

'Nothing. I was day-dreaming.'

'This was scarcely the day for it when you were supposed to be separating from your wife. Did you forget to have dinner, too?'

I had to sit while Judy went through her half of a ruined dinner served by a petulant cook.

'And as it's ruined, we may as well carry on our business now, and get both of them over.' During soup we eliminated divorce, although she was

73

in favour of it: 'You'll certainly need it one day; and Jane might. Why not have it now?'

I said I would arrange it whenever Jane wanted one; but that I certainly preferred to leave things as they were, not too definitely broken.

'You're wrong; but let's talk about the settlement,' and she asked the girl to bring in whatever was left of the fish.

I suggested we left things as they were, but that Jane should receive a portion of the total income corresponding to her original estate, and that Harris should be instructed to do this without any formal legal document being drawn up. 'Harris will be sure to find legal arguments against it; but never mind.'

Judy said that Jane would like to have her rooms at Peterley left for her, since Misham was let on a long lease; and, as Father would certainly wish this too, I agreed. Dinner and the discussion over, Judy said: 'David, you're going to be much poorer from now on; I'll treat you to a cinema,' and we went and sat gloomily through one of the long-drawn-out attempts of the British film industry to tell a story on the screen, until we could endure it no more, and, 'For heaven's sake!' said Judy, 'let's get out of here and go back and have a drink'; and we went back and sat talking till one, when I rose to go. 'Next time I ask you to dinner, never mind the Brompton Road; and, David, don't make a second mistake. And if sometimes you feel terribly lonely, and I'm alone—and I often am—you can ring me up and come here. And you needn't perhaps always leave so early in the evening.'

'Darling, you're very kind.'

'Not at all. I should enjoy it too.'

Fifteenth

Unable to use my ticket for the Wigmore Hall last Tuesday I sent it to Miss Morel but had no acknowledgment. Next time I will buy two, and keep one so that I can turn up at the last minute beside her. For Christmas I've amused myself by a stratagem that has involved Peterley and the Church of England. I have persuaded Father to subsidize the Rector's Christmas concert in the village, instead of holding the usual servants-and-friends party in the house: we will provide half the cost of refreshments and all the cost of entertainment and will have the servants driven down and back. I am to find a conjurer and a pianist. But will she come? The programme can be so timed that the last train to London will have left;

74

we shall have to put her up at the house; and she will surely stay for Sunday following; and a week-end at Peterley may do more to my young lady from South Norwood than the occasional dinner in Town. For I think it is time my life were ordered better, and I cannot think of a better ordering than a young and attractive mistress who can play as well. But, with my present income, we might have to share a flat; and thus in avoiding the legal Charybdis of matrimony we run on to the Scylla of cohabitation.

But I must have music and I am beginning to feel that I must have Miss Morel too. She has a dangerous coldness; and when she looks indifference I am already more than half won over. Judy noticed a change in me and asked what had made me come alive again; and I said I was working hard; which is true, having finished the Cleveland and being launched on Bold.

Nineteenth

We met for our private concert yesterday, and I heard the Schubert sonata played delightfully, just as well, I think, as Glock played it recently at his flat, and Glock has been Schnabel's pupil. 'But I practise awfully hard for you,' she said when I congratulated her, 'I hope you realize that.' At the hour's end, as she was collecting her music together, she thanked me for the ticket, and remarked that the pianist had been poor—'But you couldn't help that,' she added generously. She seemed a little less business-like than usual, and I mentioned that I was having a quick dinner in the City and if she cared to have it with me . . .

'If it can be near Blackfriars Bridge Station, it would be convenient. I catch my train there.'

'Right; if you show me the station, I'll try to find a restaurant.' I stood waiting for a taxi.

'Don't you ever take a bus?'

So we took a bus.

Twenty-sixth

After the music hour we went a few doors away for tea, and I mentioned casually a musical job for which she could earn in a quarter of an hour much more than in two hours with me, if she was willing to waive a scruple or two. 'I could think of several ways of doing that. The answer would be "No" every time.' But this, I said, would be a kind of charity and it would be doing me a service; and I explained that the rector gave a concert each Christmas for the village that I helped with, and this year they wanted a pianist, but a good one, to play for fifteen minutes; and that the rector felt it was wrong to impose a poor player on an audience merely because it had not paid for admission; and that he was willing to pay a proper fee. I knew she was in need of money; but she kept that disdainful composure that delights me: 'I am to play bad music for village yokels?'

'That's exactly what we yokels don't want: we want to hear some decent music for a change.'

'And what is the rest of the concert going to be?'

'Oh, there will be a Father Christmas distributing presents; Wilkinson will give a puppet show, and he's the Paderewski of his profession; there'll be a conjuror; and we want a good pianist.'

'And how much will the conjuror get?'

'That's what I don't yet know.'

I suspected conjurors were expensive; and so did she, for she replied: 'Right. I'll come if I'm paid as much as the conjurer.'

I agreed; and hoped inwardly I could find a cheap magician; and added casually: 'It's fairly late at night, and there may be difficulty about getting back to Town; but you will of course get an invitation to stay at Peterley.'

'My dear Mr. Peterley, that is out of the question.'

'But for heaven's sake, why?'

'For one thing, I haven't anything to wear; and, for another, I don't think I'd care very much to.'

'But you can wear anything you like. You'll only need a frock for the concert—and not too fashionable a one, for our yokels—and a change of tweeds for Sunday.'

'Don't you realize that a change of tweeds is exactly what I haven't got?'

The argument finished by her dictating terms: she would come if the fee were the same as Magnifico the Magician's; she would return to London if there were a train; if she had to stay at Peterley it would be understood she wore just what she pleased. I offered to drive her back to Norwood, but she declined; put her music under her arm; said, 'You'll let me know about the conjurer?' and walked away; and I drove slowly back to Bina Gardens, tormented, with a sudden jealousy as to why she would never continue these meetings and to whose company she was at this very moment hurrying. My longing grew with every encounter that proved I was drawing no closer to a woman whose attraction was increasing with each step she took away from me. The truth was simply that, for each step forward I took, she retreated an equal distance, and we were in the same relative position as when we first met. I shall have to trust to this Christmas Sunday to change all that.

December

Third

Innes Kay, the solicitor and the great friend of Brennan who did so much to carry on the salvage scheme I started with my letter to the University of Sydney, writes to me as one of the original benefactors to tell me of Brennan's death:

'I have to inform you that Chris Brennan died on the 5th instant (October) from cancer of the stomach after what was fortunately a very short illness. As you were so much *major pars* in the initiation of the movement, I am happy to report to you that during the last two or three years he has been very much improved and very comfortable. He was buried with full honours. All the people who would not help him in his lifetime, and those who did, turned up to do him justice at a requiem mass, and at the graveside, and I'm getting a lot of pleasure out of making them pay for the funeral. He was received back into the Church some months before he died, and passed away in a state of grace. He made a will under which he appointed me sole executor and beneficiary—a responsible job as all he left behind are some manuscripts and verse, and a rumour that somewhere there is available in manuscript a text of Aeschylus, which I can't find. Brereton delivered a eulogy at the graveside on his literary services, but nobody either in print or anywhere else said what a loveable man he was, and how openly generous with his scholarship. The usual stuff about him has appeared in the *Sun* and the *Herald* and the *Bulletin*. . . . I thought it was all very poor. . . . I don't think there has been much literary production in the last ten years. All he left was a small library, most of which belongs to other people. During his life he got into the hands of the Jews and owed them some two or three hundred pounds and

Dr. Moran paid them out, recovered the library and presented it to St. John's College.

I saw him the afternoon before he died. He was very calm and philosophic and not in pain. The wastage had refined his features— taken all the grossness out of them, and you could see what a remarkably handsome young man he must have been. Chris died in Lewisham Hospital at 11.30 on a Wednesday morning the 5th October as ever was, beating Falstaff by one day. He mentioned nothing about green fields on the Tuesday but specially invited Wilkins and me to have a pint for him at half past five—which we did. He was taken into the hospital on the preceding Monday so that he was not there more than forty-eight hours altogether.'

Lower Misham has never known such a saturnalia of presents, puppets, poltergeist, and pianist. It went, indeed, very well. Magnifico, who was born Jackson of Rotherham, almost conjured the eyeballs out of the villagers; and Wilkinson charmed them with puppets who made fun of City men, clergymen, sportsmen, and politicians. These hand-puppets are purposely crude, and the dialogue is of the most childlike; and yet the adult audience and I myself laughed, and were as rapt from this parish hall as though by the most breathtaking of melodramas. There must be some philosophy of marionettes; and it should be looked into. They are not all they seem. They have a power the débutantes and cinaedi of the London stage have lost.

In the human theatre the action must remain within reasonable limits, that is, within the probabilities of normal human life; for the actors are still humans, and what they do must be such as we in the stalls recognize as being natural to their humanity. The stage is a world, and the players merely men and women. Even the extremest farce must be the normal exaggerated. But with the puppets we are free of that human limitation, and the puppet theatre is not of this world. These small people are kin to elves, goblins, the Sidhe, gnomes, kobolds, leprechauns, and those small persons that Giraldus Cambrensis heard of when he went into Wales in 1188. They may be the surviving representatives of some early small race that was driven into the mountains by tall men from the East, and became legendary as the metal-workers in the mountains. They may perhaps have a more sinister ancestry. Puki was an evil spirit in Iceland; and Puck, as Langland well knew, was linked with the Prince of Darkness. The

78

marionette has no human limitations; and when he walks on, Aristotle flies out of the window, and we are left without a guide in a terrifying world where anything may happen, and does. Chaos is come again, and a monstrous Uberpuppen stalks with malevolent intent, throwing down the godly from their seats and exalting the proud and wicked. And all our baser nature rises up to applaud. Our black passions surge from the dark caves of our being. The murderous, sly, bestial men we once were a million years ago crawl back along the arteries and sinews, and reanimate these civilized bodies. As the club cracks on the poor woman's skull the old Adam stamps with our feet, claps with our hands, and shouts approval with our voice. I must look more closely into the puppet world. There is something else; an even more sinister subtlety: these marionettes that are never realistic, that always just avoid the human likeness, that move mechanically, gesture grotesquely, grimace fixedly, are in fact the devilish caricature of the human being. The Evil One is mocking the divine creation with these absurd mannikins that ape us so wittily, and move in a world where all values are reversed.

Where are the Punch and Judy shows that Cruikshank drew? Gone, I fear, with tasty sausages, and hot saffron cake, and nettle beer, and good ale. I was quite carried away by the puppets; and so, surprisingly, was my young pianist, who grew jolly and human, and laughed, and at one moment turned to put her hand on my arm, but seemed to remember whom she was with, and refrained. So that by the time she had to go up on the platform and be introduced by the rector, she had forgotten her dislike of public performances, clergymen, country people; and she sat down and played with none of that tightening of the muscles that comes from being ill at ease.

She was astonished by the applause. Some of it, of course, was due to a rather lovely, and to villagers very sophisticated, young woman in an evening dress such as they had seen in the illustrated magazines; but some I think was for the music. Knowles took and held her hand a little too long, and beamed rather too widely, and seemed unwilling to let her vanish from the platform. She came back to her seat and asked me if she had been as good as the magician, and I nearly retorted that she should have been, since she was getting as much; for my enjoyment of her playing was tempered by the knowledge, unshared by the others, that this was one of the costliest amateur performances ever known—or rather, ever unknown, since it was assumed by everyone that Miss Morel was giving her services free.

I brought John and Grace and Miss Morel back first; told her that

Grace would see to her, and that on Sunday breakfast was at nine; and then went back for the others. Father was pleased with the whole evening, and ignorant of my motive congratulated me on the idea of co-operation with the Rector. He had not, I think, taken to the pianist. The uncompromising artist terrifies him, and he must have felt that between himself and this young musician there was an unbridgeable gulf; and, even if he did not identify Sydenham behind the serious and unconventional face, he at least knew it wasn't Gloucestershire and Sussex Square; and, as I foresaw, he didn't come down to breakfast.

I found her wandering in the study next morning, and asked why she hadn't begun breakfast, and had she slept well. 'The silence was too much for me. I woke at five, and couldn't get to sleep again, and had to read a most peculiar book I found: *Unclay* by Powys. I'm not sure I liked it.' I remembered now that Dorothea had discovered the Powys books and had taken them all up to the bedroom when she was here, and there they had apparently stayed since then. Dorothea had revelled in these primitive, these autochthonous fables; had hailed each lapsed virtue and every senile ruse. I remember her saying that the prose dripped with satisfaction over rural wrong-doings. But those were summer days when Dorothea had laughed with me in these gardens, and shared my idle reading at Hampton, and shared an intimacy that was real even though never physical. It was this same year; but it was another age; and here I was now in the same room contemplating a new order in my life with a young woman who was as far away from me as Dorothea in her Australian home.

I had to recall myself to the present and to conversation, and asked if she would like a walk through the woods afterwards, although the night had been rainy and the countryside was dank and the ways mire. She very truthfully replied that she wouldn't care for it very much, and said she ought to go back home, if there was a train. But I doubted if there was such a thing as a train; it would be almost improper to expect one at Missenden on a Sunday; let alone to board it; and that in any case I would drive her back. Peterley suddenly seemed to be the most unsuitable place for broaching this question of a liaison: she did not seem at ease; and when we went into the morning-room and stood looking through the windows at the wet lawn and the dripping trees, the sight of the winter earth drinking the rains for its hidden seeds probably meant only uncomfortable dampness to her, for she walked over to the fire and warmed her hands. I might as well take her back to the London she was longing for; so I said that I would, if she liked, be ready to leave at eleven.

'Oughtn't I to thank your father for putting me up?'

'I doubt if we shall see him this morning. Write a little note, and leave it in the hall.'

As we turned out of the drive into the road, she looked round at the house, and at its old stone soaked to a darker grey by rain, but made no remark, and settled herself down in the seat in silence. I found it difficult to open the conversation to which all this complicated week-end diplomacy was meant to lead. 'Polly, it was really very good of you to come. I suspect you didn't enjoy it much.'

In a very low voice, which I had not heard before, she answered: 'Why do you think that? As a matter of fact, I've been surprised to find I loved it.'

'What, even the platform and the rector?'

'Well, not that particularly; but the rest of it, certainly.'

'Would you come again—not as a concert performer?'

For some time she did not reply; and then said, 'That's a difficult question I don't know how to answer; but I rather wondered if you'd ask it.'

I drove on without saying anything more, down the hill to the main road, and turned towards Amersham. Miss Morel, I should have recollected, could be depended on to see the meaning behind the formal words. We had left the little town behind and were on the way to Chalfont before she spoke again.

'I ought to tell you that I'm going to Edinburgh in about three weeks, and it's possible that I may be married in the summer. Does that answer your question?'

What is that stab at the heart, the chill in the veins, the sensation of the floor of the world falling away from under your feet, and an emptiness where there were trees, fields, and people before? Does all the blood drain away from the mind at such a shock, and leave the eyes sightless and the brain thoughtless for an instant? I was conscious again of the wet road surface, and the bare hedgerows, and the turns, and knew immediately that the idea of a new life with this woman, which I imagined to be still only a picture in the mind, had quietly, unconsciously, been gathering to itself, as it were, enveloping layers of emotion, becoming a 'complex' of the psychologists, and it was now not merely an idea that could be dropped at will, but was a hope, an ambition, a desire that I would have to fight for; since its loss would leave a dangerous wound in that delicate personality that accompanies each one of us and is made up of all these emotional longings and desires, which by time and will become not merely something outside ourselves, wished for, but really a part of our being. We are made up of all the things wished for as well as all things achieved. In that moment, against all reason, and by an act of volition stronger than the will, I wanted this woman more than anything in the world; and knew that a future without her was impossible, since she had become for me identified with the whole future. Whether I was in love with her I did not know for certain.

I skirted the village green at Chalfont and saw to the right the tower of Milton's village church that stood over against his cottage; and I remember suddenly thinking how far away this poet was from my actual state and how empty was all his work of this human passion.

'You say it's possible you may be married soon: it isn't certain?'

Her answer, thank heaven, did not come straightway, but after a moment or two: 'I suppose it is fairly definite.'

'But you can carry on with our recitals?'

She turned her head round to look directly at me. 'But do you want to, now?'

I took one hand off the wheel and pressed the hand on her lap and said I should miss them too much, that I had almost no other music, and that I hoped she would continue.

She said: 'Very well. But I don't think I understand you.'

We drove on without speaking, and the lanes became rows of detached cottages of the dormitory towns, and then crescents of semi-detached villas of the outer suburbs, and the winter mist thickened into a whitish fog, and the tramlines led to streets of closed shops, and we were in the slums; and then the Harrow Road and Marble Arch. I put her down by the Crystal Palace. She leaned through the window to say goodbye and added: 'I really have enjoyed it. More than you think.' I said I would send her cheque tomorrow. 'Do you know, I'd almost forgotten about that,' and she smiled and turned away.

So the week-end has not been quite as I planned, as happens when a campaign is based upon imperfect intelligence: I had not allowed for an engagement, and yet what was more likely? And now I'm caught in my own plot: the very thought that she is not free, and for me, has made her far more desirable than she was before. How this passion thrives on obstacles, like an unnatural plant that stays stunted or withers in full sunshine, but when a cloud passes over the sun shoots up with sudden rank overgrowth of stem and leaf! Marriage would be unthinkable: one does not go to Sydenham for wives. Yet does one choose a mistress for musical ability; especially when this is so great as to be able to furnish more pleasure by itself than any shared accomplishments? And then, I must admit, she has no regular beauty; not quite tall enough; short as most Frenchwomen are; and that pale skin with those dark eyes and the curved full lips are alien: I shall be asked about the Spanish dancer picked up in Madrid. But, when well dressed, she draws the eyes in restaurants of men who look from their companion of the evening or their wife and think how pleasant the change would be. As I do now, seeing her in imagination beside this shadowy fiancé.

To Billam's in Gray's Inn, he busy with a play of that unglamorous world of bank clerks, and business men who never succeed, and small-part actors, the inhabitants of boarding houses in Clapham and Lewisham. I wonder that he thinks it dramatic material, and wonder more that he can make these people behave interestingly and talk naturally, as he can, and as I cannot, through keeping to a narrow footpath in a private park. I know nothing of life in that vast Babylonian desert of baked clay that stretches south of the Thames and east of the Farringdon Road; or of how people live in Glasgow. The life of the village and of the small country town I know and love, and think the only life worth living: the life of the industrialized world is a blank; and books on economics and sociology therefore have no meaning for me, and the plays of Mr. Galsworthy bore me, and I cannot share the conscious worries of Fabian reformers. If the village hind leaves his rural paradise for the nominal wages of the factory and for the cinema and dance hall of the city slum he gets no sympathy from me: he has riveted his fetters with his union card and has embraced slavery. Let the Webbs mourn. They are, after all, the professional mourners of our civilization.

All the same, my world is a small and dwindling one. It's the rural society built upon an agricultural economy that interests me: the farmer, the ploughman with his round-ploughing, the reaper who can make a sheaf-bond, the shepherd, the village carpenter who can build a Wood-stock wagon, the village mason who can build a cottage. This, if I must live in England, is where I would be. If I cannot be behind a restaurant table in the rue des Saints Pères I would wish to be in a village inn. So Miss Morel from Sydenham has for me all the charm of the mysterious and misunderstood. I can't imagine what her life has been like; and her ways of thought are not my own. So I suppose a Circassian slave would mystify and elude and fascinate the Smyrna merchant who had acquired her. Which reminds me that I haven't done so yet.

Another quiet Christmas at Peterley. Jane is in Yorkshire. I invited Henry Banks and Sally Satchwell and Judy and Cousin Richard; all good walkers and talkers. We sat late on Christmas Eve in the Card Room as the custom is and had hot punch there, and Richard agreed to read the midnight story. This time he read one he had written himself, and explained that the whole incident, almost to the very words, had come into his mind during sleep and all he had to do was to write it out the following morning. Only one thing had escaped his memory, the name of the town where it happened; and he had since then searched the guide-books for the region and found one that corresponded to the scene; but whether it was coincidence or not he did not know.

It isn't a ghost story; but it deserves to go into the record:

THE TOUCH OF TIME

He came over the hill and rode slowly down into the valley, making for the old stone bridge over the river, crossed, and turned his mule into the dusty white road that led up to the town.

The white houses along the walls shone hot in the late afternoon sunlight, and even in the alleys within, through the archway, the air was still and tepid. The women, sitting in the doorways or under awnings stretched over the merchandise, looked up as he passed and noted the southern darkness of skin in a young face that otherwise did not seem a foreign one. He rode with no apparent purpose through the maze of by-streets, noting the one or two inns, and slackened pace momentarily before the Hôtel de Plaisance. But surely there was an inn, somewhere, better adapted to a light purse.

The street ran downhill, past small shops and deserted houses to railings and a railway line below, and at the very end, on the corner, stood a yellow building shuttered against the sun and bearing the faded sign of Hôtel de la Gare.

84

The cobbled courtyard was open and he rode in and put up his mule in the empty stable. It was not a pleasing house: neglect was shamelessly displayed in peeling plaster and paint, in disarrayed curtains and the dirty litter of the yard. He knocked, but no one answered; he pushed open the door and entered, but found nobody about, except, in what seemed the bar and dining-room, a man asleep by the fire, an empty glass on the table, and the heavy smell of anisette in the air. Going to the bottom of the stairs he called up in a French that had a strong Spanish intonation and asked if anyone was in.

'Coming; coming!' shouted a woman's voice from upstairs. She came, stout, dirty, and pinning up her hair, and eyed the young man with no welcoming gaze.

'You have a room?' he asked.

'You are from Carpitelle?' she answered, as though it were not possible for anyone to come from any other place on such a midsummer's day.

'No; from near Santatierra.'

'Ah! Spanish, then?'

He shrugged his shoulders and said he wanted to put up for the night, and so did his mule, if there was any room.

'Will you come up?'

He followed her up the boxed stairway into a large apartment, shuttered, dark and cool, with the usual heavy double bed, the huge dressing table, and the unnatural wallpaper. 'Twenty francs,' she said. He shook his head and said he would have a smaller, cheaper room.

'I can't bother to make up another room. The girl's out. I'll let you have this one for the price of the other—seventeen francs.'

'And dinner is how much?'

'Eight francs, *vin compris*. Do you want any dinner?'

'What have you?'

She hesitated doubtfully, as though in response to such an unreasonable demand something could be done, but what she couldn't at the moment think. She replied vaguely, '*Pot au feu*,' which meant, he knew, a mixture of ingredients uneatable in themselves but rendered somehow edible by fusion.

'Fish,' she added with a hint of doubt. But that would mean river fish that had hung all day in the dry dusty air. He said he would have *pot au feu*, and cheese, at eight. She went downstairs murmuring, '*Pot au feu* at eight,' and he stretched himself along the bed, glad to be out of the mule saddle, and soon fell asleep.

.   .   .   .   .   .

Eating the poor dinner, he listened to the talk of the few people round the hearth, a discussion that was occasionally interrupted by querulous remarks from the man with the anisette aroma. If this dingy scene is town life here, he thought, he preferred the country roughness round Santatierra and the friendly whitewashed room in the wine bar at the village. Here everything was sordid, except the young girl who waited on him. And she, it seemed, found his softer southern speech charming; she met, she said, so few strangers. She, too, loved the country. In the end he invited her to sit with him over the wine, a suggestion that pleased and alarmed her a little.

'I must ask the old woman if she minds.'

'Oh; but surely . . .'

She vanished and came back without her apron, and sat down beside him. Her vivacity was delightful and she looked pretty in a simple way. He leaned nearer to her suddenly and whispered some words in her ear. Her high laugh startled the group of drinkers, and the man with the anisette turned round and glared at them, muttering something doubtless impolite.

'Who's the grumpy fellow with the drink? Is he always here? He's not your father?'

'Oh, no, no. He drinks. . . .' She tipped her elbow, pushed out her lips, let her eyes close, and sagged in her chair. 'Like that,' she woke up and said.

Her sprightliness pleased him. He drew closer to her, touched her hand and said quietly, 'What about showing me the town tonight, or a walk along the river?'

'I don't think I can get away.'

'The old woman won't mind if she doesn't know.'

The disagreeable man by the hearth had eyed him often since the girl had joined him, and now he rose, with difficulty, and came across the room to them, leaning heavily on the table edge with one hand.

'What do you want with her?' he asked, looming from behind a cloud of anisette. 'She ought to be working, not drinking with strangers, the young slut, the young slut, the young slut.'

The stranger sat still, looking up at him, deliberately saying nothing in reply, and not moving. He continued looking in the man's eyes until they wavered and at last turned away. 'Was warning you,' he mumbled, 'only a friendly warning. No offence. You're all right; but as for her . . .'
And he went back and relapsed into a gloomy silence.

'Don't listen to him; he's drunk as usual.'

'Is he usually rude to strangers?'

'No; it's only because you're sitting with me.'

'Well; what about tonight? When I go out to the stable, slip out and join me then.'

'Perhaps.' She withdrew her hand from his and went away.

Down by the river they walked under the trees, the great foundations of the abbey rising like a fortress above them and the river below moving with broken ripplings in the clouded moonlight. Past the town washing-place, across the open square that had once been the Roman quay, and along the shingle banks where the river's bend had piled up the smooth pebbles in dry shoals, they wandered, and a few late-straying townsfolk saw her out with a tall stranger in a Spanish hat.

'Looks like the girl from the "Railway",' said the man dragging for *langoustine;* and his companion, hauling on the net, saw the familiar figure go by on a stranger's arm. 'Reckon she doesn't mind the old trouble at that place,' he answered as the two lovers passed by, oblivious of the shadowy form of the boat bobbing on the water.

The closed inn, when they returned, gave them no welcoming light. The door creaked as they went into the passage. They stood listening; there was no sound; but from the door of the bar shone a thin line of light on the opposite wall. He stole up, holding her by the hand, and looked through the half-open door to see the empty tumbler and the lamp upon the table and the man sitting, open-eyed, staring ahead of him, yet seeming to see nothing and to hear nothing. Each stair cracked as they went up, and at the top they stood to let silence descend again. He turned suddenly to her, held her fast, pressed her close to him, and kissed her again, again. He felt, as in the river copses he had known, the responding ardour of her lips. 'Do not go yet,' he whispered. 'You do not want to go.' He forgot his French speech and poured into her ear his native endearments for her eyes, her lips, her throat, her unbound hair. She laughed softly; said she would not come for the world; leaned her head back; said that in any case the old woman would hear them, and that the man downstairs wandered about the house and would see her slipping away. So he lifted her up and pushing wide the door carried her into the large gaunt room.

The night was so warm and still that when he opened the shutters no breath of air came in, only the diffused light from the veiled moon.

They sat on the narrow balcony and talked in low voices, looking out over the railway yard, the black shadows and the white roofs of the moon-lit town.

Later, it seemed hours later, the silence of the house was suddenly broken. Downstairs a chair fell over noisily, a door opened, and shambling steps sounded along the passage, and ascended each creaking stair-tread. He stirred. 'Ssh!' she said. 'He's only going up to bed.' The steps came nearer. He turned round and put out his hand to the belt that hung from the chair and felt along it to the handle of a blade covered in a woven sheath. The moving steps halted a moment outside the door. The two lay still, listening, breath held, and caught the sound of muttered phrases. He could feel her heart beating wildly against his own. And then the steps moved on, and he felt her relax. He drew in his arm, and turned towards her again.

'He's gone. Why are you so terrified of him? Who is he?'

'He makes me shudder sometimes,' she said. 'He's so eery, as though, he's got the evil eye.'

He kissed her eyes and laughed.

'Well, he's nothing to us. But why does he stay here?'

'He's been here ever since I have, and years before that, so I'm told. They tell all kinds of things about him; but what the truth is I don't know. He just sits and drinks, and doesn't say anything all day sometimes, but sits staring straight in front of him, as though he's done something awful and is thinking of it all the time.'

'Perhaps he's escaped from prison; or from over the border.'

'No; what they told me once was that he came to the town a long while ago, quite a young man—he's not old now, though he looks it—and he put up here and fell in love with the daughter of the old woman that kept the place in those days. They say she was very pretty. It seems that he was so infatuated he couldn't leave the place, and so he stayed on; and then later they married and she had a child.'

He pondered this for a moment, looking out through the shadowy room and the open window. 'And what happened then?'

'I don't quite know how it all happened, but there was some kind of trouble. Perhaps he'd been drinking. But he came in late one night and started quarrelling with the girl. She was in bed with the child. They say he'd a temper. He came from the other side of the border: he wasn't from these parts.' She was sitting up, leaning against him, engrossed in her tale.

'Oh, they're not all ferocious over there.'

'No; not all of them,' she replied, turning to brush his cheek with her lips. 'But he was jealous, I think; and I suppose she'd said something to him. For as they were quarrelling he suddenly drew a little dagger from his belt and struck at her with it. They say you could hear him shouting in Spanish at her. The people downstairs rushed up as she screamed, and held him back; and somehow the matter was hushed up. But the girl and her mother left the town taking the boy with them. She'd not been touched at all. He'd aimed wildly. But the blade had caught the child's leg, they said, and made a deep gash all down here . . .' and she drew her finger down his leg, lightly at first, and then with a fearful deliberation as she felt, running from knee to ankle, the wrinkled surface of a long scar.

1934

January

Thirtieth

Who makes the past a pattern for next year
Turns no new leaf, but still the same things reads,
Seen things he sees again, heard things doth hear,
And makes his life but like a pair of beads.

But I am not yet sure that a new life is beginning. In the three weeks since the return from Peterley there have been three recitals followed by three dinners at the Restaurant d'Italie, the Escargot, and our old-fashioned steak house in the Strand. There have been two concerts and a performance at Sadler's Wells, all casually proffered and all quite naturally accepted. But she sits beside me and is miles away.

On Thursday she took the train to Edinburgh, saying she would be back on Sunday morning. It was my own future that was being discussed by these two indifferent strangers in Scotland, and, to avoid thinking on it, I buried myself in the Thomason Tracts at the B.M. all day, and at night took Judy out to supper where we could dance into the early morning and I could drop into a thoughtless sleep the moment I came home.

On Sunday I rose in darkness, dressed, and walked in the cold and stillness of the early London morning across Kensington Park and Hyde Park to Euston to meet the seven o'clock train from the north. She did not expect me, and was a little annoyed. We went into the hotel for breakfast, and while we were waiting I asked if she were engaged. She said yes. The pale face and the dark eyes were calm as she added, 'I shall be married in a few months' time,' and the red lips were as disdainful as ever as she blew, too theatrically, the cigarette smoke through them. She watched for my response, and I tried to conceal my feelings by asking if we could continue to meet as before. She shrugged slightly. 'I don't see why not.'

To shorten the interview she said she was not hungry, but thanked me for the breakfast, 'the last one we shall have together'; added that she did not think I need have come all that way to meet her; and was gone with a 'Until Thursday then?'

February

Four Thursdays have come and gone, their four recitals followed by four suppers, and all were succeeded by an hour of companionable wandering through the quiet side-streets that lead to Blackfriars Station. We began to talk of other things than music, and at the station we usually found the conversation unfinished, and each time she left with a little more reluctance the lights and liveliness of Soho or Jermyn Street to pass through the grimy terminus to the darkness of South London. She became less indifferent to my invitations, and as we neared the moment of separation she would take my arm; and one evening as we came down the hill from St. Paul's twelve o'clock struck from all the City steeples, and with Campbell's poem in mind we kissed to commemorate our second midnight, although she pretended to laugh it off as a childish silliness.

I have offered to take a large flat, which I do not need, so that she could use the drawing-room as a music-room; but she refused: 'You must remember I'm an engaged woman.'

'I'm sorry. There are moments when I forget.'

'Oh,' she laughed, 'those kisses don't mean a thing. Did you think they did? It's only that I'm so happy now.'

This studied insolence is so provocative that I feel for her an emotion of desire and hate which is unhealthily strong. All the same I think I shall look for a new flat: my soul is getting mildewed in this sunless area of South Kensington.

I was in Maggs' today, looking over some art books and turning the pages of a recent work on Delacroix, who has been over-praised for the wrong qualities. I was thinking how great an artist he remains when the romanticism has been stripped away, when I suddenly saw Moira looking up at me. She is the *'jeune amoureuse au piano'*. Little more than a mono-chrome wash, to judge from the reproduction; but it may be an oil in his favourite yellow and browns. It has some of the charm of Lawrence, but more human character. It is Moira to the life, looking round at me as she plays some passage she wants me to appreciate, her soul in her eyes as they plainly say, 'Cannot you forget me for a moment and listen to what this music is trying to say?'

It was just such an expression I remember one evening when she played the piano part of the second movement of the Mozart Concerto in D minor which she was maintaining could be as philosophical as any of my Beethoven. She had the serenity of mind of the saint, which comes probably from the completest selflessness; and probably in much of her life with me she was moved by pity for my outcast state at the time when my marriage was breaking down; and once when she was kinder to me than I had ever ventured to hope in words, it was with such a lovely humility, with all the modesty of a Botticellian virgin who must one day submit to the brutalities of the real world. We had passed the autumn afternoon at Kew. Everyone is happy in a garden; and we had been ecstatically happy, and closer than ever before. There was no rhetoric of lovers' letters to separate us; each remark of mine she caught, and tossed back with just that right mingling of amusement, and reserve, and incite-ment which is the charm of lovers' conversations. We sat opposite the home of the Percys and read from her favourite *Spirit of Man*; we walked down the long avenue; we went for dinner to Richmond; and when we came back to her flat and threw up the window to let out the warm air of the room we could see the last of the sunset over London roofs. Moira had shaken out her hair and put her arms round my neck, and looking in my eyes had said with the naturalness of innocence, 'David, I would like you to stay with me a little longer.'

Someone walked across the floor, and I realized that I was still in Maggs' shop, still staring at the picture of *La jeune amoureuse* in the open book. I closed it, and went out into the air and 1934.

Judy has found me a large flat in Kensington Park Gardens that looks across to the two lethargic lions guarding the steps of Landseer's old house. It is time to immure myself between bookcases and commence the literary life, since there seems nothing else to do. My bibliophilic cousin says a man can get along with three thousand books; and the drawing-room and the study here will take that number: the rest can be sought in the B.M., where I seem to be as constant an habitué as an old, enormous abbé, who seems so timeless that I wonder if he came in the Sloane Collection. He sits at some distance from the table, so as to leave space for a pendulous stomach that rests partly against the table edge and partly on the chair, and he must consort only with the Fathers, for none of his books measures less that fifteen inches in height.

Events have forestalled me, as they often do if you leave them time to work out. Yet strangely, when they do by their own workings present you with the situation you have ardently wished, you do not feel the pleasure that might have come from a triumph of your own contriving. The woman who is concierge for the house knocked on my door this evening, opened it, and said there was a young lady to see me.

Assuming it to be Judy, I told her to send her in. But it was not Judy; and as the door closed behind her Polly came straight to me, took hold of my hands and said with the first real feeling I have ever heard in her voice, 'David, I had to come to you; I am so miserable; you can't think what has happened'; and when I held her closely she broke down and cried quietly against the old smoking-jacket that must have smelt strongly of the tobacco she had always said she could not endure. For the first time I felt compassion for this girl whose pride and independence had so far amused me. Her private world had obviously fallen to pieces and she could not go to her family for consolation. I stroked her hair and remembered how often I had had to face her arrogant regard. She must have built up that cold reserve out of her confidence in her musical gifts; out of her disdain for all the young men who would be attracted by her southern type of beauty and would care nothing for her art. But it was a narrow base for so much independence, and at the first shock it had all come tumbling down, and she was a pathetic young girl in tears who had rushed to the rival waistcoat for support. She lay down on my sofa and dried her eyes, and looking up at the ceiling told me her story.

She had gone to Scotland to see Richards. They used to meet for recitals at the B.B.C. and he was now playing in Edinburgh. It was to settle their engagement and to decide on the date of the wedding. He had apparently expected her to spend the week-end with him, and she had refused. 'Perhaps it was a mistake, and I should have agreed.' She was on the edge of tears again, at the thought of her restraint. But the meeting had been a happy one, and she had returned, as I well knew, sure of the engagement, since in her confidence she had not troubled to conceal her indifference to me. And then, this morning, a telegram had arrived at her home saying that a letter awaited her at a Shaftesbury Avenue post office. She had rushed there and read a brief note saying that, while he was still in love with her, he no longer wished to marry.

I realized for the first time how much she had been in love with him. When she had finished, she lay there listless, still staring at the ceiling, her black hair contrasting with the yellow of the sofa, and scarcely, I think, aware of me at all as I sat smoking on the other side of the hearth, admiring that clean profile and wondering how much this was a tragedy of wounded pride and whether perhaps Richards himself had suspected that Polly's affection was nine-tenths possessiveness, and that she inspired a desire she was not interested in satisfying.

My table, littered with papers, stood in the window, a silent invitation to 'the quiet and still air of delightful studies', as another student* wrote who also had had his matrimonial troubles; and here I was in the middle of an affair of someone else's heart. I rose and said I thought a brandy and soda would be a good idea, at which she turned her head and answered, 'You know I never drink spirits,' which annoyed me so that I retorted that I didn't care, and that she was going to drink some now. She was so startled by my unusual firmness that she meekly replied that she would have some if I insisted. It was a strong one, and she drank it down, and began to return to her surroundings, and gazed round the room, and looked up at me, and stood up: 'David; I shouldn't have come here; but I've been wandering through the streets ever since I read that letter, and I was so tired. Will you take me home now?' The car was at Peterley, so we went out to find a taxi, and drove in silence across London. She put her hand in mine but stared fixedly out of the window, and made only

* John Milton.

one remark: 'Do you know why I agreed to play for you? It's amusing to think of it now. It was only to make a little money for clothes for my wedding. I did not really think you were interested in music; but I needed the money so much.'

'You were wrong: it was the music I was interested in.'

She pressed my hand: 'Are you sure you weren't deceiving yourself, too?'

I dropped her at the corner of her dark street and said that she knew where to find me at any time; but to avoid any more words she merely waved and started walking quickly downhill, and I told the driver to turn and take me back.

Caught a chill in that flat which had never dried properly after the re-painting, and I have been for the first time in four years spending a week in bed, at Peterley; and as the spring rains are falling outside, it is no bad place to be, especially if the Lady Murasaki's *Tale of Genji* is by the bed-side. Father fished out the four volumes from under some military history in his study. He said Commander Longford, whose father had been military attaché in Tokyo years ago, had commended it to him; and that although he never reads novels he made an exception to this since it was about eight hundred years old. 'I assumed that at any rate there'd be no nonsensical psychology in this; and I was wrong. The psychology was there; but it wasn't nonsense and it wasn't modern. It's rather like Malory writing in the 1760s.' I read it through with a growing excitement I have scarcely ever felt for a work of fiction and am inclined to place it with *War and Peace* and with Proust as one of the three epic novels of the world.

I wish now that when in Sydney I had cultivated more the acquaintance of Sadler, who was professor of Japanese at the university. He was learned in the art of flower arrangement and in Cha-no-yu, and had carried his studies as far as marrying a Japanese, and had the tact not to impose his Western style of life upon her. She would not appear unless invited; but upon the clapping of hands would come in, make the proper obeisance, and bring in the tea. And when Father mentioned Malory the other day, I recalled Ryonuki Saito in the diplomatic service whose favourite childhood book these tales had been. He told me that an old statesman from the Meiji Restoration had given a copy to him with the remark that it showed that the Western World had once shared the chivalry of the Samurai. I imagine the accent had been on 'once'. I ended the period of convalescence with Murdoch's history of Japan, and am left with the conviction that Iyeyasu was one of the greatest rulers in the world, seeing that he succeeded in stabilizing and fixing a civilization for two centuries and a half. Useless to regret that Perry's cannon blew it all away: history is a record of inevitable things and can never be a judgment as to their goodness or badness: these two words have no historical meaning.

A letter today from Polly asking if she can change her mind and accept my old offer of a room in my flat as a music-room. I write her an authorization to move in, and I think I will move in too and change my emotional environment. This place has too strong a power to evoke emotion, as have all places where a family has lived for generations; but it is an emotion that induces lethargy and melancholy that are allied to accidie. I have been walking in the winter copse all afternoon after rain. Everything seems approaching the final state of liquefaction and decay, and it seems impossible that these sodden glades can ever become crisp and fresh again with new life, and bright leaves uncurl from these rotting branches. I walked here when Moira was in Scotland, and with the same thoughts; and I fear that the path winds downhill all the way.

I took the train to Town today determined to find out what was the state of the Kensington flat. It was empty and lifeless, but in the back room was a shiny grand piano, and a stack of music in a corner, and on the wall opposite a large reproduction of a Kiyonaga. Any irritability I may have felt at pictures being hung on my wall was cancelled by surprise that it was Kiyonaga that was chosen and not the more customary Utamaro or Hokusai. So Polly is an admirer of these slender women leaning in lovely curves against the wind that blows the leaves of autumn away behind them.

But what happens if she comes in to play when I am settling down to work, or when Judy and I are settling down on the sofa to exchange scandal? Can you keep a woman half-way? I wrote asking her to come and see me.

It is the defect of a journal that it never records the normal happinesses, the levels of content. These diary-keepers give the impression of a life of violent contrasts, like the performance curves of an ill-regulated motor that rises steeply above the median line and descends to an equal depth. A fortnight has passed of quiet and settled life with Polly, who has moved in, bed, books, and boudoir, and lives in the same apartment without living with me. We do not meet often, and only by accident or invitation; and it is agreed that she does not play when I'm at home, unless asked to. We take Sunday breakfast together because on this day we rise at about the same late hour. Judy disapproves, but is amused, and does not believe the association is innocent.

An extraordinary coincidence yesterday. I bought some books at Blackwell's, and among them was Gosse's *Life of Swinburne*, my own copy having long since been borrowed by a friend. When I look through it here, I find a discoloured letter with a printed heading:

'THE UNIVERSITY OF SYDNEY

6th August, 1917

Dear Jose,

There was no gift that could have been more delightful especially as copies are so rare in Sydney that I am the only one up at this shop who has one. And as a gift certainly not to be looked in the mouth. But as a life of *our* poet—well, it's what one ought, I suppose, to have expected. But it's strange that Gosse, who came to London about 1869, in time to feel something of the great first wave of excitement, can't give us at all, but only leaves us to gather, the immense and overwhelming impression of genius that A.C.S. made on everybody. He can give the weaknesses and the waywardnesses (and generally he always has excelled at catching the funny little trivialities of a subject) but nothing of the power. Now take the case of Villiers de l'Isle Adam: his total achievement cannot be placed anywhere near Swinburne's; but read any account of him by his contemporaries and that impression of genius, of something out and above all men of his generation, is transmitted to you. Whereas here, you get stuck forward on the front plane Lord Houghton, an estimable and worthy person, of whom one may say that he did his duty in that position to which it pleased God to call him, viz. by working the political ropes for the benefit of men of letters; but, at this time of day, he has no right to go round patting

'Algernon' on the head, for 'Algernon' is now the dead Swinburne and Lord Houghton is not even a memory (why, since his son became Crewe for being a blameless nonentity nobody knows that there ever were any Houghtons). What is good in Gosse's book is that he shows what an awful beast Watts-Dunton was: I hope that some day some-one will rise up and call him the calamity of English literature. Quiller-Couch went for him in his Edinburgh article, but the article was a scandalous thing; to raise a boo-whoo-whoo like that over the grave of Swinburne! Gosse has defective taste, or he'd have said more of, e.g., *Songs of Springtides* or *The Tale of Balen*; and he makes a lot of slips in matters of fact; and he plainly hasn't the scholarship necessary for the reading of Swinburne; and it's plain that he can't write a life unless someone has done it before, and he can add some personal details, as in the case of Patmore. We're still left waiting for the life of A.C.S. and, I suppose, the legend will keep going on.

C.B.'

I did not need to puzzle over the initials; it is Brennan to the life as well as to the delicate handwriting. Jose is Arthur W., the historian of Australia.

Richards came to London to see Polly, and I arranged to leave the flat to them for the evening, but warned I would be back at midnight.

They were still there, when I did return, for I could hear faint voices, and I was seized with an annoyance which may have been jealousy, and could not sleep. So I got up and went down to the sitting-room and read *Le roi Pausole*. Their voices came occasionally through the intervening wall, and as time passed I began to feel less tolerant of the intrusion of this rejected fellow in my flat. I could not read, but sat there in an agony of impotence, longing to interrupt them. I was ready to promise Polly any-thing on condition that he left; but at the same time I realized that this was merely a jealous emotion; except that 'merely' is the wrong word: this is the fiercest of all emotions; stronger than the simple wish for possession; much stronger than the pleasure of possession; and felt in its intensest by the intellectual, for whom physical consummation is an anticlimax and all the delights of love are in that building up, in the mind, of an imaginary world in which you and she, as principal personages, play out a comedy of *marivaudage* with the ultimate, the inevitable, misconduct to give a savour and an edge to your words.

I had felt this agony twice before, when Trumble had taken Dorothea away that evening of her quarrel with her husband, and I had sat waiting for their return through these same early-morning hours; and once when Penelope had told me that her husband had at last presented his ultimatum and there was to be no more complaisance. It seemed as though this keenest of the emotions can be felt only for the wives of others; and, after all, it would be slightly ridiculous to feel it for one's own. It is, by the way, one of the themes of Restoration comedy, and Vanbrugh and Wycherley might well be worth rereading for this point of view. But last night I did not think of them.

I could think of nothing but the suddenly awakened desire for this girl whose future was being decided in the next room and in such a way that I was powerless to intervene. I knew that if he relented and changed his mind, she would walk in and tell me calmly that all was well. And she knew that she need not trouble to thank me for anything I had done. It was half past one when I heard him go. Before I could move, Polly had knocked on the door. She came in, in the evening dress she had worn for the theatre—it had been Bergner's *Escape Me Never*—and her pale face was white and drawn and there was bitterness in her look, and I knew at once the answer. She flung herself down at full length on the sofa, and neither of us spoke for a minute or two until she said in a flat voice: 'I've sent him packing; if you want to know.'

'So it's all over?'

She nodded and added, 'You take it very calmly.'

But my calm was the reaction to an hour's agony of jealousy and impatience that she had not guessed; and I was also thinking of her contemptuous indifference that morning at Euston when all had seemed so sure; and I was a little hurt to realize how much she must have fought to keep him, for this was the bitterness of defeat. I sat on the other side of the fireplace and watched her without replying, until she sat up suddenly and said: 'David, it was horrible: he confessed things to me that make it impossible for me to see him again. I knew about the middle-aged woman he used to go to concerts with; but she must have been ten years older than he was, and she's divorced, and she dyes her hair; and I never thought it was serious. But it is true they spent a week together in Scotland. I don't know how that could be possible. And, what's worse, he admitted that he had been out with prostitutes, and that I can't forgive.'

She was magnificent in her anger with her dark eyes alight with feeling and the red lips curved in hatred as she shook back her black unfastened hair. She was young and unworldly and suffering her first great disillusion, and in her emotional state exceedingly attractive; and I felt a new desire for her which this was certainly not the moment to display. She told me all their conversation, which had been appallingly frank; and it was evident to me that Richards had determined at all costs (even perhaps at the invention of wholly imaginary misdeeds) to break and regain his freedom from his too-imperious young woman. She was still too taut and self-contained in her anger to make it worth my while to say anything, and I sat and listened to the story of her first love affair.

'He had been begging me for months to sleep with him. When I came back to London I decided I would. I thought in the train that it was ridiculous to take such a thing seriously; and I was just going to write and tell him I'd changed my mind when that letter of his came. Do you know I was going to ask you if we could have this flat for a week-end?' She laughed with an attempt at cynicism at the recollection, and I was on the point of asking if she thought I was foolish enough to agree; but she evidently had thought so, and I realized how derisively she had ignored my own feelings. But the battle had been won for me: why should I trouble now? She got up and went towards the door. 'I won't be able to sleep; but I suppose you will want to,' and was gone.

I didn't feel like sleep either, and picked up *Pausole*, but found it flat after the emotions of the evening, and looked along the bookshelves for a soporific. At the sight of all these neat cloth and sober leather bindings, I thought of all the various passions neatly preserved in these charming containers, seasoned, spiced, and pickled for posterity, all the coarse peel pared away, the untidy guts eviscerated, the pips and stones thrown out; but the sweet jams meticulously jarred that the literary merchants hawk are a long way from the harsh fruit of the country orchard. 'To Jane with a guitar' sounds delightful; but here I was tied to Miss Morel with a grand piano.

It was another half-hour before I decided to go up to bed again, and as I passed her door I listened to find if sleep had overcome that lovely and disillusioned head. The stillness of the house was not complete: I could hear a stifled sobbing behind the door. I turned the knob gently and stepped on tip-toe into the room, It was so dark I had to stand still until the piano took shape as a darker blackness and the curved stage-property in the foreground turned into a sweep of dress over a chair. Along the bed was the stretched-out figure, its face hidden in the pillow that muffled her crying.

I sat on the edge of the bed, and in a few minutes she turned over and looked up. 'David, is that you?'

'Polly, darling; it's over and done with. Forget it. There's a lot of time still to come.'

'But it's such a waste of happiness. We had such a wonderful time; and we were going to become lovers. You've no idea how much I wanted him, although I kept refusing. It would have been perfect.'

'But how do you know?'

'What a silly question. When you feel as deeply as that, it's bound to be.'

She was so indignant that she forgot to cry and began to collect herself, and I sat and stroked her heavy hair.

'But it wouldn't have been what you imagine: he obviously didn't feel as deeply as that. And the first love affair always seems so wonderful because it's the first.'

She turned her head round on the pillow to reply to me: 'You're speaking from your mind. Do you think that is any help?'

Which was true; but I did not know what to say, for I was not sure what part one played in such a scene. It's all very well to say the world's a stage: unfortunately the parts haven't been written out, and we are amateurs having to improvise on the spur of the moment and under the disadvantage of not knowing what character we are playing. I remember thinking, as I sat on the side of the bed in this dark room: what was the rôle to play? 'Be yourself' is no answer; for the whole doubt is what the self-in-these-circumstances is, and whether it 'is' or whether it 'should be'. I could imagine the scene played by others, and guess at Angel Clare's performance, or Willoughby's, or Henry Crawford's, or even Canon Slope's. . . .

There were a number of ready-made parts to hand, supplied by the theatrical dealers, Messrs. Corneille, Racine, Marivaux, Musset, Courteline . . . but these theatrical costumes sometimes do not fit. I stood up and made my way over to the window and looked into the blackness of what would be the garden in three hours, a lightless world in which I scarcely seemed to be a separate personality: perhaps the 'I' would return with the garden and the roof-tops and the smoking chimneys, unless it would return as an emotional reaction to this lonely figure on the bed. At the moment I was, as Polly recognized, only someone making a choice of phrases and not picking the right one, because it didn't exist. I fetched two blankets and spread them over her—she had on nothing but her dressing gown—and said goodnight and that I would expect her for breakfast at eleven o'clock, and went up to sleep. At a quarter to eleven that morning she came into the room where I was working, in a new dressing gown of dusty blue, and turned her cheek for me to kiss, and said, 'I've come for breakfast,' and our domestic life began, of cohabitation in only one sense of the word.

Spent the day in the B.M. looking through the work of Sir Henry Bishop and coming away at closing time with a much higher opinion of a neglected composer, less clever than Sullivan but much more pleasing.

Richards is still in Town and I asked him to lunch with me at the Club. He turned out to be a pleasant well-bred fellow, too well dressed to seem the musician he was, too intelligent to be the tailored nonentity he at first sight appeared. We had the courageous talk two men can have about a woman in her absence. He asserted that he had made the decision to break with Polly solely because he feared that her possessive character would interfere with his musical life: 'You may suspect—and you may be right —that I'm afraid of her stronger musical talents. If we lived together I'd either have to give up music, or we'd quarrel continually. I tried to persuade her of this, but didn't succeed.' I said that for the time being I would keep an eye on her, and do what I could to help her musical career; and he was glad she was away from her family: 'You'll find her a delightful companion.' We spoke of the disappearing *Week-end Review*, and of Debussy, and of Polly's compositions; and he left to return to Edinburgh.

This is a double life, very precariously balanced. I breakfast with a woman I haven't slept with; she lives with a man she does not love. My desire for her still annoys her, and she endures it only because she cannot endure her family. I try to keep it in the background, but it sometimes shows itself as small kindnesses which she resents as intrusions on her private grief. And there are moments when I am on the edge of rebellion, as when she pretends to be amused at my humiliation. I was reading *The Times* at breakfast this morning when, for lack of a conversational opening, she asked if it was polite to read the paper when I had company. I said I did it solely as a help in navigating a difficult passage in the day's journey; to which she retorted that it was insulting to display the indifference of a husband when I was pretending to be passionately in love with her. I replied that I thought it was the passion that she found insulting. 'I can't think why you are willing to put up with this ridiculous situation,' was all she had to say in answer.

I have been trying to identify that novel of Gide's of two adolescents, the young man of nineteen and the girl of seventeen, who retire from what seems to them the coarseness of their bourgeois family life into a charming companionship where they read poetry together, and discover that their fathers bear little resemblance to Sempronius Gracchus or their mothers to Cornelia. At almost the same moment, for both of them, there comes a disillusionment more sharp than usual: his father is implicated in some municipal scandal; she sees her mother leaving the apartment of a notorious philanderer at a time when she was supposed to be *chez Madam un Tel.* They weep together that evening over the sins of their parents, and, unable to endure any longer the real world of Rennes, they leave that night for a better world which, with the help of a railway time-table, they locate at Carcassonne. Even the elopement is conducted on the highest principles, and each night they sleep chastely in each other's arms. For a time they lead an idyllic existence; but slowly each becomes aware, independently of the other, that the real world extends as far as Carcassonne, and may even be world-wide; and each tries to keep the other as long as possible from making this discovery too; until, of course, the moment comes when almost without any explicit acknowledgment of defeat they together take the train back to Rennes.

It is assumed at home that they have enjoyed a guilty liaison, and it is expected that they will announce their engagement. But they never do. He goes to Paris and marries the daughter of a senator; she stays in the town and becomes the wife of a middle-aged and wealthy manufacturer.

Polly is recovering her cheerfulness. She plays more; has begun composing again; and has bought some new clothes, including, I notice, a diaphanous nightdress. This ménage is becoming absurd; and one or two evenings I have been tempted to go down and knock on her door. But the very ease and nearness makes me scrupulous.

I have ended this agony of indecision by leaving for Peterley.

.   .   .   .   .

On Wednesday last I spent the whole day uselessly in the Reading Room of the British Museum, unable, in my unsettled state, to concentrate on these verbose pamphlets of the Civil War, and too often gazing up into this dome, grand in its simplicity and weak in its colouring, looking in vain for help from the illustrious names in the scholastic zodiac. They were all frozen in immortality, while I needed some warmer-blooded comfort. I dined uninvited with Judy who reluctantly put down the novel she was reading to make me an omelette and listen to the story of my caged nightingale. She applied a caustic instead of a salve: 'You'd better start satisfying the expectations you've disappointed, and the sooner the better'; and when I objected that that was a crude simplification of the problem, she retorted that if I didn't want commonsense advice I should go to a psychiatrist: 'David, that's your mistake. Life is cruder and simpler than you imagine. Get into bed with the girl; you've got to sooner or later, why not now?'

I took another day to think over Judy's advice; and on Thursday evening went into Polly's room and said it was time to end this separate life. We talked for two hours; and at eleven she got up and asked if I wouldn't let her go to bed. In some annoyance I went out and upstairs, my mind divided—one half determined to be done with her for good, the other half feeling more strongly than ever the desire for possession; but both halves uncomfortable at the thought of Judy's derision if she could see me now. I went abruptly back and found Polly reading in her bed, and not as surprised to see me as I had feared.

It was all that an attempted seduction should not be—an unsatisfactory conjunction of will and indifference, and her indifference won. I could not endure her contemptuous: 'You can probably seduce me if you try hard, but I don't think you'll find it pleasant. I haven't the slightest desire to sleep with anyone now, and I certainly don't intend to start tonight if I can help it. And if you succeed, I shall simply leave the house tomorrow.' I realized in time how unromantic the situation was, and retreated to the edge of the bed, still contemplating with far too much feeling the young woman who was even at this very moment extremely desirable, her pale cheeks flushed with colour, her eyes bright with anger, her hair dishevelled.

She sat up, replaced the wholly diaphanous nightdress over one shoulder from which it had slipped, and, propped against the wall, said quite calmly that I was making a mistake in trying to force a love affair out of a sensible arrangement for living together. 'If you want someone to sleep with, you'll have to find someone else. Your cousin Judy, for example,' she had the malice to add; but immediately tried to soften the

103

remark by saying that if I could accept a quite unsentimental life together she would at least promise to remain, so long as I was interested in music. 'And who knows? It's possible that I might come to care for you in another way.'

'How possible?'

'Perhaps not very. But one can never tell.'

I felt less than ever in the mood to accept this business-like arrangement by which Polly had lodging, and I music but nothing else, since I was beginning to be less interested in the music and more in the musician, and would certainly be much more so after this revealing evening. We talked for nearly another two hours, but at the end Polly was as inflexible as at first, and her final words were that she just was not interested in making love unless it was done passionately and naturally, 'and I don't feel like that. And that's an end. And now I think I'll go to sleep if you don't mind leaving my bedroom.' I thought it unwise to remark on that 'my', and left her, and went in some annoyance upstairs.

Back in my room I stared through the window at the inauspicious stars over Kensington Gardens, and reflected that these affairs had been so much simpler under the Australian sun; and without further philosophy got into bed, and went soundly to sleep in spite of an unquiet conscience.

I woke, and my conscience woke with me; and I had to face daylight and remorse. How often these two march together like London policemen! Somewhere in the apartment was this young woman, either sullen and resentful or active and vengeful, I did not know which; but hostile, I was certain. It might be better to breakfast early and alone, and seek sanctuary in the Museum Reading Room where only ticket-holders were allowed.

Polly surprised me half-way through *The Times*. She was in her light-blue dressing gown; her lips were heavily rouged, and I think there was mascara on the eyelashes. With her pale skin the effect was startling and lovely; but the emphatic make-up may have concealed the tears and sleeplessness of the night. She sat down opposite me at the little breakfast table, and said in a quite natural voice, 'Would you like to kiss me good-morning?' so I obediently went over and kissed the cheek she turned to me, and she took away *The Times* from between my fingers and put it on the floor beside her chair, which removed the chief source of conversation. 'And what are we having for breakfast?'

I replied that I hadn't expected her at all and was having my usual toast and coffee. 'Then I'll have toast and coffee too.'

It was a domestically peaceful scene and I felt some pride in my lovely breakfast companion, with whom I was at least much better acquainted than before; but knowing also her reserves of contemptuous disdain I was still uneasy. I suggested a morning's shopping and lunch in Town, and she agreed, but added: 'I don't really need a thing, except a new nightdress to replace the one you tore last night. You manage to waste more time than anyone I've ever known,' but she smiled as she said it, and I accepted it as an observation and not a criticism.

The antique shops in the Brompton Road did not interest her much, except for a spinet in one shop, that had been converted into a dressing table, but she could not decide to be amused at the change or horrified by the sacrilege. I could not tempt her to anything in Harrods; and at the last minute she changed her mind about the nightdress: 'We are not yet intimate enough that you could make me that kind of present,' and said that what she would like was some music. So to Chappell's we went, the same shop where six months ago I had watched her altercation with the same assistant, and had gone away with the impression on my mind of this lively profile, like the Arethusa on the Syracusan coins. We lunched at the Club, and I debated inwardly whether to put off my return to Peterley tonight and as a matter of courtesy stay a second but proper night with a woman who was still in love with someone else. Would she be more displeased by the suggestion than offended by the omission of it? Over the coffee I remarked, as unemphatically as possible: 'I'm supposed to spend the week-end at Peterley; but I'd much rather stay in Town with you, if you have no plans for the next two days.'

She considered that calmly, blowing cigarette smoke up into the air, and looking at one moment directly into my eyes before she answered: 'I think if you're expected, you should go. I think I'll have a quiet week-end at the flat. Don't worry: I shall be quite happy by myself'—which solved the problem for me, and for a time, and meant that I'm forgiven, but that the question of our extra-marital life is left hanging in the air. In cold storage, rather. All the same, she came to Marylebone to see me off; offered me the same cheek to kiss; and hoped I would be back on Monday.

April

Came back to London in the slow train through Oxford, reading again the delicious *Tale of Genji*. The late declining sun shone level across the Thames valley and threw a tempered light over Oxford spires; and on trees and hedgerows was a green spring haze. The late afternoon, the slow train, the novel were perfectly in harmony. Transportation should be slowed down rather than speeded up. I should not be surprised if there is not a relationship between speed and the cultivation of the mind; an inverse one, of course.

Back to London and to trouble with a most unlikeable German, a mercenary type for whom perhaps the new Reich is not so sympathetic, who has bought this house and is objecting to the grand piano. I assign the flat to a charming Mrs. Talbot—of all the names that it should be that one! —and the new owner objects; and I have to call upon old Harris to take up the quarrel legally; which he does so effectively that the newest recruit to our Anglo-Saxon society is glad to drop the whole matter. Unfortunately, Harris discovers that I am not quite alone in the flat, and there is a great deal of legal humming and hawing that even went so far as to concede that if Jane should think of a divorce, it was conceivable that there was already evidence enough. 'Is it necessary for your apartments to be so contiguous?' was how he phrased it.

So I must move, and I discover how a grand piano hampers one's movements, and how insensitive landlords are to music. Reading by chance that Burne-Jones lived in the North-End Road, I went to see the district, and found a house there to let. But what a nightmare of uniformity is Barons Court! Straight streets with unit frontages endlessly repeated, the architectural equivalence of the repetition of aphasia and feeble-mindedness. Can anything be more surrealist than these rows of identical houses, built by business men who would regard themselves as normal and anything artistic as abnormal? All the same I must find a shelter for this grand piano and a roof over a not quite so grand passion.

Twenty-seventh

It is almost like the evening of life here at Peterley, so much I think of the past and regret pleasures which seem irrevocable now, so quiescent in a state of obscure poverty have I become. It is too painful to read in these

volumes of the days of sunlight and sailing in Sydney. There are pages of
nostalgia for England and Peterley; and now I walk in the Peterley woods
in an unhappiness deeper than the old Australian melancholy and in a
solitude I never knew before. It may have been from seeing Elizabeth
Bergner the other night in *Die traumende Munde*: she was so startlingly
like Dorothea in figure, face, and manner that some of the turbulent
feelings of those lively days were renewed in recollection. I found the
solitude in the woods too much to bear, and came back to London
yesterday, and took Polly by surprise and out to lunch, and spent the
whole day with her, and finished with a dinner at the Berkeley. She
began to respond with some show of feeling for the first time in our
acquaintance, and when we parted on the platform at Marylebone, she
admitted she had enjoyed the interlude, but added: 'Do you think it's
fair to disturb me like this? I'm not used to being treated like a mistress.'

As the train drew out, I looked back and saw her, a slender figure in
black standing on the edge of the platform, and suddenly felt sorry for
her. There was no necessity for this abrupt return to Peterley: it was only
that it gave a neat ending to our encounter; but while I should wake in
the Buckinghamshire woods, she would be alone in that dismal house
in Barons Court.

July

Twenty-third

Just returned from France. The June weather and the Buckinghamshire
countryside, vulgarly fertile, riotously vital all around, had been too
much for my peace of mind. I could not endure the London streets, and
Polly was becoming merely a sensual escapade. Father suggested I went
over to see the Durands; rang up the line that ships the cognac for his
dealer, and got me a cabin on the little *Swallow* that left Tower Bridge at
one o'clock on June 30th. And so for the second time in eight years I sail
down this ignoble estuary overlaid with mud and history. There was a
sunset over Deal; the Goodwins were just uncovered; and Dover Castle,
that had been warmly tinted by the setting sun in the best Turner style
when I was on my way to Botany Bay, was now lit up by electricity
like a commercial advertisement. It was a fine clear evening, with no
wind and a smooth sea, and I stayed on deck until eleven.

Sunday came with a hot sun, and a calm sea covered with a heat haze. We passed Alderney at 11.30 a.m. and the Gasquets at 1.30. I turned in early for a short sleep, and at two in the morning went up on the bridge to watch the navigation of the inner Ushant channel. A tricky passage, but there was a calm sea and a bright moon, and the various leads were very bright. The lights changed colour through sectors; and at one moment the number and differences of colour gave the tortuous channel the appearance of a railway junction. Dawn broke over the Breton mainland, and at 5.30 the passage was completed, and the sun rose over the Brest estuary. The Bay on Monday was at its stillest, a continuous sheet of silvery water with patches of haze and few fishing boats. We made the Gironde early on Tuesday morning; took on the estuary pilot, then the river pilot, and finally the harbour pilot—which ensures employment to the locals—but then it is a shallow sandy channel heavily buoyed. On landing, I went to the Hôtel de Bordeaux to meet the representative of the firm, a young fellow who turned out to be the grand-nephew of the one who had negotiated the delicate affair of Uncle Matthew's daughter.

I walked down to the harbour in sunlight, relaxation, and freedom, surrounded by the tongue I love to hear, and felt at home again. It was the heavy calm of summer and all seemed peaceful. And then I noticed a scribbled poster announcing a Nazi purge. I bought a paper and read of a blood-bath of more than oriental amplitude that the National Socialists have been enjoying. There seems to be less of the Puritan Ironsides about this new party than Cousin Richard would have us believe, and than I had hoped, unless this is a weeding out of unworthy members.

I decided on a walking tour, as the weather seemed promising; but what it performed was a fortnight of the hottest summer heat, excessive even for the sun-drenched côtes; and wherever I came—St. Emilion, Cadillac, Barsac, Podensac, St. Croix de Mont, St. Maxainte (where I saw a lovely young child drawing water from a well, whom I should have been content to adopt), St. Macaire and Longon—everywhere the vineyards, the taverns, the farms, the dusty roads in the still air seemed drowned in a sea of heat.

A most surprising warm letter came from my cool young pianist:

'David,

J'étais desolée à ton départ. I wanted you not to go, so much, so suddenly, so sillily. You dissatisfied me before: you don't now. I can't understand it. I'm not thinking any more about the future—it has such a variety of possibilities—since we shall have a month together when you come back. I feel now no longer numb and immovable inside. David, are you thrilled that my feelings are changing? It's so new, and whether it will last or is simply due to loneliness, I don't know. Rest well, and be happy, but not too happy.

P.'

The letter I had longed for since last year; and when at last it comes I am on this sun-drenched terrace looking over the family vines. The ink looks faded in this sun of Aquitaine. It is some small consolation to know that she feels something; but how much more this would have meant to me earlier and in the wet beech woods of home!

The *Swallow* brought me back to London Bridge, and there surprisingly on the wharf was Polly. We went straight home to the house, where I found an excellent dinner prepared, and this was something she had never done before. She confessed that she had been unhappy through these weeks of absence: 'The separation has made quite a difference to my feeling for you.' Which was delightfully true, for she was pleasant and friendly all evening, and played what she knew were some of my favourite pieces, including the Haydn sonata, and I suspect that she had been practising them for me. I stayed in London for four days in order to enjoy this new companionship.

[I received at this time from France one of Peterley's typical letters, which I think worth including here.]

'One of the great advantages of living in France of course is that one finds *The Times* with its crossword on every bookstall. There are other benefits, one being the total absence of drinkable water. It is water indeed that separates us from our friends the English, I thought, as I refilled the two glasses with a vin jaune d'Arbois of Louis Cartier after the iced melon that began the more modest of the two lunches offered by the Hôtel de la Poste to the passer through Pontarlier. As yellow, but not as perfumed, as Oncle Theodore's Lavigny which accompanies his fromage de Morbier.

It was probably raining outside all the eating houses of Holborn while the Jurassian sun shone on the vine in the courtyard beyond the curtained window and they brought in the Terrine maison, which, though of such base ingredients as veal, pork, liver and truffles, was so alchemically transubstantiated as to be as distinct from the originals as uranium from pitchblende. Vine and animal had been nourished on the same hillsides, like Lycidas and his poetical friend, and, not far apart in life, they were beautifully undivided after death. It's not only water that lies between us: there's the kitchen stove. And from the kitchen now came a brochet du lac around whose tender flesh, as flowers in a Russian funeral, lay wreaths of onion intertwined with tomato. In the golden mayonnaise piquancy struggled, but genteelly, with the softness of oil and cream. Frustrated pike probably still lingered in the darkness of English canals hoping in vain for such a transfiguration.

I refilled the glasses with the yellow wine, that, falling goldenly into the open glasses, reminded me inevitably of the loose pictures of Danae, especially as the young woman opposite to me . . . But there are—to return to the original thought—other differences dividing us. The young admirer emerging from the Bank with his companion could not so enjoyably have run his appreciative hand down his young lady's spine (most of which was hygienically exposed) had that been Barclay's Bank. Few couples in Piccadilly pause to embrace under the trees—but then there are no trees; or form in cafés and parks an immobile obtuse-headed triangle.

I recalled my wandering thoughts and approached the brochet with the friendliness of one Jurassian to another.

In due course the pike's skeleton was removed to the kitchen, and there followed a pause for the choice of wines. The next dish was Escalope de veau, Sauce maison, garni avec champignons—but not those ghastly simulacra that droop on the damp floors of abandoned railway tunnels in England, but lusty, lively-tinted growths that push up through the hairy recesses of the pine-woods. With it came a Château-Châlon from the slopes fifty kilometres to the south-west. Oncle Paul would have fetched up something *plus furieux et fort*, had indeed fetched it so often that at seventy-nine it will not be long before he descends into the cellar where there are no bottles. Jurassian as I am, I cannot help feeling that, but for the seduction of the Côte d'Or, he might have delayed that final descent a dozen years or more.

The Côte d'Or reminded me of the Morvan through which I had

approached it the other day. It was Quatorze Juillet. The cities were full of young couples—it is a rejuvenating time; the roads and restaurants were full of them; and so, it turned out, were the country inns. So that when we came by car, myself and two young women, to Lucenay there were no rooms free. We were in the Morvan, a country of little villages. There was Autun beyond; but the venerable Bibracte would be full of gastronomic Gauls needing a long sleep after a long dinner, and full of those other citizens, whose emotional life was still centred at a lower level and who would also need a bedroom. We pushed on to the Lac du Setton, but it is a romantic spot, and the inns were all taken. We tried Maligny, a dull village, but its prosaic aspect had not diminished the demand for couches. It was dark as we came into Chassey-en-Morvan which is the name for three farms, a turreted and mediaeval manor, a stream, one church, and an auberge. We were extremely fortunate: there was a room and it had two beds. A delicate and long discussion followed with our hostess. She argued incontrovertibly that we had arrived late, without notification. — We could not deny the hour; and in these matters time is significant. But there were three of us, and my companions were insistent. More even than I. Although it was a question of only one night. — It might be thought we were really attaching too much importance to the matter. But we gained our point at length I am glad to say. — A certain obduracy in negotiation is respected among the French. — And we could all feel at ease now that we did not have to accept the pot-au-feu, but would be provided with an omelette aux fines herbes, saucisson, salad, cheese and fruit, even if the wine was only a vin ordinaire from Dijon.

After a walk in the darkness of the summer night past the manor house, the farms and by the stream, invisible but musical over the hidden stones, you may imagine with what contentment we returned to the room so long sought and so ardently desired. The stars over the Morvan are particularly fine; and I decided to regard them a little longer, so that my companions might be given the choice of beds. . . .

The Escalope de veau in itself was simple enough but its attendant sauce was of the simplicity as of air that comes from the admixture of many elements, and it served as setting to the champignons of the local woods. You have no idea how well this dish goes with a Château-Châlon. Afterwards my companion took fruit, and I some fromage de Septmoncel, although the waitress politely suggested that it might not be the ideal month for this cheese which in warm weather tends to a fatty over-ripeness. I think, now, on reflection, that she was right and that a Comtois would have brought the lunch more cleanly to a close. But one makes these mistakes. Napoleon delayed too long at Marengo. . . .

We lingered amicably my charming companion and myself in the deserted lounge behind the closed shutters; and if Hitler had at that moment been reported crossing the Rhine I doubt if I should have been disturbed—a philosophic state of mind shared at this hour by all good Franc-Comtois. In fact my thoughts were so far from international affairs and so close to my amiable companion that I judged it might be prudent to retire—from this too comfortable, too somnolent, too suggestive hotel.

The square outside was deserted. The Pontarlissians were sensibly reclining in shaded rooms from the Burgundian sun that tapped on church tower, on the affiches of a coming circus and the National Lottery, and equally on the unpainted tin of the public lavatory and on the classical dignity of the Hôtel de Ville. We were alone and unregarded, my charming young Frenchwoman and myself, on the steps of the hotel, the dusty road in front of us, the corridors and the twelve bedrooms of the inn behind, and between us the dismal shades of Knox, Prynne, Wesley, Praise-God-Barebones, Mr. Spurgeon and other famous and forbidding English saints to cast a chill on my kindlier thoughts. I slammed the car door somewhat savagely and started for the Genevan lake, where—shade of Lord Byron!—things might be better ordered.'

September

Tenth

To Judy's for dinner, Mark being back from China. Drank a rose-red liqueur which in fact both tasted and smelt of roses, an elixir prepared by Dr. K. an Austrian anthroposophist whom J. has been entertaining recently. She has never approved of my irregular life with my second singer, as she calls Polly, and after dinner spoke about the timeliness of settling down with someone respectable. I admitted I might try the experiment again, if only for family reasons; she replied that there were plenty of young women, like Mrs. Manning for example, who did not care much for the sporting and high-living crowd they were brought up with, and would prefer a quieter type. I asked more about the young widow whom J. obviously has in mind. 'Oh, I'm only using her as an example. I hold many briefs for Susan as a charming, efficient wife (not necessarily for you), but none for you, darling, as a ditto husband.'

Left at 1.30 and walked in the warm night air from Bayswater to Barons Court balancing the alternatives of remarriage and return to Peterley or of single existence on a yacht in the Thames estuary. The more fantastic notion is probably the safer one. I enter the long nightmare of the street which is not my home, and feel restless and chilled by the loneliness of a London without Polly. She went, against my wishes, perhaps because of my objection, with the Robinsons to a summer cottage near St. Malo. The eldest son, who is musical, pretends to be interested in her music, and writes her letters which she always hands to me over the Sunday-morning breakfast table. If I had been sensible, I would have raised no objection to her going; but in a moment of jealousy, which immediately afterwards I knew to be absurd, I said that her acceptance of the invitation would imply acknowledgment of Master Robinson's suitorbility. She looked at me quizzically and directly, as she does, and said: 'I don't regard myself as bound to you in any way. But if it interests you, I may say that I could not possibly let anyone make love to me as long as I'm sharing this house with you. I shall certainly accept the invitation because I need a holiday.'

She had left the following day when I came in for dinner; but on the table was a friendly note and a box of my favourite lollies that she must have gone especially to Knightsbridge for.

Fifteenth

This being the day of my annual pilgrimage to Radlett,★ I walked there from Edgware through Elstree, past the new cinema studios that have a sordid air as befits the source of so much unnatural glamour and false emotion—the brothels of the modern mind. Coming down the hill into Radlett, I passed Kendon's house, but saw it all closed as though untenanted. Had tea at the Red Lion, and, talking with the old serving woman about the locality, I asked if she knew that Radlett was the home of Kendon the poet. She replied that she had never heard of him but that the town was very well known because of the fire brigades and cycling clubs who came here for their annual picnics.

★ For the explanation of the annual pilgrimage to Radlett see the Note on p. 216.

Back in town I went to the *Telegraph* office for news of the America's Cup, but only the half-way result had come: *Rainbow* leading by two minutes.

October

Second

I drove to Bath on Friday to pick up Judy, and we came back via Market Medford, where I was introduced to her pretty widow whom she has decided I am to become acquainted with. She grew less certain of the wisdom of her procuring as we neared the village, and warned me for God's sake not to harbour any of my romantic notions and not to hold her responsible for anything that may or may not happen. Mrs. Manning is a distinguished young woman, excessively well bred, with those pleasantly regular features of the English upper class that go exactly with their light tweeds. The house is the square, early nineteenth-century building of plastered brick, with long windows opening on the lawn. The interior is conventional in the best manner—the walnut writing table, the chintz easy-chairs, the mahogany dining-room suite with the silver candlesticks on the sideboard. I have seen it so often before; and Mrs. Manning herself flowers all over southern England from Wiltshire to Norfolk, from Gloucestershire to Kent in a thousand Halls, Rectories, Manor Cottages, and Park Houses. There was the China tea, the hot buttered scones, the thin slices of seed-cake, the saunter round the garden—'the stocks this year have been poor'—the walk through the village to the church and as far as the wooden bridge over the stream. She gossiped with Judy about common friends, and with me tried to turn the conversation to hunting until she found it no longer interested me. We stayed for dinner, and I began to find my hostess more accomplished than I'd thought at first. She has a quick mind and the agility of a ballerina in performing conversational pirouettes. When she smiles, that placid countenance becomes radiant like a lake rippled by a sudden breeze and reflecting the sunlight from a thousand wavelets. She has all the virtues, and seems chaste as well; and has a neat little mind that does not upset her orderly life. What am I doing here?

Fifth

I have sent, perhaps just a little too tardily—Unconscious art thou walking there below?—a precious note of appreciation to the lady of the manor house, and to Judy for her kindly meant services a box of the small cigars she affects.

November

Several polite letters and some more than polite have passed between here and Medford, and a few of an airy sentiment have passed in the other direction; and I asked Mrs. Manning when next in Town to lunch with me. She came up today, and we had an excellent lunch at Fortnum's, which I can ill afford, but do not grudge, as it is still agreeable to flirt publicly with a woman who is so perfectly a mistress of the art of conversation, so correctly dressed, and so obviously the product of a well-run nursery and well-paid governesses. But if I have to set her in a Fortnum frame the only suitable place for hanging is the morning-room at Peterley. She asked me for the week-end to Medford, but I have accepted only for the Saturday.

To the Club with Cousin Richard, and after dinner we were joined by Iolo Williams, who happened to remark that the T.L.S. had asked him to review Nichols' *Fisbo*. I mentioned Nichols' present wretched state of health and the need for sympathy, since it was precisely a remark of a brother poet's (aggravated by N.'s behaviour) to the effect that Nichols was not really as ill as he thought, or let it be imagined he was, that caused so much resentment in N. as to become the ultimate origin of the poem. In that poetic process the figure of the poet of real life had swollen and bellied into the Fisbo of the poem. Nichols had written to me only a few days before:

'Kuranstalt, Neuwittelsbach,
11 Romanstrasse, Munich.
4th November, 1934

Dear Peterley,
        Thank you for your letter. What beautiful writing you have now, very much like that splendid poet Edmund Blunden's. Your

115

letter was the more welcome as I am lying ill in bed here. I shall try and finish one more work—my play in verse, a *Don Juan* on which I've been busy for six years—and then I shall never write again. It's not worth it. One has no life. One is only a pen. And it takes from one all that makes life worth living: one becomes a freak. I shall give up writing and I hope [to] be able to get a job that pays a normal living —it takes me two years to write a book and then I get £45 on this side of the Atlantic, and possibly—if I sell it in the U.S.—I haven't sold *Fisbo*—£45 on the other. And so one cannot have what normal men have: a wife and child. And one becomes more and more unhappy; and if one is continually and unceasingly unhappy one doesn't write what is fresh and clear. So, like Prospero I shall break my wand. If I was as good a lawyer or electrical engineer or solicitor as I am poet, I'd make quite a decent living and be able to live like other men. But I can't; and I've had enough. So since I've been so long on this play I'll finish it—and then silence, and a chance to enjoy this life like other men before it's gone. For I'm quite a capable sort of chap and should be able to get a normal job. Thank you for your note.

Yours sincerely
Robert Nichols'

December

Ninth

Our acquaintance has ripened fast since that lunch a month ago. Too fast, too smoothly, I am beginning to think. She has left no doubt that she would welcome my attentions; but I am afraid they will have to be whole-hearted, constant, and unremitting. I am still a little surprised that this fastidious Englishwoman, frozen with good breeding into a mute reserve, can, after some eight brief meetings, make a surrender of her sentimental feelings. Of nothing else, *bien entendu*. The letters are still the clandestine correspondence of the girls' school; and I am an outcast from that pale of orthodoxy in which she moves. And her sensitive approach shows she is ready to fly back into her social life if once I strike the wrong note. I shall have to surrender everything; for she thinks that what she has to give, a woman's exacting loyalty, is worth the whole world. I was thinking this today when her letter came telling me how much she had enjoyed the week-end solely because I was among the guests—'You seem to do for me something the others don't—revive a spark of life I think was getting rather low—show me interests I had not thought of before. Perhaps I should hope you don't unsettle me too much.' Her kindness made my contemplated palinode seem ungracious; I could not send it, even though I think it would be wiser; and in my indecision I fled from Polly and my problem to Peterley.

I spent the week watching the rain on my fields, walking the windy lanes, and in the evenings talking with the Old Man. I have always admired his reticence, but this is a time when I regret that it makes impossible any discussion of emotional questions. But if I call up the vision of Mrs. Manning, the unlaid ghost of Jane will rise up too, and that would pain him too much. Yet patch my life together somehow I must, before he goes; and this time there must be no mistakes. As he grows older, I notice he seems to grow into the past, becoming part of the house and the dead family. He talks much of Matthew's *Notes on Peterley, the House and Family* which he wishes me to correct for the press; but I point out that to bring it up to date would mean putting Matthew into the picture, and that might unbalance the composition. The Old Man thought on this a long while before he added, 'Yes; one couldn't very well include Morez.' For the moment I tried to remember who that was, and then realized he was speaking of the town in the Jura. 'But why not mention Morez?' He made no reply and I did not press the question; he was so clearly far away in his recollections. Later that evening I asked if he would like a Christmas gathering as in the old days. He inquired quickly whom I had in mind, so I mentioned only Henry and Sally, the Warners if they were free, Cousin Richard, and Judy and Mark.

Polly writes that she hopes I'll be in London so that she can spend Christmas with me instead of having to stay with the family or accept the Robinsons' invitation 'which has been a very pressing one you will be interested to hear'.

I am more interested in the humility and loving kindness of this young woman who eleven months ago had met me at Euston and rebuffed me for my solicitude. Time brings in its revenges with a grim precision; just as it derides us by fulfilling our wishes, at the wrong time. I reply regretfully that I must be at Peterley for Christmas and the New Year; and regretful I am in truth; I would rather spend even the Winter

Solstice with my vain, variable, cold, young pianist than in that draughty mausoleum among the wet beech woods of Buckinghamshire, or even with the County crowd at Market Medford. True, we have our violences and our days of indifference; and occasionally there are glimpses, in her words or actions, of South London, which shock me into an awareness of our precariously balanced ménage. We quarrel about music; the other day listening to her playing of a Schubert sonata I made some remark about her fingering and unluckily mentioned Schnabel. 'Schnabel!' she retorted angrily, 'that highly paid conjuror! I'll show you how he takes you ignorant people in.' She played some bars to demonstrate what she called his conjuring tricks, and then said that if I was going to be so critical I had better hire another performer, and out of the room she went. After such scenes she would keep to herself for two days; and during my negotiations for a resumption of friendly relations she would assert that I was debasing her musical life and that it was time she went away and made an honest pianist of herself, which she would never be if she stayed with me. Which would trouble me if I thought she were serious; since she has become so much a part of my intellectual and musical life and so wholly my social one. And she, in turn, knows, but does not admit, her own advantages: she meets people through me; she has my library where she reads for hours; she attends all the concerts and sees the plays and ballets, and does not have to go alone. She is, I think, contented, and no longer resents too sharply my suggestion that our relationship should become a closer one.

Fifteenth
To Medford on Saturday. We stayed indoors most of the time because of the continual rain, but on Sunday walked across the fields and along the river-side, past the copse that she is having thinned, and talked very circumspectly of the prospects of a settled life together. The Agnews came in for tea that had last been at the house when Michael had unsuccessfully proposed, and just after the Colonel had asked, 'Where's the new lover, Susan?' I, unsuspecting, walked into the room and into a strange silence. I drove her into Cheltenham for a party on Monday before coming back to Town. An unusually emotional parting at the station, Susan saying that she was still unwilling to go away with me, but that if I wished she was 'a little more than three-quarters willing to consider marriage next year if a divorce was quietly arranged'. I viewed this theoretical future all the way back to London and found the pros and cons so nicely equal that the scales refused to kick the beam and solve my hesitations.

.   .   .   .   .

A rather bitter argument with Polly, with flashes of anger generated by the heavy emotion of the separation. She hates being left alone for Christmas and being barred from Peterley and dislikes going home or staying with the Robinsons—'they are too rich; they make me feel shabby'—and she upbraids me for spending so many week-ends away from London: 'And you don't always go to Peterley. I rang up the other week and you weren't there.' I was annoyed at this; and she retaliated by mimicking Griffiths' voice: 'Mr. David Peterley is not, I believe, at home. Would you care to give me your name?' Which proved, I said, that I was there, and that Griffiths is merely the obedient butler refusing to disturb me, as he has been told. I had been, in fact, at Medford.

When I came in to breakfast this morning Polly was already at table drinking coffee and reading a book. She looked lovely, fresh, and lively as she always does, even after our late nights of coffee and music and prolonged conversations. She had put on her blue robe over her pyjamas, and had bound a ribbon through her black hair, and her lips were of that excessive scarlet which she knows gives her the licentious look which is so exactly the contrary of her fastidious and moral temperament. I have come to enjoy the contrast as much as she is amused to flaunt publicly this deceptive allurement. I stood for a moment tying the cord of my dressing gown and looking with admiration at the young woman with whom I had succeeded in establishing so peculiar a relationship. We enjoyed the same books and music, plays and pictures; and she was quite content to drift with me through the antique shops and second-hand booksellers instead of gazing in the shop windows in Regent Street. It is idyllic right up to the middle of the idyll; but all the later chapters are missing, and will, I think, remain unwritten; the next step to Peterley can never be taken. She graces a London apartment, but would be out of place in Buckinghamshire. I cannot see her managing the diplomatic *pourparlers* necessary to extract a dinner out of a recalcitrant cook whose only concern in life is not gastronomy but four needy children. I can hear the inflection in Griffiths' voice as he replies to some suggestion of Polly's: 'If you wish it, Madam'—an inflection that would absolve him of all responsibility for this step down to chaos or this betrayal of a tradition which he, alas, is now the only one left to uphold. Servants are proud people. And Gurney, discovering that Polly knows nothing about gardening, and cares as much, would quietly continue his horticultural dictatorship and no longer make even a pretence of discussing any contemplated change. Nor would it help the difficulty of getting the right kind of young domestics. Old Mrs. Mereweather is certainly not going to allow her granddaughter to come to the house for a few years, knowing that under Polly she will never learn to qualify for Shardeloes or Tring. And the Women's Institute; and the Rector's wife's sewing party; and relations with Knight's wife, a countrywoman of enormous character; and small-talk at Hampden; and the local hunt . . . Jane did all this perfectly. The comparison would be humiliating.

I went over and kissed her goodmorning, and took the book out of her hands. As though she had been following my thoughts, she said, quite naturally, 'Mr. Peterley, I'm going to leave you.' As I assumed she was not serious, I took little notice and merely asked when she wanted to go. 'I decided about a fortnight ago. It's not that I want to, but that I ought to. You don't mind this aimless kind of life we're leading: you've never had any other kind. But I'm losing my music; and I'm not getting anywhere.'

'But you know my circumstances. I'm not in a position to marry you, and you won't consider any other relationship.'

'No; I don't think I will; and at least you must admit I have never hinted at marriage. I've decided to take the job of music mistress at W. next term while the regular mistress is away: she was with me at Cambridge.' She spoke as though she was talking of a visit to the dressmaker, as was her way: and while once I used to think she did it to annoy me, I've come to believe it is merely her preference for the direct, the clean-cut statement. She is adept at putting these verbal stoppers on any emotion that threatens to bubble over. As unemotionally as possible I said that our life together meant much more to me now, that I had no other life I wanted to live—'except Peterley' she corrected—and that I could not easily bear to lose her.

'David, whenever you want to see me you can come; not too frequently, of course. And as long as you are interested in seeing me, I don't think I shall want to see anyone else, if that is any satisfaction to you. But you must realize that my music counts a great deal for me and I'm afraid of losing that, and my independence.' I sat thinking that, after all, it was a sensible idea; that it would save our ménage from becoming stale with monotony; and that it would certainly simplify the problem of my absences at Medford. I said I would agree, provided we could meet regularly and that I could run down and see her. Polly however had thought that out already, for she replied that it would be unwise. 'We can't meet, in that way, in the neighbourhood. I've got to keep up appearances. I'll have to get a small car, and we can meet for the occasional day in some country town.'

We spent the day shopping, and she came to see me off at Marylebone. I felt sorry she was having to spend Christmas unwillingly with her family in South London, and she was, at the last moment, reluctant to let me go; and there was a sudden fervour in her embrace as we kissed goodbye on the platform. She turned and walked quickly away, and I entered the carriage and faced for the first time a Christmas homecoming with no pleasurable feeling at all.

Susan Manning writes that John the handyman and gardener is in trouble and has given notice. Gladys, the plump girl who used to stand at the bottom of the garden, twisting her handkerchief in impatience as she waited for him to join her for the evening, has let it be known as publicly as possible that he will certainly be a father in about seven months. This, adds Susan, is her second mistake, the first being four years old. He imagines Mrs. Manning does not know, and seems to want to hide his shame from his employer by giving up his job. He has nothing to go to, and she asks me if I can do anything in London or possibly get him a berth on one of Chatwin's ships. I am amused at the bodily naturalness of life below stairs compared with our mental flirtations above. Susan foresees him returning from his voyages to find unaccountable babies littering his rural hearth. As she writes in her bedroom she hears unwonted music outside and looking through the window sees a dozen villagers on the lawn serenading her with carols, and at the door they wish her prematurely a happy New Year. 'Do you think it will be a happy New Year, my dear Mr. Peterley?'

1935

January

First

I am writing in my old room, the curtains drawn against the night and the two candlesticks alight, and the Michaelangelo drawing, Nichols' Christmas present, on the wall beyond them. I have opened my journal, as do all good diarists on this annual occasion, but in a state of mind far different from those earnest determinations to be more conscientious in future keeping of it. I am disposed to close it for good. The records grow darker each year, like those late entries in the *Anglo-Saxon Chronicle*, and make the Australian annals seem paradisial by comparison. Three hours are already gone of a year which I cannot hope to be better than its forerunners. 'Do you think it will be a happy New Year, Mr. Peterley?'

The trouble is with that word 'happiness'. Sought, it eludes you; unsought, it is present all the time, but you do not know it until too late. Perhaps a journal has this one virtue: it transmutes the unhappy present into a future pleasure; and I am amused tonight to read of that truant young man who cursed the stars of the Southern Cross, but who, with chambering and sailing and the luxury of melancholy, passed a pleasant enough apprenticeship to idleness. I do not think these present years will read as well in 1939; and if I eviscerated the birds on the stone altar in the garden I doubt if the omens would be propitious.

All the same, it has been a successful Christmas. The household is asleep, I imagine, by now. Henry and Sally separate, probably, in the two East rooms—it would be simpler for their hosts if they married instead of living so faithfully together apart. Judy and Mark share the large Green Room. Cousin Richard is in the Chintz bedroom, and in the Chinese sleeps Mademoiselle Françoise Armand-Périer. She arrived, as only a Parisienne can, after two railway journeys and a Channel crossing, looking like a model from a *maison de haute couture*, tight costumed and elegantly contoured, a perky hat tilted over a face enlivened with rouge and lipstick, and with neat ankles perched on curved shoes. The countryside was wintry and without the sparkle that the cold clear air sometimes gives; but Amersham delighted Françoise, and I went by way of Shardeloes and Hampden to show that there were patches of cultivation in our wild recesses.

She had never been to Peterley before, and when we turned into the drive could not believe at first that this was the house. She thought it seventeenth-century, but I explained that our stone weathered more than did the French stone of the north and gave a look of greater age to our buildings. Father greeted her a trifle pompously in his French, saying that he was happy to welcome to Peterley the daughter of his very old friend the distinguished deputy of the Doubs '*l'un de mes deux pays*'. Françoise replied rather aptly that it was only the Peterley foyer that could have tempted her to desert her own for the New Year. These ceremonies concluded satisfactorily to both parties, she was delivered to a wide-eyed

Grace, and the new gardener's boy was called in to deal with the impedimenta from Gaul.

I was amused by the effect her presence had upon the whole house within twenty-four hours. Grace told Griffiths that the two maids spent an extra half-hour over their toilet the next morning. Even Judy, who cares more for the turn of a phrase than for the cut of a petticoat, complained to me after tea that, had she known, she would have brought 'something to wear'. Even Sally, who is content to fill her tight dresses with her magnificent figure, knowing that to add anything to this would be a waste of effort since it could add nothing to the first effect—Mark's descriptive phrase of 'Venus in a wet bathing suit' is almost certainly Judy's coinage—even Sally, who lazily ties her ash-blonde hair loosely in a knot behind and leaves it to droop negligently at the sides, had, I noticed the next morning, called it to order and coiled and transfixed it immovably behind; although she had not accepted the cosmetic challenge and her light blue-green eyes were still the only spots of colour in a pale face. Even Father had discarded his coat, that bulged at the pockets like the pack-saddle of a mule, for something smarter. But the most metamorphosed of all was my Nazi cousin, who, abashed by this so complete a representative of Parisian society, did not appear in his plum-coloured dinner-jacket ('After all, Arnold Bennett wore one.') and seriously asked me if he should cut the silver buttons off his ridiculous shooting-jacket, like a Jaeger's from the Thuringian forest.

Françoise did not carry her Anglophilia so far as to go to church, and I stayed at the house with her, amused at her delight in watching the household depart solemnly, at decent intervals, down the drive towards the village: George, the gardener's boy, with young Ronald, Gurney's grand-nephew, both constrained in clean suits and overcoats, and uncomfortable as colts in collars. And then the young maids, Peggy Updike and Violet Wormleighton—ah, these incredible rural names!—with Grace some paces behind, buttoning her gloves; and—longo intervallo, as the great Julius said—Griffiths, who alone does not look ridiculous in Sunday best. Father drove Judy and Mark and the others down.

Cousin Richard said that going to church on Christmas Day was only a social observance, and he was not a society man; so he joined us in a walk round the park. Françoise asked to see the summer house that Rose had spoken of when she stayed with the Périers in the Jura. The little Temple looked damp and pallid among the black trees; and weeds and grass had pushed between the flagstones before the door. We peered through the window-panes and saw the tomb-like interior untouched since her day: the books on the shelves, the writing desk, the chair with its embroidered seat, and the tiled stove. It seemed macabre to the French-woman, who remarked the contrast between the sombre thicket where she had read her Italian poets and been happy, and the hot streets of Rome where she had died. 'All the same, it is very charming and romantic. Your father was very kind—or very sentimental.'

We all separated on the sixth, Françoise staying on at Peterley. I drove Cousin Richard back to Town; and, as we approached Harrow, he referred overtly to what I am sure had been on his mind for a fortnight to judge by his conduct. He had recovered from the impact of that first meeting with Mademoiselle Françoise a changed man: he had become himself again, and the affectations of the Teutonified Englishman vanished. He forgot he had visited Munich and attended the Party rally at Nurem-berg. I had watched him the senior by six years succumb to the intellectual maturity of the younger Frenchwoman, and congratulated myself on the success of my experiment; and I wasn't surprised when with unwonted seriousness he broached the subject as we came into the outer suburbs, and wondered if it would be permissible to invite Françoise to dinner at his Club: 'It's a bit of a political centre: she might be interested in meeting some political people.' I replied that I doubted if someone who was invited to the Elysée would be impressed by an introduction to the ghost of the Liberal Party, but that he could try.

'Don't put on a stiff shirt. Remember she's been three years with the Sorbonne crowd. See that the dinner is good, and pick a good play after-wards. And whatever you do, don't be romantic. The romantic part must come much later in the novel, if at all.' All he replied was, 'Oh, probably I won't trouble after all.' Which made me sure he was in earnest.

February

'3 Upper Cheyne Row,
3rd February 1935

Dear Peterley,
I am now back in England and looking forward to seeing you. But first I must get properly settled in. And I am far from that. It isn't easy. Thank you for your efforts over Belloc. Alas, I have

never received his letter. Let me say this; don't expect much of me. I'm not an intellectual any longer. I cannot think consecutively. Indeed latterly owing to illness I haven't been able to think at all. I am in addition a queer fellow without tact. I blurt things out. I have little reserve. I have on top a certain facile way of feeling; then a layer of indifference, and finally a fountain of feeling not under proper control. I am a timid man who over-compensates. Neglect and loneliness have made me vain. When one has a success one naturally becomes humble and sensible. I have had only one success in my life (*Wings over Europe* in New York 1926). I talk sketchily because my heart undoes me in the midst of my talk. I seem a monster of egoism—and am constantly so informed—but that's because my egoism is—that's to say I regard myself as an instrument not for myself but for "man". If I am my own "favourite character in modern fiction" it's because the poem seems to me to stand for all men.

I am particularly difficult just now because I am uprooted and moody. But I believe, I really do, I reward patience. I would add that anybody can see my faults. I may cry out to all the winds. I seem never to have leisure or pertinacity to correct them. That may be due to want of character and to laziness and to a certain confusion of mind, but it is even more due to my interest in furthering certain qualities which I believe I possess. The keeping alive of these seems to prevent me getting at my faults.

I warn you I have grown dull these last years. I don't know why. Perhaps it is a fog which like a country mist is necessary to a certain quality of later illumination. Maybe it's because I'm very tired within.

It is necessary that I become as fresh as I can contrive to you, because you love the things I love and because you honoured my compositions with admiration.

I sleep a bit better. I must somehow lead myself back into the world and see that world, sanely. Let us meet next week. Maybe I'll be less tired. I hope so.

Very sincerely yours,
Robert Nichols

Sorry my fist is so awful today. I am dreadfully tired.'

Seventh

Robert Nichols back in England and came to dinner with me this evening. He startled me a little with the physical change: the face thin, drawn, pointed, anxious, nerve-racked; the eyes tired but restless. He was obviously ill, and tense with mental strain. But he talked as always, continually and fast, and with vivacity and interest; much of himself and with some complaint of his unrecognized work—'It is not admitted I am writing anything of value. I suspect it's assumed I can't write anything more'—and some bitterness of his wife, which is probably the result of his nervous state. We were speaking of the young moderns, and when I said something of the young Huxley's reintroduction of flippancy and the unhappy influence of *Antic Hay*, he disagreed; he said the book was in fact a pillory of the young people who admired it—a view he had tried to make Wells recognize, but without success. We talked of Frieda Lawrence's book this very morning published. 'I was one of those who buried Lawrence,' he said, 'there was Aldous and Francis Hackett and myself. I could never feel sympathetic with Frieda, because I felt she did not really understand the Lawrence I knew. But in these matters one is at the mercy of one's personal feelings and the Lawrence Frieda lived with may have been only in part identifiable with the Lawrence I knew.' He mentioned B.M. and said he was going to warn X., whom B. was trying to seduce, against his blackguardly character and his addiction to drugs. 'People today have no standards; and when I get up to protest, I'm told to be more tolerant. But I'm afraid the older I get, I don't grow wiser, but only find more things to disapprove of.' He would not agree with my suggestion that wisdom might consist in leaving affairs to follow a chance path: 'No; you must have some standards to regulate life by.'

I had ordered a good dinner, but he was on a strict diet and could eat little. He rashly took some white Burgundy, and the cigarette he tried to smoke after coffee was too much for his throat, and the coughing it caused continued at intervals throughout the rest of the evening. He had to sleep early, and we drove back to Upper Cheyne Row where at the moment he is staying.

March

I took the late train from Paddington on Friday night and was surprised to find Mrs. Manning waiting at Didcot with the hired taxi. I did not feel as grateful as I should have felt at this thoughtfulness, for Judy had recently communicated to me her fear that Susan was beginning to live beyond her income and was working too hard in an effort to maintain her old standard of living. I was consequently a little annoyed at the extravagance of bringing Rumbold and his taxi all the way from Wantage to Didcot and back to Wantage via Medford. She may have been aware of my feelings, for she said after ten minutes of silent travelling along the wet and windy road: 'I don't think Rumbold will mind if you hold my hand. If you care to, that is.' So I was forced to show more tenderness than I felt, which made me even less cordial. And throughout the week-end Susan was almost perversely affectionate; and before I left late on Sunday evening complained that if I did not show more interest in being with her she did not see why I should trouble to come at all. I could not, unfortunately, explain that I had intended to run down to see Polly, it being her Saturday off, and that as a result of Susan's entreaty on Thursday evening to come to Medford, I had had to cancel my day in Gloucestershire.

Back in London I regretted my coldness, and the wasted week-end, and this morning arranged for flowers to be sent to Polly for her rather prim sitting-room.

April

Twenty-ninth
Susan tells me of Alice Peers' wedding to a Mr. Hartland at Abingdon with the spice of malice of one who, I think, would willingly have been in the bride's place:

'It was not a great success except from the legal point of view. It rained, of course; but if you will marry in April can you expect June weather? Quite chilly, too; and the bridesmaids who were plain to start with did not improve in the cold air. The bride, who is rather highly strung like all you literary people, left us all in doubt throughout the whole ceremony whether she would choose to faint, have a *crise de nerfs*, or simply be sick, and then in the end disappointed all our fears. But at least she succeeded in inspiring an extreme solicitude in the bridegroom which became him very nicely. He and the bride's naval brother made a handsome pair. If only there had been two pretty women in the neighbourhood! The united couple have gone to test their incompatibility in Ireland. The rain, they say, is softer there.'

She goes on to wonder whether there should not be a school for prospective husbands, and thinks she might like to keep one: 'but then there certainly ought to be a branch for prospective brides'.

July

First

A scolding letter from Medford complaining about my melancholy on the phone:

> 'I couldn't gather whether you'd really like to see me on Thursday or not. I feel you might be a little more explicit on the subject. I shall not attempt to meet you unless you show more enthusiasm about it. See a doctor; go to Ramsay who is expensive like all doctors, but really good like few. I cannot exist like you in a miasma of melancholy. Tell me you are going to revive, and stop being vague and distant, and don't thank me for my "kind letter". I am not accustomed to writing letters of the kind I sent you a week ago, and receiving merely that in reply.'

She writes much better when angry. Still, she treats the state of accidie too lightly, forgetting that it has its source in that very paralysis of will which prevents your voluntary escape from it. You know you do not any longer have the power to shake off the blackness in the mind. You act as you do not really wish to act. You choose the words that will wound your friends the most; but you have no pleasure from the bitterness. And, as you speak them, you feel the urge to explain that they are not really meant; but at the same time you also feel the check of the bridle holding you back from the confession. I remember my father once casually remarking, 'You should beware of the black mood of the Peterleys,' so I suppose he must have known it too. It is probably the disease that Samuel Johnson attributes to his father: 'an unconcern about those things which agitate the greater part of mankind, and a general sensation of gloomy wretchedness'. It comes without apparent cause, and will go as suddenly. It has persisted this summer longer than usual, and unreasonably, for it has been a lovely season, and there have been many happinesses with Polly. We have scattered our meetings capriciously over the southern counties and seasoned them with archaeology, choosing the old towns, following the Roman roads, visiting ruins and earthworks and the literary shrines. It is wonderful how the figure of a young woman can improve the view. Silchester benefited a great deal from a vivacious young woman to talk to; and Salisbury Close had never looked better than when we walked across it together in the evening light. We have sat and chatted in the shadow of every abbey and minster—at Winchester, Romsey (the ale at Romsey was memorable too), at Christchurch and Malmesbury. I am not sure Miss Austen would have welcomed an unchaperoned Polly at Steventon; our normal pleasures might have displeased Beckford at Fonthill; Hardy would have been tolerant, but we, on our part, were shocked by that graceless house of his own designing. The Jeffreys country was as charming as his prose; we saw Stonehenge by the declining light of evening, when the monoliths cast longer shadows and the lichened stone grows a still older russet brown; and on an idle hill of summer we sat and looked towards Salisbury and the Plain, and watched the light clouds in a hot sky move along the distant ridges.

And when term was over for Polly she wrote saying how much she would have enjoyed being 'misconducted leisurely and lovingly from inn to inn back to London', but adding that she would prefer the 'mis' could be eliminated.

I have come to Peterley; but the moment Polly left me the melancholy returned.

This journal read over is strangely one-sided. All the memorable things are omitted—the convivial evenings with friends, the walks through the countryside, exchange of letters, silences over a book in front of a fire, the nervous interchange of conversations by telephones, hurried lunches, meetings, and partings—almost everything except the delicious wantonings with women. As a record of living it is absurdly false. Are all diaries equally so? I suspect it; for I do not believe that the choice of entries for a journal is made à votre insu by your subconscious, and therefore is a true revelation. For myself I state herewith that much of the unrecorded life —those convivialities, those solitary studies and walks—have been of more significance to me than all the emotional exchanges with all the women in these volumes—all but one. No one, reading it, would guess the pleasure I had each year from re-reading Emma, Selborne, Crotchet

Castle, *Tristam Shandy*, *Dominique*, or Boylesve, or from the daily reading of second-hand booksellers' catalogues, or listening to Italian opera, or going into a popular restaurant and watching the human being perform; or—best of all—casting off from moorings in a harbour and feeling through the tiller the yawl come alive in the push of the wind.

Found one of Susan's letters in a drawer, and, rereading it, I recalled that our occasional meetings in Town and my week-ends at Medford are assuming for her an importance I still cannot make up my mind to give them myself, but probably should be doing.

'You say that you need my affection. Do you really, darling? Is it something that you've longed for and hoped for and feel that you cannot be complete without? Is this on the way to being the core and centre of real loving, which is so much more than being in love? I should warn you that I'm avaricious of both, and of the joy and the glory of loving and being loved, and being in love. You might perhaps, sometime (if you cared to), write and tell me what your own opinion is. I should love to hear it—or anything else you feel impelled to say.'

Ah, if only I felt impelled to say anything! But each time we meet I accept the excitement and the amusement of the moment and try not to think of a future. This respectable courtship can continue only if we are to marry; otherwise it is meaningless; and I still have not dared to put the question to myself, or taken any steps to find what Jane's opinion of divorce may be.

Meanwhile, our week-ends at Medford have become almost maritally calm. I alight from the train and find her waiting in the paraffin-lit twilight of the little country station that is two generations and a thousand leagues from London. We drive back for dinner as though I am back from the City after a day's work. We discuss the week's gossip. We talk or play piquet till eleven, and then decorously we kiss goodnight, and I walk through the black unlighted village to the Parkers' cottage where I have a bedroom. I sink deep into the feather mattress, and looking through the lattice window at the stars over the sleeping Berkshire downs I wonder what I am doing here.

August

I have been under-gardener for a fortnight to Gurney and feel better for the exertion. We break off at eleven and take a pot of beer on the terrace and survey the long flower border, a little thinner for our trimming. He is a taciturn man and only by fits and starts reminiscent, but yesterday he began remembering his young days when he was a bodger at Chesham, making wooden toys for children, mostly spades for the seaside, and hoops. 'They make tin ones now for the little brats to cut their faces open with. And they've got bicycles now and the cars run 'em down.' In Gurney's eyes clearly the economic decay of the bodger had been properly avenged by Providence. He said he was learning to become a chair-bodger and whittle the spokes for chairs in the woods themselves, when one day Great-grandfather had come upon him seated on his wooden bench in Morgan's Fee woods and started a conversation and learned that Gurney's ambition was to be a gardener. 'It was good-paying work,' he said, referring to the chair-making, 'but plants are more human, if you know what I mean.' As Gurney is a misanthropic man who avoids the human race, I didn't. I found out from his talk the reason for one thing that had always puzzled me—his care for the pansies, which I have never regarded highly as flowers. The ones here which are so tenderly nurtured are descended from those produced for the first time not far away at Iver when Lord Gambier the sailor bought the house there. 'A friend of Nelson's, the admiral, he was; and a fair gardener.' Gurney said he had developed the pansy from the wild heartsease, which I suppose is likely.

The O.M. would occasionally join us, and with Gurney become almost loquacious. As he ages, he grows friendlier with the old gardener, as though their ways are converging, as indeed they are, as far as the lych gate, where the latter will turn right into the churchyard and the former carry straight on into the church. Which reminds me that some thought should be taken about a seemly tomb. (Lutyens has done a fine one at Savoy for Lady C.M.) Matthew's plan for the grounds shows a mausoleum at the end of all the rides in the wood. He used to go over to West Drayton when Bodley the architect had settled in the Georgian house beside the church and try to interest him in the scheme; but they quarrelled over the style. Matthew wanted the tombs to be in the historical sequence of style and Bodley rightly insisted they match the house. Nothing of course came of it; and Matthew who intended to lie under a soaring canopy of Gothic pinnacles lies under a plain slab at Morez in the folds of the Jura.

A letter from Polly yesterday asking me to meet her in Town on Friday; and adding in the feminine postscript, 'This is rather important.' I have never connected myself with anything important in Polly's life, and could make no guess at what had prompted this cool, reflecting woman to write urgently. I had no reason for harbouring such sudden fears as those of my unknown diarist who had from time to time consulted the calendar after receiving a letter from his Doris. I could almost envy him his perturbations. Unsanctified paternity might not be a bad thing if it ensured the succession. Dynasties have often enough taken a left turn. Bastards have been historically eminent. Is it merely an old wives' tale that sons are more likely this way instead of the string of daughters lawful unions are so often blessed with? And it would certainly be amusing to see the *brio* of the rebel Polly reduced to the long *andante* of motherhood. I remembered one of the few occasions that the Old Man had spoken of family affairs after the separation from Jane: 'I should have no objection to an illegitimate grandson, if there is no hope of an ordinary one. The troublesome problem, in these cases, is the mother of course.' Detaching a young Peterley from Polly would by no means have been easy.

The young woman in the summer dress, cool, slender, and with some assurance of sophistication, waiting for me at Buzzard's, naturally had no pre-natal worries, and I did not like to mention my theories of left-handed unions. But it was with some anxiety that I asked what was the important occasion for the meeting, and I was immediately disappointed when she said: 'I wanted to see you because of the Robinsons' invitation. They have taken a house in the south of France and have invited me for three weeks. I needn't ask you what you think, but you notice I do.' I disliked the idea of Polly being for three weeks in a provocative climate and equally provocative bathing dresses with Henry who proposed to her on alternate Saturdays; but, as I knew she would in any case go, and only wanted to test my feelings, I agreed she should go, but on condition that she didn't misbehave with the love-sick son. 'You, of all people, ought to know that's impossible.' I offered to drive her down; but she said that would make the separation difficult. 'If we could be together in France, why should I go with the Robinsons?' And the young woman who means more to me, I suppose, than anyone else now, smiled, waved, and turned away in Oxford Street to stay with strangers she cares little for.

Twentieth
Polly in the bosom of the Robinson family writes:

'David,
Why aren't you here? It's foolish that so much time and loveliness should be wasted. I have been to St. Tropez, a little port, very old, with narrow steep streets, and odd archways and stairs; with a *château fort* on the hill, a round tower at the end of the curve of the bay, and a seventeenth-century chapel on the hill beyond. You expect a ballet to emerge in front of this scenery, or a curtain to come down at sunset.

And between the warm blue of the sea below and the vivid blue of the sky above, the mountain ranges retreat into a deepening blue-grey-green distance. The chapel is filled with votive offerings from sailors saved from the sea—you would love the model ships—but I came out scared of seafaring. Don't go out in your little boat while I'm away, will you?'

She seems happy. She makes no complaints against the pertinacious Henry. It may be that the transition to Mrs. Robinson will not be too difficult when Mrs. Manning moves into Peterley; and I think that as a married woman Polly will be more accessible in her disillusion than she would have been in her wounded pride as an abandoned spinster.

I turn from the southern brightness in the letter, cross the cool hall, and come out into the milder sunlight on trim lawn, and become again a part of an elegant composition in an ordered landscape. Gurney is stooping over some calceolarias; the dog under the wicker chair on the terrace is sleeping with one eye and watching a butterfly with the other. By the stables the new boy is washing down the paved court and being talked to by the younger maid; and white pigeons wheel in and out of the turret on the roof. And what is unseen I know as clearly as this sunlit scene: Father with his black coffee in the study; Griffiths in his pantry with the morning's newspapers and his pot of tea; and Cook tidying herself up in the determination to be out of the house by three o'clock and catch the bus to Wycombe and its shops, which have for her all the fascination the bazaars of Damascus would have for us.

I walked down the lawn past Gurney to the flagstones round the base of the statue that isn't there, and sat and looked back at the house, at the long low rectangle of stone that was so subtly divided into three portions by the four pilasters; and each portion so pleasingly spaced with the long windows that imprinted a black-and-white pattern on the grey stone. And on this, the garden side, Roger, if Roger it was, has developed the door-way fancifully and lightly and not richly and martially as in the front. Placidity and restraint. But these were not eminently the virtues of the early eighteenth century, and yet they are embodied in their building, heaven knows why; and their classical homes sit as naturally in our romantic landscapes as a young girl who has not yet become self-conscious before the photographer. One could not imagine the shire without Hampden, Shardeloes, Denham and Peterley and Wotton.

Polly has been bathing at Cavalaire, and is beginning to love the sea; is even willing to come sailing with me which she has always before refused. 'But I do not know how much longer I can stay here. Henry is becoming tiresome. He has formally proposed. I had a difficult hour. I kept thinking of our times together. But I felt sorry for him; he is terribly serious, and he certainly cares for me much more than you do, Mr. Peterley. If he persists, I may have to get you to send a telegram from my parents calling me back home.' I am not sure I am ready to marry her to the well-meaning Henry just yet and I shall have to do it very diplomatically. He is interested in music, and a good amateur musician himself: it might not be so ill sorted a match. And when I remember her passionate devotion to Richards and her early indifference to me, and how she changed, I do not see why she should not change again, if Henry plays her skilfully enough. I walked down to the farm with a mind full of images of a brown woman swimming in a warm blue sea.

September

Eleventh

Landed at Dover yesterday with Polly, and leaving her in London came back here to Peterley to recapture if I can the peace of mind I had before I left hurriedly for the south. She had written suddenly that she could not stay longer with the R.s and would I meet her if she came back? I suggested she take a ticket to Lyon, change there for Grenoble, and go to the Grand Hotel where I would join her. She came in while I was sitting reading in the lounge—a startling figure, brown as a Polynesian, in a white linen dress and bare legs and sandals, with lips as bright as hibiscus flowers and her heavy black hair cut shorter but as untamed as ever. She said very calmly: 'Well, here I am. Shall we go upstairs?' And there, once the door was closed, she surprised me by flinging herself into my arms, and then immediately laughed, as though to excuse so unnatural an impulse, and said: 'It's just that I had to run away and recover from the strain. It's been so difficult; or rather Harry has. You know what I mean.'

I knew only too well what she meant, and felt a sympathy for the unhappy and unsatisfied Harry who had hoped that the sea, the sun, the south of France would have effected what his own persuasion had obviously failed to achieve. He should have been more forthright—he may have tried. But I was happy to realize that he had succeeded no better than I; for here was Polly back with me in a renewed companionship, gossiping calmly in a hotel bedroom, and, as she always was when we met after separation, free and relaxed and full of spirit.

We must have talked for nearly two hours, for the sun was already behind the Vercors summits when I got up to open the iron volets, only to find that the air outside was as warm as that within. I looked out above the roofs of the old city to where the Mont Rachais, lit on its western slope by the level sun, towered over the cathedral spire, and then looked down to the square below. It was ten years since my last visit, and nothing, except for the new apartments near the Military Hospital, had changed. The city would always, I hoped, remain small, provincial, and restfully old-fashioned. I watched some students wheel with a clangour of bicycle bells from the Place Grenette into the rue Montorge and miss a Citroen, turning from the Grande Rue, only with the help of the car's brakes. Workmen, their coats slung over their backs, were crossing towards the cafés behind the market; and two women in black on their way home with the evening bread were exchanging soliloquies by the spouting dolphins of the fountain. We could spend some days of relaxation here hidden from the world. We could take the *téléférique* up to the Restaurant de le Bastille for lunch, and in the evening search in the city for my favourite dish of quenelles. We could even spend a day looking at the Stendhal manuscripts in the city library. But Polly had thought I was meeting her here with the car so that I could drive her back to England; and I wasn't sure she would accept the compromising delay. When I asked

if she would like to linger a few days here, she was straightway suspicious; but I said I had long wanted to see the Stendhal manuscripts at
Grenoble and that she couldn't deny me this after my long journey. She
may have sensed the innuendo in my remark, for she agreed, 'provided
. . .' And I retorted a little sharply that I knew all the provisos by this
time.

So we stayed. Lunched in the hotter sunshine at the restaurant on the
Bastille. Ate excellent quenelles in an inelegant café. Walked in the
Promenade de l'Île Verte and along the quais; and I was allowed two
days to look at the Stendhal manuscripts. I think homage in such circumstances would have pleased the vanity of that other persistent, unrepentant
romantic, pursuing—'faint but pursuing'—the twin illusions of fame and
love, and finding little of either in his life. He might, I thought, turning
over these papers, be a subject for a study. There is little on him in English.
But can he be treated fully and frankly for an English audience, and in
the English language? To those sentimental inhabitants in their sheltered
island, his insistence on passion and his honesty of analysis make him un-
sympathetic. And how can one philosophically harmonize for them the
baldish, ageing, syphilitic pursuer of women with the creator of genius
without getting involved in the problem of the physiology of literature?
And that would please them less; although I cannot see how any literary
criticism—any art criticism—can be valid without the preliminary medical
history. Literature as a pathological excrescence on the normal life? Why
not? Thought itself becomes in its highest reaches an aberration, since,
pushed to its furthest limits—theological, philosophical, aesthetic—it
threatens the destruction of the human being producing it—a fatal
parturition. Except that man rarely follows his thought to its extremity;
but, with an instinct of illogicality, turns back to the sheltered valley of the
normal world, full of professions of faith in the reality of those creations
of his own disordered mind. Out of the see-saw of his instability he makes
hell and heaven; and stays safely half-way between. Books are not the
hospital of the soul, but its temperature-chart in illness.

The weather stayed fixed in sunshine. Polly was happy and friendly
and in no hurry to return to England; so we went up the valley to Geneva
and the lake; and I took rooms in the old Ecu de Genève, and from my
window looked out once more on the Île Jean-Jacques Rousseau, but not
in such melancholy this time. Polly gazed at the swift river, the leisured
swans, the hurrying people, the boast of hostelry and the pomp of civic
pride, the white sails, and the steamer going aft from the pier, and the
plume of water from the fountain that rose like a geyser and fell grace-

fully away in a plume against the background of the Alps. This, I told her, was Uncle Matthew's finest scene in the world, to which she replied that the old fellow must have been unbalanced; it was fine but there were finer. I said I thought it was all the characters in front of this stage scenery that really fascinated Matthew: Shelley with Mary and Claire helping the peasants extricate horse and carriage from the snowdrifts in the Jura passes; Germaine de Stael walking with Adolphe in the shady garden at Coppet; Boswell interviewing the Laird of Ferney; Gibbon wooing Mademoiselle Curchod in the little stone village of Crassier. Amiel walks with bent head along the Grand Quai thinking of philosophy and Philine and passes M. Liszt and Madame Sand who are leaving for Chamonix. The lovely and doomed Empress rides furiously past like Lola Mendez in the circus, and makes even Sainte-Beuve turn his head in admiration and forget his feeling of exile. Polly merely remarked that Matthew must have lived too much in the past; and that I was in danger of doing the same. 'Do you know, I had the feeling at Peterley of being in another century? As though the people there were ghosts. I remember when Grace came to waken me in the morning, I'd been awake for three hours without hearing any sounds and I nearly asked her if there were any other living people in the house. I never thought I'd see any of you again.'

I showed her the great Protestant monument which is one of the few successful ones in the world. We climbed piously the stairs of Amiel's apartment house. We visited Jullien's and bought some books; and on the third day I hired a car and took her along the western shore through Versoix and Sauverny to show her Germanie's château and the grave-yard copse, and the little ravine where the brook flows down from the Jura into the lake, a deep romantic chasm where the elms meet over the rustic seat on which she sat with the captured but not captivated Benjamin. When I was on the road to Gex I felt a momentary temptation to go on climbing; for twenty kilometres farther on and a thousand metres farther up I should be on the Faucille Pass, and there below would be Lamora and Septmoncel and the zigzag descent into St. Claude, and I should be back in my boyhood again. I thought better of it, and turned on to the Divonne Road. I showed her Nyon, and St. Cergue and took the hillside track to Arzier and St. George and Gimel. We stopped for lunch on the roadside beyond St. Oyen where the road begins to drop down sharply on horse-shoe bends to the level of the lake; and while Polly rested in the long grass I walked to the brow of the hill and looked left and right along the whole length of the Genevan valley. A summer haze softened the outlines of the shore and hid Lausanne and Vevey; but the lake surface was silvery with the diffused sunlight, and a steamer made its slow way from out of Rolle below. Across the lake the first mountain chain rose clear from the mist, and above and beyond these black peaks were sharper summits more faintly etched; but the Mont Blanc remained veiled in a cloud form that assumed the shape of the rock beneath. I looked right, and, twenty kilometres away and below, saw the white *jet d'eau* at Geneva that rose and fell away to the side like a girl's brushed hair. A blue storm was coming up from Annecy, and its edge rested like a lid on the sides of the Jura, darkening the lake's southern end and threatening a summer storm.

Here was the world's—my world's—most beautiful valley, caught in the stillness of a summer siesta, the fields that had been ploughed for as long as man had been in Europe; the vines, like the dwarf oaks of Japanese gardens; the stone terraces that held the soil on the hillsides; the roofs burned brown by centuries of sun; and, looking down on this hot plain, the dark pines of the Jura that entangled the wisps of cloud in their branches and strained their moisture on wild strawberry and mushroom below. If ever natural landscape could have a moral influence, this surely spoke whole bibles; this was the true Pisgah-sight: for here below me, without allegory, was peace and plenty, and the fruits of industry, of tolerance, of the absence of ambition; the pride of this people bursting only into the flowers of window-boxes, their covetousness snatching only another pasture from the forest. The fires of persecution had long ago gone out in the city of Calvin; and if blood had flowed at Morat and Grandson over the hills to the left, it was in defence of liberty against a tyrant. If only the world could be like this paradisial valley; if political passions could become no more serious than cantonal elections . . . I felt moved to tears by all the fine sentiments this panorama of lake and plain and mountain inspired; and then I reflected that it was all very well to feel so nobly; but what in fact had I done to increase the sum of human happiness who had never handled a plough or grown a vine? Jane sits unhappily at Peterley hoping I will one day return; and Polly is lying here by a Swiss roadside looking at a foreign sky and wondering what uncertain future she can expect with me. It is all very well to moralize over an erring world. I am cutting as ridiculous a figure as Shelley, who preceded me by a hundred and ten years on this pass to Geneva in the company of Miss Godwin and Miss Clairemont, and mixed moral indignation with abduction and fornication, with more success than I, but with an equal lack of humour. Were these waves of sentiment healthy; would I repent and return to Jane; would it be really beneficial to anyone to do so? I walked back to where Miss Morel was still lying, kissed her tenderly, and began to pack the picnic things into the car as the first drops fell of the storm I had seen over Geneva.

Fifteenth

Walked from Edgware to Radlett in a keen wintry morning air, reading from *Aurelia* occasionally, but for the most part thinking of this day's significance. She has probably wandered as much, if not as far, as I have since then—I hope with more content. I do not think Radlett has had any meaning for her, and if we met again she would not recognize me. Yet, I wonder: their senses, their memories, are stronger than ours. We are encumbered by the paraphernalia of civilized living; we move feebly in our hard carapaces, cockroaches scurrying over the asphalt we have laid over the green grass. If we met and touched hands, that magnetic current would surely flow through our fingers as before; and it is not impossible that at some village fair I might go into the gypsy's tent for my fortune, and that our eyes might meet.

I lunched at the King's Arms and in the afternoon walked over the hill to the lane where we used to have our few meetings; and did not come back until the level mists were rising from the fields and showing like a white putrescence on the autumnal woods.

Twenty-third

The evening of the twentieth was Amersham Fair, which I have often watched from the windows of the 'Crown', but this year attended as Arthur Machen's guest. We drove down, the Warners and I, in a darkening evening that began with a curtain of crimson across a threatening western sky, a crimson that turned to a glowing blue, until the dark came up over us from Denham, and Amersham in the distance was a glare of lights and coloured flares. Upstairs to Machen's sitting-room for the first ceremonial libation of his secret punch which he pours into a goblet from a huge earthenware pitcher. It is at first taste the most innocent seeming, the least apparently alcoholic, the mildest of beverages—left over, surely, from a Church bazaar; or what the Vicar daringly concocted for his bridge party—without character, indefinable, certainly impossible to analyse, perhaps a little too much cold tea to too little spirits. You drink more deeply. The round countenance of Machen smiles and he says disarmingly, 'A private blend of my own,' and refills your glass. You drink again. You do not know it then; but from that moment the transformation has begun to operate and you will not rejoin yourself and the ordinary world for twenty four hours.

He is fashioned on the lines of the oblate spheroid and would look like a Confucian sage if he did not look exactly like a Welsh wizard, which he is. The smile and white locks of Lloyd George are a mediocre imitation; for the politician is wholly of the present world, but Machen quite beyond it. He might be an emanation from the soil of Caerleon, but that I fancy he is really a character from *Kulhwch and Olwen*. Daughter Janet was there, and the Greenwoods, and F. the archaeologist and his wife, and others whose faces and names were later blurred in my memory. We ate and drank and looked down from the window on the flaring booths stretching along the middle of the village street. The air was full of the hissing of the roundabout and its jingling organ; the shouts of the fairmen inciting to impossible feats with hoops, pennies, and balls; the crack of rifles and broken glass; the ring of the bell as the strong man swung the hammer and hit the peg. The linked ranks of the young girls were broken by the phalanxes of the young men, and from the mêlée couples formed and slipped away into the outer darkness.

I managed to have a good talk with him on what had greatly interested me: the persistence of oral tradition, from which we drifted into a discussion on the Mithras cult. He told me of a village in Hampshire where one man remembered his father speaking of a golden bull supposed to be buried somewhere in the parish, and where quite recently they have unearthed an underground room of Roman workmanship which is thought to be a shrine and devoted to Mithras. Here is a persistence for 1500 years. He said that he knew of a historian who visited the field of Naseby and passing the time of day with a labourer asked him if he were aware that this was the site of a great battle? Aye, that he were, and the long field had been in oats that year and they were all trodden down.

We went out from time to time down into the street to shy for coconuts or break a clay pipe with a rifle, coming back for more punch and more conversation. Amersham was now like an allegory by Bunyan illustrated by Bosch. The faces peering through the smoky air looked less human; the laughter sounded diabolic and the wavering flares turned the street into shaky scenery that might vanish at midnight with the whole phantasmagoria. The engines hissed evilly with steam. The rolls of music were swallowed greedily by the mechanical organ. The wooden caryatides clapped their cymbals and beat their bells. When I reached the little upper room and saw our host pouring his punch, I had the impression of a necromancer who had conjured up the unnatural scene outside; and thought that at any moment he might put down his jug and leaning out of the window utter the cabalistic word at which the noise and the carnival would become moonlight in an empty street.

He was speaking of his days with the Benson touring company and had some stories of the stage-carpenter who had never read Aristotle and so tried to reproduce the realities of life on the stage, and once so cleverly made his stage ship roll and pitch that the actors began to feel seasick and the leading lady had to leave the stage. His round full face is wonderfully mobile; his deep voice very pleasantly liquid; and his lips purse to an O as he makes his points. He goes round with his jar of punch, a short plump figure in a brown suit, either gesticulating with his large pipe or sucking gurgles out of it as he listens to your remarks, his bald dome above the silver locks nodding agreement and implying a sagacity in your words they surely do not have. He seemed a literary creation by Machen. The man is the quintessence of his works.

When I came back on one occasion, there in the hall, unwrapping a veil from her hair, was Frances, who, I thought, was still in Delhi with her unlikeable husband. I should normally have been embarrassed at meeting so suddenly so close a friend of Jane; but this was not a normal evening and I was not my ordinary self, and without wondering what on earth she could be doing at Machen's, I said, 'Darling, I have been waiting for you since eight o'clock.' She went up to greet her host and partake of the punch, looking much too well-dressed for this literary occasion. She had two glasses of punch and we descended to the lounge of the 'Crown' for a quieter talk and a commonplace drink and for reminiscences of India. She was much less irresponsible in her chatter, I noticed, now than in the old days, when she had been the terror of political tables with her indiscretions; and she referred only once to my life since her departure: 'I gather from Jane that you have amicably separated.' I said, 'Yes'; and deciding to risk a move myself added, 'Is Claude staying in Delhi?' She replied, also, with a simple 'yes'; which told me (I think) what I had rather hoped to know. I had never liked my Lord Pantalone.

They turned us out long after the legal closing time; and we went up to the sitting-room filled with the smoke of Machen's tobacco and the noise of everyone talking too much and simultaneously. At two o'clock I thought one might decently say goodbye and I offered to drive Frances back to London, but she sensibly said that I was no fitter than she was to drive twenty-five miles in the dark; and so I went down to telephone the Rickmansworth Garage for a taxi.

I opened my eyes in a large bedroom and looked up at the ceiling fifty feet above me and thought it did not look familiar. I looked past the three tall windows, and then knew I was not at Peterley where no bedroom has three windows. The ceiling was now at a more usual height and I turned over to inspect the inner side of the room, and saw Frances sleeping peacefully beside me. I should have expected a leap out of bed or some violent action by anyone confronted by this situation; but the mind marvellously makes its decisions almost ahead of you, and it apparently accepted so very tangible a fact with a placidity that astonished me; and I sat there trying to reconstruct the events of the night before— or rather this morning—unless we had slept for twenty-four hours—or for three days. But where were we? Frances had surely not been foolish— or mischievous—enough to bring me to her husband's house? But she was capable of it; and this time panic overcame me, and I got up and drew aside the curtains. Wherever it was, it was not, thank heaven, Upper Brook Street. In a new office block opposite I could see through a window a business man busy with the columns of the morning newspaper. Slanting to the right was a quiet street with some greenery and a statue at the end. It was all unidentifiable, until a bus went by below with its route listed on the front, and I guessed then that this was Victoria and that we were at the Grosvenor Hotel.

Frances was still asleep, confident, I was sure, that she was safely at home. I sat down at the dressing table to dredge my memory for the forgotten happenings of the night; thought that a cigarette might help, and found some monogrammed ones of Claude's in her case, and through the blue smoke contemplated the quiet room, the sleeping woman, and the ridiculous situation.

It was amusing now to remember that Frances was probably the woman I should have married. When I returned from Botany Bay we had resumed our friendly contacts, which had always been those of cousins who see each other frequently and for whom the family relationship takes the place of the sentimental one. We were always at each other's parties; we rode together; and we were continually meeting at the same houses. When I went to stay at Aunt Emily's, she would be there; and I was always invited to Clifton. I remembered, as I stood looking through the window at what I believed were Grosvenor Gardens, the time when she had driven over to Peterley for lunch, and I had told her that Jane and I were to be married. 'I think it's a good idea. Jane will make an excellent wife.' But she added, 'And what do you feel about it?' I am remembering now my answer which seemed so silly at the time: 'The only thing I feel is the desire to run away with you abroad.' I think she laughed, and said that was the usual reaction of bachelors. Too late I realize that these sudden spontaneous outbursts that seem at the moment so stupid or misplaced are indeed our real uninhibited self making its ineffectual protest against the course of action our will imposes. The set and currents of the sea's surface move in quite other directions than the sea's depths. I began to wonder if the repressed idea had persisted for four years, and had still had enough power to bring us at any rate as far as the right station.

I took another of Claude's cigarettes, which were too full of Turkish tobacco for my taste, and decided to ring for breakfast, and then realized I had better wake Frances first. I saw she was wearing one of my pyjamas, which mystified me; but, then, I couldn't understand how I came to be wearing one either. She opened her eyes, looked up at me and said without too much surprise, 'My God, David, are you still here?'

'But do you know where you are?'

'Of course. At the Grosvenor. What time is it?' I said I hadn't the least idea, or even which day it was. 'Well, I hope it's Saturday. Hand me my bag.'

She sat up, looked at herself in the little mirror and began imperturbably combing her curls: 'Have you rung for breakfast? Black coffee and cream and toast for me. Whatever was in that brew of Machen's? I haven't the slightest headache, but I certainly woke up in the wrong bed. How do you feel?'

'Quite normal, except that I can't remember a single thing after leaving Amersham.'

Frances had a clearer head than I, for she apparently remained conscious throughout, and I learned that we had driven to the top of Park Lane with the idea of dropping her at her house. The night air must have cured my sleepiness, for we went over to the Lyons Corner House at Marble Arch, but found only a coffee-bar open. We tried the one at Leicester Square, and that too was only serving coffee. I had then, according to Frances, suggested we turn in to an hotel to have some sleep, and had decided on the Grosvenor as the one where we were not likely to be known; and on the way we had picked up the pyjamas and a large suitcase at Bina Gardens. The Grosvenor at four in the morning had very tolerantly admitted us and given us what must have been a suite reserved for Rajahs and not in frequent use. The maid came in to open the door to the sitting-room, where breakfast had been laid, and there we sat for an hour drinking coffee and talking of the past years.

I learned how she had come to be at Machen's: the old fellow had wanted to thank her personally for helping to have his Literary Fund grant increased. 'It was a miserable sum. Enough to keep in him tobacco. I'm ashamed at the way we treat our artists. Actually I worked on Claude and he worked on B.' I asked when she was returning to Delhi. 'David, if you mean are Claude and I separating, the answer's "yes". It's going to be an amicable divorce, with a manufactured adultery. We haven't quarrelled or anything like that. Claude is full of rectitude and dullness, and I've never been used to either. As you know. As you can see.' I went to shave while she sat smoking and planning a return home that should look natural. Eventually we decided it would appear much more convenable to stay and have lunch.

I went out, to cash a cheque, into a London where shreds of mist were still hanging on trees and buildings as though left by a celestial stage carpenter. I had the feeling of not being in the world I had inhabited the night before. Machen's party seemed a shadowy fantastic rite performed in the light of torches to the clash of cymbals and the shouts of Bacchantes, a long way off in time and space. I began to think that if I were to ring him up to make sure it really happened he would probably answer: 'But, my boy, there must be some mistake. I haven't had the pleasure of seeing you for three weeks.'

Frances meanwhile had persuaded Judy to ring her house to say that she had left Frances at Peterley, where they had both stayed after the Machen party, and would the maid bring down her things this afternoon. 'I thought that was rather clever.' But when I asked if she had warned Father that she was under his roof in spite of non-appearances to the contrary, she airily replied that she was leaving that to me. 'After all, it was your silly idea to come here.' So ended innocently and pleasantly enough, without headaches and ill consequences, the night of Machen's punch.

Twenty-ninth

This was bailiff's day. I don't know how old the custom is, but once every three months there is a settling of accounts, and Knight comes up from Peterley Farm, and Harris makes his trip from London for the hour of business before dinner. It was some years since I had been present. 'It's good to see you, Mr. David,' said Knight. 'We need all the hands we can get nowadays'; and the lawyer's greeting was equally significant. Griffiths brought in the sherry and Father his account books, which were spread on the long library table with the others. I find that financially Peterley is sound, but only so long as we continue to lead the present modest kind of life. There are no longer any encumbrances on the estate. The Buckinghamshire rents keep the house and gardens going. To Jane go the rents from the Bournemouth property in return for the farms that came to Peterley in the marriage settlement. 'Mrs. David gains financially by this arrangement,' Harris commented to me, 'but in the long run you will benefit by the consolidation of farming land here,' and Harris almost licked his legal jowl at the thought of such a lovely stretch of 'meum'. I was interested to learn that I myself was living on the Newbold rents at Rugby, and I discovered why I had to live so economically. Most of these rents had remained unchanged for twenty-five years, and the small houses in the side-streets were still letting at seven-and-six a week. Harris was dissatisfied with the situation and pointed out that although the rows of houses were well built, repairs were beginning to eat up much too large a percentage of the rents: 'In fact, if it were not for the two licensed houses, the shops, and the cigar factory, there would be a net loss. And some of the tenants are already demanding gas lighting or electricity. If you could sell, I should advise it.'

'To some stranger who would immediately raise the rents? No!' replied Father.

I was thinking about Rugby, and how I had played on Great-grand-father's farm, and waded in the Avon which runs shallow over pebbles alongside the Newbold Road after it has turned the mill-wheel which has been turning for Rugbeians ever since Danish days, the mill-wheel over which Wycliffe's ashes, floating down the Avon, must have fallen, and the blood from Naseby field. Later, this mill-pond was the favourite bathing place for the boys of Rugby School; and then the new railway from London to Birmingham was built and they had to throw a bridge over the road just above the mill; and the School gave the company a thousand pounds to erect a stone structure in the Gothic manner, with turrets and battlements, so that their pleasant walk should not be dis-figured. It isn't there today; and I suppose it was taken down when the line to Crewe involved the widening of the track.

We had dinner at eight, and I noticed a Givry-Clos St. Paul was brought up; and I deduced that Harris in his day had drawn as many corks as codicils.

Afterwards when we were sitting smoking I reflected that it might be the moment for finally settling down. Peterley was unencumbered and could support a family, and even two horses, and my own income could pay for a small London flat if Susan insisted on one, which I doubted. And Polly as Mrs. Robinson would not, of course, need financial aid. There was a long talk about local history when Harris said something about the country being as conservative as one could wish, and the Old Man agreed it might be so now, but that in the past it had been the centre of radicalism and disloyalty—there were the Lollards to begin with, and quite dangerous ideas they had for those days—Wycliffe held the living of Brill over the hill. Some of them had been burned in Great Missenden—Hardy in Chesham merely for owning a Wycliffe Bible—Tylsworth in Amersham for professing Lollardy. And later it was the Quakers: they were surprisingly strong in the county, as though all the burned and buried Lollards were rising from their graves as Friends. The Penningtons had the Grange at Chalfont St. Peter and intermarried with the Penns. Jordans the Quaker shrine is only five miles from here. Father went on to say that Matthew had been fascinated by Buckinghamshire heresies and had made notes for an article that, as was Matthew's way, he never wrote.

He went up to look for it and read some extracts on regicide in Buckinghamshire. Matthew had found that an astonishing number of the regicides of Charles I were county men. Cornelius Holland of Creslow, two Fleetwoods of Chalfont St. Giles—Colonel Thomas and his brother George—Thomas Scott of Aylesbury, Simon Mayne of Dinton, Sir Richard Ingoldsby and John Bigg of Waldridge, Thomas Chaloner and his brother of Steeple Claydon. He had also jotted down, as though it almost amounted to regicide, Colonel Richard Beke's marriage to a niece of Cromwell, and the descent of the Russells of Ellesborough from Cromwell's daughter Frances. There were three postscripts: 'In all the county, only two landowners joined the King, a Verney of Claydon and his relative a Denton. Query, what part Lord Wenman, of Twyford, played in Gunpowder Plot?' and (as though the bald fact were self-explanatory): 'John Wilkes elected M.P. for Aylesbury.' Matthew had gone on to seek the causes of this continuing heterodoxy with the help of forced parallels with Provence and Franche-Comté and had decided that it was due to the persistence in the Buckinghamshire hills of the Celts who had survived the Saxon settlement. He may be right: there are still the short, dark, wiry men to be seen about the county;

but whether here more than elsewhere I doubt. And they would have to be an even earlier kind of Celt than the Belgic ones that Caesar knew, who were certainly not short, dark, and wiry.

October

'Lynwood,
Amersham,
Bucks.
16th October

Dear Mr. Peterley,
Sixty-five—or it may have been sixty-six years ago, it was Christmas and pigkilling time at Llanddewi Fach Rectory, Carleon-on-Usk. I remember very well standing in the kitchen and watching the sausage making and the admixture of savoury herbs: I remember even better the rare flavour of the sausages at next morning's break-fast. Since that day in '69 or '70, I have not met that memorable taste—till this morning. The sausages are exquisite indeed: thank you very much.

Has it ever struck you? This, I believe, is an eminently material age; and oddly enough, all the "materials" have gone bad. As you say, the sausage no longer exists—save in Leicester. I wish you could come down the hill and see us. A journey with only a cup of tea and a drink at the end of it; but how about Saturday next? I should like to have your views as to the medal or badge by which the Hermit recognized the Knight in the Grand Saint Graal.
Yours very sincerely,
Arthur Machen.'

I explained in my letter that daughter Janet and I, with others of less note, had been discussing 'things violently destroyed or things silently gone out of mind' when we naturally fell to thinking of the sausage, and one of the company recommended a firm in Leicester whose product could be eaten by a man of taste. I had ordered some for Peterley, and had asked that a parcel should go to Amersham for a second opinion.

147

Twenty-fourth

I open this evening's *Standard* and see Miss Peters' face smiling at me from the page, and find she is appearing under a stage name with Leslie Henson at the Gaiety in *Seeing Stars*. My first interest in her was theatrical and was not, after all, misplaced.

Mrs. M. thinks it might be diplomatic if we were occasionally seen together in public, and I went to Tidworth with her, and we rode and talked of plans for the future. She has decided to come to Town once a week; has even arranged for a sitting-room to be available every Thursday at a hotel I had never heard of—'It's rather clever of me to have found it. I'll never run into any of our friends there, and yet it's quite near to Paddington.' What disturbed me more was that she has decided to take old Shipman's advice and reinvest her capital in the M. concern, which I suspect to be shaky. Naval men are children in business matters. I could not dissuade her. 'Shipman's the most honest man I know; and, what's more, he's investing heavily himself.' It was unavailing to reply that completely honest men were usually foolish, and that retired admirals knew as much about investments as stockbrokers did about azimuths. 'David, I don't like your cynical way of looking at things. One would think you'd been dogged by misfortune, instead of living an easy and comfortable life. Besides, I don't find it amusing. You carry it too far.'

December

Eighth

Arrived at the White Hart, Braintree, at eight o'clock after a fine walk from Dunmow. There was a night breeze that blew the thin clouds across a cold moon. After a grilled steak and a bottle of wine I relax in the smoking-room and feel like an amalgam of Hazlitt, R.L.S., and Hilaire Belloc, apart from a numbness in the legs which I hope will be gone by morning. I must do twenty-five miles each day. Essex so far is rural and dull. I hope Suffolk proves richer.

Ninth

By the time I had come through Halstead to Sudbury, my feet were blistering, and, what was worse, the north-easter had increased in force and biting power, and the cold was colder. I put up at the Four Swans, drank some hot punch and thought of Gainsborough and tried not to think of the walk tomorrow to Bury St. Edmunds. But the mediaeval pilgrim was capable of it, and so ought I to be, with more sins to justify the penance, but no real reason at all except caprice for this determination to walk from London to Norwich. No; perhaps not caprice. The desire to do something as an escape from doing something else.

There was fortunately a crowded house at Peterley this Christmas in which I could lose myself. Great-aunt Emily brought Celia from Yorkshire; and Uncle Roger, in order to see his daughter, came over from Annecy, tactfully leaving Madame de C. behind. Mark and Judy came; and Sally *sola et casta*, Henry being in India; and so I invited Cousin Richard who adores her just this side of loyalty to Henry.

There was one evening after dinner when we went down to the 'Polecat' on the Prestwood Road as a friendly gesture to the local pub, and ordered pints of ale for ourselves and the regulars of the public bar. We built the log fire into a blaze and sat round in a semi-circle. Billam had come down, and Warner; and Cousin Richard was in a boisterous mood, and had been inveighing against the Scots, and asserting that there must be something in mountains that makes men morbid, moral, and misanthropic, to judge from Norway, Geneva, and Scotland.

'And Wales, and Wales,' asserted Warner. 'Let me not let slip an occasion to denigrate the moral Welsh.'

'And Wales,' amended my loquacious cousin, who went on from the unhealthy puritanism of mountaineers, by way of a pint of beer and a non-sequitur, to the dangers of being a genius, maintaining that good writers were bad men and that the converse held true too.

'Literary historians have carefully neglected this, or have tried to conceal it, so that the unsuspecting student has the impression that Shakespeare would have been fit and proper company, or that no harm could come from an evening spent reading poetry with Shelley. How dangerous these assumptions are we can realize if, removed from the hypocrisy of public platforms and official histories, in the sanity of our own study with a meditative cigar or a philosophic wine, we reflect on those biographical facts which are lightly treated or not at all by the literary gentlemen who are trying to make a living for a wife and two daughters by writing an unnecessary study of Milton or Marlowe.'

'You need not go further back than Geoffrey Chaucer who has been called the "Father of English Poetry"—"in literal truth" says the scholar Pollard, who thus qualifies for his diploma in journalism.'

'In which case,' interjected Warner, 'its mother must have been a French professional.'

'We can pass over the fact that he owed his early promotion and worldly success to his having prudently married the sister of John of Gaunt's mistress—or as one writer decently puts it "the sister of the Katherine Swynford who ultimately became John of Gaunt's third wife". You will observe the reticence of that "ultimately".'

'We can even excuse his defalcations or mismanagement in the Customs Department, because Customs and dishonesty are inseparably connected. The one produces the other, as Sycorax Caliban. Whatever happened, he lost his official appointments, for which his poetry does not give us any reason to believe he was particularly qualified.'

'Shaken a little by this turn of Fortune's wheel, the poet forsakes Venus and Ganymede and Cressida and other such persons of doubtful respectability and begins writing about Truth and Steadfastness and Marriage and such-like duller but more moral subjects. But one should not conclude that his conversion was complete: among the last scraps of information we have is the charge of rape brought against the elderly father of English poetry.'

Here Sally looked startled and interested, and Cousin Richard paused to empty his tankard. But Billam, who has a bright legal mind, could not help an interlocution: 'We are in the fourteenth century and the documents will be in Latin. Raptus can of course mean simple abduction, or forcible possession, not necessarily for pleasurable ends.'

'We are beholden to you,' said Cousin Richard. 'You are correct. "*De raptu*" is the phrase. I compliment you on your perspicacity (although this was not quite the word he pronounced). "*De raptu*" is the phrase, and it could signify merely forcible possession of the young lady's person—but the whole person, not the part, if I may so put it. But then you are faced with a graver problem. This would not be a case of a gentleman of poetical temperament losing his elderly senses over a young sprig of womanhood, like our friend Willy B. Yeats——'

'But without benefit of Voronoff,' said Warner.

Cousin Richard nodded in his direction in acknowledgment: '—like

Willy Yeats, which would be understandable, natural, and a pardonable *crime passionnel*. It would be a piece of sordid feudal financial trickery—the seizing of a young heiress whose fortune you could play ducks and drakes with until she came of age and married the first comer who would relieve her from her feudal guardian. Chaucer, having lost the fruits of office, tried to recoup himself with a well-oiled ward; and since no one had thought fit to entrust a young heiress to the creator of the Wife of Bath, he tried to remedy the omission by force. You tender moralists can take your choice: rape or rapacity.'

He was brushing aside with a sweep of tankard the minor miscreants of the next two hundred years when I protested that we should not leave Malory out of this gallery of ignoble wights.

'After all, the rape in his case was a genuine one—on Joan Smyth, a farmer's wife of Monk's Kirby in Warwickshire. And after conferring knighthood on Mrs. Smyth, he carted away some of her husband's property, which is not the act of a gentleman. But in any case, even without these two feats of prowess, he would have qualified for our roll of dishonour, and qualified at an earlier age than Chaucer. For at the age of thirty or so he was already being accused of theft. In his maturer years the charges varied from theft, robbery under arms, cattle raiding, extorting money with threats, and an attempt at murder (unsuccessful it is true, but of a duke of all people). The only pleasing incident, among these rather professional crimes, is the stealing of some bags of coin and some religious gewgaws from the Abbey of the Blessed Mary at Coombe. But then he may have had anti-clerical leanings, since he helped a fellow freebooter to remove some of the worldly possessions from the unworldly brethren of an Essex abbey, and stole a horse from a vicar.'

My nomination of Sir Thomas Malory was unopposed, and he was enrolled among the good writers. And so was Skelton *nemine contradicente*, and Greene, who, after, as one literary historian put it, 'surpassing Marlowe in creating noble women types', died from over-eating pickled herring at a party. Which brought us to Marlowe himself, of whose pretension to decency Warner made short work: 'A Government informer in the pay of Burleigh, the Himmler to the Gestapo of those brave Elizabethan days, who compelled my university, I regret to say, to give him an unearned degree. "How he occupied himself after taking his bachelor's degree is not known," writes his biographer. Unfortunately it is: he occupied his time abroad spying on those Englishmen who for good reasons of their own had sought safety on the Continent from the heavy hand of the Virgin Queen. This creator of noble women types came to a fitting end in a drunken tavern brawl after trying to stab his cobber from behind. A magniloquent writer; a sordid rogue. I should have liked to hear his comments on Miss Dane's playlet.'

'When we come to Shakespeare,' announced Cousin Richard, putting down his mug, 'you might reasonably hope to be done with the frailties of human nature. Your hopes would be vain. The National Bard is almost appallingly human. Some critics, like Hallam, shudder and pass by; some bury the human interest in footnotes or appendices; the majority of our literary historians decently forget it and concentrate on his mind and art, his universality, his rhyming couplets. One must take it as an article of faith that the creator of Perdita and Miranda is good all the way through. Now these two ladies, in particular, who are usually brought out as chief exhibits in defence of Shakespeare's goodness, seem to me to be very damaging evidence indeed. They are, to anyone who looks at them closely, the signs of repentance of a penitent sinner, the wish-fulfilment phantoms of a mind morally shaken and now sincerely longing for the youth and innocence it has hopelessly lost. As Jules Lemaître said of Paul Verlaine: "I sometimes wish I had sinned as deeply as that man, so that I could as sincerely repent." If you have any doubt of the kind of life Shakespeare lived, read the last plays; but do not fall into the error of those literary critics who would have you believe that after the storm and stress of the great tragedies Shakespeare emerged at last into the peace and serenity of the final dramas. Behind Perdita and Miranda stands Caliban. There is no peace and no serenity; evil remains as strong and durable as good; there is no finality to that world-without-end struggle between darkness and light which makes up our human life.'

After that prologue he called for more beer and took a quick look at the career of Shakespeare before turning away in disapprobation. Looked at in the dispassionate way my cousin has of looking at *idées reçues*, it does seem to be such as would disqualify anyone from becoming a city councillor or president of the local Y.M.C.A. It begins with a serious crime. The story of the deer-stealing may not be strictly true: but legends must be in character. If they told stories about Shakespeare's stealing— and we should make no bones about it: stealing deer is stealing, and it must be presumed that, if Stratford had been a port, young William would have pillaged the wharfs—then it must have been because that was the kind of thing Shakespeare did. It is then asserted that he advanced in life by holding horses outside theatres; and when we remember that theatres in those days, to the respectable members of the community, ranked with the houses of prostitution which they adjoined and to which they served as adjuncts, this is not an occupation to which we would apprentice our sons. Our next record is that he received a large sum of money from a fashionable and dissolute nobleman. He certainly came rather suddenly into a fairly large sum of money. What services a young hanger-on at a theatre could render a wealthy nobleman may be left to our ingenuity to imagine. The problem (if problem there is) is not made simpler by the fact that this same young man wrote some sonnets, which are now well known and misunderstood. The dark lady can claim only a third. Many of the others are addressed to a man; and most literary historians, with some lack of discretion, strive to show that the man in question was the very nobleman who had been so strangely generous to the young author. Of Shakespeare's later life in London we know little except that he soon became wealthy and invested his profit in property, both in London and Stratford, although we still find him living with some Displaced Persons from the Continent with no very sound standing in the community. And almost the only contemporary anecdote of him is, from what we have seen, very much in character and concerned with a visit to a brothel.

His end was, according to report, as irregular as his life. He died from over-drinking at the age of fifty-two after being incapable, for the preceding five years, of any serious dramatic work.

'I do not,' my cousin continued, washing the dust of Shakespearian studies from his throat, 'want to bury my theme in examples, and I will travel lightly over the seventeenth and eighteenth centuries, remarking only the fact that while religion and romanticism were strong in the earlier seventeenth century you will find a greater depth and power of villainy than is to be found in the period of irreligion and classicism from 1700 to 1800. The greatest of the Jacobean poets, Donne, in his early days lived such a life as needed fifteen years of devotional asceticism to atone for. The Reverend Mr. Herrick, our charming lyric poet, was apparently only too well known (though not necessarily as a poet) to all the young ladies of his country living. The puritanical Milton obtained his first wife of three as part of a money debt owed him by her father: the father bringing pressure on the daughter to marry this priggish fellow and so reduce the financial obligation, the wooer using his status as creditor to win the father's consent to the misalliance.'

'Down with the regicide,' stammered Warner in approbation, who is descended from the Protector's brother.

'We are now,' said Cousin Richard portentously, 'approaching the Romantic Revival and Lord Byron, and the ladies may, if they wish, leave the room, for the details I am about to narrate of the lives of these great

153

writers of this wonderful literary renaissance are not fit for feminine ears.'

'But surely,' Sally objected, 'we ladies may stay in court, since there must have been feminine co-operation in these misdoings, somewhere?'

'Ah, it is that "somewhere" that worries me.'

And Warner, perceptive as always, and amused, shouted, 'Capital! Capital!'

I hurried in with a plea that it would be too easy to include Byron; but Cousin Richard disagreed: 'He is too magnificent a writer—of prose, of course—to be left out. And I must point out that he was in fact even worse than the Victorian moralists suspected, since his principal misdemeanour was hidden from them. That semi-incest with his half-sister, Mrs. Leigh, is a trifle I can overlook. After all, he had a respectable precedent in the case of Admiral Burney, who eloped with his half-sister, the novelist. I doubt if he did it from diablerie. I suspect she was the one woman for whom he felt both a sensual and an intellectual attraction. I can almost feel it myself, after all these years——'

'Whose?' interjected Sally. 'Hers or yours?'

'For that interruption, I will deprive you of the satisfaction of knowing the more serious charge; and proceed to the legend of his sacrifice in the cause of liberty that I cannot subscribe to. The English ridiculously confuse the Greece of petty brigands and exporters of currants with the Greece of Pericles. He went there to escape the boredom of his mistresses, and he died from his life of excess which had made him incapable of withstanding a malarial fever. Yes; it is too easy to use Byron as an example. Let us look at two other great geniuses of that time. No poet has a sounder reputation for morality than Wordsworth. It rests upon public ignorance. As a young man he can only be described as an unprincipled wastrel. Given an expensive education by his guardians, he neglected his studies, failed to qualify for any good employment, and wasted his own time and his guardians' money in turning himself into a revolutionary of the most ridiculous extremity of views and an admirer of the French Jacobins.

'Thinking apparently that, if the Golden Age was really about to begin, there would be no need to work at all, he went to France to study the workings of liberty, equality, and fraternity at close quarters. He celebrated this new emancipation of mankind by seducing a young woman who had befriended him at Rouen. When a daughter was born and Wordsworth was faced with the duty (even in so completely liberated a country as France) of legitimizing it by marrying its mother, the future laureate left hurriedly for England. When he had become a poet and able to colour

154

these crude realities with charming phrases, he spoke of being "dragged back to England by a chain of harsh necessity", the said chain being the cruel insistence of his guardians. As we know that he had wholly disregarded his guardians' wishes during the previous four years and had gone where he pleased, we find it a little unconvincing that he should, just at this moment, hearken to their voices, just at this very moment when he should rightly have disobeyed them and done his duty by staying in France and making an honest woman of Annette Vallon. "Stern daughter of the voice of God, O Duty, if that name thou love, who art a light to guide, a rod to check the erring, and reprove," he wrote a few years later. But when the occasion came for him, he didn't bother very much about that guiding light or that stern daughter. Later, while living on the income from a capital sum given to him by a wealthy friend, he wrote, among other things, sonnets on the "corruptions of the Higher Clergy", on "Monastic Voluptuousness", and even on "The Marriage Ceremony", with that lack of humour for which of course he is justly famous.' When he had finished with Wordsworth and with his pint of beer, he turned to Shelley and another pint.

'Let us leave the rustic moralist for someone else who also shared the ridiculous notion that a revolution will inevitably bring in a new era of peace and righteousness. Let us consider for a moment a young man who thought that human nature was capable of perfection, that men would be happy if only they were free, and that romantic poetry was somehow superior to hard work. The record of Master Shelley is worse than that of young Wordsworth. Expelled from Oxford in circumstances that do discredit only to himself, he forthwith abducted the very young daughter of a wealthy publican and stifled her scruples with the doubtful legality of a Scots marriage. He soon found her intellectually incapable of absorbing his theories of the perfectability of human nature, and, after she had become the mother of two children, he abandoned her in favour of the very young daughter of the philosopher Godwin, whose ideas the poet had borrowed.

'But Godwin, however much a philosopher, did not let his philosophy obstruct his common sense. Whatever annoyance he may have felt—or shown—at Shelley's debauching his wife's daughter, he reflected that the seducer was heir to a baronetcy and a fortune, and he compounded the misdemeanour for a loan—or rather, for the first of several loans.

'Not only did he sell his daughter once, he repeated the sale at frequent intervals, whenever he was desperately short of cash; and Mary Godwin must have proved one of the most expensive young ladies ever purchased.

Meanwhile, of course, realizing that the protector of Miss Godwin and the father of Miss Godwin's child would never return to her, Harriet Shelley, whom Percy had promised to emancipate from false ideas, threw herself one winter's day into the Serpentine in Hyde Park. *To a Skylark* and *The Triumph of Life* are well known, but there is a piece of homely prose that has not found its way into the anthologies: it is the official "Information of Witnesses on View of the Body of Harriet Smith, December 11, 1816". Harriet Smith, of course, is Harriet Shelley.

'Young ladies still respond, I believe, to the verse of Shelley; but when they next quote *The Sensitive Plant* they might do well to remember that winter morning when Harriet Shelley flung herself into the icy waters of the Serpentine. They may then console themselves with the spectacle of inescapable Fate overtaking the poet six years later. Unhappy even with the daughter of a philosopher, Shelley was already discovering that the wife of his friend Williams would be the ideal companion for himself, when something tempted him to set sail across the Gulf of Spezzia regardless of the coming storm. The sudden squall upset his boat and flung him into the waters of the Mediterranean, and Harriet was avenged.'

He ended with Shelley, whom he seems specially to detest; and he made it plain he ended because it was closing time and not because he had run short of examples: 'A rogues' gallery, if extended too far, becomes tiring like a museum. But it is amusing to see these figures, round which time and the inaccuracies of hack writers have cast a romantic glamour, as they really were. It is salutary to see the hand that wrote *Hamlet* farming the rates of his native town. Salutary that is to say if it checks that ridiculous human aspiration to rise, like a hot-air balloon, to the stars, and that transcendentalism that leads us only into the clouds and not above them. "On and on and up and up" as our fatuous Prime Minister has said leading us towards war. "Excelsior," shouts the bad poet. To which I would reply, "Oikadé—Homeward." '

The 'Polecat's' door closed, fifteen minutes late, behind us, and we stepped a little unsteadily out into the cold air. I ought to have realized that we were in no condition to take the short cut across the fields. Oliver insisted on displaying his skill in balancing, but slipped off the five-barred gate he chose for the experiment, and tore his coat on the latch; and when we came to the ditch behind Kyle's farm, which had once I think been a Ha-ha, Cousin Richard assured us it could be jumped. He supported his statement by saying that his cousin Kenneth at Emmanuel was the champion for the long jump, and to show that this skill ran in the family he took a leap across, but miscalculated the width in the dark, and landed in whatever was at the bottom. It sounded like a thick mixture of scum and water-weeds, and a startled frog.

1936

January

This twilight of two years, not past nor next
Some emblem is of me or I of this.

Eighth
But it is time this state were changed. Whatever else this year will bring, I am determined it shall bring order into what has been for too long now an unpurposed way of life. I must, at whatever cost to myself, tidy things up; trim, cut back, and weed. There have been signs, even on the estate, of neglect, as though my own personal decay has its physical image in the house and gardens. The buildings are not kept up as they were once; there are loose tiles on the roof; there is much repointing to be done on the brickwork of the stables; the gate to the farm is sagging; the dove-cot has not been painted; and the vegetable garden is not the neat patchwork it used to be. The leather harness goes ungreased and the brass unpolished. Even the Tempietta is falling back into its old state.

If only to restore this little world to health, I must put my life in order, since the one can never be anything else but the reflection of the other.

We are all scattered again after Christmas. Susan is with her family. Cousin Richard has gone skiing with Mademoiselle Françoise, although I suspect his skiing consists of wearing embroidered braces and leather pants in a well-heated hut. Frances fortunately stayed a few days and walked with me in the drives as we used to do years agao. She listened to my resolutions and doubted if I could carry them out.

I am writing this at the Club in a room looking over the Embankment Gardens to the rain-swollen Thames, brown with mud and stringed with barges and ships waiting to go up under the bridges. It rains, and at five there will be a moon's eclipse, portending astrologers know what.

Twenty-first, 12.55 a.m.
The death of kings.* For an hour ago the King died. I had waited at Gray's Inn, at the Billams', thinking the news might come through, but left at twelve with Finley. As I came in to Bina Gardens, the Miss Tennyson who has the ground floor emerged and spoke to me, thus marking the portentousness of the occasion, and asked had I heard the news? I replied that at a quarter to twelve he was dying. But she was imparting information not acquiring it, and said, 'He died at two minutes to twelve,' and retired into her room. In all my long time at Bina we have never spoken to each other before.

Susan, with all the common sense I had feared in her, writes what she says she did not have the courage to say yesterday:

'I want you to think and give me an answer—if you can—on Wednesday. This sounds ominous, but it isn't really. What you say may hurt me—but be truthful. Do you, my dear, really want to marry me? What I mean is, do you really want to spend the rest of your life with me? And even have children? You say "I want to try the experiment out first," but only years will really tell that. Do you really feel that I am the person you really need in every way, or that this is just a very intense episode, one of many equal episodes? I did foresee that matters would come rather to a head, but I didn't think they would so quickly. Do you think you will be able to love me with that inner tenderness which is quite apart from passion? Marriage is only a good institution in those rare cases when it turns out to be a success! But it is a fence that protects one's inner life from all the slights, slanders and social problems that otherwise would make for unhappiness; and I couldn't come and live with you without it. Don't think me selfish or that I'm unwilling to sacrifice anything while you go through the sordidness of a divorce for my sake. Is it all worth while to you; and are you willing to wait until everything

* In the diary this entry follows immediately on the previous one.

158

can be done properly? This all sounds very sententious; but I must put my side of the case to you. I shall quite understand if you do not share my point of view; but I doubt if we could—if that were so—continue our very delightful companionship.

Your letter has just come while I am writing this. Your doubts are absurd: you must know what you mean to me, and that to hear your voice on the phone is—so nice that I sit up late sometimes in the hope of hearing it. I would love to see you. Try to understand this letter; and if you can say "Yes" to my questions ring me up. I long to know. Aren't we rather crazy? But it is delightful and one day it might be lovely.'

Ah, but these are precisely the questions that I cannot answer, but shall one day soon, whether I will or no, have to say 'Yes' to.

The Wednesday afternoon visit to the small hotel in Bolsover Street has become a ritual, like that weekly visit of Samuel Butler, according to Festing Jones, to Handel Street (how appropriately named!) just across the Tottenham Court Road. But mine is with different intentions and different results. We gossip, discuss the future, have tea—China with toasted scones—and, in the half-hour before she leaves to catch her train at Paddington, we, rather ridiculously, I think, continue to behave with all the propriety of a couple in Jane Austen illustrated by Brock. But all the same, Judy's advice is still in my ears; and many of these final half-hours have been spent in importunities to her to come away with me for a time. She will not agree. Not from prudery; since she knows well the nuances of physical expression, and all the evocations of sensibility that may range from the frivolous to the passionately restrained, and be now amusing, now adoring, and at times brutally possessive or bitter. She will come to Bolsover Street, but no farther—and I suppose that, from M.'s daughter, is a great concession. I am too much committed now to change my mind; nor do I think I want to: she is the most admirable of demure young women, witty, and with so much character as never to be boring. She might have been fashioned expressly for Peterley.

March

It is March and the snow is gone; the frost has broken; and rifts of blue are in the sky over the Trent valley where a warmer easterly blows. A winter sunshine gives a pale life to the flat landscape. I am staying with Cousin R. at Four Oaks. We skirt the damp copses and cross the frozen ridges of the ploughed fields, and see Tamworth tower four-square on its castled hill, and the slender spires of Lichfield through the bare trees. He remarked that civilized life could exist only among the ruins of the past which represented its stages of slow development, just as the grown man kept some relic of his childhood and hung the atrocious photograph of the Eights crew on his study wall. 'This for example,' and he swept an arm over the view in front, 'is only moderately fine as countryside. There must be much finer scenes in the Dominions; but they can never be as satisfactorily habitable as this. They can never content. Or if they do so, then the contented colonist is living at a lower level of receptivity. He is not obtaining from the country all that a settled country can give. The land isn't yet humanized. He can't see further back than the general store or the stone trading post.'

I was amused to hear him theorize an emotion I had experienced in the antipodes. It was true that all that was lacking in N.S.W. were the Roman ruins, the abbey churches, the battlefields. 'But here,' he went on, 'I shave within sight of St. Chad's shrine and the spires of Lichfield, and put on my trousers in view of Tamworth tower and think of Ethelfleda, Alfred's daughter, who inherited his trousers and drove the Danes out of the valley—so much for the subjection of women in the old days. I buy my tobacco at the village store which Johnson passed when he walked in to Birmingham to try and cure his hypochondria. It doesn't, of course, improve the quality of the tobacco, but it gives a flavour to the transaction, like buying from a purveyor to royalty.'

Walked with him today in to Lichfield. He insisted on the walking: 'You can't decently enter a cathedral city in a stinking car, any more than you can play Handel on a pianola. You have to be tired and thirsty to enjoy an inn. We're not a Band of Hope picnic in a char-a-banc.' I remarked that it was better to travel hopefully than arrive; but he pretended not to hear. And so, along the road I had driven with Dorothea two years ago, I walked in an unfriendly wind and listened to him talking about Erasmus Darwin as though he had spent most of his evenings in the Botanic Garden, and with a most unnatural affection about the Swan of Lichfield. But he may be right that there was a higher cultural standard in the provincial towns of the seventeenth and eighteenth centuries than existed later: London had not yet eaten them up. They were the centres of their little world; and a little world is not necessarily a petty one; Frankfort and Weimar nourished Goethe, a world genius who never knew the world capitals. We are all citizens of the world today, but we remain little men, ridiculously out of scale.

There was some sense in his theory about walking, for we ate a seven-mile meal at the 'Crown', washed down with ale which he said was not the concocted chemical fluid of the Birmingham University School of Brewing: 'Not for nothing was Burton built on Trent. A School of Brewing! Leading to the D.D.—Degree of Dilution. It's as impractical as a Course of Courtezanship or a Seminar in Seduction, that would grant a B.A.—Bustuarium Amicus; the M.D., or Magister Diabolarium; a Ph.D., Philandriae Doctor; or even, if one survived, a D.C.L., Doctor Cunni-Linctu.'

I objected to his Latinity, and he called for more cheese and ale. By three o'clock he considered we were in a proper state to pass through the cathedral portals into the Middle Ages.

We stayed for Vespers, as I had stayed once before. I love these dead ceremonies, offices that have lost all meaning by repetition, but have gained instead a pacifying perfection like that of Byzantine frescoes or Raphael paintings that soothe but not inebriate. My thoughts were away at Cremorne in summer, where on Saturday afternoons everyone came to rest on a shaded verandah and the only sounds in a hot still world were the grasshoppers and the tram that each half-hour clanged down the dusty hill to the ferry and climbed slowly up again.

I came out of the Australian sunlight into the wintry dusk of Lichfield Close, where my untidy nostalgic emotions were out of place and the sash windows looked down their eighteenth-century brickwork in disapproval. The episcopal pediment frowned as I passed, and I scarcely caught the murmured, 'And your lawful wife?' The deanery was equally critical, 'And Mrs. Manning?' A light went on in the Precentor's house and a blind lowered like a winking eye, 'And Polly?' The architectural restraint was carried to the point of frigidity; and I nearly shouted, 'Baroque to you'; and the cathedral behind me would have fallen like the walls of Jericho at the sound of that word. We walked down from the Close towards the light of the market square, past the house where a plaque commemorates a Roundhead who leaned out of the upper window and shot the Royalist major who from the cathedral towers was training light artillery on the town; and we came opposite the most humorous statue in England, the effigy of James Boswell, self-confidence in marble, the cocked hat, tilted nose, the perky sword, the hand lightly reposing in the breast: 'Good citizens of Lichfield, behold in me the Laird of Auchinleck and the friend of the illustrious Johnson who, I am sorry to say, did not inspire his sculptor to a masterpiece to judge by the hideous statue opposite. In my life I was vain and conceited. I often made an ass of myself. I was frequently drunk and I committed adultery on very many occasions. But I had a kindly heart and I wrote a good book, and my memory may outlive your cathedral. And where I dwell a shade in the fields of asphodel, I am happy, for I converse with witty men and I have not yet been rebuked by a bishop.'

'And Belle van Tuyll de Zuylen?' I asked. 'Do you remember her? Or are the dead happy because they have forgotten?' He did not even seem to see the point of the question.

A pity, I remarked, that we did not have Johnson's *Life of Boswell*. 'It would have been a failure,' Cousin R. replied, 'but we have something just as good: a miniature pen-portrait.' I said I couldn't remember one. 'Ah, no; you couldn't very well remember what you've never seen. It has never been published. It's in a curious manuscript I'll show you at home.' I thought he was joking, but he quoted parts of the Johnsonian character sketch; and later, at the house, I copied it out:

'It is not possible for the candid biographer to assert that his conduct in London was at all times consistent with Christian principles: but who among the meretricious distractions of the metropolis can escape unscathed? It affords some satisfaction to reflect that if his lapses were flagrant his repentance was sincere; and few men have combined such consciousness of rectitude with so many divagations from its pursuit.

His natural gifts were wasted by diffusion and too often impaired by application to the grosser pleasures. Failing in any original achievement he was content to transmit the affairs of others to posterity and being a man of easy familiarity with the learned and the great he allowed little to elude the vigilance of his observation or the malice of his pen.

He was of a race that by nature possesses no qualities to endear it to foreigners; but long residence among the polite society of

London had mitigated much of the Northern coarseness and qualified him to be the friend of Reynolds and the intimate of Beauclerk. He did not so much attract by the lustre of his conversation, which was discursive rather than deep, as by the cordiality of his spirits. Mirth is more contagious than melancholy, and he who can disseminate pleasure will not lack friends. He carried no valuable freight of ideas and could make no substantial contribution to talk; but he had the art of imparting momentum to it, as a horse will give motion to a coach without sharing the discourse inside.'

The shops were closing and the streets were darkening. I raised the question of a local bus service and the time for leaving: but he said the time was fixed by the hour of opening of the pub at Shenstone. 'It opens at six. It will take us fifty minutes to reach it, walking moderately'—that word 'moderately' chilled me, since my cousin and moderation were strangers to each other—'So we leave at five-ten.' It was already five-fifteen, and we left. At his home that evening he showed me the 'interesting MS.'. It was a collection of the lost curiosities of literature which he had been thoughtful enough to rewrite. I can remember only some of the fragments. There was a letter from Rhodope to Charaxus complaining of the dull nights with Sappho; some extremely unflattering testimony by Xantippe at the trial of Socrates, which Plato had thought it wiser to suppress; a letter from Lancelot to King Arthur while the latter was at Rome; and many extracts from the registers of the Roman aediles* which, according to his recension, contribute a great deal to the biographical history of the early Church.

It has been settled that I am to prepare a case for Jane to get a divorce. Old Harris was as nervous as a spinster with a burglar in the house when I discussed it with him, and at one point put his hands over his ears and begged me 'not to put it that way: you must remember that collusion between the parties wholly vitiates any application to the courts', and then as though to mitigate the directness of the statement blew his nose loudly into his large handkerchief. 'I am to assume that you will be in no position to defend the action?' I said that that was an assumption he could make with safety. He is to let me know what terms Jane will propose as

---

* The aediles were the Roman officials responsible for keeping the registrations of the licensed houses of prostitution and their inmates.

to division of the estate; he imagines they will be merely the ratification of the present ones. He started a question; stopped, as though reviewing all its implications; and changed it to, 'Have you considered residing, yourself, at Peterley?' I said I would move permanently there in the autumn. 'Ah; good. Excellent. A wise decision. I'm happy to hear it.'

We went, Polly and I, to Greatham this Saturday and spent a pleasant afternoon with Wilfrid Meynell, who was at his reminiscent best, full of good-natured anecdotes. We drove back to London through a chequer pattern of sunshine and storm, Polly in the highest spirits from this literary encounter, and envious of Viola's model cottage. 'If I had one like that in the country, I think I could be happy; and you could come every week-end.' I dared not tell her of the even older one at Peterley Corner where the gamekeeper used to live, with its little casements peering through thick ivy and the leaning apple trees in the garden like old men bent with rheumatism supporting themselves on sticks. You could not keep a mistress on the estate, with Susan at the house. I was coming to fear it would be impossible to keep one anywhere; and I knew the moment was approaching when I should be forced to tell this young woman for whom my desire was as strong as ever that we could no longer continue this charmingly unconventional life.

We celebrated at Gray's Inn yesterday the acceptance of Billam's play. Mitchelhill had taken it and given it to Priestley to read. He was quite enthusiastic; said it needed only some rewriting in the third act; and offered to do the revision himself. Billam has agreed to the changes, and J.B. insists that the collaborator appear on the bills under a pseudonym: he is not willing to risk his own name, yet. The changes are to be mostly in the dialogue; but there will be one character modification.

April

Seventh

Judy is back in town now that Mark is in the Mediterranean, and we have taken to dining together twice a week, before a theatre on Tuesdays and before her small parties on Fridays. Frances joins us occasionally with young D., who came over to see about the sale of the family Armagnac and has apparently stayed on to see more of Claude's wife. Judy has thought it her cousinly duty to talk to me seriously about Mrs. Manning. She confessed she was worried. 'Susan has obviously decided that you two are to get married; and this move to London is meant to make certain of it. I'm sorry she's giving up Park House; she'll never be happy in Town. What are you going to do?' I said that I should probably in the end decide to do as she wished. It would please the Old Man; would suit Peterley; and would be generally approved. Judy looked thoughtful and leaned over to pour a little more wine into her glass. 'Have you slept with her yet?' and when I shook my head, she added: 'Well, for God's sake do, before you decide. What have you been doing all this time?' I said nothing about our meetings in Bolsover Street, and defended myself as best I could by confessing I had been suggesting the idea frequently and recently to Susan, so far without success. 'Probably,' Judy said, 'because of your musical doll. You may have to get rid of her first.' She finally decided we ought to go away for a summer holiday, chaperoned, and out of England, where Susan would have no fear of being recognized. 'And if it's a success come back and get married and off my hands.'

Twenty-second

'Dear Mr. Peterley,

What a noble gift. I assure you it was most highly appreciated. Thank you very much. There's a judicious character in Dickens who says: "A bit of savoury pork pie would lie atop of anything you could mention, and do no harm." How right he was—though his remark must be taken as a meiosis and be read "much good". You are right: that is indeed an enchanting quarter, that region that lies to the right of the Gray's Inn Road. When I first saw classic Baker Street going up to Lloyd's Square I realised those emotions of which Keats wrote—"upon a peak in Darien". I have been trying to capture the essence of the place for forty years. In vain, of course; but I think my nearest approach was somewhere in a story called "A Fragment of Life". But do you know Barnsbury? If not, lose no time, or it will have turned into residential mansions. Semper aliquid novi: the last time I was there, in '29, I took two Americans, and came into a street that was absolutely new to me, though I had wandered about Barnsbury off and on for thirty-five years. It ran down a steep hill, and each doorway was guarded by a pair of Egyptian Sphinxes in peeling, chocolate-red plaster. The Americans were awed and amazed. And then, there is the 3rd Pointed square, executed in whitish-grey brick according to the lights of 1830–40. But, there is no end to marvels.

With many thanks and all good wishes.

Yours sincerely

Arthur Machen.'

May

The Hartland marriage that Susan had witnessed at Abingdon, and described to me, has broken down. It was an ideal match, and they were by far the handsomest couple that one could imagine; she tall and graceful, with masses of that copper hair that captivated Rossetti, and with something of the face of Miss Siddal except that the nose was too thin for beauty, and with an extreme pallor of complexion that made her eyes seem green, as they may indeed have been. Her eyebrows unfortunately were too light, almost of a light reddish tint; but it was a defect that men who met her were probably not conscious of among such abundance of other attractions; and particularly as she often, with the careless generosity of the richly endowed, left open for admiration some perfections of a bosom which I agreed with her in thinking it were a shame to hide. Alice Peers was freer of any false modesty than any woman I have known except Cousin Judy. She has found refuge with a publisher and I write to congratulate her on finding work where her literary gifts may have some scope.

On Whitsunday with Polly to Windsor, and we walked down the Long Walk to the statue of George III which, viewed from behind, looks like all statues in all Russian films of the revolution of the proletariat. Thence by Virginia Water to take tea in the garden of the Rising Sun, I took her to see Cousin Richard in his new quarters in Bathurst Street when we came back into London, a dwelling somehow characteristic of him. The ground floor is an empty shop, and the second floor is empty too. As you climb the stairs your footsteps echo in the empty room. But once his door is opened you are in the cosiest of apartments, which he shares with Warner: thick carpets, old walnut furniture, and sagging easy-chairs covered with cretonne covers. There are books everywhere, and tins of John Cotton, and on the mantelpiece two magnificent jugs, one of them printed with a design of the famous Ironbridge in the Severn valley. He was enraptured to welcome Polly to what he called his nooko-tine; showed her his book rarities and his collection of prints of the early railways. I suspect him of being excessively thrilled at entertaining some-one he assumed was a kept woman; and was amused at his venturing to show her one of his illustrated Catullus when I remembered the much more daring volumes *à tirage limité* she had brought back for me. They seemed charmed with each other, and she accepted his invitation for supper. We went up another flight to a small dining-room nearly filled with a long refectory table. I remarked its ridiculous antiquity, and he admitted the deception: 'From the Abbey of Tottenham. The worm-holes are made only by the finest marksmen.' But he had two fine pewter candlesticks, and his Swedish china from Gustavsberg looked well on the unpolished wood. The walls were a flat white and the only decoration was a carved figure of dark wood wrenched from some cathedral stalls. He gave us a good fish kedgeree, some sage-flavoured cheese from Dorset, and, as a savoury, Bath Olivers covered with reindeer paste. Polly seemed willing to stay indefinitely, and I had to bring her away at half past twelve, to our host's disappointment, who showed his pleasure at the evening's encounter by asking me as I turned to descend the stairs whether I should like to receive an invitation to the next Party Rally at Nurem-berg. I felt bound to refuse this so flattering offer, and rejoined Polly in the street below, who felt that the evening had finished too early.

June

Sixth

I have written goodbye to Polly and have never done anything so unwillingly. I have told her quite truly that she is the only woman for whom I have any passionate feeling; but this must be poor consolation to someone who in the next breath is asked to go. 'It was all very well to dissemble your love, but why did you kick me downstairs?' There was a time when I foolishly imagined that Miss Morel of Weymouth Street or Mrs. Robinson of Queen Anne Street could still remain as much a part of my life as Mrs. Manning at Peterley; but not only would Susan object, but I should be disconcerted if she didn't. I am sacrificing the possibility of passion with Polly for all the certain difficulties of a second marriage. I am losing those Saturday retreats into the countryside. We shall no longer lie together in a fold of the Downs on summer afternoons, or walk a gorse-strewn lane that was once a Roman road, or meet under the gas-lamps of a railway junction. We shall become worse than strangers; we shall be two people who can never meet.

Tenth

Polly had rung me and asked if I would call on her this evening at Weymouth Street. I had been dining at Sally's and couldn't leave too early; and it was eleven o'clock when I turned from the Marylebone High Street and knocked on her door. She was wrapped in a dressing gown and said that she had given up hope that I would come and had gone to bed. She had a bed-sitting-room, a small narrow one, rather poorly furnished for a block of flats in this district, as though the tenants were all virtuous. She was wearing black silk pyjamas which I did not like; her taste was generally simple and good; and I was surprised by this sudden lack of it. She was nervous, and kneeled uneasily on the bed. The black clothes contrasted too sharply with the exceptional whiteness of her skin.

It was an embarrassing meeting. I knew it was Susan I should rightly be abandoning, not Polly; and it was no consolation to remind myself that she was only reaping the harvest of her two years' refusals, since, after all, the only proposal I had made was not strictly an honourable one. But while I had unwillingly accepted an unsentimental relationship, and had gradually recovered from those early impetuosities, Polly had gradually developed for the one person who was admitted to share her loneliness the affection she had scornfully assured me she would probably never feel. And by having rejected the passionate relationship that I once demanded, she had now lost all possibility of attaining it in the only way, the legal way, that I suspect was her real desire. And now she was aware that not even a full surrender, a life together on any terms, would save the situation. I said that I had made up my mind to settle down at Peterley with a wife, and that I had to give up some of the pleasures of singleness. She was curious to know who it was, and annoyed when I replied that she wouldn't know her. She began to cry a little, and pleaded with me not to break off our life together. Her weakness was rather pitiable compared to that contempt and pride of her encounter with Richards, and I felt a little sorry for her: she looked worn, tired, and woebegone in these detestable black pyjamas, her lips unreddened and her eyes red. At twelve she made some coffee and we drank it in silence, although neither of us, I think, really wanted it. She demanded if I couldn't really consider life together 'on any terms. I should not expect marriage, if you would be unhappy'; and I assured her that nothing would have pleased me more than to have lived with her, but that sooner rather than later I had to come to terms with the family.

'And they wouldn't accept me?'

'It's the other way round. You wouldn't accept them and the kind of life they would insist on. You would run away at the end of a year; and I would not blame you. Living at Peterley would be a waste of your time.'

'And this woman—she fits in with all that?'

'It's her kind of life.'

'But you're not in love with her?'

'That's not a question you can expect me to answer.'

'I can't see how you can be, considering the times we've spent together when you should have been spending it with her.'

At one o'clock I got up to go. She stood up and held me back and said vehemently: 'David, you're making a mistake. I think you've grown out of Peterley without being aware of it. You are going to regret this attempt to go back. And serve you right.'

I agreed that this might be true, but that I didn't see any alternative. I had for once in my life to act prudently and sensibly and do the right thing and not the romantic one. I asked what she was going to do, and she sharply replied that that was her business now, and would I go. So I went down the stairs into the Weymouth Street I had once imagined as the scenery for quite a different story; and felt so spiritless and irresolute that I went on mechanically walking through Manchester (shades of the shady Hertfords!) and Portman Squares to the Arch, and across the Park without one solicitation or one comfortable thought.

Rehearsals for Billam's play in progress, and I attend sometimes with George and his co-author, although Priestley does not like rehearsals watched. He has chosen Peter Goldsmith as his pseudonym and is keeping the collaboration a close secret, probably until it is known if the play is successful. I am perplexed as to the real personality of Priestley behind the successful writer. I still remember with affection his *Brief Diversions*, long and undeservedly out of print, and wonder what became of that brilliant young man. Today, the idealism of the writer is out of keeping with this hearty countryman who possibly plays up his Yorkshireness for his audience; and he seems to share with that other provincial writer who likewise forced his Muse to support him by walking the pavements of Fleet Street and who also emphasized the earthenware beneath the glaze—to share with Bennett too great a respect for worldly success.*
Priestley's eye for theatrical effect is wonderfully keen, and so is his sense of what is dramatically appropriate; and yet I doubt if he has it in him to give the stage anything more than the contemporary problem play or the sentimental comedy.

The casting has been excellent, and Billam's play, which, in any case, was almost actor-proof, would be safe with Basil Radford and Louise Hampton and Arthur Sinclair, and I am in love already with Nancy Hornsby who is playing Madge and is always in the arms of a young fellow as repulsively handsome as handsome young men on the stage always are.

There is a satisfaction from activity; a sense of power from achievement. I've started to order my own life, and feel more tempted now to order that of others. I am preparing the case for Jane to go to court with; I've decided to take leave of Polly. I'm taking to regular hours at the B.M.

* Peterley might well have revised his opinion had he known the strong anti-Establishment line Priestley was to take in later years, and which does not at all make for worldly success.

in order to finish the Cleveland and Bold essays and tidy up this sprawling bibliography of the seventeenth-century editions. Perhaps I'm dining too often with Cousin Richard who's always as full of the hot gospel from Munich as of Niersteiner. If I find myself eyeing the riding-whips at Peterley I shall be worried.

But Susan was not I think displeased by a show of resolution on Wednesday. We have taken tea and toast and talked about the future too long in the extravagance of a hotel sitting-room; and I have always felt aggrieved that the hotel takes the cash and certainly gives us the discredit for behaving quite otherwise than we do. I told her that all was being arranged for a divorce, and that there would be no obstacle to a marriage after the Absolute; but that I was determined that we should spend these summer holidays together, even if virtuously. She began by objecting; she said we had discussed and settled all this already; that she did not like these probationary honeymoons, and in any case did not intend to play the part of a probationary bride. I replied that I considered it would be much wiser if we spent our summer leisure together, even if she did insist on a chaperone; and she may have scented in my words the threat of an alternative for me if she refused; for she said: 'You're asking an awful lot, David. Of someone, that is, who doesn't go in for that kind of behaviour. Why do you think it's so important?' Which was a ridiculous question from this scented and pomaded young woman with her expensive coiffure and every fold of her dress suggestive in its restraint. She said she'd think it over. I replied that all she need bother about was where we should go, but certainly out of England. 'Oh, but of course,' she added; and I was amused to notice that she had already unconsciouly accepted the idea.

A note from Polly:

'David,
        I hate to bother you, but I must see you for a few minutes; and it would be better for both of us to meet in public, so I suggest the Lyons at the end of Shaftesbury Avenue at seven tomorrow. Can you try to come?'

She was already there when I arrived, startling as always, with that pale, rather imperious, face under the heavy black hair. She was calm, friendly, and mistress of herself again; gave her order and turned to me: 'David, if you're still serious about this marriage, then I want your advice. If there's nothing in the future for us two, if you go through with this marriage, or if you just don't think we're likely to resume any kind of relationship, then I think I shall marry Harry. But I want to know what you think.'

I once thought that it would be the ideal marriage of convenience for us; but I knew now that was the kind of dream fantasy one constructs for the future. Polly was making me make up my mind once and for all. But time and indecision and Susan had already made it up for me, and I no longer had the power to save Polly from Mr. Robinson. I answered that the marriage was not certain, but that I felt I should eventually decide for it, and that I couldn't expect her to wait for the mere possibility that all my plans might collapse and leave me free. 'But not to marry me, darling?' she retorted but without any bitterness. She was right; and I said that if she wished for the stability a marriage would give, then she should accept Henry, who was a very decent, serious fellow, and wealthy, and slavishly in love with her.

'Yes; David, but . . .'

'But what?'

'Well; never mind; that will be my affair.'

She made little attempt to eat; but smoked several cigarettes and drank two cups of coffee, and for a long time said nothing; but at last: 'If that is your advice, then I'll take it. You won't mind? You won't misunderstand when you see it announced, and think that I'm in love with him, or anything like that?'

For a moment I felt my old love and admiration for this girl revive; for a second could almost have leaned over the table and thrown away my doubtful future to save her from her own. I had only to say four words, and she would have thrown Henry to the winds. Instead I stared at the hideously veined brown marble of the wall and said nothing. We got up and went out. She refused a lift; held out her hand; and said good-bye and walked towards the Underground.

There was once a countryman who, disdaining to follow traditional pursuits and earn an honest living, decided to go up to an Academy of Learning. Here he soon came to the conclusion that it was necessary for the welfare of the country that the chief ministers should be removed, preferably by assassination. Pondering the means of achieving this post-graduate aim with the least discomfort to himself, he concluded that the patriotic missile must travel a considerable distance to enable him to be modestly retired; and for this a knowledge of ballistics was needed. He devoted himself forthwith to the subject and, entering the College of Ordnance, gave himself up so zealously to this science as to win the approbation of his superiors and to be speedily promoted. From the command of a single battery he proceeded by degrees to General of Artillery, and finally won the gratitude of his government by his spectacular defeat of those rebellious subjects who had ignorantly conspired against the established order.

Seventh

To Southsea today with the Billams for the first performance of the play, now called *Spring Tide*, at the King's Theatre. The acting is excellent: the actors are sure they have a winner in this gold-plated fairy tale. It is produced by H. K. Ayliff, with scenery by Paul Shelving, both chief magicians once in that lovely palace of illusion in a back street of Birmingham where Barry Jackson presented to our wondering eyes the drums and tramplings of a thousand tragedies, and Mr. Ayliff called up all the heroines of history in front of Mr. Shelving's scenery, so that I could adore Miss Ffrangcon-Davies in all her Pythagorean transmigrations.

Sixteenth

We—for I have been so long with this play that I can almost use the plural —opened last night at the Duchess Theatre to a full house whose final applause promised a long run. The Billams and I sat in the second row; Priestley hid shyly in one of the rear boxes and made George take the final curtain alone. I opened my programme, and there was Stella, the whole elegant length of her, posed in an evening dress in a Marshall & Snelgrove advertisement.

We went with Gordon Harbord's crowd to the Savoy for supper, and afterwards Billam and I decided to walk back alone to the Inn and discuss the new play he has in mind. We were coming up Southampton Street, and paid no attention to a young woman who seemed to appear suddenly ahead of us and as suddenly vanish; but as we came to where she had been we heard the sound of a baby's voice. We looked round, and there was nothing to be seen in the street at all, and we both decided it must be an auditory illusion in this empty street at this time of the early morning. Then we heard it again, quite distinctly, and had no more doubt of its being the cry of a small baby. But it's a short street that runs up from the Strand to Covent Garden, and even a baby would have been visible; and we stood there mystified not knowing what to do. Perhaps under the impulse to do something however haphazard Billam went over to the public telephone kiosk, opened the door, and saw the baby wrapped in a woollen shawl in a woven basket on the floor. We stared at it, and jointly said we would be damned. The baby stared up at two men in long black tails and tall white collars and smiled happily at the peculiar sight. We both now recollected the young woman who had for a second appeared and vanished. The opera hats and the cigars had deceived her—it may have been a similar deception to that former one whose fruits we were now viewing—into thinking that this struggling barrister and this unemployed *flâneur* were two wealthy bachelors whose hearts would melt, etc. I'm afraid they didn't.

Billam, a married man, contemplated the return home with a baby he could explain only by saying he found it in Covent Garden; and as a married man he rejected the idea out of hand. I would have no more success with Susan, who was doubtless aware I had a mistress and would certainly refuse to include the child in the marriage settlement. We felt extremely silly, dressed as we were, taking turns at carrying the clothes basket with the baby in it, and must have looked it as we searched for the nearest police station. The sergeant on duty did not find our story too incredible. He opened the shawl. 'Fine child,' he remarked, as though inspecting abandoned babies had made him expert. 'Striking resemblance too.' Billam could not help asking to which one of us; and the humorous sergeant reflected and said: 'Well, now; that's difficult. Perhaps it was a joint effort?' But he made no fuss about jotting down the particulars and seemed to take our word for the occurrence, and we disclaimed paternity and responsibility and he jotted down that too. We gave him one of the Savoy's cigars and departed for Gray's Inn and sleep; but once there we mixed some milk and whisky and settled down to discuss the new Australian play, and so sat till half past three.

I arranged to rise early and go out for the morning papers; but early proved to be nine o'clock and the Billams were still asleep, and it hadn't occurred to me that I had no change of dress here, so that I had to emerge into the morning bustle of the Gray's Inn Road, clothed for the theatre, and buy the morning papers at Chancery Lane Station. The notices are all good. The *News Chronicle* speaks of the exquisitely comic moments, and J. L. Hodson adds: 'If London has finer comedy acting I should like to see it. The piece has its imperfections, but it will be odd if you do not spend a very jolly evening with it.' The *Post*: 'Though at the heart of it just another boarding-house fairy tale . . . this first play of a new pair of dramatists is at the same time a brightly written human comedy. It won the heartiest possible reception.' The *Daily Herald* puts Louise Hampton's red wig in its headlines, but admits that the new comedy made a considerable hit with a full house. The *Daily Telegraph* says:' Only great courage or complete inexperience could have led two dramatists to write a play as simply and unashamedly romantic as *Spring Tide*. . . . As I know nothing of George Billam or Peter Goldsmith I cannot say whether they are heroes or tyros. All I know is that they have, against all the odds, pulled it off.' We opened *The Times* with trepidation and closed it with satisfaction: its approbation was almost benignant: 'There is nothing against this play except that every word of it cheerfully, indomitably and gaily sobs.'

We were still discussing the reviews at the breakfast table at midday when A. of the *Express* came in from his flat below to congratulate the author and to arrange for a personal page in *Cavalcade*. Before he left, Billam told him jokingly of our encounter with real life in Covent Garden this same early morning. The journalist in A. almost jumped out of A.'s clothes, and did in fact throw A.'s hat on the floor in vexation. 'What a couple of goddamned fools! You should have rung me up. Why, that's the kind of publicity you wouldn't get once in a thousand years; and you throw it away!' I don't know if he referred to the publicity or the baby. 'You should have arranged to adopt it. We'd have had headlines: "New dramatist finds real drama in Covent Garden." "Stepping out of the Duchess Theatre last night, the applause of a first-night audience still in his ears, George Billam ran smack into a great tragedy of real life. . . ." O my God, what a story lost!' He sat down to brood over the loss to journalism until he realized he ought to be on his way to the office; picked up his hat, and went out a sad and disappointed man.

At dinner at the Étoile with Cousin Richard and Henry and a Swedish engineer who talked most of the time about the possibility of there being such a thing as non-axiomatic mathematics, maintaining that it was in fact impossible, that the axioms must exist whether in the shape of formal logic or as unformulated psychological assumptions or intuitions. I was uninterested in these refinements, and I asked Cousin Richard where, if one wanted a really secluded holiday, one could go nowadays. 'You know your Europe,' I flatteringly prompted. He lit one of his cigars which he says he gets cheap from Germany, and gave himself up to serious thought. 'I can think of two places ideal for your purpose: Tatranska Lomnica and the west of Ireland. Both are at the ends of the known world.'

August

Thirteenth

Rabbit Island, Lough Corrib, Co. Galway. Cousin Richard was right. This is the world's end. I am surrounded by the waters of this weird lake that lies in the hills of Galway; and in this solitude, this inhuman desolation, you feel already in another world than the one you left, but the world of Childe Roland rather than of faery.

I crossed to Dublin with Susan four days ago in bitter cold, with a heavy wind and a choppy sea. Dun Laoghaire was but old Kingstown writ large, and Baile Atha Cliath only a more bedraggled Dublin. The other Susan was already at the Shelbourne waiting for us. We drove across the country to Headford, which is as far as the road runs or the Republican postal service will reach. From there we had to walk the mile down through stony fields to the pebbled beach of the lake, and wading in the shallow water launch the boat and row over to the island. The water passage is a tortuous channel, and at one place is just five feet wide between two rocks that are visible only from the wash of the petty waves on them.

The island is wooded, and lies about a mile out. There are no beehives and no bean-rows, only a wooden cottage, and, but for the lapping of the waves and the wind in the thin trees, a silence that lies everywhere like a cold mist. The owner, an eccentric peer, must have invested all his common sense in this miniature property, for he has built a stone pier for the boats, has set his verandah to face the post-meridian and setting sun, screened the cottage with trees, and built into the living-room a wide brick hearth for the log fire. We are as hidden from the world as we could wish; and if we could forget it—or if I could—for four weeks, we might be happy. But when you surrender something you do not forget it: renunciation only makes it more desired.

In the mornings I chop wood for the fire, and the two women cook. On fine afternoons we walk or drive on the mainland or fish the lake fishlessly; and in the evenings read by the glimmer of the oil-lamp or talk in the firelight. A quiet, a pleasant, but not a passionate life. Susan still wants to put off to a later stage the intimate relationship she would prefer to follow marriage; and now ironically I am no longer the importunate and impetuous lover of the private hotel and the Berkshire village. My life is now all in order, tidy, swept, and garnished—and as desolate and empty as this flat lake and these stony mountains. The past was finally wrapped up and put away two days before I left, when the books and pictures came back from Polly, with my letters still in their envelopes as women love to keep them. But there was also a pencilled itinerary on a visiting card: 'Aug. 19 Bristol Hotel, Oslo. 20–22 Maristva Hotel. 23–26 Kviknes Hotel, Balestrand. 28–30 Vatnahalsen Hotel. Then Molde and perhaps Trondhjem.' Astonished, a little uneasy, and greatly hesitant, I sent back a card in turn: 'C/o Miss Kenny, Cloonkeely, Headford, Co. Galway.'

Sixteenth

We have been here six days by the European calendar but about a fortnight by the Irish one. There has been one fine evening and some days of thin rain when the hills vanish and the lake seems a part of the falling water, and the inhabited world shrinks to a patch of grass 600 feet square. We are no longer quite alone. Looking out of the window yesterday morning I saw a donkey grazing by the little garden. But why a Headford farmer should have thought it worth while to ferry him over to this thin pasture, I cannot think: it does not seem less credible to imagine he fell with the last shower.

We live peaceably together. The other Susan is the woman who has never had to do anything in her life, and is contented in doing nothing, except that she misses her horses. She has tried to read a book, but decided that it was an over-rated pleasure. She admitted however that she had read all, and even re-read some, of Lever; so I have wired Greene at Dublin to send Jorrocks. The library here is mildly amusing: some Birmingham, all Somerville and Ross, Sale's *Koran* (my landlord is a convert to Islam), some Yeats, and one treasure—Emily Eden's *Semi-detached Couple*—which is as unexpected as that piece of carved jade that a Kerry man once told me was found deep down in a west of Ireland peat-bog. Yeats who reads so well in London, as he did in the long music-room of Bulli when we talked of Ireland, is not, I discover, the reading for the glimmering evenings of Galway; and I am glad I brought some Duhamel.

We picnicked yesterday at the ruins of Aghanore Castle, a square unbuttressed keep whose military grimness—smooth stone with one single opening like a black eye-patch—was testimony to the brutality of the Norman soldiery within and the brutality of a cowed peasantry without. The walls of the enceinte are heavy with ivy, and bushes sprout from the fissures of time. Norman and Elizabethan and Cromwellian have gone, but the tolerance of their successors has not worked any better; and the Celt remains sadly, unsuccessfully, a little anachronistically; shadows in a shadowy country—the living ones are all in New York or Sydney or London.

Nineteenth
I walked up to Headford for the mail this morning and at Miss Kenny's saw the familiar handwriting on the envelope.

'16th August.
On the way to Newcastle. I have sent some more things to Bina Gardens that I must not keep any longer. They are infinitely precious to me, and I parted reluctantly with them. I turned off the dull North Road to see Peterborough that you used to speak of, and found it all you described. We passed through Lincoln and are making for Durham. Another eighty miles tomorrow morning. If only . . . but I must not say it. I am writing with difficulty while waiting for the car to be ready.'

'Durham. 10 p.m. This is surreptitious writing. Henry has gone out for a walk, and I have pleaded fatigue. I must admit that I have begun to long for your company now that it is too late. Norway will have to be interesting for the three weeks to be endured. I cannot bear travelling now when I am not with you. I am faint with all the recollections of our two years together. If there is any change in my feelings, it is in intensity. Forgive me this last extravagance, and do not let it pain you. If I write again and write less warmly, you will know that it is only that I must not let myself be so moved. We sail from Newcastle at four tomorrow afternoon. If only . . . it is too late now for anything but letters—but may I have one?'

On the stone wall outside Miss Kenny's cottage I sat down and stared for a long time at the letter. Its hurried scribble was as full of meaning as its words and both were an accusation. It was a letter that should have never been written; that could not have been written but for my brutality, that had wrung this cry of pain from her. What was worrying me now was whether I had not been worse than brutal, and been stupid. When she asked for my advice, I should have known that her spontaneous heart was incapable of the kind of marriage of convenience I was willing to undertake; but I sacrificed her for Peterley, and left her to pay a price that may be too heavy for her. And now, when it is too late, I am doubting if I made the right decision. Would she, after all, have been so wrong a choice for Peterley? If she can steal away on a honeymoon to write to the man who has abandoned her, she might make a perfect wife; and if she would have fled from the Rector's wife and Mrs. Knight, that is what I always feel like doing myself and lack the courage. Perhaps Peterley needs someone to upset its Byzantine formalism, shock Griffiths, and break some unwritten rules: it might not be too much to pay for a lovely and adoring wife. But I'd already made the decision in the London café. Perhaps it is only because I am in another world that it seems the wrong one . . . *nos et mutamur in illis.*

I could no longer sit still, and began walking the road to Galway. I thought of telephoning Oslo—but would she still be there? Where was that pencilled itinerary? And what would I say? 'Abandon husband and come back stop All is forgiven.' It was ridiculous. And I should have to send a telegram to Rabbit Island too; which reminded me that I was supposed to be hurrying back with the island's mail. So I turned about and made my way across the stony fields to the beached boat. I fished all day, to avoid conversation; and spent a gloomy evening smoking hard and dreading the inevitable remark from Susan when we parted for the night. I could only reply that a touch of the sun when I was out on the lake must have brought on the headache.

Twentieth

I betook myself and my journal into Galway, and in the hotel there wrote what is probably a dangerous letter:

'I have received the letter which you should not have sent and am sending you a reply I should not write. Like you, I am already regretting the decision I had to make; but I knew beforehand that I should regret it. Now that it is impossible, I would willingly reverse it; for the certainty that I shall never touch your hands, your lips again has made the future that I planned seem not worth the sacrifice I made. If it is any comfort to you, I can confess that I have longed for your company every day since our separation, that the memory of our days together has been as great a torment to me as you say it has to you; and that you can be certain that my desire for you as a woman to make love to, to talk to, to quarrel with, and be jealous of, and be near, is returning now when I had thought it subdued, and returning with overwhelming intensity. We are both finding that the life we abandoned was perhaps the happiest we shall know; but there are two seas between us now and there will soon be two marriages; and I must try to forget the happiness of two years that you gave me, and learn that I lost it by my foolishness. If I wrote more it would be what is better unsaid. Our moments of silence were once the happiest of all: now silence has become wisdom.

Once my heart's darling, farewell.'

They tell me there is an air-mail in the Free State. Perhaps it would be better if the letter never got to Oslo at all.

I met an old man yesterday who stopped, as all do, to speak and said, 'I beg your pardon, Sir, but what part of Ireland do you come from?' When I replied, 'Antrim,' he said, 'Now did you see such crops as these in that part of the world?' and pointed to a field of beet that De Valera's import restrictions on sugar had forced them to sow. And when I said I was going to row across the lake to Oughterard—three miles away —he mused and remarked that it must be a fine town now, but he had not been there for twenty years. It is a straggling street of poor cottages and licensed bars. I said, talking of the world, that I had been to Killarney. 'I have heard say it is a great place with lakes.' 'There are five,' I admitted. 'Five!' he said, astonished, although there were five hundred just behind his back in Connemara; 'And seven churches too, I've been told, thanks be to God.'

I am still astonished at the poverty of this people. No shop I have been in yet has had change for a pound. They live on ducks, fowls, pigs, and cows; and bacon-and-eggs and potatoes are their unchanging diet. Every shop is a bar open from ten to ten and licensed for seven days a week. Went this afternoon to Clifden, the very westernmost and least habitable-seeming place in the British Isles. These grey houses, overtopped by form-less rocks and grassy mounds, look like the last ditch of a primitive and forgotten civilization. Edward Garnett with Sean O'Faolain had left the day before and I missed them. E.G. had been the last person I wrote to before leaving England, about a new publication for the Nonesuch Press. I had to row back from Oughterard at half past ten, and it was already semi-dark, with rainclouds sloping from the hills. The lake was a sheet of silence with no wind to stir the waves, dark everywhere with no lights, and I had pains to find the island.

'Kviknes,
24th August

David,
Your letter came after me here. I would not have it unwritten for worlds. I shall have known, at least, that you still loved me. I am not alone as I write. I dare not say—I should not say . . .'

'Morning. Darling, I had to stop. It is another day, and my misery is as unbearable as before. I should not complain, since he is the kindest of husbands to a woman who is as difficult as I am. Darling, I cannot help being unkind to him. I am completely cold. I avoid all intimacy. I have scarcely spoken for three days. I walk furiously, climb moun-tains, drive fast; but I cannot escape. My only refuge is the thoughts of our life together, and that's dangerous. For the last time perhaps let me say I adore you in every way. You are life itself to me. I am sending back your letter.'

Scribbled in pencil was an afterthought: 'I am keeping it. It is my last treasure in this world.'

Since that first letter I have tried to behave as though I hadn't a care in either world—Gaelic or human—but the holiday spirit doesn't fit me well, and the continuous gaiety must have worried Susan, who surprised me yesterday by saying as we kissed goodnight, 'Do you want to go back to England, David?' I said good heavens no, I much preferred this country; and that I thought I'd take a long walk in Connemara if the rain held off. She agreed it was an excellent idea, though perhaps she wouldn't come herself, but that Susan could drive me up to Cong. There is a road from there between the two lakes to Leenane, where one could possibly sleep, and return by way of Kylemore Pass to Clifden or Glendalough. There would almost certainly be no train, but one could hire a car from there to Oughterard.

September

Second

Two days later the rain lifted, and I walked over to the Connemara coast, a route march I could not possibly have done in any ordinary state of mind. Susan, who is tact and common sense themselves, probably thought the healthy exercise would cure me of whatever romantic fancies were disturbing my peace of mind; and, if they had been of the light and fleeting kind, the cure might have succeeded. I recommend to all lyric poets and songwriters who chatter about the blue hills of Connemara or the glens of Mayo to walk for twenty miles through them. These stony places hold no comfort for the sentimental heart. You come through them, and you go quietly back to cultivate your potato garden.

I have returned unchanged, that is to say resigned and miserable; except that any dangerous temptation to fly to Norway was exorcized by these bleak hills. The more I thought about that unwritten scene from an Ibsen tragedy, the less real it seemed. And yet it was an action that could follow quite logically from the situation as it was at the moment. There was nothing to stop my flying over, travelling to Vatnahalsen, wherever that was, and saving Polly from the honeymoon she loathes. But it is a possible action you do not take because it is so melodramatically untrue to life. One does not solve these emotional problems so neatly. This one will have to be solved prosaically and slowly by resignation and gradual forgetting; or by Polly voluntarily leaving her husband. It must be a step she takes of her own free will. At Oughterard I had to call out my Gaelic boatman to ferry me across in the half-dark, as I do not know the channel. He has little English, or else uses it rarely; and after pushing off made no conversation at all through the three miles of darkness until he wished me goodnight as I stepped ashore on what seemed a lifeless island.

Third
Our life resumes its peaceful round of morning work, picnics in the afternoons, and somnolent evenings before a wood fire. We may stay longer here if this sunnier weather holds.

Sixth
A terrible third letter from Norway, scribbled in pencil and nearly illegible: 'I cannot endure it. I feel desperately ill. What am I to do? My heart's desire, I can find no solution. I am numbed with the pain of longing. I adore you.' I cannot now remember the other words; she went on to regret that I had not written again; assumed that my letter must have been meant as a final farewell; swore she could not submit to an intimate life with anyone else; complained that the memory of the past was haunting her. She recalled our days together with such emotional intensity that I burned the letter as I rowed back to the island, and left the black fragments floating on the water behind.

The passage from the mainland is first of all down the narrow inlet and then straight ahead until you see the island almost in line with the hill behind Oughterard. Then you describe a half-circle back towards the stretch of small rocks that carries on the line of the promontory into the lake. In the middle of this is the five-foot width of deep water between two rocks that are barely level with the surface. Once through this gap you are safe in the deeper water of the lake. With each step down the stony track from Headford I had tried to make up my mind; and as I started to row away I knew I must come to a decision before reaching the island. I watched the charred bits of paper float away, and swore I'd decide by the time the narrow gap was reached. There were two hundred yards of clear water before the final choice.

I brought the mail to Susan where she was reading on the lawn, said that I'd had a letter from Peterley which disturbed me a little and that I would have to go in to Galway and try the Irish telephone. She replied that Susan would let me take the car, that the hand-brake didn't work, and did I want her to come? But I said I'd be back quite soon.

I sat down a second time in the un-aired, un-dusted parlour of the Galway hotel where I had composed that other letter to Norway, which

183

I thought a mistake because it said so much and now knew to be a mistake because it said too little. I determined this time to speak clearly.

'I have just had your third letter. I ought not to have written to you before; but now I must write, whatever the consequences may be. I did not, my darling, understand how deeply you felt, either happily about our own life together and unhappily about your new married life. I think now that you are right; that after sharing two years of happiness we cannot now separate simply like two adulterers who have gone through all experience and have nothing to look to in the future.

If you cannot endure the physical travesty with another, I doubt if it will be possible for me either. Come back, and let us live together, as we ought.

This present perplexity will face us later if not solved now; for the union of our two selves cannot be broken without ruin to us both. I should have known this before; but I was foolish. I know it now bitterly. Is it too late? . . .'

I wrote more in this vein until it all seemed rhetoric and a waste of time, and time was becoming precious. I tore it up, and instead I have sent a business-like note:

'Polly, if you are sure your marriage cannot succeed, abandon it now; come back, and when my divorce is through I will ask you to marry me, when you in turn are free. I have instructed my bank to wire you money to Oslo and to wire you at the Bristol Hotel there and at Vatnahalsen the name of the bank to which it has been sent. Take a plane if there is one. I will go to the Red Lion in Bedford and wait for you there. I want you to make your own choice; but I hope I shall see you in Bedford.'

For safety I put Judy's name and address on the outside as the sender. I came back with a lighter heart along the Headford road. At last, and for good, I'd put my life in order; a little late in the day, but just in time to prevent the ruin of four lives.

I announced to the island that I had to leave immediately for Peterley. Susan had enough discretion to ask no questions, and the other Susan who knows nothing at all about anything outside Ireland but knows everything inside said she would drive me in to Athlone in the morning where I could catch the Dublin train. On parting Susan looked down for a moment, traced a pattern in the dust with one pointed toe, and said, 'David dear, if you come back, think very carefully first won't you?' I pretended not to see the meaning of her warning and said lightly that I would send her a wire. 'I think I'd prefer a letter.' I waved goodbye. Susan was smiling without any joy at all. I do not in fact know how I am to break the news to her, although she must have gathered that the break with Polly had not been successful. I imagine she had learned through Miss Kenny that all my mail had the funny stamps of three little white lions rampant on red, green, and blue grounds.

If Griffiths was surprised to see me, he did not show it. I do not know why, after all these years, he keeps up this ridiculous pretence of polite indifference; but I suspect it is because he regards it as a kind of play-acting that makes his job more exciting, as a small boy will behave as though there are bandits behind every bush. It is his custom after asking about my health to issue a brief bulletin on my father's; but I noticed this did not follow. I guessed he was waiting for my question, and I knew he could play this game better than I, so without further skirmishing I asked it. 'Your father is abroad,' he answered, as though it was the most usual of occurrences, whereas he never goes across the Channel at the holiday period. I said I was surprised. 'I was surprised myself, at the decision and at the destination. He received an invitation from the German Embassy to attend some kind of reception after the Olympic Games.'

'But he surely didn't accept?'

'He was inclined not to at first. And then one morning he said to me: "Get my things packed. I'm going to see what these bastards are up to," if you don't mind my quoting his own words. He can be reached through——' and Griffiths suddenly realizing he was faced with one of these foreign names drew his little notebook from some part of his spare figure and read, '——the Leinfelder Hotel, Munich.' Perhaps it is just as well he is out of the way while I so drastically rearrange all my family plans.

Eighth

Now that there is likely to be new life at Peterley I have gone over the house and grounds. They were busy in the stables, and all that has had to be countermanded. There won't be any need for stables under Polly. Ridgley was at work repairing the woodwork of the stalls and racks, and it occurred to me what a magnificent music-room this long range would make with the floor new-tiled and the walls repainted and the old harness, the lamps, and whips left hanging, and the stalls combined in pairs to form alcoves. I told him to continue tiling the concrete floor which I had ordered stripped, and to use a small dark-red tile, and to repair all wood-work, taking off the paint and varnish and rubbing it down with white paint and oil. 'We'll only keep rocking-horses here, then?' was his only comment.

When I came back to the house for lunch Griffiths said that Frances had telephoned to find out where I was. 'I was in a dilemma,' remarked Griffiths, 'as I did not know if you had officially returned.' I said certainly not. 'As I thought,' he added. Apparently Frances had been ringing before. I rang her London house, and she was overjoyed to hear my voice, so that I knew I would be asked to do something particularly difficult, discreet, and deceptive. She said she could not tell me now, but would ring exactly at three; which meant that she wanted to be sure that no one was listening in on one of the other phones, so I said I would call tomorrow on my way to . . . Dorking, as I corrected just in time. 'Oh, dear; how difficult life can be,' was her typical comment, and I wondered what tangled indiscretion she had contrived for me to untie this time.

Thirteenth

Bedford

I have been here at Bedford for three days waiting for the slight vivacious figure to come through the folding doors of the lounge of the Red Lion and say calmly: 'Well, David, I am here. Shall we go upstairs?' As she did at Grenoble. But it was full summer then, and she was sunburned, and almost as unclad as a surfer, and our abandon was in keeping with the latitude. Here, it has been raining since I came, and this provincial street looks merely sodden without looking clean, and, if she came in, it would be draped in a mackintosh and shaking out her wet hair that she would have neglected to cover. Bedford-by-Bunyan is perhaps not the fit place for a scandalous rendezvous. But it is strange there is no word from her. I still cannot believe that last letter was only a young woman's hysterical reaction to a honeymoon. Whatever feelings she had were deep and serious and willed. She must at the last moment have decided as a final act of courage to accept the consequences of our two decisions, and remain the wife she had become. Which means that I am renounced forever; for, knowing her well, I am sure she will never slip weakly back into a change of mind unless Harry is unbelievably stupid. She will have made her decision; and the only proper thing for me to do is to respect it. But I doubt if I have the strength of mind. I shall weakly wait for chance to throw us together again. But at least I have discovered how unreal was my scheme of replacing Jane by Susan. I should have foreseen that the same virtues would have the same defects.

[At this point the diary comes to an end for the time being, when the writer learned of the tragedy that had taken place in Norway. He learned it unexpectedly at a dinner at the Barcelona, the Spanish restaurant in Beak Street, where the plump Basque waiter used to demonstrate how to pour wine down one's throat, from a distance, from a bottle with two spouts. In the party was O., a musician, who was a great friend of Robinson and played duets with him; and half-way through the meal when they were discussing music O. happened to refer to 'poor Robinson and his personal tragedy'. Sally Satchwell was there and tried to turn the conversation aside by inquiring of Peterley how his father had fared at the Nazi gathering after the Olympic Games; but he ignored the question, and, turning to O., asked him what he had meant by the phrase.

It was a tense moment, since everyone there knew the truth except Peterley himself, and no one had had the courage to tell him. O., apparently, was not aware of the connection with Mrs. Robinson, but was intelligent enough to sense the tension in the group, and tried to tread carefully. He explained that Robinson's young wife had had some kind of nervous breakdown while on her honeymoon—'It sometimes happens, you know,' he rather fatuously added—and without warning had left her husband and returned to England. She had turned up at some friends' in London, who had taken her into the country; and there she still was, not ill, but very quiet, and refusing to see anyone at all. All Peterley said was, 'And when exactly did this happen?' and O. replied that it must have been the very beginning of September. No one made any remark; and O. looked round at all the faces for some enlightenment. The silence was uncomfortable, until Peterley broke it by saying very casually: 'I'm not sure this Spanish cooking agrees with me. I'll go out for a breath of air.' He asked Warner to settle for him; said goodbye to O.; and walked carefully to the door, and out.]

December

Twelfth

At the Johnson Club dinner yesterday with Iolo Williams, who read a paper on some minor references to Samuel in eighteenth-century literature and on some unnoticed Johnsoniana. Afterwards we listened to the King's speech announcing his abdication, on a wireless set that Victor Rothschild had set up in the famous Dictionary Room. A fairly good speech. Written by whom? Churchill?* Sir Edward Boyle opposite to me was much moved. 'A terribly scandalous business,' he said. Old Lovat Fraser much affected, too. I suggested to James Laver a short story of how, in the years to come, travelling from one European capital to another, Edward and Mrs. Simpson might in the rooms of some old hotel meet the similar ghosts of the young Pretender and Clementina Wilkinshaw. 'If only they could have sailed away in the *Nahlin* and been lost at sea!' he said. Wilde's son, who sat beyond him, seemed indifferent to it all. The elder brethren took it very much to heart. I could not, without hypocrisy, agree, holding that the old notion of the divine nature of kingship having been destroyed, the question of his moral conduct was a private matter, and that a true marriage, even if founded on 'sensual lust' as one elderly gentleman, long superior to such low feelings, told me, would have been better than the loss of an intelligent man as King.

I shall long remember the shudder that ran through the celebrities in this almost sacred room when the phrase 'the woman I love' came so awkwardly out of the mechanical box. I felt it too.

There was no reason for thinking that Christmas at Peterley would have been a success this year. Father is usually re-converted to misanthropy by the spurious good nature of the season; and I needed no conversion. He arranged for the staff to attend the Rector's carnival, and betook himself with Gurney to Matthew in Yorkshire. I did not wish the quiet house to remind me of noisier anniversaries, and went with the Billams to Cousin Richard's at Shenstone. B.'s play had come off in mid-October, a Priest-

---

* Opinion at the time was that the speech suggested Mr. Churchill's practised hand; which must be gratifying to H.R.H. the Duke of Windsor who has since revealed that he wrote it himself.

leian idyll that caught and then strangely failed to hold the public fancy.

The weather was fine and warm, with soft westerly winds and faint sunshine. We went in to Lichfield for the carols on Christmas Sunday. The choir sang a Byrd motet behind the High Altar, a Holst carol at the West Door, and several other carols at carefully chosen unsuitable places in the building. I was a visitor from two worlds, that of my present and that of my past, and I was meeting my old selves in the Gothic shadows and finding what thin spectres they were. I think a Credo resolutely proclaimed would have exorcized them quite. They may have looked at me and seen in me the ghost of my own future. I listened to the carols without hearing them, and looked at trefoils and pendants, at spandrils and mullion, and up at the cross-springer of the roof groining.

Had I once watched here the ballet of the springing arches, the fanvaults spreading out like the full skirts of sylphides, and the line of triforium pirouetting upon pillar'd toes in a Gothic twilight in this most theatrical of theatres? Had this frozen music once melted for my ears? If, then, I had responded with a joyful heart it was only because it had been filled with the love for Dorothea or Polly, and I had entered into His courts with praise, but not of the sacred kind. Is there really a distinction which can be weighed and measured between the *sursum corda* of the Psalmist and that of the lover? And was my responsive and exultant heart worthless when compared with the emotion of the nun? For who knows whether her ecstasy is not most mystical when nearest to the passion of the lover? In those unregenerate days I had surely been more acceptable in the sight of the Lord than now when I sat unfeelingly among these cold stones.

'How beautiful it was!' said Mrs. B. as we came out. 'Don't you think so?'

'I thought so once, when I didn't really believe in it.'

'And don't you think so now?'

'Now, I only feel that if it's true it's terrifying; and if it isn't it's grotesque.'

' "Sir, said Dr. Johnson," ' said Cousin Richard, ' "I never heard so much blasphemy in so few words." '

1937

January

Eighth

When I returned to Peterley yesterday Griffiths informed me as he took my bag that my father was well, but had some sad news, and I learned that Frances had died of influenza quite suddenly and surprisingly. I shall miss her probably more than anyone else will. I found her irresponsibility amusing and loveable; her family found it exasperating, and her husband intolerable. The memory of some shared adventures will stay with me all my life, and I shall remember her when greater friends and much more important people have been forgotten. She participated in real life as much as a butterfly, that floats through the window into a meeting of company directors, shares in the operations of the company; and yet she was more real than most persons of substance who because they are serious think they are alive. She had obtained her decree nisi in October. Sylvia was to have kept her company in court but was away in Barcelona helping the government forces. Sally went, and afterwards, in telling me of the case, mentioned her Counsel's asking the court to take into sympathetic consideration the incident of the Grosvenor Hotel, 'which although unconventional was not the occasion of misconduct' as Counsel phrased it. Sally said that the Judge was just about to scratch his head in bewilderment when he remembered he had his wig on, and instead screwed up his face in either disbelief or disgust. I went up to my room and finished O'Hara's new novel *Butterfield 8*.

At the Club John Burns told me about the medal he had received from the Pope for his loan of books to the recent Thomas More exhibition and how he had avoided the appellation of 'His Holiness' by the phrase 'the illustrious donor'. He discussed with me the disposition of his library, and I suggested a tripartite division into 'More' for the Bodleian, 'London' for some London library, and 'Other' for sale. I went up for an evening in Warner's flat. Austin, Finley, Williams, and the Alice Peers who was or may still be Mrs. Hartland, there among others. Mulled claret laced with brandy. I heard what had happened to the O'Hara novel, which has had to be quietly shelved in view of the difficulty of getting past the English laws concerning published obscenity with one incident, but that a crucial one in the story.

A long discussion about the quality of Tennyson's writing, which made me realize how little I had thought about the question. Oliver pointed out that we had a sure guide to the poet's feeling for poetry in the *Golden Treasury* which, as Palgrave admitted, reflected Tennyson's taste, an admission confirmed in the official life and letters. Alice Peers very scornful of my lack of clear opinion: 'My dear Peterley, the matter is simpler than you think—if you did care to think. Take those lyrics which are certain to be reprinted a hundred years from now. Count the lines, and find what percentage of his whole output they are. Do the same for, let us say, Arnold and Housman. You will be surprised.' I asked her if she had done it. She smiled and said no, but it was just the job for someone like myself who had nothing serious to do. When we all left I offered to drive her home, and she rather tartly answered that she liked walking by herself because she liked thinking, 'And I don't think you would be much help there.' I apologized for not walking by pleading the distance I had to go. 'And how far is that?' I said, 'To the other side of Amersham,' and that I should do a modest amount of thinking on the way. She looked at me again and was about to say something, but changed it to, 'Goodnight, Mr. Peterley, goodnight.' Which I think was meant to be final: our paths diverge, and always will, was the unspoken phrase.

But going home I thought about Alfred first Baron Tennyson, and today have been up to Matthew's attic to look for the works. They were all there including a copy of the two volumes of 1842 which he had had bound by Tout in a full, dark-green, grained morocco with rich madeira-coloured doublures. Inside on a fly-leaf he had written: 'All that need be preserved. M. P. Divonne, 1897.' Which I incline to think not so erratic a judgment as it seems at first sight. And all today, out of my annoyance at Miss Peers' pretensions to the literary Bench, I have written a reasoned statement of the Tennyson case, which I will send her.★

The house is becoming oppressive: it is strong, abiding, and successful. The gardens are dispiriting for I can bring to them no feeling at all, and they remain wet and wintry. They are portions of a past which came to

★ There is among Peterley's literary papers one called *Tennyson as a minor poet* which must be the one referred to here. Ed.

nothing; and they will stay embedded in those regrets, and each year look more like a wood-cut in a Victorian magazine for Sunday reading. Rose's little temple reminds me not of her happy death in the sun but of an unhappy life in the north. The unrestored stables are a monument to a double failure: there will be neither horses nor music there now. Gurney, whether aware or not of these human happenings, goes on planning flower-beds, although there will never be any children to pull the flowers up roughly by the roots or anyone to cut them for the drawing-room and break the tradition of flowerlessness. Father makes no observations on my idleness, and leaves me to discuss the house with Griffiths and the garden with Gurney, and doubtless hopes my state of mind will uncloud.

There has come a characteristic reply from A.M.P.:

'If you want to convert me to your opionions on Tennyson you haven't succeeded yet; and if you really want to make a practice of conversion, may I convert you to my belief in suavity rather than dogmatism? You go very boldly half-way. You say poor old T. has no ideas, and you may be right. But you haven't analysed at all minutely the *Idylls*, and you should have done. I doubt if there's anything in them, but I should like some evidence that you have looked. You are also caught in your own emphasis. You say he's a minor lyric writer, and then you end with a formidable list of his imperishable lyrics. *Sapristi*, my dear young man, if all this is first class, so is their writer. When next you go back late at night to Amersham, go a little more slowly and think this out again. Still, and all the same, it's well written, and gave me some pleasure in the reading of it; and but for its wilfulness and onesidedness would be printable. And now that this question is settled, I suppose this correspondence may as well cease.

Yours
A.M.P.'

Kyle's unsatisfactory tenant is being at last eased out of Farm Cottage and is going to Repton, from whom we have concealed his worst faults. I've asked Knight to arrange a lease for me. I must escape from the weight and reproach of Peterley, from the range of empty rooms that remind me of my failure to have them used; and from the silence that is, like murder, horribly vocal—and every accusation I know is true. When we sit in the long drawing-room for tea, there are too many unoccupied chairs and a figure in each. Frances is sometimes sitting there, pale and, for once in her life, seriously worried, as she sat after our silly escapade into Wales, waiting for the fury of her family to descend on her (and me) with their arrival. We did not know they were only rushing down in haste in the political emergency, so as to be near Chequers in case . . . And the P.M. did not telephone; and in the political excitement and deflation, Frances and I were forgotten. When I see Jane it is while she is reading out loud the beginning of a letter from Scotland. The other insistent image is of a stranger to Peterley walking through the rooms still unwarmed by the winter fires and hesitating to sit down to breakfast by herself on that Sunday morning after the Rector's Christmas party. If I remain I shall start speaking to these figures. . . .

The formality of the house begins to get on my nerves. These stilted rooms should have been modernized. Jane left them as they were because that was how she had always known them, and they reminded her of her early days. The false elegance of the interior decorator is over most of them: they need a feminine hand to spoil their symmetry and make them humanly habitable. All but the Chinese Room, which has become a museum piece, as things do which were once fashionable à l'outrance. It must have been the envy of George Augustus Antonio of the Chinese tea-room at Shardeloes that led him to cover the panels with the apple-green paper that portrays slender bamboos shooting up from the banks of little streams that slide in neat waterfalls over grotesque rocks, and trees harbouring strange birds, and cows and dragons ruminant and rampant in the meadows, and the red of peony and yellow of hibiscus vivid amid the foliage. In the alcove formed by a fretwork of trellis is the fretwork bed with its imperial yellow silk hangings looped up with crimson cords. There are frail chairs the eighteenth century imagined to be Chinese, and on thin stands are undoubtedly real and unquestionably most lovely Chinese vases of blue designs on the whitest of glazes. I bedded Mademoiselle Françoise here who was a comparable work of art; and, earlier, Dorothea who was as enchanted as a child with its fairy-land décor—Dorothea who is the only happy ghost flitting along these corridors and laughing.

The Card Room, too, which we haven't used since our last but one New Year's party, should stay untouched. Its white-painted panelling, with each tall panel surmounted with its swag of fruit and flowers, is the

Augustan restraint at its most polite. The small drawing-room I had once thought to turn back into a library for myself; but this turbulent world so shakily governed by open covenants openly arrived at is not likely to let me acquire many books, and I'll let the Victorian furnishings symbolically remain.

I should be sorry to leave the Old Man alone if I thought he would notice my absence. While I am here he makes conversation, which would not qualify as such across the Channel; but if I went it would only be one social obligation the less. He has successfully formalized our co-existence. The opening remark at breakfast is usually a mild criticism of the error in yesterday's *Times*: the mis-spelling of an Indian word or the use of 'averse to' or dissent from a new theory of the origin of Stonehenge or the Polynesians. Anything nearer in time and place he passes over in silence as being too heavily charged with an emotional potential—the Bishop's ideas on Prayer Book revision, family allowances, or an elected Upper House. But an announcement that the Holy Grail has been discovered by an Arab in Antioch, or a Scandinavian sword dug up in Michigan . . . these have been washed to the bone by time, sterilized for use, made safe for discussion.

Twentieth

On Monday evening at the Casa Prada with the Billams for a final dinner and talk about the two plays he has in manuscript, before he leaves for Pau. I saw them off on Wednesday morning by the eleven o'clock boat train at Victoria. An unusual throng round the bookstall; and of a sudden the flashing of magnesium lights; and from the crowd emerges Anthony Eden and joins the rest of the delegation to Geneva. The train moves out and we all turn back to London. I hear a tall official saying to his diplomatic cobbers, 'There is a delightful Chinese proverb that even a journey of a thousand miles begins . . .'* and I fail to catch the rest of the sentence and spend the next half-hour trying to fill in the missing words. A scene from a C. E. B. Jones novel. Victoria Street was clear with winter sunshine, and flecked with the white of wheeling pigeons. I wondered why I stayed in England.

. . . . .

* Evidently Mr. Peterley did not know his Lao Tsu. The saying, 'The journey of a thousand miles begins with a single step', is in the Tao Te Ching, and the curious reader may find it in Sohaku Ogata's admirable translation in his *Zen for the West*, p. 159 (Rider & Co. 1959).

Had a talk with Cyril Connolly before he leaves. He is going back to Valencia to test the currents and sound the depths of the troubled Spanish waters for the F.O. I am eager to have him appointed editor of the new magazine Chatto are meditating. I have already discussed it with David Low, who is sympathetic but thinks that what is needed is not polite and social humour but something with a bite in it; or rather he felt he could be of use only on the biting side.

March

I move from Peterley House to Farm Cottage, Peterley Corner; and whatever symbolism may be in the move, to Quarles and Spenser with it. It would be the ideal cottage for the lady novelist or the young gentle-man author who wears lace on his prose instead. Cleansed of traces of the previous dwellers it looks like a birthplace preserved by the National Trust or prettified by members of the commemorative society. It needs a plaque. I am half tempted to put one: Here at his death came D.P. to live.'

It has four latticed windows symmetrically placed on either side and above the front door through which I must stoop to pass. It has insect-laden ivy clinging to the walls, and time-darkened tiles on a sagging roof. It stands back from the country lane behind a low brick wall and a white gate, and on both sides and behind is garden, flower-beds and vegetable plots, and an orchard with trees so old and bent and crooked that the apples are shrivelled to the size of horse-chestnuts.

It is older than suspected. The thick flint walls are possibly of the middle seventeenth century; the red-brick addition was certainly put up a hundred years later, for the carved wooden canopy over the door is eighteenth century and so are the windows with their wrought-iron frames that enclose the leaded panes which are set square and not diamond-wise.

The front door leads straight into the living-room, where the heavy beams of the ceiling are black with smoke from a fireplace that has been beautified by bright tiles that hit bucolic taste eighty years ago. The other large front room to the left is the kitchen-dining room; red tiles on floor, white plaster walls, and beams black as the enormous stove. There is an oblique step up to the older back part of the cottage and to the huge larder which, with its thick flint walls, was probably designed as refrigerator for a gamekeeper. The stairs go up by three stages to the four bedrooms above and these upper floors dip and rise with the warping of the long elm planks that the scrubbings of years have worn to the colour of pale silver like sea-washed and sun-blanched wood.

In the scullery is a cast-iron ungainly pump bringing water up from the well below the floor sunk deep into the Chiltern limestone. There is plumbing but no bath. I refuse to run gas-pipes and electric light into this model cottage, and install an oil-stove and Aladdin lamps. By day all is prettiness and light; but on moonless nights when I cycle back from Missenden and the midnight train, the scene is changed. I fly down the long slope from Prestwood, into the black tunnel through the beech woods, and emerge into the other darkness again by the 'Polecat', and see the signpost at the crossroads looking remarkably like a gibbet. Behind it is the cottage, a slouched shape in the background. An owl cries in the Peterley woods; and a bat sweeps and swerves in the open road. But closer, more pervasive than the darkness, is the silence, a deep black stillness which can be felt sensibly, as one might be aware of a hidden watcher in ambush.

My bicycle lamp picks out the gate and a black window. I unlock the front door and am almost on the point of calling out, 'Who's in?' There is a minute, when the door is closed against the night outside, and I am locked in the inside darkness, feeling for a match for the paraffin lamp, when I feel a foreigner on the frontier between two countries, both hostile. I light the lamp. The flame runs slowly round the circle of the wick, and goes from yellow to blue, and I turn it up into white, and the room is re-created: the Victorian sofa, the rows of books, the easy-chair, the water-colour over the fireplace. I draw the star-patterned curtains, and march from this outpost into the dining-room to listen for sounds upstairs. On such nights I have to reoccupy the house, room by room, and reassert dominion over the darkness and empty spaces.

Twenty-third

To Paris for the week-end with Cousin Richard, and glad to see Françoise and the Armand-Périers again. Lunch *en famille* avenue Victor-Emmanuel: quiche lorraine, pâté en croute with its meats marinated for days beforehand in wine, a Brouilly, and Kirsch afterwards, but from the maid's uncle's Alsatian establishment, not the commercial brand. For Sunday supper, to a students' restaurant at the back of the St. Germain market. I notice my cousin is almost silent with admiration for Mademoiselle Françoise. It is not undeserved, since she is easily and gracefully and unself-consciously one of the most striking women in Paris, being tall, slender, a magnificent figure, with black curling hair and a face of remarkable regularity: dark eyebrows like pencil lines (perhaps artfully reduced), dark-brown eyes, a straight and classical nose above the fullest and reddest (or reddened) lips that have a rather humorous as well as a lovely curve. When she and Mademoiselle Laval are together, the effect is formidable.

Simone Monnet was there, Provençally vivacious and full of her new passion, which I do not share, for paintings. One of her ideas might be workable: a bureau in Paris to undertake research for scholars, galleries, or libraries; to answer historical or technical questions; trace works of art, photograph them; check references. But why such a lovely, rich, and lively young woman should want to run a scholastic inquiry office for professors mystifies me. But then the European woman manages to pack more interests into her personal life than either the English or the American one. Jacques Diemer came, with young Millot from the Quai d'Orsay, and Vermorel, and Sigaux* who was rather youthfully full of wine and philosophy, and is always full of words, and perhaps was eager to shine before strangers, and was egged on by Françoise; and as a result there was a noisy half-hour when Jacques and Simone were shouting art criticism across the table, and Sigaux was expounding the ideas of a professor of philosophy at the Sorbonne for whom, it appeared, the word 'cause' has terrors undreamt of by the unthinking.

Sigaux, in fact, substantialized by a good dinner, was becoming metaphysical and trying to convince Annie that he was nothing apart from his fears for the future and his remorse for the past, although he was not wholly willing to admit any distinction between 'past' and 'future'. But Annie, who is not philosophical, inquired if there had not been good dinners once, and if that did not give ground for hope that there might be good dinners yet to come. But he would not accept so comfortable a solution: 'It is the fallacy of the old philosophy, that chain of probability, of cause and effect. . . .'

Millot, who had begun to listen, said 'Pouf!' very loudly; but Sigaux maintained his paradox that there is no inevitable continuity and that living is the living of each moment newly and freshly, since each new moment presents us with a problem: the dilemma of choice. 'Existence is the risk of choosing; without that choice we should be nothing. And

* Gilbert Sigaux now the well-known novelist and critic.

having that choice we are the slaves of the anxiety it occasions.' But Vermorel protested that by the intellect one could so manage as to avoid the fatigue of making continually fresh choices, and formalize one's life on an agreed pattern, as most people do. 'True,' Sigaux replied, 'if you are willing to compress your living into the strait-waistcoat of the intellect; but the measurement of an individual's significance, in philosophy, is the intensity of his feeling in his moments of choice.' Vermorel refused to be serious: 'So you bring back passion into philosophy and make it respectable?' 'I refuse to admit either passion or philosophy is respectable,' he retorted.

I was taken by one remark he made. He was still debating with Millot the notion of the individual as something not belonging to a fixed scheme or hierarchy—in which I completely failed to follow him. 'We exist,' he said, 'in a moment of time which includes the future as well as the past, because at that moment we are all our hopes for the future as well as all our regrets for the past; and the being that we are in that moment is conditioned as much by the one as the other.'

I am not sure now, ten hours later and sober, if I have remembered him correctly, but I think so, and for the reason that his words echoed something I said or thought or wrote at some critical moment in my own life, and a moment of choice too, but which moment I cannot now remember. Sigaux became slightly boring with his neo-Bergsonianism or whatever it was—he used to be called 'the philosopher' when young— and he was also slightly inflamed by the wine and by Vermorel's indifference and Millot's baiting, and there was an occasion when he felt that philosophy and he had to stand up and fight back, for philosophers had been accused of picking out those beliefs that suited their own inherited temperaments. Sigaux stood up, towering two feet three and a half inches above the restaurant table, and brandished his crumpled napkin like a thunderbolt of Zeus: 'If I insist on being an agonising existence between a past which is nothing apart from my sorrow and a future which will deceive my hopes; if every present moment is a moment of painful anxiety because of the burden of choice, do you think I believe this because it pleases me? If I sacrifice my happiness, it is from respect for philosophic integrity.' 'Ah, you are right,' replied Vermorel with a mock solemnity, 'let us drink to philosophic integrity.' Sigaux, placated, refilled his glass and sat down and pulled back in place the black tie that had begun to creep round his collar.

Françoise turned to us. 'Gilbert my cousin, you must not take life so seriously: it will ruin your digestion.'

But he answered: 'It has got to be ruined before I can become a writer; or [and he looked at me and smiled] I shall be in danger of writing like Boylesve. I have to spoil my digestion, quarrel with my mistress, marry unhappily, borrow from my friends, and refuse honourable employment. And then I may become someone my friends will be honoured to know, that a publisher will employ, and that fashionable women will invite to afternoon tea and press to stay when the others have left.'

I came back on Monday. Heaven knows why, I had nothing to look forward to.

The prospectus marked 'Strictly Confidential' has been issued discreetly for the new humorous weekly which will supply 'the lighter reading of the upper middle class public' which at present has to choose between *Punch* and *Razzle*. 'But *Punch*,' the prospectus truly observes, 'by very reason of its unique position as a national institution is compelled to pursue a cautious and conservative policy . . . in the character of its contents. Inevitably, therefore, it is behind rather than ahead of the times and to some extent out of keeping with the spirit of other contemporary entertainments such as the modern cinema and theatre.' The publication must be weekly, at sixpence, with 48 pages which would include 16 pages of advertisements, and with Chatto as producer and distributor. Nearly £10,000 has already been subscribed (mostly by Cazalet I believe) and another £5000 will be needed. But Graham Greene has been picked as editor, and I am a little saddened. The very excess and uniqueness of his literary talent will not necessarily fit him for this job; he is the romantic pure and simple, the imaginative artist. I had backed Connolly for this position, for his is a talent of a different kind, that of the critical intellect.

April

Crossed a North Sea without a ripple. Ostend 3.15. A quite good dinner served as we passed through Louvain and Liège. The German Customs inquisitorial to an unpleasant degree, going methodically through baggage and all one's money, fingering, shaking, pressing, prodding, unwrapping, and holding up to the light anything not open. Hot in Cologne; deep shadows in the cathedral; dusty shafts of sunlight in the narrow streets; and glare of the sun on the fast-moving Rhine. Airplanes continuously noisy overhead; too many blue-uniformed soldiers and far too many brown-shirted villainous-looking S.A. men. The Labour Corps units smartly turned out, all very young and innocent-eyed. I stay at the *Ewige Lampe* in great comfort and spend the days walking round the city and taking trips into the countryside.

After a slow progress up the Rhine I come to rest in the Hotel Leinfelder and find Munich still as enchanting as ever, without the grace of Dresden or the Baroque romance of Prague, but amusing, and, if a little pretentious, yet with that Bavarian bourgeois good nature that robs the extravagance of any offensiveness. I sit in the English Garden when the morning has warmed it up at ten o'clock and think of Nichols sitting here three years ago and trying like myself to settle his mind and to find something firm to stand on; although it was not by his own fault that his world had come apart.

A week ago, at R.'s, a dinner of publishers, with Alice Peers taking an unfair advantage of all the women present with those waves of bronze hair and those green—if they are green—eyes. She was all in white, which heightened the effect almost beyond the permissibly dramatic. I may have shown too openly my eagerness to claim acquaintance for she said: 'You, Mr. Peterley? But I thought you were a writer.'

'You think the strangest things when you walk home alone,' I answered, and left to speak to Warner who was with Rosamond Lehmann.

But two days later, repenting of my rudeness, I wrote and said I rather wished she might find it possible one week-end to come here for lunch or tea. One of her tart letters comes back by return:

'Dear Mr. Peterley,

I don't think much of "rather wish". Can't you be a little more acute? Besides, you don't state (with diagram) where "here" is, which is very important, viz: looking for a quotation, in bed, at a Board Meeting, on a Nature Ramble, etc. I have many capacities. Being queasy when I have meals with strangers is one, and not a convenient one. So I don't expect I shall come to lunch on Sunday, not out of any consideration for you but only for myself, so far. Nor shall I come at all with husband, because like so many others I have found marriage all a little difficult and having no capacity for perseverance and unselfishness I have withdrawn from the struggle. But I feel it very probable that I might appear some time in the course of the afternoon, after the local pub has closed or before it opens. But it is no good relying on me for a four at bridge, or a three at poker, or a two at sex, because I am both unreliable and unsatisfactory. I hope it will be fine on Sunday.

A. M. P.'

She did not come, and with even more diffidence I renewed the invitation, to which she wrote back:

'Mr. Peterley,

Sir, meiosis and I are old enemies; likewise moderation, the golden mean, balance, good sense, reasonableness, reliability, humour, and almost all the other fine old English traditions. If you have any others, please include them as above. Taste, personal prejudice, and as much as I like of them, are my stars. If it's fine on Sunday and I come (see "taste", "personal prejudice", *supra*) I shall probably make a day of it in the country and *not* take the 2.30 from Marylebone, though it is kind of you to suggest meeting me. Prowling through the fields and studying Nature is an attractive prospect, and I shall probably arrive at some odd time by some odd way. I shall neither deliberately forbear nor deliberately imagine.

Yours sincerely,
A. M. P.'

I don't know what the 'M' stands for, unless it is Mordant. I did not by now believe she meant to come, and asked a few people down for the

Sunday. We were all sitting under the apple trees at the back when she came down the path from the cottage, confidently, as though she were on familiar ground. She was in a well-cut coat and skirt of mottled green with a white blouse, her bronze hair loose in the wind; and I did not really think she had been on a ramble. She distantly acknowledged the introductions, sat silent for about half an hour, and rose and said goodbye. I walked through the garden to the road with her; but all she said was that the country was getting very crowded now in the week-ends, but that she thought the cottage charming. She shook hands and was gone. I refuse to take her theatricalities seriously; but all the same I would have preferred her conversation to that of all my other five guests, and I was slightly annoyed that they had unwittingly driven her away. It is probable that she is unhappy and that her literary sensibility has developed into an abnormal sensitiveness as a result of the failure of her marriage.

'Dear Mr. Peterley,

I was relieved to get this morning a note which I imagine you thought I had received before the week-end. I had, I admit, done you an injustice, for I had accused you of deliberate inattention to my known reluctance to come when you had strangers. Now I see it was only incompetence. Your note also removes the fact of the shock of intrusion, the extreme anger of self-reproach and the extreme irritation at you for exposing me to be the intrusion. It removes the fact but not the illusion, the psychological bad taste in the mouth. That could only be cured by your note's having arrived sixty hours earlier, and must therefore work out its own antidote. I only hope that my violent agitation and sense of blunder did not escape the hold I put on it "between the hand on the handle and the opening of the door".

Yours sincerely,

A. M. P'

June

Twenty-third

I still feel uneasy in conscience about Miss Peers that was Mrs. Hartland for so short a time, and I have written today suggesting that she might like to spend a week-end at the cottage, as she obviously needed some quiet and some seclusion. But I was not clear in my mind whether I was sorry for a young woman who had to put up such a heavy scaffolding of independence round her personal life or whether I was fascinated by the hauteur and the insolent wit.

'Dear Mr. Peterley,

I feel I ought to be unable to accept, but I can't think why. The feeling can be nothing but a shade of a code not now in general use, that if I pass a night—were the upholders of the code able to be immoral only at night?—under your roof, even in your absence, I shall lose my reputation and you yours; assuming that either of us has one to lose; and that your only reason in accepting was sexual intercourse. Both of which seem to me assumptions in the most exact sense of the word. It seems that that is a little absurd, for two reasons: (1) that if any such desire existed it would make itself known without any such arrangement of circumstances—though I don't deny the power at times of circumstances, but times are rare; and (2) that if it did not exist, no number of nights passed under the same roof would produce any shade of it.

The only possible reason for you to ask me is that you would in general like it if I came, and for me to come that I should like to do so. And whether either of us would like it as soon as we had got it is a matter for the Universe and our temperaments. The second is at least calculable, the first not; and so there can be no answer. The one at the back of the book will certainly be wrong.

I assure you the axle of the business is my stomach. Like Housman, though not yet so finished a poet, my reactions are gastric. He composed verse while shaving, I understand, and was in constant danger of death because of the jerks which his diaphragm produced when his brain had conceived a peculiarly felicitous phrase. With no relation

203

to emotion, my diaphragm is as independent and unreliable, and it would be a great bother if it decided, as it has done against uncles, mothers-in-law, friends and strangers, against you. It is incalculable because it is disturbed sometimes by happiness, sometimes by unhappiness, by distress or by peace. It has been good for a long time now, so I distrust it.

But as I am living in digs on my own, it would obviously be very nice to enjoy domesticity and conversation for a week-end. I go to lectures on Dante on Fridays at 7.30 so it would have to be a late train on Saturday morning. But I shall probably come before the summer is over—unless by sheer pressure and exhaustion of the system I am re-collected into family life.

Yours sincerely,

A. M. P.'

She didn't of course come. But on Tuesday came a letter:

'You must forgive me. The trouble is that I really enjoy writing letters and I adore hunting a trail, and when the two combine the result may be genius but it is certainly fantasy. I think you are charmingly serious—I don't know whether you are seriously charming, for as I said before I know nothing about you. No; it is unlikely that I shall come next week-end. Nor can I drink sherry with you tomorrow for I am to drink it with my Lady P. instead; and Wednesday and Thursday I won't because of the two previous evenings. So, except for any stray flights of correspondence, our acquaintanceship must languish.'

Thirtieth

The launching ceremony for *Night and Day* was held this afternoon at the Dorchester, and in spite of my profound disappointment at the choice of editor, I went, and had the twin pleasures of prognosticating doom and of noticing that my Alice Peers, or Mrs. Hartland as I forget she really is, was the most striking woman in an assembly that included, besides the literary ladies, some fashionable ones. Not the loveliest certainly; but that height and figure, the coils of bronze hair, the green eyes, and that clear white skin of face and bosom were together more than any other woman could boast. True, the crowd could not know the bitter mind behind; but I thought that if I ventured into the middle of that paradise I could not complain at finding a serpent's tongue there.

Ich sah dich ja im Traum
Und sah die Schlang, die dir am Herzen frisst . . .*

July

First
As unexpected as all things connected with A.M.P. are, was her letter that came today:

'Dear Mr. Peterley,
I am wretched this morning to find everything a cause for rage, so when I consider you you become the same. If facts are not turmoil they are disappointment, and vice-versa; and all I desire is to be placid —to live in Ely or Ludlow, some place where the early summer mornings have the still expectancy of London with a blissful certainty that the expectancy is of nothing. Not village life, for there though nothing happens, it happens under a microscope and the artificial impact is more strongly felt—as art is on the whole more effective because alien, than experience. The first stage of dullest civilisation is my ideal, a small country town. I am full of rage and empty; and so naturally I say No to anything you suggest; that's obvious. And when I think that you have seen my signature some half dozen times and spelt my name as often and never once spelt it right, my rage roars up on something it pretends is a ground. I do dislike you acutely, no not even acutely, and where shall I meet you if I want to on Friday?
                                                        A. M. P.'

Seventh
There comes another letter from A.M.P. criticizing my rewriting of the Genesis story and very justly, saying that, although I begin by writing

* 'In dreams I saw you, and the serpent that Feeds in the blackness of your heart. . . .'

from the outside of the story, the sterility and ruin in the story are taken Teutonically, Saxonly, instead of in the French style, the more hopeless because buoyant and brilliant. She has an interesting remark:

'I wonder if the female really is the more eager for sexual intercourse. One only judges from experience of so narrow a group and type, but I have overwhelmingly found women to delight in skirmishing and to evade, or at best put up with, the act itself. And that skirmishing of course *may* be genuine physical pleasure but is usually the clamour of vanity. D. H. Lawrence remarks how few women take any interest at all in a man's body, in the way of admiration and detailed delight which they expect from him towards their own, and I am wholeheartedly in agreement with him. I know it is true, and it is that which has angered me with so many women in their amorous confidences. The whole thing has been missed, thrown away in a wild concentration on vanity. There is no thought of intelligence in it, the real emotion and intelligence of the senses. If you read my novel, which I doubt, you may remember that some faint groping after that was part of the concern of it—the apprehension that some extraordinary knowledge, delight, ecstasty, power lies through the flesh somewhere, and in some mental approach to it which is not commonly used. But one has to take the body seriously, in a way entirely different from any that I have yet met, a gay seriousness, a serious gaiety. No, both those are off the mark and I can't find the word. Perhaps it's because I have not yet found the articulation of the flesh. I wonder if homosexuality may be the way to find it. If so, it must be only one way and not the only one. . . . The real advance from the universal fevered unintelligible excitement that everybody knows and that results almost always in the satiety and distaste you describe so clearly in your Genesis tale, to the really shaking mature experience which I dimly feel is just off the road or round the corner, is not to be easily made in very intermittent nights of tumult and uproar. The state so facilely described by half-good novelists of a French flavour, and I believe, so rarely discovered, or practised, or entered into, in experience, when the mind and body are really joined and really illuminate each other and the whole experience moves to a different music altogether though appearing outwardly the same, that state is not, except for rare flashes and moments, to be achieved except by prolongation of some kind, not necessarily of continuous time, though probably more readily.'

206

And she adds a marginal note:

'The immortal and exact description of it: The soft outstretching of her hand was like a whispering of strange words into the blood, and when she fingered a book the heart watched silently for the meaning.'

I think I see the influence of C.W. here.* She writes from Ludlow still, and has a postscript:

'No one in Ludlow knows who Housman was. Nor does any shop display his works for bibliomanes or low brows; and as I couldn't find my S.L. before leaving London I only have the damp dynamite in the inaccurately echoing caverns of the brain. I wish you'd send me a really cheap copy of S.L. or L.P. to the Post Office, Ludlow. If you sent me a copy I thought expensive I should send it straight back. I slept from 9.30 to 8 this morning with no break and hardly know myself today. I am off to Richard's Castle and various rivers. Do I wish that you were here with me? I hardly know. I have a pleasant feeling that you are. The moon will be increasingly lovely all the week here over the river and cliffs. I shall take some night walks.

I remain yours sincerely still,

A. M. P.'

Alice Peers wrote unexpectedly, as I might have guessed, that she would like to come down at the week-end, and that she might travel down on Friday evening.

'But if I do and you are travelling by the 6.30 train too, please I don't want to travel with you. I'd rather be alone. It would be nice if you went a wee bit earlier and would meet me on the edge of that wood reached across a big field from a path that runs back by the railway and then past a Quaker graveyard. But probably you'll have to go much later and I'll wait for you in peace in your garden. I'll let you know if I'm not coming by wiring you at the Club or something.

A. M. P.'

* C.W. is probably the late Charles Williams.

And this morning came the scribbled note that was unexpected even from the unpredictable Alice Mary:

'I am impatient for this evening. Yet, can you be as charming as your letters? Do not let us forsake them, even if we can't live up to them! You'll not forget the condition of my coming, that there shall be no passion, but only poetry. I offer you the job of using your intelligence to make this relationship unique and unsentimental. It will not be easy, and frankly I don't think you will succeed.'

I do not suppose I lived up to her literary standards; but I passed (and I suspect that she did) a completely happy week-end, with no passion, and, if with poetry, not so as you'd notice. We had a simple dinner at the cottage, and walked out afterwards to sit on the shoulder of the hill where it dips down to Missenden. It was a luminous dusk with summer stars, the air still and warm. We talked, it must have been for two hours, and came back by way of the old pub to find it was nearly midnight by my Swiss clock whose ticking was the only sound in the cottage. I left her in possession and went by the fields to occupy my old bedroom at the house. On Saturday I joined her for an early supper, according to the agreement, and we sat in the warm evening under the apple trees of the garden. She had recovered a serenity from the day's solitude and from the writing which she had at last been able to do. Questioned about being alone in the cottage at night she said she had not been sensible of any 'atmosphere', as I had often been. 'I only found it utterly peaceful. Your astral body must have a vivid eye and strong senses generally, which I should not have expected from the Saxon appearance of your physical one.'

On Sunday morning I walked over, to peer through the open lattice and see her busy at the long dining table. She rose and faced me through the window, and said she had had the most wonderfully peaceful night.

'But this is the real country. I wonder if you deserve this heaven. You don't have to work for it, as I'd have to do.' She refused an invitation to lunch at the house, but agreed to walk with me in the gardens, 'provided I don't have to meet the County'.

'They are all at church.'

So she came.

As we rounded the west side of the house into the long flower garden and saw the southern front, she remarked, 'Ah, I see why you will never be a serious writer.'

'I'm too deeply embedded in all this? I'd have to escape first?'

'If you haven't escaped by now, it's too late to try now: you won't succeed. And after all, why should you trouble to? There are plenty of unhappy creatures scribbling in furnished apartments. You're condemned to be normal, Mr. Peterley; and if you were not so fascinated by the spectacle of yourself, you might be happy.'

When she uttered these opinions, cold and pointed like icicles, her voice remained clear and pleasant but took on the sharpness of her judgments. I was on the verge of retorting angrily to this bronze-plumed serpent-peacock trailing her literary affectations across Gurney's trim lawn, when it occurred to me that her insight might be the artist's intuition and not the feminine defensiveness. Those sharp eyes, too small perhaps to be beautiful, under the pale eyebrows, saw the joints in your mind's invisible armour and her tongue inserted the acid irritant that would eat away, as was intended, your placidity. So I answered very casually: 'You may be right. Have you a cure as well as a diagnosis?'

'I don't think there's anything I can do to help you. And if we tried, I don't think it would be successful. Your over-developed ego would keep getting in the way and I'd give up in desperation. And I should insist on a standard you would find too exacting. Besides, my writing would suffer.'

'And for that you would sacrifice even marriage?'

'But it's you we are diagnosing, Mr. Peterley, not me.'

So we walked down the long lawn to the pedestal without its statue, and turned right to the artificial lake, where we startled a swan in the reeds that took to flight with a whirr of wings and made a landing at the far end, leaving interlocking semi-circles on the water where his trailing feet had rippled the surface, semi-circles that interlaced and formed temporary patterns that spread into a complex grouping and then subsided and left the surface still again, reflecting a pale sky. Having reached the end of firm ground, and nowhere farther to go, we turned back through the woods to the main road and so back to the cottage where we cleared papers from the table, and lunched like two poets on cheese and beer. And afterwards, fearful of company arriving unannounced, she decided to go; bundled her manuscripts into her attaché case and brushed out her thick bronze hair. She said, I think sincerely: 'It has been a successful week-end, Mr. Peterley. You carried it off much better than I could have expected.' And with no more ceremony she picked up her case and went out.

I watched her walking down the road to Little Missenden, her coat over one arm, her bronze hair glowing in the sun, and the white blouse open to the winds and the censure of the modest peasantry. I went in; emptied out the ashtrays; put back the books she had taken from the shelves; and sat for the rest of the afternoon reading under the apple trees. I was grateful no one came to disturb the solitude of the garden and the mingled serenity and disquiet of the mood. When, that night, I went up late to bed and looked into her room, there was her nightdress lying forgotten over the unmade bed. But I decided that this was absent-mindedness, and not a symbolic gesture; the forgetfulness that goes with the over-furnished literary mind.

I do not know why I have not been at ease at the cottage all this week; and even at the house on Friday I was so restless that I decided to go abroad. I think I will go to Naziland, but not, as my cousin would have suggested, to read the *Völkischer Beobachter* in Berlin, but Kleist and Hoelderlin in Bavaria.

'Leinfelder Hotel,
Munich

My dear A.M.P.,

Your just reproaches have reached me here and distance has made them even juster. I knew that nightdress would come between us one day; and now that it has, you must be relieved to find me safely in Bavaria. It has been on my mind for a long time, and I agree with you that it should be on a more suitable object. It is still where you left it. I toyed with the idea of returning it, but that natural delicacy of senti-ment with which you refuse to credit me restrained me. To send it back would have been brutally abrupt, and might even have seemed like accusing you of absent-mindedness. I had to let a decent interval elapse; and to consider the proper procedure for a young man faced with a nightdress in his own home. There is surely an established practice. It must have happened before.

The Post Office was out of question: you could not coarsely wrap such a delicacy in brown paper and string like a flitch of bacon. And if you had to declare the contents? And there is probably a regulation against the use of His Majesty's mails for the transport of night attire (feminine) except as from one married woman to another.

By this time, of course, there no longer seemed any urgency at all, and the problem became quite a fascinating one to contemplate. My departure for Germany gave it a new aspect, and I could not make up my mind whether to leave the relic there unguarded, or to wrap it up (in samite) and take it with me; but I remembered the travels of the young man in the Portuguese novel who had gone to seek a relic for the chapel his devout aunt was building, and, after a relaxing interval in Cairo, had brought away with him as a sentimental memento a pink nightdress wrapped in brown paper; and how, after obtaining for his wealthy aunt no less a relic than the crown of thorns which an obliging Arab let him acquire, he had wrapped it carefully in brown paper; and how the wrong parcel ends up on the altar of the new chapel on the day of its consecration; so that when the archbishop unwraps the precious relic which is to hang in the chancel there is unfolded to the eyes of the faithful . . . I wonder if it was of the same delicately light pink as . . . I decided it was safer to leave yours in Buckinghamshire, although I am unlikely to endow a chantry *pro salute meo*. Still, I recognize that there is now a numerical problem; that your store of dresses is less by one; and so I am remedying that with the parcel (without samite) which I hope His Majesty's Customs will allow to reach you without too much immodest chaffering; and when I return your stock will be increased by one, so that the unjust implication of your letter, that the cottage is purposely baited, will be removed.'

[The letters between this irritable pair increase, and so does the dissonance. They cannot avoid writing and wounding each other in the process. In the rough drafts which interleave the journal here his bitter refusal to accept the emotional implications of the acquaintance is proof that he is seriously fascinated. She in even bitterer replies explains why he does not deserve the generosity of her letters, and each day declares she will write no more.

Now seems the language heard of Love as rain
To make a mire where fruitfulness was meant.]

August

'Dear Mr. Peterley,

Your letter reflects a dim awareness of having fallen hopelessly short of a desirable standard of morality, or behaviour in any given situation, and for such I salute it. Though the blasting awareness of nothing in the diagram but yourself prevents you from having an awareness—inevitably—of the diagram of any other part of the pattern.

Do not think for a moment that I am not fully, exactly, and continually aware of your passion concerning yourself; the terror that one strand of you may become attached, one thought of yours become committed, one fraction of your sovereignty of fear over yourself be abrogated. You fight stubbornly and determinedly to have nothing but yourself, and that is exactly and appallingly what you have. You do not even have it with gusto. . . . Though I can believe there is a blind hope buried in your black treadmill, while you put no key into my hands I cannot even unlock one lock, much less let air and light into the habitation of despair. Assuming that you would wish me to; assuming that I had any wish to. Both being assumptions that need not concern us, since both are impossible so long as you only offer me suspicion; suspicion that if you admit you like, love, or desire me, I shall fix a talon in you and begin making claims or demands on you limiting your freedom of thought or action. And although a knowledge of your suspicions helps to mitigate their effect, yet if again and again I am met with a formula which destroys progress, gradually and inevitably any progress will be destroyed and so cease. And you will blindly add another, as you call it, proof to the unsatisfactory nature of all relationships, never admitting that you chose and ordained and persisted in the production of that proof.'

Our two unhappinesses recognize each other and stretch out their hands imploringly. But sometimes that of Alice Peers calls with an accent of longing I cannot associate with that too imperious beauty. We have attained by means of letters an intimacy that months of cohabitation would scarce have produced; and letters from her have been unmerciful in their critical analysis, and from me exasperating in their fantastic evasions. By accusing each other of being incapable of honesty, intelligence, and feeling, we have almost talked ourselves into behaving with all three. It is a situation that would interest young Sigaux with his ideas about the deceit implicit in all acts of life, where the 'being' is a 'being acting a part'.* But if I am deceitful, it is because my fear is real.

'Your letter, my dear Mr. Peterley, showed signs of life, had buds of growth, almost tenderness. You'll repudiate the phrase. It nearly made me think twice before answering. But I know it won't last, and that you will transfix me with a wry witticism in your next, and step back in terror when I step forward in welcome. So I am going, my dear Mr. Peterley, to step back myself, out of reach, out of sight, out of earshot. It won't matter any more that your eyes sometimes had such gleams of kindness in them, and your voice a quality that warmed and moved me in spite of my caution. I'm really saying goodbye to that frozen caricature of yourself with whom I have had to consort. You insist it is your real self. Very well, I'll take your word for it. But it's a pathetic figure, made up of renunciation, and pessimism, and fear, with an awful lot of disdain and self-love. If that's you, I don't like you at all. You made the situation more tangled for me, although more interesting for you, by the insinuation that I should assume that you were really someone frank, tender and generous whom a great grief had embittered and closed up. Right; I'll assume it. But my dear Mr. Peterley, in that case you are taking the wrong cure. The only way out is to burst through the restraint, the terror, the self-pity. Expand, not contract. Give yourself away; even your heart, before it withers. Be rash, impetuous, foolish. You could have been all three with me. Alas, you never made a false step. Your goodness was of the negative kind that makes God love sinners, and makes me lose interest. You can still save yourself; but it is more difficult as time goes on. There's only a medical mission in Africa left for you now, or being drowned trying to rescue a dog in the Channel. But I can't wait to share either triumph with you. Adieu, my dear Mr. Peterley, adieu. You are alone again. You have wished it. Hereafter, in a better world than this, I hope to have more love and knowledge of you.'

[* I assume this is a reference to the discussion in the Paris restaurant, and that M. Sigaux was expressing the Sartrian distinction between the 'Being-in-itself' and the 'Being-for-itself' of L'Être et le Néant. Ed.]

September

[There is another gap in the journal. The next entry is for September 2nd when he records that he is back from Bordeaux. Inserted in the volume are some loose sheets headed Biscay Ballads, 'so called' he notes 'not because of their rollicking and care-free nature, but because they were written during a crossing of the Bay in calm weather and a tempest of mind'. He went over apparently with Chatwin who had a ketch of about nine or ten tons and was his frequent sailing companion. The series of poems is of a most gloomy and sardonic character, and undoubtedly expresses his state of mind as a result of the breaking-off of his friendship with the A.M.P. of the letters. I quote the two last ones, as they were the final verses Peterley wrote.

The sea-change is over. Here at the Bay's end,
subdued by sun-fire and by salt, the sailor
emerges from the waters that befriend
the land-weary, the willing exile, the lover,

and all who ever place their hopes to westward
pursuing still a still retreating shore
the round seas bring back home without illusions
or leave upon the ice of Labrador.

When we have served apprentice of the seas,
all Eldorados and old loves forgot,
we come contented to an orchard plot,
happy to watch the sun climb over trees
to warm an old dog scratching for his fleas.

Palinode

And yet the last word is not said.

The cynic bark of dog or fox
from farm and covert in the dark;
the spring of trap and cry of dread;
owl's screech, and almost noiseless track
of snake on dried leaves in the brake—
these, though the sounds of night, are not the night.

Over the night there broods a peace that sings.
The silence in itself is musical.
Still chime the turning worlds; and all things
move to the measure of mind that bends within
the circle all the paths of men and stars,
and brings to birth and ripeness and decay,
and brings the wheel of fortune slowly round,
and the lost traveller home at fall of day.]

Third

Very disturbed by what the Old Man said about the tempo of affairs in
Germany. He had had a letter which Frau von B. had forwarded from
Mittenwald. I arranged yesterday a dinner with Elizabeth Wiskemann
before she leaves for Czechoslovakia to write her book on the Sudeten
Germans for the R.I.I.A. Rendezvous at Josef's in Greek Street. To her
flat afterwards for a long talk on the German question which she insists is
a Czech problem first. 'Of course Hitler will attack Russia; but he must
swallow Poland and occupy or neutralize Czecho first. Poland is not worth
fighting for—no, I don't mean that; I mean it can't be fought for; it's
not defensible. And not everything in Polish politics is pleasing. But
Czechoslovakia is a democratic nation; and, what is more, a well-armed
one with the will to fight; which is more than you can say for this happy
isle of amateur sportsmen.'

She told me of her recent talks with M. Masaryk, and of Witos the
Polish peasant leader. I have liked her ever since we met last year at
Rosalie Mander's. I came away at a quarter to twelve, as she had to pack
for her journey. As I walked up Gayfere Street I thought I would call on
Janet Norton whose light was still burning, and I stopped and had nearly
an hour's talk with her about, among other things, the possibility of persuading someone to stage Michaelis' *Revolutionsbryllup* which I have been
translating and in which I longed to see her as Elaine.

Sixth

A quiet birthday at home. Great-aunt Emily here with Celia who came
out this year. The old lady very handsomely gives me the little Boning-
ton* I have always, so extravagantly, in her opinion, admired. A simple

* Later, he has doubts about the attribution, and suspects that Aunt Emily may have
had doubts too.

215

landscape, a quiet estuary with sand, a beached trawler, and a young man standing by some spars and fishing-baskets and gazing out to sea. It has the luminous quality of a late afternoon, the air warm and rich and full of sunshine; but an afternoon of the early nineteenth century, when, so we feel, days were longer, the sun was always shining, life was peaceful, pleasant, and human. The canvas gives a sensation of well-being; the fishing boats are not a depressed industry or involved in controlled marketing; the young man is not meditating suicide; and as far as the eye can see across the estuary there is not an advertisement hoarding or a trespassers notice or a barbed-wire fence. I look at it and wish it could impart some of its serenity to my own life. Was there any in Bonington's? If art is effective, it should be able to.

While waiting for dinner, I walked out through the gardens at the back and looked over the valley. I am older, but the heart is still moved by this yellow light of evening behind the hills; and the apple trees in moonlight are still, I find, as inexplicably mysterious as ever. The moon has not become less beautiful by familiarity, and the clouds do not cease to surprise by their infinite renewals of splendour. We, as we worsen, marvel the more at the too lovely earth. I turn back ten years in the journal and find the words 'self-communing' and see myself watching the sunset over Sydney harbour from the heights above Neutral Bay.

Fifteenth
This was the day I should have made the annual pilgrimage to Radlett. That I didn't go is the measure of my changed life. I do not think it was from indolence, but because I realized that such a formality as this belonged to a world that has passed away. But when it passed away I am not sure; nor whether it was merely my world that has vanished, or the world of all the people around me. I suspect the latter; and that it was almost certainly the Führer who uttered the spell that dissolved the baseless fabric.

And so the damp lane through the wood will go unvisited. I never really expected to meet them there again. They have certainly returned after the first encounter; they probably make the same circle every year or two. It was a pious visit to a family grave—my own: here was buried the being who was all the emotions of that moment, the hopes, the desires, and the affections, and who vanished with them. The sad journey into age means that one day you leave the family graves behind untended.*

[* There was nothing in the journals to explain the pilgrimage to Radlett or the meaning it had for the writer, and the original event must therefore have occurred before 1926. But

Sixteenth

A card from Rosalie Mander holidaying in the Zakopani highlands in Poland, and absorbing oxygen and romanticizing the peasant after minority meetings in the towns. Machen writes in the green ink he affects inviting me to the Fair at Amersham on the twentieth, or rather to his even more hilarious party that celebrates it.

Warner was lunching at the Savile and I joined him, and when we came to discuss publishing I mentioned my idea of persuading Topolski to illustrate Proust. 'Think how formidable his Charlus would be! Imagine his Oriane, his Verdurin! And how well he could suggest with a swirl of boa, an elegance of parasol, a swelling of bust and train, those two supreme minxes Albertine and Swann de Porcheville. No English artist could possibly portray the scenes of Proust. Nor need he confine himself to scenes which *Punch* would approve. There are some delicate situations that might skilfully be elaborated.' He said he'd put it up to Chatto. Bierce is another publishing project I've always thought should be ventured; but he said that Cape had put out a trial volume without success. It seems to be a humour that has no appeal for our islanders.

Dorothea's present came a week ago: the Conrad Martens book that I wanted, to support my theory that at no time does the artist paint what

in a diary of his college days are some notes which probably refer to the incident that caused the annual return to Radlett: 'She was really there when I returned the next afternoon. Before, she said her name was Sophy Price. Now she said it was Sophy Cooper. She said it wasn't possible for me to join them; but I said I could buy a caravan. She asked if I meant a Romany vardo, and that they cost five hundred pounds, which I am sure is an exaggeration. She said it would have to be a "Reading". She would not promise to be there next day because she might not be able to keep her promise. We met five times altogether. She would not even let me take her hand. On the Monday when I came she was not there and did not come. I asked at the inn where they had gone and they said to Hertford; but I went there and there was no sign of them, nor, it appeared, did they ever come there.'

From which it is clear that he had met a gypsy and had even contemplated eloping with her, which might have seemed possible to someone as ignorant of gypsies as he shows himself to be. Sophy must have married a Price and have left him and returned to her own family, the Coopers, which would explain her change of name. A 'Reading' wagon is one type of travelling wagon of gypsies. Sophy's grandmother, I suspect, became suspicious of Sophy's absences and purposely laid a false trail for him when they decamped. Each year, whenever he could, he revisited the lane where they met, not, I think, because he was broken-hearted, but because he liked to create these ceremonies out of the ordinary happenings of life. He was mourning the Scholar-Gypsy lost. That he did not straightway abandon this absurd idea of joining the gypsies is shown by a letter in an early file from a saddler at Thame who quotes for a special harness 'suitable for caravan or tinker's cart, the straps to unbuckle on both sides', etc.]

is in front of him. There were two artists busy painting the colonies in the eighteen-forties: Martens in Australia and Krieghoff in Canada. These two countries are not in any way similar; their climate, their geology, their flora and forests could not be more different: and yet Martens' views of New South Wales look remarkably like Krieghoff's views of Upper and Lower Canada. Both artists were painting landscapes, and both had had the same instruction in how to paint a landscape. The academic rules were too strong for them and formed the landscape for them.

Twenty-second

To Amersham Fair on Monday; but saddened by memories of this same festivity two years ago when Frances had joined me so unexpectedly. All those others who had been with us then, Janet, Mrs. Compton Mackenzie, the Greenwoods, and Pitter, and the Warners, they were here today; and the unchanging faces made the single absence much more poignant. I spent the evening sitting talking with the Old Man, who was in good form, and had some excellent stories of Kemble the actor at the Garrick Club: the one about the 'young fool' and that about the member complaining of K.'s snores. Gave Machen Corti's *History of Smoking* and the illustrated two-volume edition of Brillat-Savarin. He told me of the little girl that T. F. Powys has with him in his cottage at Chaldon. Machen says it is his son's daughter and that Theo took her on condition her mother did not interfere. He is educating her himself, mostly, it seems, by readings of the Scriptures. We were talking about the state of letters in England which has always, I maintain, been poor for a great country by comparison with France, the literary man here receiving no respect. 'Receiving no cash,' answers Machen. 'I was telling my friends in Gwent the other day about the literary life. I made a reckoning in 1922. For eighteen books written during forty-two years I was paid £635, which works out at the rate of fifteen pounds a year. Ah, but your business man replies, but what a pleasant life (meaning by "pleasant" "idle") is the life of the writer! That, like most judgments on life by business men, is nonsense. The job of the literary man—at least I've found it so—is inexpressibly painful, nervous, laborious, with more of disappointment and despair than happiness. Only your belief in the value of the written word supports you; and it needs all your strength of will to cling to that belief in this country.' He showed me a book of newspaper cuttings: 'These are the unfriendly reviews.' It was quite a large book.

Twenty-fifth
The cottage and I get on well together. We are both withdrawn from the highway. We both love solitude. I have spent the whole week-end reading under my apple trees, without one longing lingering look for humanity. The hikers that pass down the lane grotesquely accoutred, probably on their way to stare at the house, do not help to cure my misanthropy. It has been a fine week-end after days of rain, the sun warm again, the air fresh and clear, the sky swept clean of clouds, and studded with four bright stars in the evening. No news yet from Elizabeth Wiskemann in Prague.

Went into Town to stay with the Billams at Gray's Inn, and discussed his two new plays, *Firebrick*, which is an impossible title, and *Music Hall*, with much disputation about the characters in the former, which I claim are too life-like and do not possess that slight unreality which characters in art must have, just as a statue to look life-size must be larger than the reality.

B. said he would like to attend a Quaker meeting, and asks if (as he phrased it) 'I could use my influence to get him into Jordans'; but I explained that our seignorial powers extended only over the local living and certainly not as far as the Quaker Mecca. Besides, a stranger attending for the first time would find the hour's sitting and silence rather hard to bear. 'But I can sit and think of the play,' he replies.

Twenty-ninth
Warner has bought the heavily timbered mansion at Haslemere from Sir John Leigh, proprietor of the *Pall Mall Gazette*, for the installation of Elizabeth who will reign impeccably, spreading charm at hospitable week-ends, raising rhododendrons and children with equal success; and the contrast with Peterley will be almost too painful.

The Royal Bucks. Laundry foolishly left my shirts in Prestwood by mistake two weeks ago and I have since blessed them for the error. The young woman from the cottage where they were delivered brought them to me the next day. I invited her in for the twenty minutes that she would have to wait for the bus to return, and we found each other's company so endurable that I suggested a cinema in Wycombe on the following Saturday, that being, I believe, the proper preliminary. She is not a native but from near Luton, and works in the new Tea Shoppe the Misses ffrench (lower case please) have opened in the Missenden High Street. She is the simple country girl, full of good health and fun, quite shrewd in real life, but ready to be carried away by the most preposterous melo-drama in the cinema. We have been three times now, which is almost more film than I can stomach; but Audrey has an ostrich appetite for celluloid, and I've suggested a day-long run in the country for next Sunday. Audrey thought a long while about that; but finally said 'yes' if she had the day free. She wondered why I called her Audrey when her name was Gladys: 'There was a woman in a picture called Dolores; I wish I was Dolores.'

The weather grey and windy, but to escape from the depressing company of Herren Feder, Rosenberg, and Darré I drove Audrey to the Oxford which she had never seen. I wondered if it would impress her, and it didn't.

'Why are the buildings so small?'

'They have shrunk with age.'

'Oh, you're always joking.'

I was about to lunch at the Mitre, but this would not seem very different to Audrey from her Olde English Tea Shoppe and I changed our course for the Randolph and there she was silent with admiration and scarcely said a word. I called at John's in the afternoon, and left her to wander round by herself and to meet me again at five. She was full of excitement because a young gentleman had tried to pick her up. She was looking at the coloured pictures in a shop in the High, and he stopped and looked in too. 'It was ever so funny. He said, "Do you admire gobble gobble gobble?" And I didn't know what to say because you shouldn't really speak to strangers, especially in a different town, and so I said they were very pretty, and he stared at me quite rudely and then he asked me if I would have tea with him, but I said I was meeting my fiancé—I had to say that, I hope you don't mind—and he asked me if he was an Oxford man.'

'What did you say?'

'Oh, I just said, "No, Peterley," and he was very funny. He laughed and said "You mean Peterhouse?" And then, do you know what he said then? He said, "Goodbye, Audrey." Now why did he say that?'

I couldn't very well explain that the lonely and metaphysical young gentleman had thought at first that he was greeting Margharita Philosophiae, and had recognized his mistake; so I put it another way, 'He wasn't really trying to pick you up in that sense; he was lonely and needed someone to talk to.' But I doubt if the idea was communicated, for a little later she added, 'He was too young really.' We drove through thin rain across Oxfordshire and climbed up into the Chilterns in a downpour that forbade any thought of idling in a country lane. So I stopped the car just the other side of Prestwood and turned to demand a kiss from my companion, which she very readily and warmly gave, and renewed, and came closer and said, 'It was ever such a lovely day.' So we dine in Aylesbury on Tuesday. I had supper at the House with the Old Man and talked about Oxford, but not about Audrey.

October

Thirtieth

The dinner in honour of Arthur Machen at the National Liberal Club was held last night. I went and thought it a surprisingly good show for England which is chary of literary occasions. The literary men who had been asked to come had nearly all in fact turned dutifully up, and the large dining-room was filled. The guest of honour was too moved to make a good speech—but then he never has been able to speak in public—but he gave a fine word-picture of the London to which he came as a young man—a gay, colourful, and varied city where lawyers still pleaded at Westminster, and horse-buses rolled through the streets at a brisker pace than the snorting omnibus; where Rotten Row on Sunday morning was really like a Frith painting; and where the danger of death on the Queen's highway was considerably less. Algernon Blackwood spoke well about Machen's having introduced a new *frisson* to literature, and claimed that in its genre the *Three Impostors* was a masterpiece, which is true. I forget if it was Wolfe or Jepson who put in a plea for *Hieroglyphics* as literary criticism of the best kind. Bentliff, among all these professionals, made the best speech of the evening, well turned, full of the right allusions, witty, and right at the heart of the subject. I was terrified when Cousin Richard, who had been drinking an Alsatian wine which I did not think went well with the fish, rose to his feet; but he praised Machen very soberly for his integrity of mind and laboured craftmanship, and ventured to adopt Flecker for the occasion and to say:

> 'He surely had the power
> To Le Fanu given of old
> To touch us at the 'witching hour
> And make our blood run cold.'

He added that it was a pity Mr. de la Mare could not be here tonight, or we should have seen at the same table the three masters of the art of sinister and macabre suggestion; for *The Riddle* and *The Return* rank with the stories of Mr. Algernon Blackwood and with Mr. Machen's *Three Impostors* and the *Hill of Dreams* as the best work in the allusive-mysterious that we have in English; and he suggested that if the lights were to be lowered the company tonight would surely see hovering behind the three chairs the approving shade of Sheridan Le Fanu. I was relieved when he sat down without having mentioned politics, an academy, the reformation of literature, or the need for control of publishing. He must have been less sober than I thought.

Thirty-first

'Sunday—which is known in the language which ought to be mine as Nos Galan Garaf—the Night before Winter.

Dear Mr. Peterley,

      And what a very pleasant evening we both had! I thought everything went off easily, delightfully, on oiled wheels. It was a curious and happy coincidence that planted Tomlinson, an actor in one of my small dramas, close against me. I had not seen him since 1921 when we quarrelled mildly about Ireland. We agreed warmly t'other night that we both loathed daily journalism. We got home in good order. Though Greenwood glancing at our two spouses towards the journey's end, said suddenly, 'They look like refugees.' It was quite true: huddled in the train they reminded me forcibly of the wretched Flemish women whom I saw at Folkestone, early in September 1914. All we wanted was a bird in a cage, covered by an old counterpane.

Yours gratefully and sincerely,
Arthur Machen'

It has been a difficult evening, when I have had to explain to Audrey that the intimacies we have been only too freely enjoying cannot be followed by marriage. There was half an hour of bad temper which revealed that she had harboured the thought. Stranger things have happened in the pictures. But the rebellion did not last longer; since, to this normal young woman, our misdemeanours had been only normal amusements. Intimacies was the last word for them. Her moral and emotional personality had not been involved. The spontaneous embrace under the hedge in a perturbation of petticoat was as satisfactory to her as the sophistications of the candle-lit bedroom. I said that so long as our friendship continued I would make her an allowance each week for clothes. 'Well, that's what you say,' she retorted sulkily. So I wrote out a cheque and handed it to her. Everything about her is so perfectly in character. 'What, each week? But it's too much.' And then, feeling that she had been too unguarded, added, 'It won't look nice cashing cheques.' She left, pacified at last, the four notes in her handbag. This is not like the films, but she has sense enough to see it has its advantages.

November

Twenty-seventh

I have begun listening to music again, and went yesterday to hear Schnabel play, magnificently, the Diabelli Variations. Perhaps I should not have gone. I could not sleep last night; and this morning got up as the sun was rising over the Missenden valley, and went down to the farm and took out Knight's mare and rode down to Mousely Farm and to Hitchingdon, and was on the hill looking over High Wycombe before turning home. The moon was still bright, and the fields were white with frost. Perhaps I should not have gone to hear Schnabel. There was still too much power in this music, heard before, to remind me that I was listening to it again, alone; that I was waking to daylight, daily, alone; and that there was the reason why I should never enjoy either of them fully again, daylight or music.

Nichols once tried to distinguish the various kinds of response to music, but I did not think his distinctions were generally valid. There was first the pleasure that arose from beholding (for it is almost a visual reaction) a sound-pattern; and this is the purest response. Then there is the induced emotional state in which, again almost visually, we behold images 'suggested' by the music, which can even have colour sensations associated with them. There is the response to music as to action, action in which we seem to participate and share its hopes and fears. And finally, he maintained, there was a fourth kind of response: we watched the music building up architectonically a mass of sound which moved within its own field of force rather like a miniature solar system. I could not understand his fourth category and assume it was valid for himself alone. He said his responses were nearly always of the third kind, the response to music as action; and he considers this to be, as far as his is concerned, the fullest kind of response. I think he is trying to define in another way what the Quakers call 'centring down'—the state induced, after perhaps twenty minutes or half an hour, by the silence of the meeting; a state of spiritual quiet to which succeeds—or may succeed—a spiritual content, or state of receptivity in which may occur a quite different kind of spiritual experience: a sudden lightening of the vision, a clearing of the mind, an exaltation, a sense of liberation, joy, and even a brief ecstasy—and somewhere after this, but how far I do not know, the beatific vision, the mystical 'union with the Divine'. The Quakeress and St. Theresa are together here, and it is possible that at rare times the music listener may join them.

It was a fine morning but I had scarcely noticed it, and I walked up the hill to the cottage still debating this question of listening to music. Listening to music is not simply one of two alternatives: either escaping from the world, or fortifying oneself against it. Anodyne or stimulant. 'And ever against eating cares Lap me in soft Lydian airs. . . .'

You could listen merely for the pleasure of listening, and this was probably the proper way. At least with some of the composers. Beethoven forbids that kind of listening with his introductory, 'Listen: I am going to say something.' He destroyed the simplicity of listening to music. With Mozart there is nothing but the music; there can be nothing but the music, since it seems itself a world complete with light and colour and form. It seems to take the place of the ordinary world and we accept it unquestioningly just as children accept the world they grow up in. And as we accept the music of Bach and Handel and even Haydn as complete and self-sufficient—but having no close relationship to the real world.

Yet can we always be certain of which attitude we are adopting when we are listening, and be certain at one time that it is to forget the world outside the concert hall, and, at another, that it is to brace ourselves to meet it when we come out? And forgetting with music, is it any better than forgetting with alcohol, since the two experiences are equally un-settling and disqualifying? And on the other hand, is music as a stimulant any more effective; can it take the place of the character that is lacking? The strong man doesn't need it: will the weak one, even with benefit of song, sonata, and symphony, be anything but weak? What does music do but confirm us in our preconceptions, fortify our prejudices, and make us more than ever ourselves? Had it changed either my character or my way of life? I remember Moira rebuking me once, for giving too much place to music: 'Life comes first and has to be solved by its own rules and not by music.' It's probably only when you've succeeded in living that you can listen purely to music. And I haven't yet succeeded; and it will soon be too late to make the attempt.

1938

March

Hitler has marched into Austria. We have been fooled all the time, and the Nazi revolution is nothing but a conspiracy against decency and good order. I went up to Town and called on Cousin Richard to persuade him to join me in forming a political group for the defence of Czechoslovakia. He was uneasy about the behaviour of his Führer, but objected that

Germany had given assurances the integrity of Czechoslovakia would be respected; to which I replied that Germany had been bound by the Agreement of 1936 but had scrapped it when the moment came. I promised to finance the scheme if he would act as secretary. 'The fact that we are probably too late and will be defeated is no reason for not making a fight of it.' The argument continued through dinner, although he complained that it would spoil his digestion; but as he had begun with a huge toasted cheese and a flagon of ale, I was not sympathetic. 'But what can we do?' he kept demanding. 'Baldwin and Chamberlain have just about emasculated the English. A nation of *thlasiae*.'

He was eventually converted by the specious argument that here was a chance for someone who admired the Nazi dynamic to practise it a little on his own: 'Did Hitler sit in fashionable restaurants eating enormous Welsh rarebits and asking what could he do? He went and did it. He spoke on street corners, in the rain in squares, in shady bars. The Kampfzeit he makes so much of now was merely tub oratory. We can do that too. We can be as Nazi as the other man.' In the end he agreed to act as secretary if it meant no more than signing letters. 'That's all it means. It may be signing your death warrant, of course. It may end in front of a firing squad.' 'Whose?' 'That's what I don't yet know.'

April

I have had a bureau brought over and have fitted up the smaller of the front bedrooms as a work-room. I have moved my bed back into the room that looks on to the garden at the back, and left the large bedroom for Gladys, who never sleeps there but loves to sit, before and after, combing her hair, sampling the scents I buy for her, trying on the dresses she buys in Wycombe, dresses she buys in sales, economically, of a bourgeois modesty and plainness. She has also taken to lying on the bed reading *Vogue* and *Harper's*. I think she regards their extravagance as sinful, and gets a great pleasure from contemplating it. A young woman of admirable virtue, punctilious, and well behaved. She sins charmingly and naturally upstairs after our evening meal and then insists on washing up before she goes home.

Have sent R. a list of the people who should be approached to form a committee for propaganda.

Twenty-second
With Lady Kilbracken to South Kensington for the ceremony of handing over the title deeds of the National Theatre. A cold draughty afternoon, with dust blowing about the excavated foundations; and as the Fleet Street choir began singing 'Spring the sweet Spring' a light rain fell. 'Why are we here? This thing will never come to anything. We could be having tea and muffins comfortably somewhere.' But she said one had to do one's public duty. Dull speeches afterwards; and a badly rhetorical, ungrammatical, high-falutin' appeal for money by Sybil Thorndike. The wrong site; a wasteful diversion of money from the Old Vic; a foredoomed failure; a new, an academic artificiality. I looked down and saw that I had put the wrong shoes on.

The difference in the moonlight of different nights. Sometimes it will glow sharply and whitely; sometimes bright and soft; and sometimes, although the moon will be shining in a clear sky, there will seem to be hardly any light, but all will be dim and shadowy. This has been a re-versed spring, with a warm end of March and a warm early April, and, after mid-April, cold northerly winds, frosts, and a cold dry air with no rain. The premature blossoms were scarcely whitened before the frosts browned them. The cuckoo was first heard today, Saturday, April 30.

May

Fifth
A long talk with Elizabeth Wiskemann and Dr. Kraus of the Czech Legation. I announce my plan for the Czech Committee and the line of propaganda to pursue. It is not easy. If we export our democratic notions about minority rights we should support the nations that buy them; but

227

here Hitler is using one of our pet theories about minority rights in order to wreck a democratic state. Halifax and Chamberlain pretend to take this seriously. I don't know whether Chamberlain really knows any better, but H. certainly does; and this example of shocking hypocrisy is only too common among prominent Christians, as the pagan Führer well knows.

Have drawn up, and sent to R. for circulating, a draft of the aims of the Czech Association:

DRAFT OF THE PROPOSED STATEMENT OF AIMS

The Czechoslovak Association is intended

    (a) as a centre of action for those who are alive to the full gravity of the Central European situation;

    (b) as a centre of full and accurate information on Czechoslovakia, her history, her internal situation, her foreign relations, and in particular the question of minorities.

The Association will endeavour to bring home to the British public the vital importance of Czechoslovakia

    (1) as a strategic key to the whole Danubian and Balkan problem, and therefore to the whole balance of forces on the Continent;

    (2) as a great free democracy east of the Rhine;

    (3) as a consistent champion of the League system;

    (4) as a state whose minority problem since the war challenges comparison with that of any other country.

The Association will support all efforts to promote a just and lasting settlement between Czechoslovakia and her minorities but will oppose any attempt to force upon her a change of foreign policy or any measures calculated to undermine her present constitutional régime and means of defence.

The Association will act through publications and through the Press, by public meetings, by contact with existing societies, through Parliament, and by any other suitable means.

228

The Association is an all-party organization and is in no way committed on any point of domestic policy nor on any point of foreign policy outside the scope of these specific aims.

Tenth

Lunched at the Ivy with Elizabeth Wiskemann and Jonathan Griffin. He is willing to join my Publicity Sub-Committee. A man of correct information, clear ideas, and honesty of purpose; in a democracy these admirable men are shouted down by the demagogue and the business man, and their rôle is that of the dramatic critic in the stalls whose review will never be published. We discussed drawing up a model Treaty of Peace for the conclusion of the next war; and also composed a letter to *The Times*, refuting Noel Buxton's ideas on Czechoslovakia, which that august newspaper should have known were nonsense. In the evening to the House for dinner with the Manders, I still feuding with Rosalie about her depreciation of Byron and her misreading of Mary Shelley's character. If she were not (*a*) so amusing and (*b-z*) so attractive, I doubt if I'd bother. Geoffrey Dennis, of *Coronation commentary* fame, was there with his mother-in-law, who is W. M. Rossetti's daughter. Mrs. Belloc Lowndes, a sprightly old lady, bewailed to me the rising rents of Barton Street that were now £250 for a small house, with £90 in rates, and that had once been £40 complete, in her time. 'Young men working in the B.M. used to rent bed-sitting-rooms there. And you know what wretched salaries the B.M. paid.' I talked with Mrs. Angeli about Trelawney, and about her father, and of the Shelley circle in Italy. She said that William's journal, that Garnett had edited, badly needed re-editing; but I did not gather why. She knew the original. She has a soft chanting voice, and she sometimes breaks into the conversation randomly and will continue talking although no one stops to listen.

Walked back with Rosalie Mander who tells me about her work on Claire Clairemont. I remarked that she began as the conventional minx and matured into a woman of some interest, as minxes usually don't; and R. seemed delighted that at least as to Claire we were in agreement. Suddenly *à propos de bottes* she said: 'Tell me. Why are you so melancholy? No; that isn't quite right, I mean a kind of grim endurance.'

'It's the mask for my irresponsible levity,' I answered.

'Don't turn things upside down. And you should give a serious answer when a woman asks you a serious question.'

I left her, but amicably, at her door. Walking back up Whitehall, alone, I reflected that she was right; I should have answered simply and truthfully. But I do not seem to have the power of spontaneity any longer. And confession might be dangerous; is there not something the psychoanalysts call 'transference'?

Twelfth
'Dear Sir,
        I am inquiring of a few prominent public men who might be thought sympathetic with the proposal whether they would be willing to sign for publication in the Press such a letter as that enclosed. Immediately upon publication of the letter, an appeal would be made inviting support; a Committee would be formed; and a printed pamphlet distributed as widely as possible. A public meeting would also probably have to be arranged. In the last century, it will be remembered, the Greek and the Polish Committees played a useful and honourable part in their day.
    The names of those now being approached are given below, and those marked with an asterisk have already associated themselves with this proposal. . . .'

Later. I think it is after midnight; but my clock has stopped. I did not get any further with my letter for there were two hesitant little knocks on the back door below, and Gladys was there. She comes only when I ask her; but the tedium that stalks bed-sitting-rooms on summer evenings had driven her abroad and she came to beg me to take her to the pictures. I abandoned Central Europe to its fate and sat through two preposterous fabrications of the Semitic overlords of Denham, in one of which young Englishmen covered with burnous and tobacco juice raced across the burning sands of Buckinghamshire to rescue a young Englishwoman whose dramatic frigidity would have immobilized the *gluteus maximus* of any virile male and cooled the blood even of an Egyptian. Gladys was carried away. She showed no eagerness to be back at Prestwood before midnight, and stayed on after supper, and so . . . and so . . . here am I trying to save Czechoslovakia in the small hours of the morning while the Führer is wide awake in the Berghof plotting its destruction. I wish I could feel the issue were ever so slightly in doubt.

230

[From this time on, the diary is little else than the Minute Book for the Czechoslovak Committee, but with his personal affairs intruding incongruously into the records of political meetings and decisions of committees. There are some amusing encounters with distinguished people. Harold Nicolson, for example, is asked to join the Committee, and he replies 'that the situation is so delicate at the moment and the Government are pursuing so correct a policy in Prague that I should not wish to be associated with the appeal'—and Peterley consigns him (in the diary) to perdition, and to that bottom circle he reserves for democratic theorists, Utopians, and opponents of capital punishment, although with some regret that a writer of such good prose should sink so low. Nicolson soon has Sir George Clerk for company there, after Peterley receives a statement of Clerk's belief that 'a solution on reasonable and peaceful lines may yet be realized' by Mr. Chamberlain. As he kicks Sir George down a descent that Milton's hero took nine days over he observes to his journal: 'All that Clerk says is eminently reasonable and therefore at the present time quite wrong. This gentlemanly restraint is exactly what Hitler counts on for the success of his devilishly dangerous Weltpolitik. The time for reason, caution, the play of the mind has passed; and we are in a satanic poker game with the stakes rising sharply. We have to bluff, be brazen, bold, and brandish our empty holster just like our opponent. It may sober him. This letter of Clerk's would make him laugh. It makes me sad and hopeless. But then I have embraced a cause I believe hopeless. That may be its attraction. We shall all go down; but I want to make sure we go down fighting.'

He has already started fighting, but it is against the lethargy of the Conservatives. If his Committee is to do anything to stop Mr. Chamberlain's impatience to sign on the swastika line it must represent Tory opinion—Mr. C. will listen to no other advice. And while wooing the Conservatives, he is being subjected to the more than friendly advances of the Communists who assume that anyone who is against Mr. Chamberlain is for them. They write fulsome letters and shower him with propaganda on bad paper. They send him not very prepossessing envoys, some of whom arrive via the high-minded Utopians of the House of Commons. A Mr. Clementis, for example, from Prague, who, in joining the Czech Association, obviously hopes to join the Association to himself, or whatever is behind him. A Comrade Beer embraces him on paper and offers him the columns of the *Organ der internationale Kulturliga*—'as though there could be such a thing' Peterley observes. All the same he recognizes that they alone seem to be clear-sighted and aware of the coming disaster.

There are, of course, the clergymen and cranks, Lord Tavistock at their head, who send him pamphlets about the prophecy of the Pyramids, the incidence of taxation, the meaning of Chapter XII of Revelation. And Dr. Schwarzenberger sends him a pamphlet on the economic, sociological, political, ethnographic, religious, and cultural significance of the Danube basin. An Austrian Jewess, Fräulein Komer, tries to persuade him to liberate

Austria for Jewry. M. Winter comes to persuade him to liberate Austria for the Austrians. The Hungarian Tourist Agency begs him to spend the summer in Hungary. . . .

In these whirlwinds of talk and snowstorms of paper his only relief is the occasional cocktail with Rosalie Mander and the rare evening with Janet. He has come to Town on a Saturday morning—the date in the journal is May 28th —and through H.'s legal long-windedness had missed the midday train back to the peace of the Chilterns:]

I was sitting in the Club trying to make up my mind what to do, when Janet rang announcing her return from Wales; and when Janet rings gone is the world I know, and the Hapsburgs could be restored without a protest from me. We lunched at the Restaurant d'Italie; went to see Disney's *Snow White*; had tea at her flat; saw no reason to part so early in the day, and separated to change for dinner at the Club; we dined and went to see Macgowern's new play *Glorious Morning*, and afterwards for supper to the Princess, but I found it tawdry for my mood, and we moved to the Trocadero where we had to endure a pretentiously suggestive cabaret. As I walked back from Gayfere Street in the summer night, melancholy overwhelmed me like a black wave that falls ponderously on the beach and stirs up sand and broken shells and debris from past floods, and washes away those kirtles of shallow water with their lacy fringe of foam that lay spread over the smooth sand. Whitehall is a gloomy street, heavy with the destiny of empires and the doom of statesmen, and at night dead as the Acropolis; and my own past and the past of history came up like a darker cloud in the dark night, and I seemed to be walking in the ruins of a buried civilization. Will London one day lie under the mud of Thames as Babylon under that of Tigris?

In these moods time vanishes like space; and I might have been walking through pine woods near the fringe of the snow-line of a new ice age, and thinking of the past times when the Thames valley was deciduous and warm and habited; or I might equally have been threading the ancient river marshes of Thorney that could never be good for anything but wild fowl. When the feeling of space and time is gone, you are like someone whose sense of taste has left him, and all food is the same and like powdered ashes.

Back at the Club I could not sleep. I got up and looked through the window at the night over South London, and at the unseen river, and resisted the temptation to write to Janet. Heard the clang of firebells from galloping engines along the Embankment below, and sat and read until morning came.

Tired, sad, and purposeless, I came down to the cottage today, and sat listless within, watching the continual rain, driven by a most un-May-like wind against the latticed windows. I ought to be at work on the programme for the Czech Committee; but Czechoslovakia seems one with Nineveh and Tyre. All things have happened, in the sense that what has not yet come to pass is contained within the potentiality of history; and since the future event will follow from what has already happened, it is already conditioned; it is foreknown; and being forecastable is as much part of our minds as the fall of Byzantium. The rain turns the beech leaves on the trees across the road to shining bronze; it beats down my periwinkle that I had trained along the low brick wall. It drums on the hollow roof and has pitted the flower-beds with puddles. No Sunday hikers pass down to Wycombe, and I am alone on this plateau in the Chilterns, curtained from the world with rain. If, when the storm is over, and the warm mist has cleared, I walked down into the valley, it does not seem impossible that I might come upon an antiquary digging the ruins of the past and finding marvellously preserved in her coffin the form of a young woman whose chestnut hair pillowed a face that was of an infinite distinction now in death, 'She had the loveliest grave eyes and a slow smile that could take your peace and your will right away.' He would reply that I must be mistaken; that she had been dead these four thousand years. 'But so have I.'

[On the 21st of May Peterley discovers himself attacked by the *Hamburger Fremdenblatt* for 'interfering in the internal affairs of Czecho-Slovakia', and while expressing surprise that Goebbels should have troubled, is obviously delighted that he has. But for most days the journal entries are so hurried as to be almost unintelligible, like the following one: 'Arthur Henderson to come in. Major Hills—D. of Atholl to approach. Tea with Janet on Thursday. See Dr. Ecer, Vice-mayor of Brno, Thursday. Primrose 5830—A. Salusov. The Association a non-party organization in no way committed on any point of domestic policy. Get photograph of Jaksch. Wiskemann 12.30. Clementis 2. Aufschnitt; peaches, kirsch. Kraus. Phone Mrs. Ortmans Hampstead 6398. From Dent's Book Catalogue: "And if you are in Czechoslovakia for a last look round . . ." ' He does however succeed in founding the Czechoslovak Association, and in getting together a reputable Committee composed of, among others, the Duchess of Atholl, Lord Cecil, Lord Lytton, Walter Layton, Vyvyan Adams, Acland, Geoffrey Mander, Spears, Seton-Watson, Temperley, and Wickham Steed. They meet and discuss the politics of Central Europe and agree that Mr. Chamberlain's policy is stupid, but are not so unanimous as to what can be done. Wickham Steed seems to be rather a handful at times, as Peterley complains: 'At the words Central Europe, he splashes into the

233

Danube basin, scours the Hungarian plains, and, after singeing Mr. Stoya-
dinovic's beard, is half-way to Bucharest, looking something between King
Charles I and Don Quixote.' There is too much talk, and not enough money,
in spite of Peterley's appeal in the papers. But he and Seton-Watson do get
some pamphlets printed and distributed, and make sure that correct information
on the Sudeten question is sent to all M.P.s.]

I took the afternoon train to Haslemere for dinner with the Warners
whose Old Manor Cottage is the size of any comfortable country house.
But Elizabeth had not warned me that Janet was to be there, and I had
to endure the spectacle of my young actress in a dark-blue and dull-silver
evening dress playing the part of a Pinero heroine. When she looked at
you and slowly smiled, her thoughts were as plain as though spoken:
'How I love acting! How amusing it is to be alive, and young, and
lovely, and adored—so long as it does not become serious.' I looked at
her, and decided to save myself by going to Prague. If I am at last to try
to do something useful,' there can be no time for the *douceur de vivre*.

June

Twenty-third

In Prague again after thirteen years. The city is lovelier than I had remembered, and gayer and brighter; but then they are preparing for the tenth
Sokol celebrations. The Václavské náměstí is more imposing than I'd
imagined; Na Příkopě and Národní třída fuller of tempting shops; and
the view from Smetanovo Square—but there is no change in what was
always perfect, and this is still and forever the finest view in Europe—
the Charles Bridge to the left that leads in the grand manner with a
cavalcade of statuary to the Nicholas church with its arrogant and
Baroque dome; and in front, across the Vltava that flows musically
towards Melnik, the old town that rises in a pyramid of roof and tower,
of spire and dome and terraced garden up to the castle walls, from out
of which the cathedral shoots up in pinnacles like tongues of flame. The
Hradčany is the most elegant of fortresses now, with its battlements long
since replaced by these fenestrated façades, prim as a Parisian square; but

on the east the Black Tower still stands in its mediaeval grimness where the hill slopes gently down in foliage to Letensky Garden.

The Esplanade is full or reserved for the Sokol visitors, and I have to go to the older Atlantic by the Masaryk Station whose refreshment-room serves, as in the old days, hot frankfurters and mugs of ice-cold pivo. The Heythums have moved to Na vinićneh horách and I had difficulty finding his new house in an unfamiliar suburb. It is simple and modern; plain white concrete and huge sheets of glass for the windows, and the interior broken up dramatically into different levels. A highly coloured and vigorous Prokhoskha on the end wall of the drawing-room, with a plant beside it, with large leaves like irregular pancakes. Heythum himself a modest little man speaks rarely but smiles angelically at each remark you make, as though grateful for your condescension; you could not believe that this personification of diffidence could possibly have created this assertive house with its skilful balancing of concrete and wall and window, its artful interior that was fluid and open instead of the nest of shut-in rooms that is the conventional home. But it was this charming little man who had designed the Czech Pavilion for the Brussels Exhibition which was the most successful of the modern buildings there. And just as you are wondering how he could consort with so dynamic an aesthetic, Charlotta enters in a sweep of bright-patterned skirt, tall, black, handsome, and Polish, and enfolds you in a warmth of welcome and has resumed half the history of the intervening years before you are seated. Antonin has no need to say anything, and sits smiling shyly. I walk back through Bubeneč and by the winding road under the Daliborka tower that I used to take to the Letensky Garden, and across the Mánes Bridge to the Old Town and Na Poříči and the hotel. Prague wakes early in these parts and wakes me up, and I go out before breakfast and wander the streets which are as new and exciting to me as though I had never seen them before.

Twenty-seventh

This evening to a little café that hangs out from the castle rock over Malá strana, a narrow terrace between the ramparts and a sheer drop down to the square of the Golden Fountain immediately below. Here in the warm summer evening we sat and looked down on the Waldstein Palace, on the great Nicholas dome, and on the dark river flowing between the lighted banks. The Heythums had brought Milos Novak and he had

235

brought his wife Libuse, whose English speech was more beautiful than any Englishwoman's because it was spoken in a voice softer than any in that chilly island; and what the soft vowels left unspoken the lightest of blue eyes completed, so that there seemed as much meaning in her glance as in a ballet, just as there were all the shimmering shades of corn in her blonde hair, and in her cheeks that miraculous intermingling of rose and white that poets speak of and you assume to be a lie.

We drank the Melnik wine, and talked about Weltpolitik; we sat in peace in the Golden Orb in the heart of Bohemia and thought of the German madman to the north and the heavy-footed Teutons he could set in motion with a word. And the gentle Heythum slapped the table and said: 'But he will not. The Army will fight. We shall all fight. He knows it.'

'If you fight; yes.'

'And besides; France and England will be with us.'

I dare not say what I thought of my country's eagerness to fight.

'And if they are not; we shall still fight.'

Charlotta smiled and said something softly in Czech, and the Novaks laughed. I asked them why and Libuse explained that she had called her husband 'the little tailor'. 'It is the name of a character in an old Czech folk-tale. He is a peaceful little man who is always involved in terrible situations. They were amused because they were probably thinking of the night when he wanted to show what a capable husband he was; but his wife just wanted to go to sleep—you know how it is'—and she suddenly laughed a soft low laugh—'but no; of course you don't know, do you? Well, you must try and imagine it is possible—so she pretended to hear a noise in the kitchen and said: "Husband, there are thieves breaking in. They will steal our china teapot and soup dishes. They will take my virtue. You are so brave. Go and beat them off." So he goes down, and she turns round and closes her eyes. But she is wakened by a terrible noise. The furniture is being overthrown; the pots and pans are falling; and her husband is shouting: "Out, villains, before I murder you. Thieves! Ravishers! Members of the Citizens' Reform League!" and other horrible names. She hears beatings on the table and imagines her husband is beating their heads together, and then the door bangs and everything is quiet again. He comes upstairs and says he has driven the two scoundrels away and saved her honour; and he claims his reward for his bravery. You know how men always expect that . . . ah, no; I had forgotten. Well, of course, what had really happened was that he had seen only the usual mice running about the kitchen but he had pretended to fight the imaginary thieves and had thrown the pots and pans on the floor and cudgelled the table with a stick. It is written in an amusing kind of popular Czech.'

We went on to talk, Libuse and I, about my reasons for being in Prague, and she said that it was a pity my name was David, and that if it had been Richard I could have become the second Richard of Prague.

'And who was the first?'

'Why, you should know that. He was one of Wycliffe's followers. He came over here I suppose to convert the Bohemians to Wycliffe's views, and he called himself Richard of Prague. You haven't heard of him in England?'

I hadn't and felt like the barbarian from the fringe of the Empire sitting with the society of the city and thinking the Roman women to be the most intelligent and most beautiful I had ever seen. I also realized that I knew almost nothing about the history of Bohemia, or for that matter of Europe; and that most Englishmen shared my ignorance of the Continent that really was the civilization we in our island talked about as though it was our own. Perhaps it would be our privilege to save Europe from the Austrian bandit, as we had saved it from the Corsican; or, at any rate, this lovely city that lay below us, whose towers and spires and domes showed above the luminous mist of the summer night like dark rocks from a smooth sea; or, at the very least, the even lovelier Libuse who sat serene as a mediaeval Madonna and talked of worldly matters with a worldliness almost Chaucerian. I can see I must avoid the peril of confusing Czechoslovakia with Libuse Novakova.

After a glass of slivovice we all walked down the tortuous street to the Malostranské náměsti and there parted, they all to take the tram to Bubeneč, I to walk over the Mánes Bridge back to the hotel where now I write, not in complete peace of mind. Life seems to be a continual beginning again in a new direction; and I was determined to confine it to a single purpose. I should not have hurried from England and left the Association unguided; and here, instead of touring the Sudeten districts, I am sitting in cafés and enjoying the life of the senses and the mind. But, after all, that is exactly what all politics are only the administrative machinery for making possible. The only justification for Mr. Chamberlain, Herr Hitler, and M. Beneš is that they enable me to sit under the castle of the Winter Queen on a summer night drinking wine, and wasting time, and enjoying that strange game of arranging words so as to form an image for the listeners to guess the meaning of, and feeling that emotion of contentment and quiet desire that comes from watching handsome women. But this is just what the Viennese bum is preventing us from doing, and why I am on this side of the frontier. I had better start doing something tomorrow.

Twenty-eighth

This is the tomorrow of my virtuous resolution; and if I had been tempted to waver, the letters sent on from London would have pulled me up sharp. Griffin is worried: Steed and Lytton are trying to merge the Czech Committee into a kind of European sub-committee of the L.N.U. Elizabeth Wiskemann writes sharply asking where I am, and what I am doing, if anything, and what I intend to do, if ditto. Sheila Grant Duff wants to come actively into the Committee, and suggests a visit to Prague forthwith. Janet inquires with a mild interest where I may be. She mentions that she had rung the house, and been told, 'Mr. David Peterley's present movements are unknown,' which is the phrase I suppose Griffiths worked out for himself in the privacy of his sitting-room as the correct formula. A note of gratitude from Audrey, on tinted paper with a coloured bunch of flowers at the top, thanking me for the brightly coloured woollen jumper in a highly sophisticated 'peasant' style that I had sent her: 'I'm sure it will be a great success in Great Missenden and specially at you know where'—that is to say, in the grocer's family, whose eldest son is wooing her in his clumsy way. She still addresses me as 'Dear Mr. Peterley' but ends 'Your loving Gladys' and appends three large crosses with a marginal annotation, 'You know what these stand for.'

I had a serious talk with her before I left, and hinted that I was going to be away from Peterley often in the future, and very busy; and besides it was time to think of her future. 'Oh, I'm all right,' she said. Which in a way is true: she is living in what the sociologist would call a state of concubinage (if not worse), but her self-respect is not injured since she enjoys an economic status far superior to that of the other village girls; she is seen in the Peterley car; she can go up to London at the week-end and come back with ugly bibelots on which she has wasted her money. She even has savings in the Bank—in the Wycombe Bank, which I thought more discreet. But I feel some responsibility for her, and would like to see her rising on stepping stones of her dead sins to higher things, which at the moment are represented by Mr. Grit, the grocer's son, and the young mechanic at the Aylesbury garage, where I have stopped for petrol and given them the chance to admire each other, as it appears they do. I said I thought it was time she should think of marriage. She replied that she didn't want to get married and have to do the washing and everything; but I insisted that, with me gone, she would drift into it in any case, and that it was better to think it out beforehand.

I paced up and down the bedroom floor while she lay on the bed turning over the pages of one of her picture magazines, and I tried to make up my mind which one to marry her'to. The grocer's son is dull, and perhaps stupid too, but he inherits the most prosperous business in the village. But he will assume that his money is enough to keep his wife satisfied, and that he does not have to exert himself to do so; and in time my Audrey will yawn, look round for diversion, and—if she does not over-eat and grow lazy—will have no difficulty in finding it. Where? I wonder. She is an amusing and healthy girl the young doctor might appreciate. But it is risky for a country doctor; and difficult to hide. I can foresee the scandal: the B.M.A., instigated by a jealous wife or a jealous patient, intervening, and his having to leave the country with his guilty partner. He will try to establish a practice in Algiers or Hong Kong. And as time goes on, and the novelty of exile wears off, I see Audrey yawning on the verandah or the balcony and catching the eye of a major in the garrison who is passing by. . . . When I turned round, I was quite relieved to see Audrey still safely on the bed.

And life with the garage mechanic instead? He might not be so stupid; but he would condemn her to the washing-tub and the back-yard line, the hot lunch at twelve, and, if it rains, the cinema at night. There would be no diversions: his jealousy would see to that. She would always be a little afraid of him. A life of virtue from which only death—hers or his— would release her. I found the decision very hard to make. Audrey herself gave me no help. She was busy gazing at pictures of the Comtesse de Rethy at Nice, of Mrs. Simpson in Paris, of Barbara Hutton that was, in Portugal, and of the King of Egypt dining with friends 'among whom is Catherine Cony, star of the new Megalomania picture'. I decided in the grocer's favour. I don't think that in the long run it makes much difference. And when I asked if she thought she could settle down with Albert, she said, 'Yes, as well as with anyone'; so I said I would give her two months to settle it. I also gave her some advice. It was rather like an inverted *Ragionamento** of Aretino; that there should be no favours before the wedding—otherwise, with Albert, there will be no wedding—and

---

* The *Ragionamenti* of Pietro Aretino are what Bacon would call Essayes or Counsels civill and morall for the instruction of a young woman about to enter the Profession. Ed.

that for the first six months of marriage it would be wise not to be cleverer than her husband. 'After that, you can, if you like, introduce a little variety.' She ingenuously asked why he wouldn't know these things already. That was our last time together, although I did not tell her so; and I hope she has stored my precepts in her heart. I should like to see her happy and her simple virtues rewarded in this, her own and only world.

I turn to the other letter, from Kraus of the Legation, who is just a little hurt that I went so precipitately to Prague, and now sends me the official introductions, and the booking for the Esplanade. He says that Masaryk wishes me to meet Mrs. Pamela Petschek at Aussig and Madame Loew-Beer at Brno. Dr. Kubka of the Czernin will see to the rest, and I must call on him as soon as possible—in other words before I make any mistakes.

Twenty-ninth

At my interview with Kubka this morning he gave me the programme for the Slet and said that a Czech who spoke English would be appointed to be at my service while I was in Prague, and when I said that French would suit me as well, if this were a commoner accomplishment, he added that as a matter of fact the guide had already been appointed— a Madame Novakova whose English was excellent. Perhaps I gave myself away by exclaiming: 'But I know Madame Novakova.' 'Ah, what a coincidence!' and I think that if Kubka ever allowed himself to smile, he would have smiled then. So Libuse has been diplomatically active already in the Czernin.

The inscription on the old sundial is out of date: the days are so sunny I do not record them, and so full of activity I have no waking leisure left at night to fill my journal. Monasteries, historical monuments, churches, palaces, old towers, and castles form one enormous montage, and Libuse Novakova of the blue eyes, with a sheaf of cornflowers and ripe corn, a Slovakian Ceres, smiles from the middle of the picture like the girl of the travel poster. The impression that remains is Baroque. The Baroque of Bohemia has corrected the error of regarding Gothic as the supreme style, and has completed the cure begun in St. John

Nepomuk in Munich. Our timid English shrinking from the Baroque is a defect of the insular character that cannot bear to admit that art may have its own conventions, which surpass the conventions of polite society, and that subjects grand opera and epic poetry to the test of what it calls the natural, that is to say, the diurnal commonplace. The bravura of the renaissance is foreign to the English mind which never felt the full impact of that intellectual earthquake. But, for me, these saints that on the very tip of scaffolding of twisted stone seem to leap into the air with ecstasy, these virgins that hold a fluttering robe close to thigh and breast, the Theresas who faint with the intensity of passion's consummation, or weep with tenderness as a cardinal pleads his cause at her feet, all these performers in the divine opera of art move me as much as does a young soprano in an aria of Mozart.

July

Third

I decide not to move to the Esplanade but to stay at the Atlantic as I spend only the seven hours of sleep here. To the Barrandov restaurant this evening for supper with the Novaks and the Heythums, and Joan and Jonathan Griffin who have just arrived. Here, five miles from the capital, Vltava curves round a rocky promontory, and here once lived the French geologist Barrand 'for the sake of the unusual rock formation', although I wonder if the more usual formation of a local *paysanne* may not have played its part. On the steep slopes above the river are now the terraces of the modern restaurant; and as you dine you can look down on the curving river, the water-meadows, and poplars below, and watch the moon rising out of the evening mist and silvering the ripples from the boats going downstream to Prague. Can this scene of bourgeois opulence, of dining families and dancing couples, be really part of the communistic republic that worries the great statesman to the north? Are these men and woman of a Britannic respectability the brutal dwarfs who savagely oppress the innocent Aryans within their gates, and venomously write the Czech name above the German one on the signposts? We were in a happy mood, with the wine, the music, the white moon, and the warm night, and I even went so far as to forget my reserve and sing, in what must have been an unendurable accent, 'Kdybych ja byl Selskym synkem' and 'Nemelem nemelem'. 'Now whoever taught you those, I wonder?' said Charlotta, looking at Libuse.

I should be making notes for Miss Wiskemann at Asch and Egger, and instead I have been touring the beauty spots of Bohemia with a Bohemian beauty. We have been to Krivoklat, the model of all fairy-tale castles with its tall round tower roofed with a dunce's cap, its squat keep, its chapel, its neat battlements, all huddled together on the small rock that rises steeply from the black woods that hem it in. We lunched in its shadow and talked about the ancient kingdom. We have been to Karlstejn, the castle of all feudal brutality, and lunched in its shade and talked about the world in general. We went to Lany, country house of the enlightenment, and walked in the park and talked about the universe. And at Melnik we lunched by the roadside on the way to Rudnice and in the shelter of the famous hill Rip we talked about ourselves. I do not know where we go next.

Sixth

On Wednesday was the march past of the national contingents that had come for the Sokol festival. The platform was put up in front of the Town Hall, and the Sokol flags hung behind. There were four chairs in front of the dais for Zenkl, the mayor of Prague, for President Beneš, for Madame Beneš, and for Madame Zenkl: and then the platform chair next to Madame Zenkl was for me. Kubka had given no hint of this prominence. He had said, 'The Minister wishes you to have a good view of the parade,' which may have been his humour. I noticed the English Minister was some way to my right; and that may have been Kubka's humour too.

The procession took five hours to pass by. There must have been about 100,000 Sokol members. Even Austrian Sokols came bearing the swastika banner. There were Bulgarians in fur hats, embroidered jackets, and white skirts; there were Sokol leaders on horseback in their grey capes and their eagle feathers; there were Poles and Serbs and Croats, and Slavs from Hungary and from Rumania. When not in national costume, the men wore the Sokol costume of red and fawn, with the jacket swinging from one shoulder. The girls had a well-cut uniform of fawn skirt, white blouse, and braided jacket with a round Russian cap. They blew into trumpets; they banged drums; and whistled from fifes; and sang; and the sun shone on the colours of their uniforms and of their flags as they marched hour after hour across the city square and under the Hus statue and past the presidential platform.

And here sometimes their enthusiasm broke their rigid ranks; they shouted greetings to the President; they threw garlands of flowers at his feet; the girls broke into peasant dances, and had to be sternly re-formed by their leaders and ordered on. I noticed there were often tears in the President's eyes as he stood at attention receiving their salutes.

In the middle of all this martial pageant there walked, all by himself, a middle-aged man in a dark suit, with a straw hat and an umbrella and a brown-paper parcel, probably his lunch, under his arm. I was puzzled and assumed he must be a traditional political joke, a figure from the pre-republic days, the symbol perhaps of Austrian bureaucracy, the civil counterpart of Schweik. He certainly looked the part of the sedentary office worker, his footsteps fumbling along the street, his shoulders bowed as though under the weight of official forms in triplicate. And then as he came level with the President he drew a miniature Union Jack from under his arm and waved it weakly once or twice, and smiled half-heartedly, and then rolled it up, tucked it under his arm and shuffled on. It was the representative of the British Empire. I looked at my programme and there he was: Mr. X, Secretary and Treasurer of the Frimlington Boys' Outdoor Club and Natural History Society, representing the nation of Cromwell, Marlborough, and Wellington.

But I am doing him an injustice. He was representing, ably, the nation of Mr. Chamberlain. He was expressing, poor fellow, so clearly the policy of His Majesty's Government that there did not seem to be any need for any further diplomatic negotiations. The British Minister here might just as well fall upon his umbrella. Indeed he should have done so, there and then; and I looked down the line of chairs to see if the thought had crossed his mind. But he was chatting to his neighbour apparently unaware of the double humiliation, that inflicted on the Czechs and that self-inflicted on the Empire.

In the afternoon to the Masaryk Stadium where I had a seat in the President's box for the final display of the Slet, the musical gymnastics by the Sokol members. There was a hot sun shining on the huge field and on the more than 200,000 people on the slopes around. It was said that half a million were outside watching the Air Force exercises.

I have never seen anything to compare with this exhibition for precision and beauty.

Through the five gates of the Masaryk Stadium come the first files of the 28,000 men. The ranks, in their white tunics, seem at this distance a solid mass in motion, and so far away that the noise of marching cannot be heard. The square formation advances with deliberate step, slowly sharpens to a phalanx, and then the sides turn outwards to form the shape of an enormous bird. Behind, there emerges another army from the gates, that advances and then spreads out in a parallel movement. The outer files reach the edge of the stadium; the whole space is filled; each man of all these thousands in position.

A curt order from the loudspeaker, and all the ranks turn and face the President's box. A second later we hear the swish of their tunics. There is not a single deviation in any of the radiating diagonal lines of rigid men.

From the ground, where the loudspeakers are buried, rises the music for the exercises. The rigid figures suddenly vanish. The stadium is a net of outstretched arms, a forest of uplifted ones. Then the ranks sway sideways and over, and we see a waving plain of corn chequered with shade as the light is reflected variously from the diagonals. We no longer see the actual movement of men, but only the changing light, the moving shadows over the surface of brown arm and white tunic as the ranks bend and sway. As the music develops, the movements change and seem to be proceeding according to an inner logic of evolution. There is no stiffness of physical drill: 'they move to music, and like music move'. It is, rather, a stern ballet.

It comes to an end with each man in place again. The music changes. The files move together, and close; and out of a network of lines coalesce two solid masses that part and march to the side gates. The ground beneath the gates rises in a convex curve: the solid files flow up the slope, and seem to break like a breaking wave down the incline and vanish like a wave of the sea into a cavern.

I noticed Steed among the Army generals. He told me afterwards that 28,000 men had marched into the stadium and taken their appointed places in exactly fifteen minutes; and that, when the exercises were over, the eight columns of sixty men abreast had marched out in twelve minutes. 'That's getting an army corps into a space of forty-five acres and out of it again in twenty-seven minutes, which few generals could manage. And the women, 16,000 of them, were just as efficient.'

Seventh

Le tout Prague thronged to the presidential reception in the royal park this afternoon. It would be truer to say it crawled. The cars were head to tail all up the steep and winding Chotkova silnice and along Marianské hradby in order to reach the park by the Prasny Bridge which is now no bridge at all, although I suppose it did once bridge the moat here. Even the moat was transformed centuries ago into bear pit and zoo for the royal animals. And even these had been transformed now by a Circean magic in reverse, into diplomats, generals, industrialists, writers, and society women, for the diversion of the President.

A Bulgarian lion strode through groups of fawn-like creatures, shaking his medals loudly. A Yugoslavian fox in the diplomatic stripes was talking politics to a jackal from the Hungarian plains; and moles disguised as civil servants ran to and fro avoiding the larger animals. There was an expression remarkably like that of Wickham Steed's on the face of a giraffe who was leaning over and conversing with a tiger in jack-boots who was trying to hide behind his back a two-headed eagle he had just caught. A small rabbit with a Union Jack tied to its white tail chattered with a French poodle; and in a corner all by themselves stood four bears back to back as though defending themselves against all non-comers. It may be Disney, the modern Grandville, who upsets our vision; it may be that the setting was so fairy-like, with the enchanter's castle, black against the sun, rising up in massive wall and grim tower over the trees, and in the clearing the Belvedere, that is so unreal and exquisite a building it might have risen out of the ground at the spells of an Italian magician.

I was talking to a Rumanian about propaganda and as a professed Anglophile he was criticizing the British Council's choice of faded ladies of semi-noble birth to go and speak about English culture to the Balkans, when up came the Novaks and said I must meet the President who was approaching. But I shook my head and said I did not want to add to his fatigue. Milos however objected that, as founder of the Czech Association, I must be introduced; but I still shook my head; and Libuse added, 'Certainly; there is no question about it.' I said: 'It is too early. I have done nothing yet. I will meet him when I ride into Prague with the Army and restore him to the castle.' Liba turned on me, and her full face remained serene, but her light-blue eyes were lit with a white fire, and she was just about to retort in anger, when in an instant she changed and said quietly, 'Why did you say that?' And I replied that I did not know. 'Well, never mind. We won't trouble.' And we walked away from the presidential party as it approached.

Why I did that, I still do not know; but Liba seemed to understand, and she took my arm and was friendly, and introduced me to a charming man who was a Czech historian at the university.

Seventeenth

I am back in England in the solitude of the cottage at Peterley, and instead of beginning the work that is waiting to be done, I sit in the garden and try to remember the Bohemian fairy tale which has ended. I retrace all the steps backwards from that final moment on the platform at the Masaryk Station when Heythum presented to me the bottle of slivovice, and Charlotta the cheese I had become so fond of; and when, as the train started to move, I pressed the hand of Liba and felt the pressure in return that promised . . . nothing really, because the fairy tale was ending, as they do on the outbound platforms of railway stations. But all the vanished scenes are coming back in the silence of the Chilterns.

August

Almost daily consultations with Seton-Watson who agrees to prepare a talk for the B.B.C. which could be printed as one of my Czech broadsheets; and I have asked Jonathan Griffin to write one on the strategic importance of the republic. I come back in the evenings after all these confabulations on the late, the last, train from Marylebone that creeps into the midnight blackness and silence of the Chilterns. Great Missenden is almost its final halt. I descend; and the guard waits a moment in case any sleeping passenger wakes and finds he has overslept a station or two. But no one else ever emerges from the carriages. He waves, and the train resumes its nocturnal country ramble. The sleepy porter nods to me, turns out the oil-lamp, and goes home. I wheel my bicycle up the long hill, and ride through closed and curtained Prestwood to the empty cottage. The air inside is warm and unmoving like the airlessness of a family tomb. I leave the front door open, light the Aladdin lamp, and let the night air enter and the moths flutter in that will in two days lie dead on the hot window-sills. The rooms upstairs are close and dusty like a museum in a small country town that is rarely visited. The long coloured map of Czechoslovakia is stretched across the wall of my work-room; and in the large bedroom on the floor are Audrey's blue slippers on which the dust has been settling for a fortnight.

The summer is passing but I see little of it. I am talking in lit rooms in the City. And out here the garden is unkempt; the grass uncut; the flower-beds full of weeds; and my more private garden untended too. Audrey is neglected, while I by telephone and letter and luncheon-meeting try to bring several people to decide upon a single simple action; while the single dictator can decide upon several actions in the creasing of a brow. And will all my activity deflect our gutter Napoleon from his march on Prague one day? I doubt it. His spells are stronger.

[Meanwhile, against his wishes, there are manœuvrings in London to widen the Czech Committee which he had formed into a Central European one. Lord Lytton is in favour, and has Wickham Steed with him. Peterley, a little dispirited, knowing time is running out, leaves the politicians to argue whether their interest shall stop at the Czech or Bulgarian border, and begins to arrange for a Czech Exhibition in London, with the idea of getting all the national art treasures out of the country before the Nazis move in. Prague is agreeable, and asks Masaryk to help; and the journal is more and more taken up with this project. Heythum in Prague begins listing the old Bohemian wood-carvings. And Peterley decides to include the Masaryk Library still at the President-Liberator's country house at Lany. He persuades the London School of Economics to take charge of it until the next war is over. The sudden appointment of Runciman as investigator strikes terror into all these conspirators for the continued independence of Czechoslovakia. When Peterley calls at the Legation the next morning, Kraus, the first sec-retary, admits 'We are worried', which for this imperturbable Czech is the very Tuscarora Deep of pessimism; and Peterley unkindly suspects the idea may have been put into Mr. Chamberlain's head by Ribbentrop at the luncheon on March 11th.

At the beginning of August he goes to Durnford near Midhurst to pay his respects to old Mrs. Cobden-Unwin, and finds one of the Liberal leaders there; and in an informal talk after lunch he is asked if he would consider standing as Liberal candidate for the division. In the journal he gives the real reason for his refusal: that he would hate to oppose the Labour candidate, Poulton, who is the husband of the Diana Poulton whose playing enchants him.

The amount of work that Peterley was doing at this time, and his attempt single-handed to deal with the correspondence with Prague, with the Czech

247

Minister in London, with M. Bata, who is becoming interested personally in the idea of a Czech Exhibition, with Members of Parliament and with the English newspapers, proved too much for his endurance. There is a note to Kraus of August 24th reporting on what had been done so far and announcing that he has been ordered a complete rest and that he is disappearing from sight for ten days.]

September

[There is nothing in the journal until an entry for September 7th mentions that he is back at Peterley after recovering in the quiet and the heat of Divonne, where apparently the family used to go regularly in the old days. The moment he gets back he prints another Czech broadsheet to the annoyance of Wickham Steed but with the approval of Seton-Watson; and he remarks with melancholy]:

If the Czech Association is still alive and vocal and critical, it is only because in my small upper room at the cottage, in these star-filled silences at night, I go through the correspondence that arrives from Englishmen who are becoming uneasy and from Czechs who are on the brink of despair. I send out my little broadsheets; write to Members of Parliament who are fishing in the Highlands, holidaying in Italy, or just relaxing in the country; and circulate to newspapers scraps of information that have escaped their scrutiny. Quite a lot escape it; everything, in fact, they do not wish to see. I work all night, jotting down answers for later typing; and as a summer dawn begins to define the latticed window I turn out the Aladdin lamp and go to sleep, wondering if Milton lost his eyesight from reading too many political documents in bad handwriting.

Twenty-first
I had to ring the Legation this morning and Kraus was put on the line. He was curt, and said, 'Wait, I will ask the Minister.' Masaryk's voice came on and he listened to my problem. There was a moment's silence and then in a peculiar voice he said: 'My dear Peterley, let us forget your

problem for a day or two. I will tell you something and you will understand why I do not feel like thinking about it. You do not know what has happened this morning. The British and French Ministers have—I was going to say betrayed us, but I will say behaved very unkindly. The President has had little sleep for several days. I know that. They fetched him out of bed this morning at two o'clock. They read Hitler's terms to him. Hitler got them to do that. I will tell you what those terms are. First, if the Czech Government does not immediately and unconditionally accept the Munich terms it will be solely responsible for the war that will follow. Second, if it refuses to accept these terms it will be guilty of breaking the solidarity of the powers, since Britain will in no circumstances march, even if France should do so. And thirdly, if the Czech refusal should provoke war, France will be freed of her treaty obligations. This is not the kind of message one expects to receive from one's friends. Now do you understand, my dear Peterley, why I do not feel like doing anything today? But we will talk about your problem some time.'

[Under the date of September 23rd there is a telegram stuck in the journal signed 'Griffin'—which must be Jonathan Griffin—saying: 'Come quickly yourself discourage S.', and Peterley leaves the next morning for Prague, and there are no more entries until October.]

October

Now that I am safely back in England, at Peterley, calm again in my orchard, I can look back with amusement on the flight to Prague which at the time was unhumorous enough. I booked on the plane that left Croydon at 8.45 on the morning after getting that telegram, on Friday, September 24th; and as I was to land in Prague that afternoon and could go straight to my rooms in Ořechovka, I took only an umbrella and a camera, and nothing else except the roll of plans for the Czech Exhibition in Dorland Hall. In my pocket were two pounds and three highly confidential letters from Masaryk to the Czernin. For when I had rung the Legation to warn Kraus of my sudden journey, he had immediately suggested that the Minister might want to make use of the occasion;

and at half past eleven that night Kraus himself had handed to me the three letters for personal delivery to the Foreign Office in Prague.

As I sat in the plane on the airfield waiting for the engines to warm up, my black hat (bought for H.M. King George the Fifth's funeral) on my knees, my hands on my umbrella, I thought it was really too ridiculous a parallel to what must have been a similar scene three days earlier when a more important person with black homburg and umbrella, but with striped trousers, had sat here waiting for the plane to Godesberg to start.

I had been a little worried by what Kraus had said last night about the developments abroad, and had made a point of asking the airways for an assurance that the plane really would get to Prague; but the official had regarded this as a slight upon their service, and had been slightly rude in his contemptuous reply that there was of course no question of their not getting me there. 'You have your ticket, I take it?' he had asked, as though that made it certain. We landed at Brussels; and when I asked which was the plane for Prague they were not contemptuous, but merely laughed, and said that there were, of course, no planes going to Prague. When I insisted I had to get there at all costs, they said that the Vienna plane was at that very moment taking off, and if I cared to try that way round they would signal it to stop and take me on, which they did. We came down for lunch at a German airfield where everything was satisfying—the clean lines of the terminal building; the clean restaurant inside; the clean citizens taking their leisure over their midday meal and beers. In England it would already have become a little stuffy: the card-board advertisements for Hovis or Bovril hanging from the light fixtures, the bottles of HP sauce on every table as a warning to gastronomes, the tired waitresses approaching you with dyspepsia and taking a pencil languidly from behind their ears. Here all was fresh, clean, crisp, spruce, and active. I felt already a traitor to my backward country.

I wonder now where it was: I forgot to notice; probably Munich. But aloft again, and passing low down over the towers of Melk, I saw those half-Eastern and bulbous domes and realized we were on our way to Vienna, the gate between the Turk and Slav, and now the Nazi outpost, and I began to think that it might not turn out to be prudent to advance so hurriedly into the enemy's territory with an umbrella and with three incriminating letters.

At Vienna, at four o'clock that afternoon, they thought I was joking when I asked when the next plane left for Prague. There are, of course— they said—no planes for Prague. The frontier had been closed.

I bought a map and went to the British Consulate, foolishly expecting them to be working overtime in these days of crisis; but the building was deserted except for a passport officer who had come back for some forgotten papers, and he was uncivil and unhelpful. I do not remember ever having received courtesy from British diplomatic officials abroad —certainly never any help—and I am inclined to think that the method of their selection needs revision.

I walked to the Ostbahnhof and studied the time-tables. There was a train leaving for Marchegg at seven, and I took a ticket and waited hopefully, since this village is on the banks of the river that flowed between me and Czechoslovakia; and the notion of bribing a boatman to row me across the Danube did not seem too ridiculous in the state of disquiet that I was in. The slow train, the last one that night for the northern villages, reached Marchegg at nine o'clock; and by then it was carrying only myself and one old peasant woman laden with the week-end shopping in Vienna. She opened the door on the left and stepped out on to the platform; but I thought it wiser to descend by the door on the right and walk away into the darkness. A useless precaution, for I walked into the German Army camped on the river bank. Two soldiers escorted me back to the station where the same train was on the point of returning to the capital. It carried back to Vienna myself and the pitiful old woman, with all her provisions for the family, shut out from Czechoslovakia and home, and weeping quietly all the slow way back.

As the train slackened speed, approaching the Ostbahnhof, I wondered if the military, that had speeded my journey, might arrange to have me welcomed at the other end, and, saying goodnight to the old peasant, I jumped out before we came into the station and crossed the goods yard into the street.

It was 11.30 and I was hungry, but hesitant to spend on a meal the little money I had; and in any case I found that the cheap cafés would not accept English currency; so I ended up at the most fashionable restaurant of Vienna, which agreed to change my shillings at an exorbitant rate, drinking two café crèmes, to the disdain of the head waiter who had expected something better from an Englishman with a black hat and an umbrella. There I sat as long as I dared, and at half past midnight went out to look for a place to sleep. It was chilly and growing damp from the light mist that was rising from the river. I walked to the Nordbahnhof, thinking that railway stations are friendly places for the homeless; and it was closed. So I walked back to the Parkring; and although I must have looked strange, with a camera, an umbrella, and a roll of architectural plans, several friendly Viennese ladies offered me the hospitality of their beds.

This was the one occasion in my life when the proposal was not wholly repugnant, since it would have provided security and sleep; and it was ironically the one occasion when I could not, for lack of money, take advantage of it. But it seemed almost more peculiar to continue parading the midnight streets and refusing overtures which I seemed to be inviting; and I turned into a small park from which dogs and Jews were excluded. But it proved too public and too well illuminated for any gentleman in a black hat and umbrella to be found extended along a bench; and in any case the benches were accumulating dew. So I walked back again and sat for an hour in a pavement-café chair in the Stubenring, opposite the headquarters of the Army, watching despatch riders arrive and depart, officers emerging and being driven away in cars to the salutes of sentries, and a continual bustle of men, lorries, and even bicycles. All the windows were brightly lit and where the blinds were not drawn figures could be seen passing to and fro, or working at desks, and all as sleepless as I. But such observance might not be wise, and I got up from the wicker chair, and walked to the canal, and sat for a time on a bench there, until the mist thickened and made me long for the warmth of the centre streets. So I went back and sat for a change outside the Metropole in the Morinplatz (headquarters of the Gestapo, as I was afterwards told) and from there, to shake off the increasing chilliness, went down again to the Nordbahnhof and returned by way of the Stuben-, Park-, Schubert- and Kartner- Ringen to the Aspernplatz, and then via the Rotenturmstrasse to Kartnerstrasse, trying the cafés that were still open and still finding them suspicious of my foreign small change. The wicker chairs outside the Europa were comfortable, and there I sat and watched the buses leaving; and moved at four to the corner opposite the Urania, where I managed to doze until 5.30, by which hour dawn was breaking on a stranger with an umbrella, black hat, camera, and a roll of plans of the Czechoslovak Exhibition.

So I walked, unshaven, creased, sleepy, hungry, and cold, until seven o'clock, when I knew the Lufthansa offices would open. They opened, and informed me that they would know nothing of any flights out before eight o'clock, and so I had the opportunity of an hour's walk through the city. At eight there were no more planes than there had been at seven. 'Perhaps this afternoon . . .' but they were being polite. I breakfasted at the Urania corner on a roll and butter and a black coffee and went to choose a discreet hotel. I found one in a back street near the station, the

Continental; took a room; paid in advance; forgot on purpose to sign the register, which the host was too prudent to remark; and went straight to sleep.

It was hot, sunny, and Sunday when I woke a little after 1 p.m. I left the hotel and in what was half-shop half-café and both dingy, in Schonlarernstrasse, behind the Post Office, ate a greasy wienerschnitzel in the middle of an assembly of music-lovers. The patron had placed a radio on the counter, and the Sunday-afternoon habitués were gathered round listening to the martial music. 'Pom, pom, pom' went the brass; and the barman blew out his cheeks and said, 'pom, pom, pom' and took another swig of lager. It was Sunday and sunny and the city of Schubert; and all this added to the solid food made me feel less despondent, and I lit a bad cigar. And then I learned what these music-lovers had been waiting for. The music stopped. Silence. Then a roll of drums. Then the announcement of the Speaker; and the Speaker was there, clear, commanding, almost in the room: '*Deutsche! Volksgenossen und -genossinnen! Am 20. Februar habe ich vor den deutschen Reichstags-abgeordneten zum erstenmal eine grundsatzliche Forderung unabdingbarer Art ausgesprochen. . . .*' I knew that voice. I had heard it before in days when it held an appeal and had a fascination. Its power was still there to charm men's ears, and I had to admit that I was listening to one of the greatest orators of the world— in spite of the nonsense, the insensate flow of words; in spite of this garbled and Goebbled history. 'The problem of these months and weeks is not called Czechoslovakia, it is called Herr Beneš. In this name is concentrated the fanatical determination of millions of men. . . .' I thought of the President whose defect, if any, was willingness, pliancy, peaceableness . . . .

He began to speak of the Weltanschauung of the new Reich, and I knew the oily liar: '*Wir haben kein Interesse andere Volker zu unterdrucken. . . .*' He mentioned his strivings to limit armaments and ships and bombing; '*Es war alles umsonst!*' he sadly concluded; and having thus shown his good faith he proceeded to boast of his rearmament programme. He touched lightly on Poland; wept a few tears over the unfriendliness of England; affirmed that Germany and France were now forever at peace; and that Germany and Italy were joined in '*unlosbaren Freundschaft*'. And having demonstrated how triumphantly he had solved every problem up to the present day, he came to the point: '*Und nun steht vor uns das letzte Problem, das gelost werden muss und gelost werden wird! Es ist die letzte territoriale Forderung die ich in Europa zu stellen habe. . . .*' Every new one is the last; and this will be the last until the next one; because you solve one only so that you can proceed to the one beyond it.

He began the declaration of war against Czechoslovakia, and he mapped out the opening phases of the campaign in the hearing of his thousands of listeners, and in fact to all the world, with the probable exception of Mr. Chamberlain. And when he mentioned the Czechs, there were howlings from the mob in front of him; and the beery patron beat the counter and shouted his approval. He spoke of Herr Beneš' reign of terror; and my Austrian bartender slapped his hand down and said 'the dirty swine'. And with every mention of Beneš' name the venom in the mind of the orator spilled over into his voice and my companions of the Viennese café were in a murderous heat. The spells of the enchanter were still terrible, and these fat lazy pub-crawlers had turned into man-haters, with their blood pounding in their arteries, their eyes strained and bloodshot, and their sagging muscles tightening under the stimulation of the chemical secretion of their glands.

Sunday evening was less damp than Saturday's, and there was some dancing to watch by the canal before I returned to the Continental for a long sleep.

On Monday morning I made my eight o'clock call at the Lufthansa and found them as polite as ever, and as planeless. 'Perhaps this afternoon . . .' and they smiled. At the British Consulate they were as impolite as ever; did not smile; refused to cash a cheque; refused to help at all. 'We've got enough to do with all these Jews,' the young diplomat grumbled, and it was true, they were queued up along the corridor and all down the curving staircase and were being kept in line by the disdainful doorkeeper. When I said I had some affairs to see to in Prague, all he could reply was that I had no business to be going there at this moment. I left in anger, certain that the next war was already lost on the playing fields of ――.*

As I walked through the streets I noticed the word ČEDOK above a window, and felt elated. If the British Empire can do nothing, the Czechoslovakisches Reise-und Verkehrsburo may save me yet; and I went in and picked out an obvious Czech from the staff and confided my problem to him and showed him one of the letters. He had probably not had a public-school education—I shudder to think of the kind of upbringing he must have had at Olomouc or Brno; but he was intelligent and helpful. He explained that there had once been a light train—it was not much more than a tram—that used to run into Hungary before the peace treaties shifted the boundaries and cut across its track, and now it

* I have thought it kinder to suppress the name of the school Peterley maliciously mentioned. Ed.

ended in the middle of fields. And if you alighted at a station before the terminus, and walked away eastwards, you might be fortunate enough to find yourself in Hungary, and circling back northwards you could strike the southern end of the bridge at Bratislava. 'There you will be safe: our troops are at this end of the bridge.'

I took the little rural train at 11.38 and descended at the village he had named and walked eastwards through open fields in a black hat, with an umbrella, camera, and a roll of architectural plans, wondering what Mrs. Meynell would have thought. There is a theory that however resolutely a man advances in a straight line, the unequal lobes of his brain, or the greater weight of the left ventrical, or simply the tides in the Eustachian tubes, inevitably curve his path to left or right, whichever it may be, and he describes an arc. A cow looking resolutely like a bull at a distance can have the same effect, or barbed wire, or a field of barley; and by the middle of the afternoon the sun was not where it should have been and I saw no signs that I was in Hungary. Eventually I took to a paved road for ease and walked into a military road-block of three German privates and an N.C.O. They were polite enough to receive my explanation that I was on a walking tour with nothing more than unbelief. One of them retired to his field telephone and made a call. He came back and reported that it would be necessary for me to accompany him to the military post on the main road; and we walked the four miles together, an odd pair, the Austrian Nazi with rifle, the English tourist with umbrella. At the highway was a rough hut, a motor-cyclist, five privates, an officer, and a machine-gun, and a telegraph pole across the road. I was invited into the hut, asked the same questions, gave the same answers, and received the same polite silence. They requested me to show the contents of my pockets, and I showed them everything except the three letters, by this time under my waistcoat, to which Masaryk was doubtless already awaiting the answers. They were interested in the plans of Dorland House in Regent Street, and my explanations in halting German must have sounded unconvincing. 'And what,' they inquired, 'are you photographing?' 'Nothing.' 'But,' replied the polite officer, 'one can do that without a camera.' So he borrowed the camera; looked inside; found there was no film, and was even more mystified. He did not at first accept my suggestion that if you are photographing nothing then a camera without a film is just about the best thing for the job. He suspected, I think, that there was some device for concealing the presence of the film, and he was beginning to lose his Austrian patience and politeness, and beginning to have that worried look of a man with a situation that is not covered by the regulations. Eventually, after some painful lack of thought, he said curtly, 'You may go.' I thanked him and asked the way to Bratislava. He pointed down the road, said: 'Two miles. But they won't let you over,' and went back into his sheltering hut. I trod happily the dusty hot road to freedom, and saw the hill across the river, on which the old castle stands, and was feeling elated at nearing Slovakian soil, when I heard the sound of a motor-cycle at full speed. I had a second of panic realization that they had telephoned Vienna and been told angrily that when the frontier is closed it is closed; and that they were repairing their mistake before it was too late and I reached the bridge. I turned to wait for the cyclist to emerge from his own dust. He came up; stopped; straddled his legs to support his machine; and politely handed me the roll of plans of the Czechoslovak Exhibition that I had left behind at the frontier post.

The Czech guards let me through, more by surprise, I think, than intention; and I walked across the bridge to which they were already busily affixing explosive charges and into a Bratislava that was all confusion and barricades.

In the Bratislava Station were civilians and military sitting everywhere, on suitcases and kitbags, and waiting with the patience of the Slav for the future whenever it should come. The train service was suspended. I asked to see the station-master and found a very worried man; explained to him that I had to get to Prague; and produced the three letters as justification. He said that there would probably be a troop train leaving that evening, so as to travel in the darkness to the capital, and he gave me a written statement which I was to show the military. And I too sat down to wait.

As it happened there was a change for the better. A special train was apparently put together for the soldiers and for as many of the civilians as were travelling to Prague; and we left at five o'clock. It was a hot afternoon; it was a third-class carriage; and it contained eleven high-spirited warriors and myself. One of them was more high-spirited than the rest, and when he had exhausted the usual themes of humour of the typical drunk he noticed me, and, with the intuition of inebriation and the help of the black hat and umbrella, realized I was English. Here was the heaven-sent butt, and he had no difficulty in maintaining the morale of the troops at a hilarious level for a long while, so ridiculous is the Englishman in the imagination of the European. But from the odd word I could catch here and there, I guessed he had moved on to current politics, and that he was expressing a point of view that I was sorry Mr. Chamberlain could not be with me to hear, namely that the French and English were betraying Czechoslovakia. I noticed his comrades laughing with some hesitation now and looking a little sheepishly round at me; so I laboriously phrased a sentence that I was a friend of Masaryk and not a friend of Mr. C. and that I had come here to help them. One of them spoke to me in German, and I made it plainer; and when the humorist began again they shouted him down and told him to close his pig's mouth. The train slackened speed and came to a stop at a country station: Breclav.

We sit waiting, and nothing happens; and then the word runs along the train that we all change. It is hot and still and thundery and growing dark; we are herded into the bare waiting-room lit only by a small oil-lamp high up on one wall. In the refreshment-room all lights are turned out except two and they are covered with a blue cloth that gives the most spectral of phosphorescences. When I ask why, they reply that they have been ordered to screen all lights along the frontier in case of a sudden air-raid. On wooden benches civilians are lying asleep or sitting with no apparent impatience at their long-overdue or cancelled trains; and here I sit from six o'clock of a windless summer night, bitten awake by the enormous, the surely famous mosquitoes of Breclav, and unable to phone or send a telegram. At one o'clock I ask for the station-master, flourish my letter and my pass, say I must be at the Czernin immediately. He finds a French-speaking Czech, and enlightenment comes with the Gallic tongue: there will be an express for Prague at 1.30 for the troops and he agrees to put me on it. It comes; it goes; it arrives at the Masaryk Station at 7.50 and I am at the telephone and Liba answers. I rush to Ořechovka. She opens the door and steps forward impulsively: 'David, where have you been? We heard you had left London. We were so worried.' I had to remember I was on a political mission; and instead of saying, 'Darling Libuska, I have come to fetch you away,' I bowed over her hand and said, 'I came by way of Vienna.'

I shaved and went to the Czernin on 27th of September, and handed the three letters to Kubka for placing in the right hands. He opened his own, and even his imperturbability was shaken. He rose quickly and went out; I sat there for half an hour savouring an almost perfect quiet. There was the muffled sound of feet in the corridors beyond the double doors; and occasionally an official would look in, apologize, and withdraw; but inside the room the gilt clock on the mantelpiece ticked on, and measured the silence, while I sat listening to it in the heart of the political thunderstorm that was gathering outside, and thought of the frenzied angry men in all the capitals, and all the telephone wires busy with messages, and the newspapers shouting their sensations on the streets and radios their propaganda on the air. And all in vain; for Czechoslovakia had already fallen; Mr. Chamberlain had been duped; the Nazis were marching up Wenceslas Square, and the Führer was gazing from the castle over the old roofs on which I had looked that magical evening with Liba when we still thought the future could be avoided. All the feverish activity was already too late: the words of Sunday's orator were in my ears, and every spat-out syllable was a fore-echo of the tread of Prussian boots in Prague. The politicians had heard and had not understood, and were going on talking, telephoning, writing, and scurrying across corridors. And in the centre of this maelstrom was this peaceful room in which I sat and listened to the ticking of the clock, and decided that Liba must leave for Peterley.

There was no longer any need to stay, and I went out of the long classical palace and down into the city to the air-line office, and began a discussion about plane reservations which developed into a diplomatic conference wherein important names were rather imprudently used. But I obtained a provisional booking for Liba and the two children on the next-afternoon's plane, provided the government authorization were forthcoming.

Liba and the two children left on the London plane this afternoon, Wednesday, 28th September, she in tears at leaving her country, I over-playing the air of indifference and disinterest. She had resisted the idea of going. There had been a scene in her room when she had turned on me with that fury I had for a moment seen once in her eyes in the Hradcin garden: 'I have to run away from my own country because you want it. And I must beg for permission to run away from my own government. What will they think of me? And I thought that you——' but she still had enough self-control to stop there and not give herself away. She turned and went to the window and looked out into the city she would have to leave, while I stood and felt my resolution ebbing away, and motives and emotions and decisions flowing together and mingling and becoming so mixed in my mind I no longer felt sure what policy I was really pursuing.

If her anger had held, I should have given way. But she said without turning round to look at me: 'David, you don't know what you are asking me to do. I don't know if I have enough strength to do it.' I could not give the true reasons for my insistence that she go: that the game was lost, and that I was willing to abandon Czechoslovakia, but not her. But then

I did not know what real and unconfessed motives would, in the end, dictate her surrender. We neither of us used the right words; we deliberated in silences, and took care not to approach that guarded frontier between our ordered lives and our real, our natural beings. I said that if the flow of events could still be diverted, it could only be from London now, and it was there that the last Czech pressure would have to be applied, and it was there she could be of the greatest use. I said that Masaryk believed she could help in London and had backed my plan to fly her out, which was untrue. But the lie prevails sometimes where the truth is powerless and in the end she said: 'Well, David, I will go. But I hope I never have any reason to regret it. And what will you do?' 'I shall stay here,' which pleased her; and she went to make preparations for leaving. And so this afternoon I watched the plane rise and circle and head for the Bohemian mountains with the new inhabitants of Peterley safely on board.

I reached the Esplanade at five for tea and found the Griffins there waiting for me with the printed propaganda that the Czech police had seized at the Henlein headquarters. Patšček, who had got them from the Czernin, had brought them for us to see. We studied them with glee: they were so exactly what we could use. I even wondered if they were forgeries; but apparently there were bales and bales of them, and they had come from Berlin, and they had undoubtedly been found *chez* Henlein; and Patšček had guaranteed them; and he was in close touch with Beneš, and is a completely honest and reliable man. Griffin decided to make one of them, the sheet of little maps of Europe, the subject for his broadcast this evening; and we began drafting the talk. Šafranek was tired, worried, and depressed; and the news of the coming Munich conference was disquieting enough. He left us and went up to sleep. We went, the Griffins and I, to the wireless-room at 8.10. Reception was good. He discussed the continual German expansion, and went on to attack the proposed four-power conference, 'at which one power will dictate and three powers will confer'. Afterwards back to the Esplanade basement where dinner is served to the light of candles now that a total darkness is imposed on the city, for fear of a sudden air-raid. Patšček joins us; and the Cockburns come in but do not stay after 11.30.

Patšček I remember saying that the fear of the bureaucrats at the Foreign Office was that if the negotiations were 'successful' the trouble might be that the Army might refuse to obey the order to retire from the frontier. Entrenched behind their almost impregnable Maginot Line, sick to death of the continual German threats, they knew that if they did not fight now they would not again have the opportunity of fighting as free men. Their fear was the fear of being prevented from fighting by their own allies. But Širovy had assured the President that the Sokol ethics, of obedience and discipline, would bring them back in order, if this became necessary. We could not help thinking of the contrast with that scandalous scene on the morning of the 21st, when Chamberlain and Daladier at the bidding of the Führer had instructed their representatives to get the Czech President out of bed at two in the morning and read to him the brutal ultimatum of his friends. I hope this will never be forgotten, and that whenever anything favourable is said of the British Empire, or anything about the British love of liberty, etc., it will be remembered that these lovers of freedom and fair play performed the most despicable act in modern history, in the hope of saving their skins from an Austrian wastrel who shouted loudly at them and made them shake in their shoes.

Šafranek drives me slowly back to Ořechovka. All cars have had to paint their front lights a dark blue, and they move cautiously through the unlit streets like enormous cats. I leave him on the main road and grope my way to Klidná in absolute blackness that reminds me of my late returns to bed through a sleeping Medford. I keep thinking of that Nazi propaganda sheet with those maps of Europe that show just what the Führer intends to do each spring, summer, and autumn for the next three years. At least I am content with one thing: that one person is safe from his malevolence.

When I woke the next, no, it was the same, morning, it was warm and sunny and the sky was cloudless; and the trenches that ruined the flower-beds in the park across the road did not seem so sinister now that Liba was across the Channel. I came down to coffee and thought about the Nazi map of Europe; and the more I thought about it, the more certain I was that something could be made of it. I rang the Griffins at the hotel; and without waiting for a second cup I called a taxi and went over the river to their hotel. But they did not see how any effective use could be made of it over here.

'If that piece of paper could be put in front of some of the men in London . . .' said Griffin, 'or if a newspaper would use it . . .'

'Exactly; if that appeared on the front page of a London paper, think of the shock to the feelings of all those nice-minded Englishmen who think that the German Chancellor means what he says.' Griffin thought of that with some satisfaction and then said: 'I think you'd better take it over. I think you are right. It might work.' And when I protested that I had only just come and had to settle the question of the Exhibition with the Minister here in Prague, he replied that this was a gamble that might do more than all the Exhibition could, but that it would have to come from the English side, not from the Czech.' There is the afternoon plane.'

'Yes, but you have to have a Bank clearance, which I haven't got.'

'Which we can get. Book your seat first.'

I had to ring Rakusin at the National Bank for my *valuten* pass. He said it was impossible; and then I told him of the scheme, and he said he would do it, and would tell the air-line that the pass would be ready before the plane left—'but not much before'.

I did not even have time to return to Klidna for packing, but reflected that I should be back in a few days, and this time there was hope that the plane would go right through.

We all lunched at the Esplanade, and the Vincent Sheeans joined us, and Šafranek, and Madame Patsček, who brought her husband's memorandum for Cecil and Eden for me to carry back. G. mentioned Mussolini's plan for arbitration at Munich: retirement from Spain in return for a free hand in Czechoslovakia. I jotted down some points to make clear to Sinclair, Cecil, and Barry:

(1) The Berchtesgaden terms in any case not legally binding without the sanction of a treaty;
(2) their acceptance by the Hodza Government caused that government's immediate downfall;
(3) that the cession of territory has thus been decisively rejected by the whole Czech people;
(4) that the Širovy Government cannot go against that popular will;
(5) that there must be no more talk of Czech capitulation. They have not capitulated. They have decided to fight rather than yield everything;
(6) that the Sudeten problem was solved by the flight of Henlein, the obedience of the S.D. to the mobilization, and the new manifesto of the regrouped S.D. under the old democratic leaders.

We sat talking until 3.30, when I left for the airport carrying the Sheeans' assurances to Lady F.R. and Šafranek's message to his wife, who was in the Charente. At 3.15 Rakusin had phoned to say the Bank permit was with the air-line and my ticket would be waiting for me at the air-port. And so with the Nazi propaganda sheet in my pocket and with nothing else, no plans, hat, umbrella or camera, I took off for London.

The heat over the Bohemian mountains turned thunderous over Bavaria, and about an hour later we were in the middle of stormclouds and could see the lightning through the plane's windows. The pilot must have decided to fly under the storm, for we dropped down clear of the clouds into rain that was so heavy and thick it streamed in sheets of water over the panes of glass and blotted out the landscape, except at the instant of the lightning flash. We dropped lower, as though the pressure of rain were beating the plane down. We must have been over the Ruhr or the industrialized Rhineland, for at one brilliant second when the lightning was closest and most intense I saw, lit up like a stage scene, a corner of a suburban street, deserted in the downpour except for a woman under an umbrella waiting for a tram. There was a lighted shop or tavern behind its windows steamy with the interior heat, and in the illumination of the flash even the posters on the wet walls could be seen.

The storm must have been travelling with us for we did not move out of it, and when, to my surprise, we alighted in Holland, the torrential rain had turned the empty airfield into a swamp. We were ordered out of the plane to the airport building and there told that another plane would pick up the passengers for England when the storm had ended. But when I thought of my previous broken journey and of the Nazi propaganda in my pocket and of Liba over the water, I asked if this plane was not going to continue the journey. 'For mails only,' they replied; and I said that in that case I would go too. 'We advise strongly against it'; but I persisted and they gave way. 'Very well. Will you wait half an hour in the restaurant?' But I waited in the waiting-room; and they did honestly fetch me in forty minutes. I stepped up into an empty plane, and we set off in rain as thick as ever. We were flying in a mist that hid the world from us, except for moments when through a swirl in the vapour the lightning revealed the water of the North Sea as a moving floor just beneath us. It was like looking through the planks of the mill floor to see the black water moving underneath. I had never before been so glad to see the coast of England as I was when the North Foreland light flashed below us.

From there all up the estuary, searchlight after searchlight picked us out and handed us over to the next light, so that we rode on a continuous crest of light as far as Croydon. The rain had stopped and I picked my way through puddles to the terminal building but decided it was too late to ring Peterley.

I went this morning to see Barry at the *News Chronicle;* spread the Nazi maps in front of him, and said he could have them for his front page tomorrow with all the authentication I could give him. He sat, and without a word stared at this cartographic record of Nazi triumph: Austria occupied in the spring of 1938, Czechoslovakia in the autumn of the same year, Hungary in the spring of 1939, and Poland in the autumn, Yugoslavia in the spring of 1940, and that autumn Rumania and Bulgaria, and in the *annus mirabilis* 1941 Denmark, Holland, Belgium, and Northern France, and later in the year the Ukraine. He looked at them and the more he considered their explosive quality the less he could make up his mind. He said, 'I'll have to bring Layton in on this, and perhaps Sinclair,' and he arranged a meeting for two o'clock. Both of them turned up and both were immediately aware of the significance of this propaganda. I gave them a full statement of their discovery and the hands they had passed through at the Czernin; and said that Patsček vouched for them. Layton seemed willing to print them. He turned to Sinclair, who sat regarding them in silence, and asked him his opinion.

'I've been thinking. If you come out with these on your front page tomorrow, Barry, I think that may well be the end of Mr. Chamberlain's negotiations. I don't see how he could go on if these are in all the English papers in twenty-four hours—as they would be.'

Layton asked him what he would advise.

'I would not like the responsibility of doing something that might wreck the government negotiations. And I think publication of these maps would do that.'

'So we don't print them?'

'I'd advise against it. But I'll see that these are on Mr. Chamberlain's desk this evening.'

I felt like saying that would be a great help, but I didn't, and Sinclair took the little sheets away. Barry shared my disappointment. It would have been quite a scoop. As for me, I felt as though I'd fallen among gentlemen.

I carried my bitterness to Peterley. Liba, who had mingled surprise and displeasure on the phone this morning, forgave me for deserting my post when she heard the story. She was worried about Miloš who is at

263

the front and has not yet written; but she was happy to be in the country, and Šiša and Pufič had taken possession of the grounds, outhouses, messuages, barns, columbaria, stables, etc. and also of the heart of the Old Man; and were running from his knee to the servants' kitchen for a cake, and back from the kitchen to his knee for a caress; and chasing the dogs with Slav endearments, and frightening the swans with outlandish shouts. Their plump round faces, their round blue eyes, their corn-coloured hair, have captivated the villagers, who come to their shop doors to see the Czech children go by.

Eighth
Campbell Johnson has married the young creature with the violet eyes and the air of being half supernatural and likely to vanish one midsummer eve or All Souls' night in a wisp of blue smoke when he utters the wrong phrase. I have lent them the cottage for their honeymoon; it is surrounded by woods, it has a well, and is bat-haunted: she should feel at home; and it will never serve any such purpose for me now.

I had my set of Genji put into Liba's room—she is in the Chinese bedroom—and she has been captivated by it. So much so that we have decided to translate parts for Czech readers. I write to Waley at Davos for permission, who will surely be amused to think of the mannered and archaic Japanese of the twelfth century being transmuted via his elegant English into the Czech vernacular.

Twenty-fifth
On Tuesday last to Oxford and lunched with Edith Elbogen at the Clarendon, to talk over the recruiting of members for my lost cause in this home of them, and the formation of a Masaryk Club at the university. A lovely autumn day of clear skies, fresh winds, and sunlight on the brown leaves of the trees. In the luminous air the domes and spires shone as though washed in rain and reminded me of those others I would rather see from the other side of the Vltava. When I came back to Peterley (along the road I had last travelled with Audrey) I found that Liba had not yet returned from London where she had gone to see the Legation about this still-unsettled Exhibition. She came back on the last train, and I

opened the front door for her, as I'd told Griffiths to go to bed. I was just about to scold her for being out so late, when I could see by the brusque way she took off her hat that something had disturbed her placid nature. When I asked what was the matter she said, 'Can anyone hear us here?' so I led the way into the long drawing-room and put some wood on the dying fire. Liba closed the door and sank into the sofa. 'You will not guess what has happened.'

'Prague has been difficult?'

'Not Prague; Jan Masaryk.'

'But I thought he was——'

'David, that was why I had to make sure we could not be heard. It is not the Exhibition. I have had a terrible hour with him. He is furious with me, with you.'

I was too mystified to make any comment.

'It is difficult for me to say this to you. But he thinks that we . . . that we have run away together. I could not convince him that we were not.'

She was on the verge of tears: 'I should not have come. I should not have let you persuade me. That is what he kept saying: you would not have left Prague at this moment if you had not . . . I can't repeat his words. I know I should not have come; but I wanted to see the children safe. And now it is Jan Masaryk who punishes me.'

Watching the flames curl round the fresh wood, inserting their pointed tongues into the cracks in the log—how apt is the phrase 'licking' for young flames!—leaping up on the currents of hot air, and sending out the flash of light that is reflected from mirror, vase, picture, and polished wood in the shadowy background, and from the face of Liba, lovely in repose, whose eyes are closed to hold back her tears—this face that has the serenity of all women conscious of exceptional beauty and has for me the splendour of a summer cornfield . . . but of course why should not Masaryk be even more appreciative? I remembered one afternoon after we had lunched with him at the Legation and had gone into his study, with the Scottie, for coffee, and had sat for nearly an hour talking in the friendliest manner with bursts of humour from Jan, and how, when we had risen to leave, he had spoken some words in a low voice to Liba. She had, I noticed, blushed and looked embarrassed; and I could not help asking her what Jan had said. 'Oh, it was just one of his jokes. He made an amusing reference to me and my blond Englishman.'

Thinking of it now I am not sure it was as amusing as Liba pretended; or she may have purposely mistranslated. Liba would have re-traversed this path of memory, too, during the slow journey back to Missenden; and to confirm her own suspicion I said it was obvious that Masaryk was jealous. 'He is in love with you,' and I was careful to omit the 'too'.

'Of course not,' she retorted, too hurriedly. 'You could not think that if you knew Jan as well as I do. He thinks I have deserted my country.'

'That is the way he puts it. Remember that he's overwrought; remember that he's had to be good humoured for months to all these wretched politicians while they betrayed him. With you, Liba, his reserve has broken down and the truth came out.'

'You should have heard some of the things he said,' and she almost seemed pleased to think of them. 'But all the same I must do something.'

'You will have to send him a letter, and put it in writing that his accusations are untrue. You can truthfully say that I have never at any time said anything that hinted that I was in love with you.' I felt the bitterness of this so deeply, that there was an involuntary brutality in my voice as I added, 'It is true, isn't it?'

'But of course, David,' and she opened her large blue eyes and looked at me, perhaps in fear that there was going to be another emotional scene.

'Well; you must write to him. Masaryk is the one man on earth I could not betray, and I can't endure that he should suspect it. Will you write tomorrow?' I rose. Liba was still staring at me. I repented of my bitter voice, but I dared not stay, and I said simply: 'Liba, I'm sorry this has happened. I must go. You know your way round; call Grace if you want some supper. Goodnight, Liba.'

She did not move, but still looked directly at me and answered in a low voice, 'Goodnight, David.'

With that care, that concentration upon the trivial, the mechanical that is the solace of the deepest anguish, the darkest melancholy, I released the catch of the front door; closed it quietly behind me; listened for the lock slipping into place; crossed the gravel of the drive on to the grass where my footsteps would not be heard. I was safely locked out, and that letter of denial could be written truthfully. I took the short cut by the fields to the cottage, and at every step on the wet grass I kept reminding myself that the denial would be true in the diplomatic sense only, but that, once that letter was written and sent, it would have to remain true, until, with the lapse of time, that time would come when its truth or falsity would not seem of the least importance.

266

Twenty-seventh

Liba has left the children at Peterley and has moved into Courtfield Gardens to appease Jan M.; and so I tend to stay in Town and work with her in the evenings. And when the moment comes to leave, that other moment also comes when we each of us silently, without a sign, resignedly, resist the almost irresistible desire to stay together, to put aside pen and paper, turn down the lights, and turn to one another. But the shadow of the Minister comes between us and drives me out into the sleeping Chilterns to a damp, lonely cottage and a bitterness that erodes the night.

I am arranging another rush printing job for Seton-Watson, to answer the critics of the former pamphlet of September 26. It did have some effect. It provoked some awkward questions in the House to which Sir Samuel (Abyssinia) Hoare gave a lying answer. Masaryk has supplied the information.*

November

First

Dinner with the Vojtiseks at Eaton Place and hear the latest news from Prague where English credit has fallen to the dishonourable level it reached in Europe in Napoleonic days, before Wellesley came to our rescue. Liba accompanied me, much happier now that the quarrel with Jan M. is over. She wrote the letter, and he sent it back without comment; and when we called at the Legation he was as friendly as ever. He made one remark which was characteristic of his habit of turning serious matters to a jest, preferably a vulgar one: he made it in Czech to Liba who forthwith translated it to me, how softened I don't know. He said he had had some interviews with Mr. Chamberlain, 'and if you could see my backside you would find it bright blue from the kicks I have been honoured with. . . .' I was amazed—and for the sake of this country's

---

* This is the four-page folder Peterley printed for Seton-Watson called *Godesberg and Munich*. It is now, as far as I can discover, extremely rare.

tarnished honour, pleased—to learn from something he let fall that he had been receiving most helpful and confidential information from inside our own F.O. from men who thought it their duty to be disloyal to their own Minister when he was betraying the country. I mentioned to him, in the lightest of allusive ways, my idea of having the Masaryk Library temporarily transferred to London; but had the impression Jan is not eager to see this collection leave Lany; perhaps because it would be too clear a sign that the work of the President-Liberator had been in vain. Škrach, librarian of the Castle Library, had agreed with me before I left Prague that it was worth trying, as this library on European liberalism was one of the first things the Nazis would cart away or destroy. I had a talk with Carr-Saunders on the 25th and he has given me a verbal assurance that, if Prague releases it and pays the freight, the London School of Economics will house it meanwhile. I would rather see it here than in the States where it would be easier to ship it. It might even have an ennobling influence on the smart radicals of the L.S.E.

> 'Stonedean,
> Jordans,
> Beaconsfield.
> 23rd October

Dear David,

I hope your Sunday has continued as pleasant as mine. If it were not for the uncertainty of our human fate I should almost say I am experiencing happiness again. Perhaps it is the mild autumn sun and the old garden, full of lobelias, dahlias, and the flowering shrubs, that I am sitting in. Perhaps it is the faith inspired by such places—places which move me strangely. Places which I saw in May, under circumstances so different! I keep thinking of you, and of some strange things you said the other evening. I wish I knew that anything I have done did not make you feel sad. Now that we are so close, I miss your charming letters, though I know it is better not to write and read them. I am so thankful for all you have done, and are doing, for me and the children, I am going through strange thoughts; it is like wandering through the woods around here; wondering what the outcome of it all will be. I have no ground left to build my house of logic on, and I let myself be taken into God's palm—or if you wish, drift with the fascinating stream of life: I am Christian and heathen enough to combine those two things into one feeling which fills me at present. I have to wait humbly, impatient as I am by nature, to see which way my fate is turning out. Perhaps in a few days I shall be returning docilely to Prague to start a new struggle for everyday living, and work among people who, from being friends, will have turned to be suspicious enemies. But whatever happens I wish you to feel that you have, forever in friendship,

Liba'

Twelfth

Walk in Kew Gardens with Libuska. Ourselves alone among the whirling leaves, the bare boughs, the damp avenues. The air mild as spring, and a watery sunset paled over Sion House, and over Thames flowing cold and white under the bending poplars. Darkness fell as we walked back by the tow-path to the Green. We drove to Courtfield Gardens where she has been staying since Masaryk's outburst against her being domiciled with me at Peterley. After tea I got up to go and Liba rose too and came up to me and held up her face to be kissed. 'But what will the Minister say?' She laughed and flung her arms round me. 'I don't care. And I swore to him that you had never done or said anything. And this is because you haven't.' And she kissed me and said I had better go before it became too difficult to part. I drove back to the house; saw the children put to bed, in company with the Old Man, who assists at this ceremony every night and presents the bear to Pufič and the rabbit to Šiša. I walked over to the cottage and solitude and melancholy. This Sunday morning a windy, warm, rain-bespattered morning, I pace the rooms and try to calm my thoughts and resist the temptation to go across the fields to the telephone and make the call that she is trying not to hope for.

Twenty-fourth

We have been so busy in London together the time has passed safely and prudently; but our nerves have been on edge, and once Liba broke down when we were at her flat translating some Nazi documents that Škrach had sent me. Their significance was only too plain, and as she worked at them, her country in her mind, and thinking of her semi-exile here and of her life with me, she suddenly felt she could remain reasonable no

269

longer. She threw her pen down and began to weep. When I tried to console her, she turned sharply on me. 'I can't bear this. You shouldn't ask me to work like this. You don't realize I have my feelings. And you make it worse by being here with me. You had better go. I'm not going to translate any more papers for you.' And she brushed them on to the floor. I put on my coat while she sat moodily at the table, but as I opened the door she rose quickly and said: 'David, forgive me; but that's how I feel and it is because of you. Go now; and ring me in the morning when I shall feel better.'

Twenty-seventh

There was a gale all yesterday. I watched from the window in Gray's Inn the old trees bending their tops under the wind, and dead branches being thrown across the lawns. I was sheltering not from the storm but from the world's eye. I had cancelled a lecture, a public dinner, and attendance at John Henderson's funeral: all that I had promised Liba not to do, I had done. Miloš comes tomorrow, and they will return to Prague in the illusion of safety; and I shall be left with the memory of the days with Liba, and the knowledge that they have gone forever. Even in the square of the Inn I felt shut in, and I left a dry City where the wind was blowing dust and waste paper along the streets, and came to the loneliness of the cottage. The gale died away in the night, and today a warm sun shines in a sky swept clear of cloud. The fields are washed clean, and tree-trunks glow green like properties in an Irish fairy tale; and the tracery of bare bough and twig seems in the distance a mist that half hides the dark evergreens. I walk through the sloping beech wood behind Kyle's farm, and down the deserted road in the valley, coatless and hat-less in this magnificent autumn, but so heavy at heart that the beauty of the countryside becomes an added anguish. I have never before felt so tired of a life that seems purposeless and where pleasures of hours become the regrets of years, like a great flood that ebbing leaves stranded in the river-meadows the white yacht that rots and falls away year by year in loose planks and scrofulous metal, a miserable memento of the riotous waters. They will remain in London a fortnight; and for a fortnight I must be someone other than myself. It will be difficult. We shall meet in Kensington, and under the sardonic eye of J.M. at the Legation; for that is a pleasure Jan will not forbid himself, and a penance he will not deny me.

·   ·   ·   ·   ·

A letter from a young Australian who has heard that I knew Brennan and thinks that I might have anecdotes to give him. He speaks of his own love of literature, his own admiration for 'our truly great Australian poet', and intends (although he does not speak of this) to use whatever he can obtain from me as a means of getting his article placed. I am amused to find that the pathetic drunk and sponger of my Sydney days, loveable and entertaining as he was, is becoming a legend in his native land and is emerging as the country's greatest literary personality. My begging-letter writer is almost reverent when he mentions the poet, and he clearly assumes that to have been admitted to his intimacy was a social distinction to which few could have aspired. I am tempted to reply that in the old days, when I occasionally had to drag the huge bulk of the great poet from its horizontal position on the side-walk of the city's main street, his companionship was a distinction that no one else was eager to share with me. Time and death, it seems, have transmuted the fumes of alcohol to the odour of sanctity, and the shapeless hat I have so often picked up and replaced on the tousled head looks rather like a crown of laurel now.

December

Tenth

In Australia I used to think that once back in England, with moderate means and a cottage in the country, I should be happy. I have them all and more, and am as far from happiness and content as ever. These, having been achieved, lose their power of pleasing. The only things that remain are the moments of simple satisfaction, chiefly in the late evening, as I walk the country lanes and feel the warm south-westerly wind, and see, etched on a blurred ground of scudding cloud, the bare trees; or when, getting up from my chair beside the fire, I put down my book and, opening the door, find the moon rising behind the beeches and shining on the brickwork and the lattices of the cottage with a soft light that gives to the scene the unreality of the beautiful. These seconds are the only memorable ones. And yet this transitory pleasure itself prompts the urge to give up this acquiescence in a simple voluptuousness, and take up a cause however vain, however unbelieved-in: to go out to Spain, as I went to Prague; to turn bigoted Communist; to hasten the day of the barricades. . . .

Libuska and Miloš and Pufič and Šiša left for home today by the two o'clock from Victoria. The bitterness of leave-taking was sugared by the promise to return in three weeks, if our scheme goes through for an unofficial secretariat here in London; but I fear that Liba is deceiving herself. J.M. will not further it. It is too late. There is nothing more to do. As he knows; as Liba dare not confess. Nor is there any safety in returning: England is as doomed as the Bohemian fairyland of wood and castle where we went together. They have all gone, and I am alone. Who was it said that? It is the silence of the cottage that has become vocal.

> 'Prague XVIII,
> 13th December
>
> Dear David,
>
> What a lovely surprise to get your letter! The very morning of our arrival. Thank you for your kindest thoughts. I really do not know how we deserved all your friendliness because it was you and you again who was so kind to us. And all the lovely things we discovered in the parcels on the train! I will write again. This is my first letter from Prague. My hands and thoughts quite unsteady still; letters and accounts all around; children running about speaking a funny English and wild with excitement and the telephone ringing all day. I do not know what will develop here. People say the last fortnight's developments are showing already to the good but I hope it is not only an excess of our national vice-optimism.
>
> Excuse this business letter: I will improve with time. Greetings from Miloš: Best thoughts of mine.
>
> Liba'

Twentieth

In twenty-four hours the mild weather has changed to bitter frost and wind-blown snow, and the thermometer has dropped to 26, and all water pipes are choked with ice. An easterly gale stings the face, and a frozen spray spatters on the window-pane. I have come back to the cottage after ten days of absence. It is unwarmed and damp, and in the corner of the sitting-room the rain seems to have soaked through the bricks of the outer wall, and to be suffusing the plaster. I light Valor stoves in all the rooms, and a smell of warm dampness pervades the whole cottage.

Last night, an intense vision of the road on the crest of the hill at Point Piper, where it dips down to Rose Bay, where so often on cold and moonless nights I have waited, often vainly, for a last tram after a late evening with Penelope. If the year goes out in gales and snow, it will be well enough, a fitting end to a tempestuous and bitter year.

'Prague,
21st December

Dearest David,

This is to wish you Happy Christmas, if such a wish can have any meaning, and hardly do I dare say anything about the New Year. How difficult it is to write! I do not yet see what depths we shall reach; and I cannot write a Christmas letter. If it weren't for our friendship I should not attempt it at all. I feel dead in a sense ever since I returned here. I am surrounded by absurd optimism of some people, by the stupidity of others, and by the deliberate self-seeking of the rest. There are still a few I am proud to say who go on their old way and hope to maintain their beliefs and their standards. But I admire them and cannot share their faith. Yesterday I heard that about a hundred people, including three of our best writers, and "national" at that, have been asked to leave the Club on the pretext that they have not paid their fees. The letter asking them to leave was signed by someone whom we all used to believe in and who should long ago have retired for age and not mixed with any activity any more. Forgive me: I did not think it would surprise me since I had expected this sort of thing to happen.

I can do no work. Day by day I try to steady the children, who miss their school and their freedom in England; but I do not think it would be possible for Miloš to get leave this term. There is no hope of your coming is there for Xmas? You have been spoiling me all the time I spent in England. David, I realize it only now. I miss you, although I should not tell you. I am teaching Pufič and Šiša the nursery rhymes from that lovely book you gave them and I read your poems to myself. There is dry frost and emptiness in Prague. All is quiet and subdued. It is not only winter, you feel at once. Even the faces of people have changed. And how are you, David? I hope to hear from you before too long. Do not think that you have already said everything. Remember me to people you introduced me to. Let me know what you think of the political world, and do not forget your silly,

Liba'

1939

January

Facing the New Year with the usual perplexity of mind. There are still the old unsolved problems. One does not escape them by growing up. Time leaves the old ones behind unresolved, and brings different ones we shall not any more successfully solve. Now, it is above all the problem of human relationships, and the problem of faith. One must make one's compromise peace with the world, and one's permanent peace with God. Is it weakness or wisdom that one decides one cannot always struggle against both? The difficulty is to know which God to come to terms with. The Sinai thunder-deity has passed through so many transmigrations from the Hebrew Father-image, by way of the Graeco-oriental Zeus to the Christian paterfamilias, subtilized on the way by Alexandrian neo-platonism, and finally almost argued away into a world soul or a tendency making for righteousness by our well-bred unitarians. So that it would be a waste of time to look for Him now in these stellar time-distances. He existed once by reason of man's belief that there was someone not too far away or above, 'an ever-present help in trouble'. But who can believe in someone who may be millions of light-years away; or who is so suffused through all things as not really to be there at all, except possibly to the metaphysician in his Oxford sitting-room trying to concentrate on ontology now that at last the two young children are in bed and the maid's wireless has been turned off. It is with oneself that one has to make one's peace, and either rest happy in your faith, if you happily have it, or accept the chill consequences of your lack of it and be content soon to be nothing. I think the second is the nobler.

As for one's worldly salvation, I am even less sure of that. Am I in any way a different personality now than three years ago, more mature, more highly developed? I doubt it. Less intolerant perhaps; but only because less vigorous. One develops a worldly wisdom from the struggle for existence; but this is cunning rather than maturity. There should surely be something better than this; one should pass beyond cunning to a disregard of it, to a neglect of the worldly virtues, just as worldly possessions ought to come to seem burdensome, otiose, oppressive, suffocating. Until one can say: 'Throw those silver candlesticks away, and that red crayon sketch, and that translucent china I have enjoyed so long. I have learned to do without them.' I am in danger of staying too long in the aesthetic stage, where one should not linger too much. The porphyry and the bronzes will give cold comfort at the end. One should accept the unknowable, jump into the dark, do all that you were told should never be done. It could be maintained that the value of the aesthetic lies precisely in this: that it leads you more quickly to that moment when you can put it all behind you and proceed from the sensuously perceived to the spiritually apprehended. Unfortunately, my weakness is that I do not believe there is anything to be apprehended.

Fourth

Miss Johnson to dinner this evening. She is the young woman who had had the difficulties with the waiter in the dining-car on the train to Marseilles last year and for whose . . . hell, it was just because she was so extravagantly good looking that I had rushed into a fight with the National Railway, and eventually cooled the passions of a meridional waiter and warmed the fishy coldness of the Parisian chef. Usually I do not interfere with the English trippers abroad, but prefer to watch them suffer humiliation justly for their stubborn neglect of all languages other than, and often including, their own. We had finished by lunching together; and I was sorry I had to change at Lyons. She had given me her London address. I had thought her story of the little holiday in Corsica was probably misleading; women so well endowed do not have to spend their holidays in Corsica alone, and I imagined she was joining a yacht at Monaco. She had been charming for the hour we had spent together, and under the surface ingenuousness I suspected great sophistication. And this evening she had been willing to travel to the middle of the Chilterns for dinner. So I unfolded my plan for a Turkestan journey and spread the maps over the floor. She did not hesitate when I asked her if she would come with me. She said quite simply, 'Yes.'

February

Nineteenth

A spring day of continuous sunshine on the brown budding trees and the still wintry earth. The birds are singing in the Peterley woods, and rooks wheel against the patches of blue sky. A robin waits beside me as I dig and pounces on fat worms beyond his power to lift. The snowdrops are hanging in the hedgerow and the primroses are in bud; and the rain-drenched grass lifts itself upright to feel the sun. I could stand up too and enjoy this renewal of life, if there could be an aim to live for. But there have been too many failures which I think are really one continuous one, a single one that takes many forms. Release can come now only from without, in a general cataclysm or in the lucky accident of chance, and I be saved in spite of myself. That bitter and prophetic witch may yet be right.

The Turkestan journey I have given up, perhaps because it proved less difficult than I had imagined. When all had been arranged, at any rate as far as the Georgian border, and it remained only to set out, I lost all desire to go, much to Miss Johnson's disappointment. But there must be no more mistakes; and to avoid them, there must be nothing. I must prepare an empty stage, not merely change the stage direction to read 'A Plain in Tartary'.

A rather queer happening last night. I have been waiting for Landell's reply to my inquiries about this Queensland scheme which sounds financially promising, but which depends upon a favourable decision by the State government. It might succeed; and the hope of succeeding in something is becoming a dangerously emotional one for me. Landell's letter was overdue and I was becoming impatient.

So that this morning I woke and immediately remembered the incident of the night, when I had been roused by the rattle of pebbles on the window and, opening the lattice, had seen the rain falling in the blackness of the early-morning hours. And below, in the garden, was a very small, very old man with a lantern who was looking up waiting for the window to open. He lifted up the lantern as though to shine it on my face, and waved a piece of paper, and shouted above the splashing of the rain: 'Prepare

276

yourself for calamity'—I remembered clearly how he spoke this phrase, which struck me as ridiculously theatrical—'The government has decided not to make the recommendation.' And he went away, and I shut the lattice, and returned to bed.

But it was, of course, merely a dream. Had it even rained during the night? I looked out, and the garden was certainly wet. It must have been the rain that woke me. Towards ten-thirty the village postman propped his bicycle against the garden wall and came up the path with the cottage letters. And on the top was a telegram. But I knew already what that cable said, and I was right. It said, 'Regret inform you government decided against the recommendation.' It had been lying in the village Post Office at the hour when I had my—but what was it I had had? I do not know; and I should be inclined to dismiss it, except that this is not the first experience of this kind.

There was an even less explicable one in Trafalgar Square a little while ago—and here there was no emotional intensity built up by hope or interest. I was walking across the square towards Northumberland Avenue, thinking that this really was the least successful of all squares in the world, being devoid of proportion and therefore without any feeling of spaciousness, in fact a jumble of oddments. The column was too high. The Admiralty Arch had nothing in common with the Gallery; the new South Africa House nothing in common with good taste. The Canadian Bank should be sent back to Winnipeg. The Strand façade was simple London vulgarity. The streets wandered in and out of the square like dirt tracks in a vacant suburban lot. Nothing suggested that the human intellect had been at work here. And looking down at the pavement I thought, for no reason at all: 'How amusing if I could have immediate knowledge of something that is happening now, and go to Barry of the *Chronicle* and persuade him to print it two days before it is released as news.' And, just as words run straight on in those electric signs outside newspaper offices at night, the thought continued without a break: 'M. Paderewski the President of Poland has had a secret meeting in Paris with M. Witos the Peasant Party leader to discuss a possible common course of action in that country.' Nothing could be less likely than a meeting between these two political opponents; and the knowledge that they were opposed in politics was the whole of my knowledge of Polish politics. I could not even have stated with certainty that M. Paderewski was alive. In fact, the idea was so absurd on the face of it that I let it drop and forgot it. Three days later I saw an inch of column in *The Times* under the Paris heading, which said, 'It is reported from Paris that M.

Paderewski the President of Poland . . .' but I knew how it went on. That this should happen twice is not more convincing than once. That it can happen at all is disquieting enough. The difficulty is proof: these occurrences can be valid only for the person who experiences them.

Peterley seems now to be merely the symbol of an England that is lost for ever. The *entre-deux-guerres* is joining the Edwardian age and the nineteenth century as history. There does not seem to be any present, apart from this waiting for the first shots of the second war. Time and a future may still exist abroad; but here is only a suspension of time and movement, a mere waiting. I shall go abroad.

March

Third

Have finished the legal discussions with Harris. The old fellow was in a mournful mood: 'But this means the end of Peterley.' To which I reply, 'But only in so far as we shall soon see the end of everything as we know it,' but he shakes his head over my pessimism. Strange that these old people do not notice how fast things are moving, in the wrong direction. I was surprised to learn of one thing: in his totting up of all the assets, and his calculation of what ready cash would be available for the Australian investment, he referred to the Miss Gurney fund, and when I asked whatever that was, I noticed a sudden flutter of hands and words that showed he had let that out unintentionally: 'Your father was always sympathetic with old Gurney's problem. Rose would never have been strong enough to earn her living. Hoskins had warned him of the consumption. He had set aside a sum for her if she wished to live on her own. To make her short life as comfortable as possible.' And Harris added, 'It came out of your father's share of the estate you realize.'

I thought it very considerate of the Old Man. 'And how much was it?' 'Thirteen thousand,' replied Harris, and took out his handkerchief as though to blow his nose, and then put it back when he realized—and realized his visitor would notice, too—that it didn't need blowing. There was so need to say anything more. I should one day have discovered this fund. Harris was probably relieved that it was now known, and painlessly;

and as he said nothing more, he guessed that I had drawn the correct conclusion.

I have booked on the *Brisbane Star*, a new refrigerated motor ship that makes the run to Melbourne in the fastest time of any eastern ship, with only one stop at Madeira. She leaves on April 5th.

Sixteenth

Hitler has entered Prague. This man fulfils one's worst forebodings. But then this was certain, after Mr. Chamberlain had cleared the way for him.

'Prague XIV

Dearest David,

Your note has just come which made me realize that your Australian plan is true. As things are shaping now, I do not believe I may be coming to London within two or three weeks as I had expected, so if you feel free to come to Prague and say goodbye to us before you leave for those distant places, do please. We would not like to miss saying goodbye to you, as we don't know when we shall see each other again. But I leave it to you to do what you think the right thing. Your old rooms are gone of course but you can always stay at the Sokolsky Domou, as you know. Do send me a wire. I am looking forward.

Liba'

Poor Liba; we are just too late. It is Hitler this time who has come between us.

As I was getting dressed this morning I saw from the bedroom window young Ronald crossing the fields. My one link with the outside world in

279

serious emergencies was advancing with that leisurely pace that ensures longevity to the countryman. I opened the window as he came along the garden path and asked his message. It was the usual one: would I ring Cousin Richard right away? I dressed and went over to the house and rang the Club. He sounded serious and business-like for a change. 'Are you ready to go to Prague?' I doubted if the new owners would let me. 'Quite; but are you willing to try?' 'When?' 'Now. There are sixteen Czechs that must be got out quickly and unofficially.' He said he wanted someone who could make the right contacts and find his way about the city without attracting attention. I had to object that I scarcely fitted the specifications. 'I agree. But there's no one else.' Which did not reassure me. I pointed out that I had booked on the Australian ship for April 5th, and what guarantee was there that I'd be back by then? He took that lightly: 'Oh, you'll be back long before, or not at all,' and refused to discuss the matter in greater detail on the telephone. I went in to lunch with him.

He was all prepared. He had the list of the sixteen names, and the cash for their fares through Poland to Gdynia, and the special visas the F.O. had made out for twelve, and even two domestic permits for two of them on arriving here. If they could reach the British Consul at Gdynia they would find everything arranged for their travel to England. The difficulty would be to get in touch with them. They would all be taking care not to be got in touch with. It seemed a hopeless scheme; but I thought of other things and said I would make the attempt. He said I would have to memorize the sixteen names: it would be fatal for a list to be found on me if I were searched. I would have to get a visa from the German Embassy: 'And we are not yet sure how strict they are on the frontier and whether they will give you the visa and immediately notify the frontier guards to watch for you.'

Twenty-fourth

I got the visa. I set out. I crossed the North Sea and landed at Flushing, and was handed Richard's telegram. I had been uneasy ever since the German Embassy had handed me the visa. They had asked me to return in twenty-four hours, and, when I came back, had been so polite in presenting it to me, and had apologized so much for the delay that I was disturbed, probably quite without reason. So I had rung Cousin R. and asked him to make whatever inquiries he discreetly could as to border control and the vigilance of the Nazis in Prague, and to send me a telegram to Harwich or Flushing or Podmokly if he thought there might be any likelihood of walking into a trap. And there was the telegram waiting for me at Flushing, with the phrase agreed upon.

So it was all for nothing that I had sat in the dim billiard-room of the Club, under the portrait of Mr. Churchill that had spent some years facing the wall, memorizing the sixteen names: Gunther Kalz, Heinz Ritter, Elisa Nyeste, and the other thirteen equally unmemorable ones. I wonder what will become of them? My sense of defeat is now complete. I do not think there is anything else I could possibly fail at.

[There is little recorded in the journal at this time; and no mention of a crossing to France. But it seems he went over to the Jura, possibly to St. Claude, the scene of some of his boyhood; for among the entries written on board ship is the one that follows, which he has headed *The Testament of Morez*. Morez is a small town in a narrow valley of the Jura and lies on the road from St. Claude to Besançon. Ed.]

THE TESTAMENT OF MOREZ

From where I sat I could see the plain slab of the vault that had opened for Matthew, the tomb of the Armand-Périers, Françoise's ancestors, hard-working, canny Jurassians, without the Gallic levity or the Swiss love of pretty neatness, and fanatically attached to the grim mountains that had made them pay dearly for their livelihood. So the flamboyant, thriftless Matthew had come to rest in the consecrated limestone detritus of the same hillside as these respectable burghers of a little town.

That he had evidently made his peace with the Church was not surprising in one who had regarded the separation of the English Church from the Catholic communion as a regrettable error that, as he had expressed it in his *Englishman's Guide to his own past*, had cut us out of the European community and left us open to the sectaries of Protestantism, who shared with protozoa the characteristics of fission and nonentity.

To be received into the Church would have been only a final dramatic moment in the long artifice of Matthew's life, and I think he would have been so touched by the spectacle of the Curé of Morez confessing a Peterley that he doubtless made a fine confession. Had he really had much to confess? And did it really matter? For here he was embedded in the upper strata of the Jurassic limestone among the most eminent citizens; and in a cemetery the question of good and evil seems of little consequence. And does it have any more meaning outside if you lift your view from the individual and from the moment? Below me were the roofs of this town, sunk a thousand feet down in the cleft worn in the Jura by the tumbling Bienne, and existing here only because that stream in its leaps from rock ledge to ledge had turned its factory wheels; and for this advantage it had been content to forgo for ever the sunlight of every early morning and the light of every late afternoon, and to endure the still heat of a summer valley and in the winter the sharp winds that are funnelled down from the upper slopes of snow.

From all the history of human settlement in this valley could the threads of good and evil be identified and disentangled? If all the evil were taken away, would anything that resembled human life remain? And all this view of mingled stone and tile, and latticed window and old balcony, and the Baroque of country church and the classical of prefecture, the arches by the square and the clipped trees by the river— all this was the lovely product of the good and evil in the generations. For you could not without absurdity claim that only the presence of an abbé or two had hourly prevented this scene from collapsing into a black and smoking ruin. Could you lay a hand on anything in this town and swear this was produced only by virtue and complete goodness? Even that silver knocker on the door of the Maison de la Main d'argent, could you swear that no greed, ambition, lust, or pride went to its delicate embellishment? Everything flowed from the unchanging complexity of the human heart, that would never, in spite of all the reformers or Utopians, alter to a monstrosity of complete goodness or ever lapse into utter badness, but would always contain within itself all the potentialities between the heaven and the hell that were its boundaries. Limits that in fact are not so far apart; that shift with time and sentiment and race, and are like those lines of magnetic variation on charts, all pointing in different directions but all concerned with that same imaginary point beyond the chart where there is no variation at all; limits that often run close and parallel, like the pavements of the main street in every town, between which all that could possibly happen in hell has already happened as well as all that could be conceived as of the most celestial.

The metaphysical drama, as that other Peterley called it, has been played out here in a hundred forms without attracting much notice or drawing crowded houses. The momentous happens every moment to this human creature who so often seems unaware of his true stature. Yearly the blind are cured; the lame walk; the poor are miraculously fed; the young religious reformer is publicly mocked; Barabbas is chosen mayor; the judge from Paris makes a wrong decision; some Judas betrays his master; and the masonic free-thinker on his way back from the capital, where the presidency of the government commission has slipped through his fingers, has felt that marvellous working of the spirit that brings one back into the Church. And if the young limb of Satan, of the Compagnie Colin, has fallen from the happy realms of light women and his father's allowance down to the mournful gloom of the rue de la Gare where, with the associates of his loss, he has set up a pool room; yet, to maintain the cosmic balance, the young daughter of the Lunetterie Robillard has devoted her life angelically to the care of the diseased Liberians, perhaps in gratitude for being saved by her family from the afore-mentioned limb. We tread Jacob's ladder, the *scala perfectionis*, daily; but in our relative universe, it too is curved, and only brings us back home.

I lowered my eyes from the hills on to Morez, through which had flowed, like the unstaunchable mountain torrent, generation after generation, the two tides of good and evil, leaving, like the boulders, the bedsteads, and the broken hardware in the stream, a sediment of slum and mountain villa, factory and hospital, and shop and municipal offices; calling forth the Renaud to rule over ropes and harness and hardware; appointing Chauvelot lord of pharmaceutical products; ordaining that milk and honey should flow from the counter of Madame Boutelot; but fruits and vegetables from the cornucopia of Madame Duvernoir; setting up the Colin in the seats of the mighty; and at times sending the rich headless away. But I could not see anywhere the goodly man flourishing like trees planted by the waterside, nor discern the unmerciful, fornicators and adulterers, covetous persons, idolaters, slanderers, drunkards, and extortioners perishing and being scattered like chaff on the face of the mountains.

Indeed, as I looked, the two tides seemed to merge in one and become like the pulse of a single heart; and I doubted if I should ever be able to distinguish them, even if I watched for generations the microcosm below. Rather, I grew certain that if I watched long enough any distinction would become meaningless; and I was sure that if I stood here for ever I should never see the heavens bowed and the Lord coming out riding upon the cherubim and flying upon the wings of the wind, and the hailstones and the coals of fire descending, as he thunders out of heaven; and the arrows flying that will scatter his enemies, and mine, and make them like a fiery oven in the time of his wrath. That has not once happened in the past three thousand years; and the human beings of the valley go about their business unconcerned by its possibility at this late date. They have, indeed, so long toyed with these apocalyptic visions, calling up, like a schizophrenic necromancer, cohorts of demons with one hand, and bringing down legions of angels with the other, creating uncreated deities and comprehending incomprehensibles, that these astonishing men of the valley go about their business of making spectacle-frames quite unconcerned whether or not Jehovah will appear one day in clouds of glory on the Risoux, and indeed behave exactly as they always have done and always will do, so long as the Bienne does not begin to flow uphill and turn their water-wheels the wrong way round.

I imagine Matthew's reflections could not have been so different had he been able to stand with me here now, although he would have added: 'Agreed; but this world is not run by the theories of every idle ruminant. Conformity and continuity are the virtues. Even at the risk of our disbelief we should belong to a Church. And there can only be one. Two would be excessive; more would be ridiculous.'

I doubted if Matthew had really thought it necessary to receive absolution; but he probably had thought it seemly that the humanly appointed representative of humanity should give the appropriate gesture of farewell and bid him go in peace: 'Having contributed your good and evil to this human life, go now to that other one where there is neither good nor evil.'

For all his errancies—indeed by virtue of one of them—Matthew had done more for Peterley, in creating Mademoiselle Marie-Thérèse, than I. The connection between the estate and the family has been broken for ever; for I do not imagine that she will abandon her vines of the Gironde for our wet beech woods. But the family continues; and if the continuity is matrilinear, that after all is the real one.

I owed Matthew something for having done what I had failed to do, and was glad I had climbed the steep track to the cemetery to salute his grave.

The high cliffs had already cut off the afternoon sunlight from the town, and the light was resting on the white strata of the opposite face of the valley, unhealed scars of some recent rock-fall. I looked westwards to where the valley's green end was curtained by the pleated arches of the

284

viaduct that spiralled the trains down from the heights of the Jura to the station in the ravine far below. Leftwards, under the arches, the road curved out of sight and ran along the tumbled bed of the Bienne that flowed to turn the mills of the abbey of St. Claude, those black water-wheels which as a child I had watched strike silver sparks from the dark water as it flowed and fell.

I looked east where the hills closed in and screened with pines the pass that went up by cliff paths and tunnels and hairpin bends up to the great crumbling fort at Les Rousses, that guards France from the aggressive Swiss, the pass that climbs up so high only to drop down suddenly through damp pine woods between the Noirmont and the Dole to the warm meadows of the Genevan lake. There, too, were memories that I could not yet recall with calm. I turned and walked down the track by the old church that had been made into a workers' tenement and from whose east window sprouted a long black chimney; past the cabinet-maker's workshop and the Sisters' orphanage, unpainted and unrepaired; across the brook whose summer dryness revealed the winter's garbage; and through the square where they were playing their silver *jeu de balles*; and, getting into the car, started the long climb to the Col de la Savine in the hopes of reaching Besançon before night fell.

April

Ninth

Easter Sunday. I write in—of all places in the world—the lounge of the Blue Star motor vessel *Brisbane Star*, in the eastern Atlantic between Las Palmas and the African coast. So, in exactly thirteen years and six days, I find myself bound again for Australia and this time for life-long exile. The wheel comes full circle with a vengeance, and the opening paragraph of the early volume can be quoted almost word for word. And from these thirteen years, nothing but the disillusion and melancholy of experience, from which perhaps resignation may one day come.

We sailed on Wednesday the fifth from the Royal Albert Dock; and in my indifference, I just failed to miss the boat train, racing along the platform at the last minute with a parcel of books, an untied bundle of letters, an umbrella, and a box-file of Czech documents which Cousin

Richard with great solicitude and little sense brought me at the last moment. But Hitler has beaten me to Prague; I must forget the one city I would be in, and the one place where I cannot be. I must forget. There must be no continuity between the fever of the past and the deadly placidity of the future. So I shall end this journal when we sight the flat sand-dunes of Port Phillip that chill the expectations of the immigrant.

In the cold waters of the South Indian Ocean north of Kerguelen Island. A rolling sea catches our quarter, and a biting wind rushes round the decks. Whales spout to the south. I am the only passenger to lean against this wind and gaze on the grained green water, the grey sky. The other five keep their cabins, sensibly; these seas are not part of the human world. Even the wireless waves do not penetrate here: there is a band of almost complete silence. We are, thank heaven, an unsociable company—two Jesuits going to one of the Papal colonies (Queensland); an Australian from Young; an English salesman; and a grim-looking Norwegian who says nothing.

It is the second, I think, of May, with heavy seas and an ice-laden wind, and the ship rolling and pitching like an abandoned hulk, since she is without cargo. We are getting wireless reception again, and the report of Hitler's Reichstag speech comes brokenly to us as from another planet. And I feel poised between two worlds, in neither of which I have any longer a part, and feel as though I were becoming absorbed into this wind which blows continuously round these empty latitudes. I am already dreading the hot colourless vistas of the Brisbane River where year by year I shall remember spring mornings at Peterley, and the long sunsets in the harvest haze, and moonlight on my cottage walls, and nights in the Chilterns blown clean with wind and rain. Only the knowledge that I can never go back will keep me here.